THE FABULOUS FOX TWINS

THE FABULOUS
FOX TWINS

Ken McCoy

F

1402917

This first world edition published in Great Britain 2002 by
SEVERN HOUSE PUBLISHERS LTD of
9–15 High Street, Sutton, Surrey SM1 1DF.
This first world edition published in the USA 2002 by
SEVERN HOUSE PUBLISHERS INC of
595 Madison Avenue, New York, N.Y. 10022.

British Library Cataloguing in Publication Data

McCoy, Ken, 1940
   The fabulous Fox twins
   1.   England, Northern - Social life and customs - 20th century - Fiction
   I.   Title
   823.9'14 [F]

   ISBN 0-7278-5881-5

Typeset by Palimpsest Book Production Ltd.,
Polmont, Stirlingshire, Scotland.
Printed and bound in Great Britain by
MPG Books Ltd., Bodmin, Cornwall.

To Val, who always had faith in this book

One

19 May 1956 was a day of swings and roundabouts. A date as deeply engraved on my memory as it is on that black marble headstone. I still visit the grave from time to time and I always will. It's a cheerful thing to do. The occupant would be most put out if I turned up with a long face.

For me, Billy Foxcroft, soon-to-be-expelled grammar school boy, it was a day that ended many things. Childhood, a friendship, innocence. Or you could say it was a beginning. It began with a broken window.

'Foxy!' That was Henry.

'*Foxy*!' This louder shout came from Utters.

A stone clattered against my bedroom window and failed to stop there. It punched a neat hole in the bottom left-hand corner and landed on the lino amid a tinkling of glass. More pocket money up the spout. I heard Utters say, 'Oh, heck!' and I knew I must take my revenge quickly, because Utters was a world expert on diffusing my anger. Jacky would be out there as well, with his snotty nose and silver sleeves. The sun sneaked through a rip in my bedroom curtains and it looked as though that Saturday would be yet another nice day. In a few weeks I'd be taking my O Levels at St Ignatius's Catholic College, after which the world was to be my oyster.

It was the beginning of the Whitsuntide holidays and the sun was shining. Unsworth wasn't used to nice weather. It wasn't built for nice weather. Unsworth, like most towns in the West Riding of Yorkshire, was a solidly built place, mainly built in grey. The muck doesn't show up so much against grey and it blends in so well with the climate. But that day we had colour.

1

I opened the back bedroom window and smiled an innocent greeting to my friends, then I emptied Uncle Stan's tin po over them. Anticipating such a move they took evasive action and caught just a peripheral sprinkling, but enough to provoke an anguished cry from Utters.

'Aagh! Yer dirty sod, Foxy! These are me new jeans. Come on! It's nearly eleven o'clock.'

He acknowledged my odious retribution with his usual lopsided grin. This told me he would get me back. Utters always got me back.

But not that day.

I dressed quickly and examined my face in the bathroom mirror for spots. All clear, it must be my grandma's blood. According to Foxcroft family folklore, my paternal grandad had been eaten by an Alaskan grizzly bear which had just come out of hibernation and was looking for a decent meal. The only person who mourned his passing was a local girl whom he had inadvertently made pregnant. My eskimo grandma had somehow made her way from the wilds of Alaska to the wilds of Featherstone to claim her marital rights and bring up my father. It's a tale worth telling, but not in this book, where I have stories of my own to relate.

Although my Inuit genes were outnumbered three to one by their Yorkshire counterparts they gave a good account of themselves in my appearance. It gave me an interesting look, which the ladies would find irresistible. A cross I would have to bear. I was a skinny five eleven and rising, already two inches taller than my dad, who looked much more of an igloo dweller than me. Although most of the pictures I've seen of eskimos showed them smiling. My dad hadn't smiled since mam died, and that was two years ago. It never seemed to occur to him that I missed her as well. To a certain extent I missed him – the way he used to be, that is.

The four of us strode out into the Saturday sunshine. Utters, or Martin Utterthwaite, to give him his Sunday name, Henry Hall and Jacky McMahon, who was a couple of years younger than us. Henry examined his Dan Dare watch, the one he'd won from the *Eagle* comic for a joke he'd sent in. Utters claimed 50 per cent ownership of the watch, as he reckoned Henry had nicked the joke from him, but if the truth be told, Utters had got the joke from my Uncle Stan.

'Anyway, what time do you call this? It's nearly dinner time, you idle sod!'

'You what?' I protested. 'I've hardly flippin' slept, me.'

'What was it?' enquired Utters. 'Your Uncle Stan snoring again?'

'It's every rotten Friday night,' I grumbled. 'He comes home with a right skinful.'

The three of them were now staggering around imitating drunken men.

'It's all right for you lot,' I said. 'He snores like Flamborough foghorn and farts like a five hundred Norton. I hate Friday nights, me.'

Jacky found this more amusing than it actually was. He was still laughing when we arrived at Mostyn's Fish Emporium, a converted single-decker West Riding bus which parked outside the Plasterers' Arms every Saturday lunchtime.

'Good day to you, Mostyn!' called out Utters in one of his many voices, this being his posh one. 'Once, with scraps, my good man. Lightly salted with a dash of vinegar and wrapped in mucky magazine – and might I have a look at the wine list while I'm waiting?'

Mostyn shook his head. 'You want to get him doing a double act wi' yer Uncle Stan. They could call theirsens the Barmy Buggers.'

'His Uncle Stan farts like Flamborough foghorn,' said Jacky.

'No he doesn't,' Henry corrected him. 'He *snores* like Flamborough foghorn. He *farts* like a five hundred Norton. You should try and get your facts straight.'

'He's only a lad,' excused Utters.

Mostyn stared at us for a second, then shook his head. 'Same for the rest of you lads?' he asked.

'Yes please.'

Mostyn turned his back as he scooped our order from the friers. He called out over his shoulder. 'Where is it today, gentlemen? Paris, Monte Carlo . . . ?'

'Brick Road Feast,' said Jacky.

'Brick Road Feast, eh? Life's just one big social whirl for you lads.'

'We've been saving up for ages,' Jacky went on.

'And does your mam know where you're going, Jacky?'

'His mam knows all she needs to know,' I said. 'We'll look after him.'

Jacky was indignant at this, although I meant no harm.

'I don't need no looking after,' he protested. 'I can look after meself, me.'

Mostyn turned to face us with a scoop of delicious-smelling chips in his hand. 'No, Foxy's quite right,' he said. 'There's funny folk go to Brick Road Feast. You need somebody with you. Somebody who knows how to behave responsibly.'

Utters laughed at this. 'Responsible? Foxy!'

'I suppose yer could do worse,' argued Mostyn, although he didn't sound convinced.

'He just emptied his uncle's po all over us,' said Jacky.

'Right . . .' said Mostyn, stuck for a reply to this. He stared at us for a second, then said, 'Four times, coming up.'

One by one, he handed us our mobile meals. 'That'll be nine pence each. Tanner for yer fish and threepence for yer chips . . . and there's yer scraps,' he added. 'Scraps is one of the few things in life what costs yer nowt.'

We all laughed when the top came off the vinegar bottle, soaking Jacky's fish. An act of sabotage by Utters – meant for me. But I knew his sneaky ways.

If these occurrences seem unrelated to the story I'm about to tell, it's because they are. It's just that there's at least one day in everyone's life which we can remember in every minute detail.

And this was my day.

Brick Road Feast was a conglomerate of many small travelling fairs which met up once a year on Brick Road Moor. How it ever came to be called a moor is one of those great urban mysteries. Unless of course a moor comprises a dozen or so acres of khaki grass, horse muck and consolidated pit ash amid a sprawl of factories, houses and Rastrick Street Gasworks.

The primary attraction of Brick Road Feast was its dangerous and sinister undertone. Attributable in no small way to the people who ran it. We strode among the cheap and cheerful attractions with all the style we could muster. Our ears bombarded by tinny repetitive pop songs, two songs for each ear. A bargain. Doing our best to avoid the entreaties of the quick-tongued beckoning stallholders.

'Come on lads! Three darts a shillin'.'

'Guess your weight, lads? Five bob if I'm wrong.' (This one was always tempting.)

'Here! Catch hold of this hammer. Big lads like you could ring this bell, no trouble. Show the lasses how big and strong you are! Hey! I'm talking to you. Come back 'ere, yer nancy boys!'

'Come inside and see the Crocodile Lady. The tragic result of an illegal union between an African pigmy and a crocodile! Tanner ter look, shillin' ter touch.'

Hard-faced people with short-term smiles that vanished as soon as money changed hands. We parted with reluctant coins and were rewarded with the failure to which we were entitled.

'Get stuffed, I check 'em every day!' sniffed the cross-eyed dwarf on the rifle range when Utters complained that the barrels were bent.

'Bugger off!' wheezed the frightening old crone on the coconut shy through the foul-smelling cumulus that leaked from the cracked and yellowed pipe she had wedged between her cracked and yellowed teeth. Jacky had scored a powerful direct hit, which left the coconut as unmoved as her pipe.

'They're all glued on, yer cheatin' old ratbag,' he grumbled.

She took a wooden ball from the bucket and hurled it at his head with surprising accuracy and force.

Ken McCoy

'Let's see if yer head's glued on, yer gormless lookin' little pillock!'

This is why we came. To test our daring against the Denizens of the Feast, as Utters called them. Jacky was always a great provider of amusement. Prizes at Brick Road Feast were rare trophies indeed. Many weeks' carefully saved pocket money was cheerfully wasted. Screams of terrified delight came from the Caterpillar when the heavily patched canopy closed over the whirling, rattling train. Concealing carnal goings on in there. What a wonderful place to spend an adolescent afternoon. Stomachs gorged on overpriced apples coated with cheap toffee and on candyfloss and hot dogs and McEwan's chocolate toffee bars. Jostling with coarse-mouthed girls with lipstick on their teeth and love bites on their necks. Escorted by Teddy boys with elongated Tony Curtis hair, drape jackets with velvet collars, drainpipe trousers and crêpe beetle-crushers. Girls casting longing glances at our handsome quartet as they hurried past us, whispering secret giggling things to one another.

Which we knew were about us.

Jacky won an anaemic goldfish in a plastic bag on the *Ping-Pong Ball into a Goldfish Bowl* stall. This was a sensational triumph achieved with a mixture of skill, timing and dishonesty. He waited until the nine-year-old nose-picking attendant was round the other side, then climbed over the rail and dropped his ball into a bowl.

'What yer gonna do wi' that?' I asked. 'Yer mam'll never let yer keep it.'

'Not since she found that frog down your lavvie,' added Utters.

'Frog in the bog!'

That was Henry, laughing at his own joke, which was just as well. Someone had to.

'I got a right belting fer that,' recalled Jacky, looking wistfully at the circling fish. 'It jumped up at her arse. She cacked hersen good and proper, yer know!'

'Well – at least she were in the right place!' said Henry.

6

'Didn't mek no difference,' recalled Jacky. 'When she jumped up, she cacked in her knickers! She were as mad as hell.'

I remember feeling a bit guilty for laughing at him. Eventually he joined in, which made it okay. You should never laugh at your mates, but with Jacky it was sometimes difficult not to.

'I've never had a pet, me,' he grumbled.

A small boy had been unsuccessfully throwing ping-pong balls for quite a while. Jacky tapped him on his shoulder.

'Hey, young 'un – d' yer wanna buy a goldfish fer a bob?'

The boy shook his head and threw another ball, which hit the rim of a bowl and bounced back on to the grass. A hand reached out and grabbed Jacky's fish. Another hand held out a sixpence. It was the boy's mother.

'Here, this is all I've got left. Yer'll have ter mek do.'

Jacky accepted the coin. Only half his asking price but he was still fourpence up on the deal. The small boy grumbled something about wanting to win one for himself, which earned him a clip round his ear.

'I'm not bleedin' made o' money. Yer'll have what yer given!'

Jacky watched her drag her son away, still protesting.

'I wish me mam were like her,' he said.

'Like her?' Utters never failed to be amazed at Jacky. 'How d' yer mean? She gave him a right crack.'

'I know,' said Jacky. 'But she bought him a goldfish, she prob'ly loves him really. My mam'd have given me a crack an' not bought me a goldfish.'

'Let's go on t' waltzers,' suggested Henry.

Brick Road Feast fairground folk never looked in the best of health. Grey and oily, with matted hair and brown teeth and smelling of halitosis and diesel fumes. Skinner was no exception.

As far as girls were concerned we were all at that funny age. Not quite ready. Patronized by girls no older than we were, who

7

would pass us over in favour of any passing eighteen year old, the rougher the better. But most drew the line at Skinner.

We spotted a couple of girls climbing aboard Skinner's Whirling Waltzer. Doris Day and Gina Lollobrigida. From behind anyway and maybe a bit slimmer, especially Gina. We took up stylish lolling positions against the garish green and red perimeter fence. The trick was to talk out of one side of the mouth, whilst from the other side a Capstan Full Strength would billow a casual plume of smoke straight up a twitching nostril. The speaker above our heads bellowed out 'I'm Not A Juvenile Delinquent' by Frankie Lymon and the Teenagers, and life was good.

Bounding from car to car with apelike agility was the apelike son of Skinner, a teenage Neanderthal whose role in life was to collect the money and charm the girls. A family vocation handed down through generations of Skinners and finally passed on by Skinner senior, who had touching but misguided faith in the sexual magnetism of his son.

Love and *Hait* were tattoed on his knuckles, which, when at rest, hung suspended just above ground level. Many links down the food chain from us, his age and IQ were a perfect match. Not so his eyes, which did not afford parallel vision. He was what an Indian would call *Looking Bombay, walking Delhi.*

It was hard to believe that some eighteen years previously, millions of sperms had sprung from Skinner senior's loins in that great race for life and Skinner junior had won. What on earth had all the others been like?

'Are you looking at my bird, twat?'

Skinner made this enquiry in mid air as he leapt from the Whirling Waltzer and landed with all the agility of his hairy forefathers, right in front of us. He seemed to be addressing Henry, into whose face he'd thrust his acne-encrusted nose. Henry said nothing, he was scared. So was I, but I felt I had to say something.

'Leave him alone, he's done nowt ter you!'

'Who's talkin' ter you, Shit fer Brains?' I stepped back

smartly, to avoid the spit accompanying his words. He returned his attention to Henry, who hadn't spoken yet.

'Are yer bleedin' deaf or summat?'

He had hold of Henry's shirt collar and Henry was going red. As the ride came to a halt, Doris and Gina stepped off and came over to see what all the fuss was about.

'What's up, Skinner?' asked Doris, who, on closer inspection, was no Calamity Jane. A rush of waiting people swarmed around them, jumping into the emptying rides.

'This twat were lookin' at yer!' A note of sheepishness had crept into Skinner's voice.

'So what? It's a free country.' She spat out a wad of chewing gum.

'He said you were his bird,' explained Utters, helpfully.

'His bird? His bleedin' bird? Who'd go out with him, the big daft poxy-faced pillock?' howled Doris Day.

'Sounds like the old brush-off to me, Skinner, me old tatey,' said Utters. He turned to the girls. 'I'd say there's more appeal in a leper's jockstrap, wouldn't you agree, ladies?

The broad grins on the girl's faces confirmed their agreement. The ride started up once again. Skinner should have been back at work, not standing there being humiliated by Utters. He had neither the wit nor the repartee to cope with this. Few people had. With the back of an oily hand he wiped an unwholesome-looking drip from the end of his nose.

'I'll kill yer, yer bastard!'

'Piss off, yer big daft baby!' said Utters, who could never keep a civil tongue in his head.

Skinner took a long, scything swing at Utters, who ducked and pushed him backwards into Skinner's Whirling Waltzer. Skinner was scooped up by a spinning car, which carried him away upside down and mad as hell but not as mad as the unusually large and belligerent lady he'd landed on, who was laying into him with merciless vigour by the time he reappeared. We should not have stayed to gloat. We should certainly not have given him a communal V sign every time he came round. But we did all these things because we were young and foolish and out to impress the girls. We were at that funny age.

Gina and Doris linked arms with us as we hurried happily away from the cursing Skinner and his Whirling Waltzer. Doris turned out to be a Fanny and Gina was really her cousin, Helen. It was clear that Fanny had sprung from a more homely branch of the family tree. Helen was taller, prettier and more refined; although it didn't take much to be more refined than Fanny, who had an enviable repertoire of rude words and mucky jokes. All in all they were good company.

A sixpenny investment on the rifle range earned Utters a cuddly toy. It was a better prize than his score merited but the stall was in the temporary charge of a young girl who succumbed to Utters' charm.

'Thank ye kindly, ma'am,' he said to the grinning girl. Turning to Fanny and Helen, he added. 'Muh gran' pappy used ter be called Two-Gun Tex Utterthwaite, the scourge of Tombstone.'

The girls looked at me for confirmation. I grinned. 'His grandad was ten-pint Tommy Utterthwaite, the scourge of the Plasterers' Arms.'

'Ah, but he was a cowboy when he was younger,' argued Utters.

The girls' eyes were on me once again, wanting to know the truth.

'He told me he worked down at the sewage works, man and boy,' I said.

'No,' explained Utters, patiently. 'That were me grandad Shoebottom, better known as Shit-Shoveller Shoebottom.'

Fanny spotted the danger first. Skinner was approaching.

'Ohh hell!' she murmured. 'He's got his daft mates with him. They'll murder yer, they're all soddin' psychos!'

'Right,' decided Utters. 'Best be off then.'

Fanny pushed me roughly in the back. '*Run!*'

There was an urgency in this command that told me all I needed to know. Few whippets would have made a better standing start than we did. I felt it unnecessary to look round at our pursuers. There was a coarseness about their language which was not reassuring. They gave every indication that they meant us great harm; this was a bad situation to be in. Jacky McMahon led the field by two clear lengths, but the rest of us, girls included, were hard on his heels. We made two circuits of the Big Wheel then peeled off past the Octopus and the Ghost Train, heading towards Oliver's House of Fun, where we planned to shake them off. We escaped through a loose panel at the back, which they couldn't possibly have known about, so how come they nearly caught up to us at the Hook a Duck? Jacky led us straight through the Coconut Shy, where he stopped and scooped up an armful of wooden balls, which he proceeded to hurl at Skinner and Co. To my dismay, Utters followed suit, so Henry and I had no option but to help out. The old crone was convulsed with rage, rushing between us and thumping us on our backs.

'Leave it!' screamed Helen. 'Don't make them madder than they already are!'

'Christ!' shouted Fanny, tugging at Utters' arm. 'They'll kill you when they get hold of you!'

We hurled a final barrage at Skinner and his cronies, which held them at bay long enough for us to make our escape. As we fled the fairground's perimeter I looked up to see where Jacky was leading us. A tram was stopped barely thirty yards away, its bell sending a clanging instruction to the driver. One final spurt and our momentum carried us up on to the platform and halfway down the aisle. Utters and I went back to repel boarders.

Skinner made a desperate lunging dive, landing on the platform, teetering, trying to establish his balance, cursing at our taunting as, with no assistance from us, he fell slowly backwards into the path of his three galloping cronies, bringing them down in a clattering heap.

'Get back to yer pigsties, yer mucky gyppos!' we bravely shouted, safe in the knowledge that they'd never catch us now.

They got to their feet and continued their pursuit. What

11

was wrong with these idiots? Didn't they know when they were beaten? We could just hear their oily, seg-studded boots clattering out a threatening rhythm of, *We're going ter get you, yer bastards!* on the cobbles between the tramlines. Why weren't they hurrying? We could see their faces set firmly in masks of hate. It was time to start worrying again; the tram was slowing down. The tram had stopped!

By the time all the alighting passengers had got off, our pursuers had arrived. The tram was boarded!

'Where's them bastards what got on at the last stop?' enquired Skinner of the conductor.

'Fares please,' said the conductor, who was only paid to collect fares and not give out passenger information.

'I said, where's them bastards what got on at the last stop, yer deaf twat?'

The conductor took a strategic backward step, away from the finger-jabbing emphasis of this repeated enquiry and pointed through the window, from where we six had been lip-reading the conversation between the two of them.

'Do you mean them bastards?' enquired the conductor.

'Fares please!'

He was a wise conductor, who had urged us to leave through the front door just as Skinner and Co. got on at the back. He didn't want trouble on his tram, thank you very much, and we were only too pleased to help him in any way we could. We were like that. Skinner will pay our fare, we said, but I don't think he did. Discretion being the better part of valour, we boarded a tram going in the opposite direction and decided to give Brick Road Feast a wide berth for a while.

Two

H enry, Jacky, Utters and me were the last remnants of the
Black Scorpions, a devil-may-care gang, formed when
we were about twelve. We did the usual daft things that boys
do. We once dammed up the stream in Wyke Valley Woods,
creating a lake deep enough to drown in. Only the council came
and released the dam when a park keeper heroically – according
to the *Unsworth Observer* – rescued a ten-year-old kid from a
watery grave. It wasn't all that heroic. The snotty-nosed kid
was sitting down in the shallow end roaring his eyes out because
his toy boat had sunk without trace. We'd have got him out
ourselves but he kept telling us to bugger off, so we did. Then
the parky came along to perform his heroic deed.

'Come outa that water, lad, yer'll catch yer death,' he said.

'Bollocks!' said the boy.

'Don't you swear at me, yer cheeky little sod, or I'll come in
there an' tan yer little arse for yer.'

'Bollocks!'

We were warming to this kid. The parky sat down and
removed his shoes and socks with a view to carrying out his
threat. The kid was unmoved.

'You touch me an' me dad'll come an' knock seven shades o'
shit outa yer. He's a bobby is me dad. Chief Superintendent.

'An' I'm the Queen of bleedin' Sheba,' said the parky. He
waded in and grabbed the kid by his collar. The kid threw
himself backwards and brought the parky down with a great
splash. The parky reacted with unnecessary violence and gave
the kid an almighty swipe that knocked the little sod back into
the deeper water, where he sank. Utters and Henry and me

dashed in and dragged the kid out. He was coughing and spluttering and using the foulest of language, then a woman came along with her dog and asked if she could help.

'It's all right, missis,' said the wet and worried parky, now sitting in the water where the kid had originally been. 'I've er . . . I've just had to pull that young lad out of the water.' The lady's face brightened up. 'Wonderful! I'll dial 999, get you an ambulance.' She was gone before the parky could stop her. We thought an ambulance was a great idea.

Blackmail's a dirty word, so they say. But not when it's applied to park keepers. The kid demanded a pound for his silence and we demanded free run of the woods. *Without let or hindrance*, to quote Utters. The parky agreed to our demands on condition that we, *Bugger off immediately before the soddin' ambulance comes, because the fewer people who know about this the better.* But it didn't stop him telling the papers how brave he'd been. We wandered off with the kid in tow.

'Can I join your gang?' he asked. The water had failed to wash the snot off his face.

'It'll cost yer,' said Utters.

'I've got a bob,' said the kid, holding out a shilling coin.

We accepted this as a down payment. 'What's yer name?' asked Henry.

'Jacky,' said the kid. 'Jacky McMahon, but don't ask me 'ow ter spell it.'

He was the youngest of us. He was constantly telling us how he'd be *famous one day, just you wait.* In the so-called swinging sixties, he experimented with LSD and hurled himself from the top floor of the Majestic Hotel, straight through the open sunroof of the Lord Mayor's official car, twelve storeys below. Some people said he chose the car on purpose because the mayor was the very magistrate who'd sent him down for three months for burglary. I couldn't see it myself. Jacky was never one to bear a grudge. Whatever the truth of the matter, he sure fulfilled his prophesy. Jacky's funeral was a modest one compared to the big civic affair accorded His late Worship the Mayor. But he got his picture in all the papers.

His soldier dad had spent Christmas Day 1941 in Hong Kong. Unfortunately the Japs thought this would be a very good day to move in and capture both the city and Jacky's dad, who never returned home. There was much family speculation as to why, because he'd never been officially declared dead. Whilst it was accepted that the Japs were no angels, it was also accepted that Jacky's mother was not exactly a joy to come home to.

As this happened eight months before Jacky was born, his dad would never have known he had a son. Perhaps if he had, Jacky's life would have been different. On the first anniversary of Jacky's death, I went to put some flowers on his grave and saw a man standing there. Perhaps praying, perhaps talking to the dead Jacky. For some reason, I didn't ask, but figured it could only have been his dad. He looked a nice enough chap. What a pity he hadn't been around when Jacky was alive. He'd have been pleased with his son.

The Unsworth Housing Department had transferred all our families from the mean streets of downtown Unsworth to the Robertstown Estate. There were three types of dwelling. Your common or garden brick, pooh-poohed by your average council house afficionado. The only advantage of the common or garden brick was that they seriously outlasted the other two types. Your concrete panelled house, on the other hand, was much admired. They began life as brightly painted show-offs but sadly sank into early decrepitude as the unkind northern elements left them dirty, streaky and unloved. Many of them, in privately owned middle age, were to suffer the indignity of stone cladding, to give that much sought after country cottage look. This was serious one-upmanship, especially if your country cottage half ended where your neighbour's dirty, streaky and unloved half began.

Our house was neither of these. Ours was your exposed-aggregate panel house. Pebbledash to them as knows no better. The queen of council houses. Like well-preserved women, they maintained their good looks well into middle age before starting to leak. This was of no concern to us, for we had her in her prime. The leaks will, even as I write, be dripping down someone else's neck and I have to confess to not being all that bothered. We had a garden and an inside toilet and were therefore socially middle class. Barry Armitage, next door but two, had even joined the Young Conservatives.

The Robertstown Estate was a rural estate. We were adjacent to Wyke Valley Woods and Benton Park Mental Hospital, which was handy, for many lunatics came to live on our estate. It was in the wood that the Black Scorpions had built their den.

We built it at the top of a horse chestnut tree. Such trees are notoriously hard to climb and this would deter intruders. The Good Lord, on tree-creating day, had decided to make the fruit of the horse chestnut tree into a seasonal sport. Such fruit being not much good for anything else, except for giving birth to other conker trees. The simple act of stripping off the spiky shell to reveal the cocooned beauty of the shiny sienna nut was one of the few sensual joys of my boyhood. That and Monica Pickersgill, whose sensual joys were soon to pale into insignificance. The Good Lord in his infinite wisdom had decreed that the first conker tree branch be at least ten feet off the ground to make your average conker, and the sensual joys therein, not easy to come by. This was probably to teach us not to take our sensual joys for granted – a lesson I never learned. But the Good Lord in his infinite wisdom had overlooked my dad's brace and bit, with which we drilled several holes into the trunk of the tree. Into these holes we inserted metal dowels to form a set of steps, which we always removed and hid whenever we weren't there. The Lord helps those who help themselves.

The beauty of living on a housing estate with odd bits still under construction was the availability of building materials. Most DIY enthusiasts took modest advantage. Perhaps a tongued-and-grooved dog kennel or a concrete bird bath. Materials for which would be benignly overlooked by the site foreman, who had enough to do and not enough time to do it in. Some, like Mr Potter from number twenty-six, abused the privilege and built a double garage out of Armitage class A engineering bricks, which only a mentally deficient millionaire would use for such a project. It wasn't as if the Potters were a two-car family – or even a one-car family, come to that.

After a three-month stint in Armley jail, Mr Potter took his tearful family back to the mean streets of downtown Unsworth. This sent out a clear message and many other ambitious projects were abandoned at design stage.

The Black Scorpions, who were never abusers of privilege, built a simple tongued-and-grooved platform, thirty feet up. Just big enough to take four sitting down or six standing. Our den was a great feat of engineering. Windy days would see us lying flat on our backs, enduring the heart-thumping thrill of staring up at the scurrying sky as the platform creaked and swayed dangerously beneath us. On calm days we would turn these clouds into horses and elephants and schoolteachers and Jacky's mother. Then as puberty popped its short and curly head over the horizon they became large-breasted ladies and gentlemen's appendages of unusual shape and size.

Then there was that warm summer's midnight when Utters and me sneaked out and lay up there until dawn. Just us and a canopy of rustling leaves and the endless acres of starlit sky beyond. We talked boyish things and looked up at the night sky and marvelled at the awe-inspiring bloody majesty of it all. I revealed my secret and as yet unfulfilled ambition to be a world-famous portrait painter, like Annigoni. Even at thirteen I was doing what my art teacher called remarkably mature work, whatever that meant. Mind you, I'd yet to make the transition from 2b pencil to oils.

'Is she any good then?' Utters asked, lighting up a Wild Woodbine and coughing out fumes from his thirteen-year-old lungs.

'Is who any good?'

'Annigoni.'

'It's a fella, he's Italian.'

'I've never heard of an Italian feller called Annie.'

'Are you thick or what?'

'What does he paint?' he asked, ignoring my taunt and taking a deep determined drag.

'Lords, ladies, anybody. He painted the Queen once.'

'My Uncle Stuart does that.'

'Your Uncle Stuart paints portraits?'

'Well, he paints ladies' – he paints gents' as well. He's a famous shithouse painter.'

'I bet your Uncle Stuart never painted the Queen's shithouse!'

'That's just where you're wrong, Foxy Foxcroft! Her Royal Majesty's allus ringin' me Uncle Stuart up. "Hello," she says. "Is thet Stuart Atterthwaite, the famouse shitehouse painter? Ay wender if you could pop round Backinnam Pellas termorrow – may hasband was out on the piss larst nayt an' he waiped his arse all over the shitehouse wall."'

'I don't believe you.'

'Why not?'

'Your Uncle Stuart hasn't got a telephone.'

You don't have to talk sense when you're thirteen and up a tree at two o'clock in the morning. There's a group of stars up there in the shape of a Scottie dog. Doubtless the astronomers have some fancy Greek mythological name for it, but to us it was the Scottie dog. Utters pointed up at it through the leaves with uncharacteristic sincerity. He pursed his mouth, goldfish fashion, and released an unsuccessful smoke ring.

'That's where I want to go. I want to be a spaceman. I want to fly right up there, up among them stars.' He grinned his lopsided grin. 'One day I'm going to fly my spaceship right up that Scottie dog's arsehole!'

Now that was real ambition. Well beyond the dreams of your run-of-the-mill astronaut. In later years, Neil Armstrong would never get further than the moon and as for that Yuri Gagarin – compared to Utters, he'd had a quick trip round Blackpool Tower. Utters wanted to be a proper astronaut. He was bright enough and determined enough and he was my best pal. As things turned out, the top of our tree was the nearest Utters would ever get to the stars.

But that's a lot nearer than most.

The tram containing Skinner and Co. took them off to a

safe distance. A distance reassuringly doubled by the tram containing us. We alighted and walked down the street in pairs. Fanny and Helen in the lead, me and Utters behind them, with Jacky and Henry bringing up the rear. Jacky was in high spirits. 'Hey!' he laughed. 'That were brilliant. I've never laughed so much since I don't know when.'

'What, since yer granny caught her nipple in the mangle?' said Henry, who'd had the sense to find the whole episode a bit traumatic.

'Yer shouldn't talk about me granny like that!' objected Jacky. 'She's a sight better than me mam any road!'

'Don't get yer knickers in a twist,' said Henry. 'I were only kidding. Any road, yer were shit scared, you. I could tell. Yer were shittin' green snowballs!'

Utters nudged me and grinned. He enjoyed these exchanges between Jacky and Henry.

'Scared?' protested Jacky. 'Give over. It were you what were scared.'

'I weren't scared – I were laughin', me – weren't I laughing, Foxy?'

I didn't reply. Personally I'd been scared stiff.

Jacky scoffed. 'If yer were laughin', why've yer gorra brown patch on yer kecks then?'

Utters and me howled at this, as did Helen and Fanny, who'd been listening in. Henry was embarrassed.

'I'm off home,' he decided. 'I'm hungry. Are yer comin', Jacky?'

'Nah.'

'Me mam'll make us summat to eat.'

'Go on then,' conceded Jacky.

They peeled off and crossed the road. 'See yer!' they chorused.

'Not if I see you first,' returned Utters.

Off they went to Henry's house, where Henry's mother's singular mission in life was to fatten up her skinny son. Utters and I made a fateful decision to break the golden rule of the Black Scorpions and take outsiders to our den.

Three

I'd never felt comfortable with girls. A minor personality defect I was soon to put right. I introduced myself, William Arthur Foxcroft, named after my grandad. Fanny was Fanny Onions, whose ambition was to get married to get rid of her surname. She was destined to marry Rodney Pickles but she didn't know that then. Helen was Helen Ash and I'm not quite sure when I fell in love with her but it was sometime that day.

In Wyke Valley Woods there was a high stone wall. Beyond this wall were the grounds of Benton Park Mental Hospital and a well-concealed trysting place, much favoured by nurses and their gentlemen friends. It was a wonderful place for trysting, hidden from everyone and everything – bar anybody at the top of that impossible-to-climb horse chestnut tree growing at the other side of the wall. The Black Scorpions had learnt much about the art of courting by secretly observing the goings-on down there.

Fanny shot up that tree like a monkey, with her cousin not far behind. From the back, Fanny appeared to have potential – slim and blonde with nice legs. But from the front, it has to be said, she was no oil painting. Sweet sixteen, with a small pinched face and dark-brown mocking eyes full of mischief. She wore a clinging, blue-and-white striped sweater that didn't have much to cling to – it looked as if someone had wallpapered over a couple of light switches. Her personality was as bubbly as Jacky's nose and her sense of humour was coarse. Anyone marrying Fanny Onions would have few dull moments, but it wouldn't be me, because I had designs on her cousin.

Helen was a year older than Fanny and possessed of a spine-shivering beauty rarely seen at the top of Unsworth conker trees. Certainly not *our* Unsworth conker tree. Her hair was a dark, silky chestnut with streaks made lighter by that year's summer sun, which had also given her skin a light tan. Everything went in and out in the right places. She had the darkest eyes and brightest smile; and here she was, sitting at the top of our conker tree. With us.

I caught Helen staring at me and sensed a mixture of pleasure and embarrassment.

'You're Billy Foxcroft, aren't you?' she said. To anyone else I'd have answered, 'So what?'

'That's me.'

'My brother goes to St Ignatius's. I've heard a lot about you.'

She turned to Utters. 'And you must be Martin Utterthwaite.'

'Martin *Wilfred* Utterthwaite,' said Utters. 'Named after me dear old dad, Gunner Wilf Utterthwaite, the first man off the boat during the 1944 Normandy landings.'

Helen and Fanny looked at me, assuming he was joking.

'It's true,' I confirmed. 'He jumped ship in Southampton.'

Utters grinned at Fanny. He already knew that if we were to be paired off he wouldn't get Helen.

'Fanny,' he enquired. 'Is that your real name?'

'Her name's Frances,' said Helen. 'But I don't think it suits her, somehow.'

Fanny grinned at this. 'Me mam calls me Fanny,' she said, 'after *Fanny by Gaslight*.' She turned to Utters. 'It's a book about a Victorian gynaecologist.

Utters screamed with laughter. To my embarrassment I didn't get it, not being quite sure what a gynaecologist was. My naïvety apparently endeared me to Helen. She smiled gently then said the wrong thing.

'You're not exactly a man of the world, are you? Didn't your mother warn you about girls like Fanny?'

My mother was a touchy subject with me. When I was fourteen I was off school with flu and my mam had gone to the chemist to get my prescription, only she didn't get there because she was knocked down and killed by a car. I know it wasn't my fault. Everybody assured me it wasn't my fault. Everybody but the one person I needed to hear it from – my dad. He took it very badly. He'd lost his mother and his wife in the space of two years. Never got over it really. Anyway, it's not what other people say, it's what you think yourself that counts.

Helen saw my discomfort, our eyes met. Thinking back, I reckon that was the exact moment.

'I've said something I shouldn't, haven't I?' she said. 'Sorry Billy – I didn't meant to offend.'

'It's OK. I lost me mam a couple of years ago. You weren't to know.'

She bewitched me with a smile. My feelings for her must have been well and truly on display. The four of us talked and laughed late into the afternoon. I could never remember feeling happier.

Fanny planted a kiss on Utters' mouth, taking him aback somewhat. 'I bet yer've never had any girlfriends, have yer?' Her question was more of a challenge – and was posed to both of us.

'We've had our moments, haven't we, Billy?' winked Utters.

For the life of me I couldn't work out which moments he was talking about. Utters looked over the edge of the platform into a clearing at the far side of the wall.

'There's naughty things go on down there that'd make your hair curl,' he said.

'Honest?' said Fanny. She followed Utters' gaze. 'Hey! Yer get a good view from up here, don't yer?'

Helen grimaced. 'Ugh! You don't actually watch people – actually doing – thingy, do you?'

I felt it time to change the subject. 'Did you hear about the Irish acid bath murderer?'

Helen turned her attention to me. Utters was peeling the spiky shell from a conker.

'No, what about the Irish acid bath murderer?' asked Helen, on cue.

'He lost his arm pulling the plug out!'

Helen laughed, Utters threw the unripe conker at me. I ducked and the conker flew over my shoulder and fell down the tree. I still remember the grin on his face as he threw it. Even to this day.

'Shhh!' said Fanny. 'There's someone down there.'

Down below, in the trysting place – a clearing surrounded by rhododendrons in full pink and white bloom – was a nurse of generous proportions. Not a handsome woman, but more than a match for her beau when it came to personal beauty. He was a man of agricultural demeanour. A gardener perhaps. Nine unblinking eyes watched the nurse undress. It would have been ten, but the gardener only had the one. Great mounds of liberated flesh flopped out all over the place. Down below me was the first completely naked woman I had ever seen – and a great disappointment it was. Her suitor didn't look overly impressed either. She reached inside her handbag and took out a packet of cigarettes. Lighting one as he reluctantly stripped down to his mud-encrusted navvy boots and a pair of derelict underpants. The latter he removed with much encouragement from the nurse. But she failed to persuade him to remove his treasured footwear.

'I'm not sure I want to see this,' whispered Helen, nudging me to one side to get a better view.

'Nor me neither,' said Fanny, her eyes transfixed on the action below.

Utters looked across at me and shrugged.

'He's got spots on his bum!' observed Fanny, who was leaning precariously over the edge. 'Watch out! His willy's on the move!'

The naked one-eyed Romeo posed awkwardly before his fifteen-stone, naked, lusting Juliet. His was a body unused to the sun, which reflected off his white agricultural skin. His monstrous navvy boots set at ten to two and his odd agricultural willy just coming up to ten o'clock. There was apparently something erotic about this size twenty-four Juliet that I hadn't spotted.

The nurse laid her naked body down on the grass, cigarette in her mouth, drawing her lover on top of her. She removed the cigarette and made to kiss him, then paused and asked in a voice that carried right up to us, 'Have yer brought a contraceptive?'

'Pardon?'

'A Johnnie,' she explained.

'Oh aye. I've got one in me jacket.'

'Well, it's not much good in yer jacket, is it?'

A short bout of confusion followed as he ferreted about in his coat pocket for the required bit of equipment. Followed by a second bout as he tried to put it on his apparently deflated organ.

'Oh heck!' he said. 'It's gone back down!'

The nurse stubbed her cigarette out on the ground and reached between his legs. 'Oh good God, Bernard – give us it here! It's all right for you, I'm on me tea break.'

'Nay, I'm doin' me best.'

'Well I just wish yer'd frame yerself, yer dozy bugger!'

A further bout of manipulation and she lay back again. 'Try it now,' she said. 'It'll have ter do.'

We always kept various handy items in our den. One such item was a whoopee cushion, which Utters was inflating, for reasons best known to himself. Bernard drew his spotty bum high in the air and was about to make his initial downward plunge when Utters tucked the cushion under his armpit and squeezed out a foul-sounding razzberry. The copulating couple froze.

'Was that you?' asked the nurse, indignantly.

'I thought it were you!'

'Yer know very well it weren't me, yer dirty sod!'

'Well, it weren't me neither!'

'It's not very nice when yer gentleman friend lets one fly halfway through sexual intercourse!' said the nurse, indignantly.

'I'm tellin' yer,' protested Bernard, 'it weren't me.'

'That's what's known as fartus interruptus,' whispered Utters.

The argument between Bernard and the nurse ran for some time, until lust got the better of them. Bernard's bum arched upwards once again.

'*Plunk!*' A dried pea bounced off his left buttock. I always kept a peashooter handy for moments such as this.

'Ouch!' said Bernard.

'Good God! What's up with yer now?'

'Summat's bit me on me arse!'

'I'll bite yer arse meself if yer don't stop messin' about!'

Bernard stopped messing about and started again. Up came the spotty bum and I fired a second pea, which, more by luck than skill, jammed itself deep within Bernard's cleavage. Utters gave me a congratulatory pat on the back. Out of the corner of my eye I could see the girls' shoulders heaving. An investigative finger probed the target area to remove the missile. Three eyes examined it and accurately identified it as a dried pea.

'It's a pea! I had a pea stuck right up me arsehole!' Realization dawned. 'Someone's shootin' peas at me arse!'

An urgent, whispered conversation followed. The nurse trying to hide her ample nakedness beneath Bernard's bony frame and Bernard, bless him, doing his best to protect her modesty at the cost of his own. Her head peeped out around his Danish pastry sized ears and she squinted up towards our tree. We had the sun at our backs, we knew we were unseen.

'Bleedin' pervert!' she shouted, obviously thinking we were but the one pervert. Our giggles must have reached her ears.

'I can hear yer,' she yelled. 'So don't think I can't!'

Like mating crabs they scuttled backwards into a bush, where a further discussion took place before Bernard darted bravely back out, still naked and erect, to retrieve items of scattered clothing.

'I just hope yer satisfied,' yelled the nurse from behind the bush, 'cos I'm fuckin' not!'

'Neither am I!' shouted Bernard.

This was too much for the girls. Fanny broke first. Sort of a pent-up, hiccuping scream. Helen joined in, an octave or so lower. Much more ladylike – if you can have ladylike hysterics. We all clung to each other in howling, face-aching delirium. I've had many a good laugh in my life but none to match that. We were still at it long after the failed fornicators had left, hurling more abuse in our direction.

Fanny managed to stop laughing long enough to give a passable imitation of the nurse. 'Was that you?' she asked of Utters.

'I thought it were you,' protested Utters, accurately mimicking Bernard.

'Yer know very well it weren't me, yer dirty bugger!' howled Fanny.

Then it happened.

The platform broke. Or rather the platform beneath Utters broke and he disappeared from view. He was still laughing as he crashed down through the branches. We weren't. A thing like that is very sobering. I climbed down first and sat on the bottom branch, staring down at the lifeless form of my best pal. He was acting, of course. Acting the goat. Playing dead. Typical Utters, trying to scare us like that. He didn't fool me, of course. I winked at Helen's worried face and whispered, 'He's always doing this.'

I sat on that bottom branch doing my bugle imitation. No one could do 'The Last Post' like me. Even Utters had to admit that. Come on Utters, you've been rumbled. He couldn't last out much longer. Any second now we'd see that daft lopsided grin of his. Helen gripped me tightly on my shoulder. She didn't say anything. She didn't have to.

The three of us jumped the last few feet to the ground. Helen leaned over him to see if he was breathing. I tried his pulse, only having the vaguest idea of its whereabouts; then Helen tried; then Fanny. One of us would have found the right place, but there was nothing. No breathing, no pulse, no sign of life. I remember thinking this was the first time I'd ever seen him without a smile on his face. One of his shoes had come off and he had a spud in his sock and I knew he was dead.

We just stood there, useless. Tears rolled down our faces where there had been tears of laughter just minutes before. We didn't know about the kiss of life in those days. There was artificial respiration, but that was only for people rescued from drowning, or was it? To give us credit, we had a go. It was Helen's idea. I knew how to do it. I had a bronze medallion for lifesaving. I don't know how long I did it for. Not very long, because I had no faith in what I was doing; or maybe I felt I was desecrating my pal's body or something. Helen took over half-heartedly before I pulled her gently away.

'I'd better get some help.' My voice didn't seem my own. It was tiny and strangled and tinged with a mixture of grief and panic.

'Would you . . . would you wait here with him, please?'

The girls nodded, ashen-faced.

And weeping silently now.

My dad's legs were poking out from beneath his Austin Ten when I arrived.

'Billy?'

My breath was lurching out in great sobs. He came out from under the car and looked up at me, wiping his hands on his overalls.

'Now then,' he said. 'What yer been up to?'

'It's Utters, dad.' I was struggling to get the words out.

'Oh aye. What's the daft beggar done now?'

'He . . . he fell out of our tree.'

My dad shook his head. 'Has he hurt himself? If he has, he's nobbut himself ter blame.'

'Dad,' I said, 'I think he might be dead.'

This had him taking me seriously for a change. 'Right then,' he decided. 'I'd best ring for an ambulance.' He started towards Mr Rosenberg's house next door – we didn't have a phone in those days – then he half turned, looked back at me, and asked gruffly, 'This isn't another of yer daft tricks, is it?'

'Course it's not.'

I suppose my tears convinced him. There were times when I just wanted my dad to hold me and tell me everything would be all right. This was one of those times.

A few minutes later he came out and said he'd rung for an ambulance and would I wait there and direct it to where Utters was and he'd go and tell Mr and Mrs Utterthwaite what had happened.

There are many folk who might have baulked at such an onerous and unhappy chore. Not my dad. He had his faults, but shirking his responsibilities wasn't one of them. Unless of course that responsibility involved me.

I rode in the front of the ambulance, taking them up the dirt track that ran within a few yards of our tree. We arrived to find a tragic little group, standing or kneeling around my pal's body. The girls were standing quietly in the background, arms around each other, not wishing to intrude on family grief. Mrs Utterthwaite was silently cradling her son's head in her lap. As still as stone, petrified with grief. She reminded me of a picture I'd once seen of Michaelangelo's Pieta. One of the ambulancemen knelt beside Mrs Utterthwaite to check for his life signs. He turned to his colleague and gave an almost imperceptible shake of his head. The two of them stood back to allow Utters' mother her time with him.

My dad stood, head bowed, with his arm around an inconsolable Mr Utterthwaite, who wept great buckets of silent tears. It was as though he didn't want to disturb his wife's quiet, dignified mourning. Utters' sister, Maggie, knelt beside her brother, clutching the rosary she always carried, praying for the repose of his soul. She was good at praying, was Maggie. Mind you, knowing Utters, she'd need to be.

The Utterthwaites were Catholics like us. Perhaps their faith could help them at a time like this. It had to be good for something. A police car arrived. Its siren respectfully switched off as soon as it drew close enough to assess the magnitude of the situation.

Apart from my mam dying, it was without doubt the blackest moment of my life. So how much worse was it for Utters' mam and dad? Jesus! That didn't bear thinking about.

One by one, me and the girls were asked to sit in the police car to tell them what had happened. We all told the same story without the need for collusion. None of us mentioned the nurse and her boyfriend. Perhaps to avoid embarrassment, or maybe out of respect for Utters' memory. We just knew it was the right thing to do.

Four

After they'd all made their sad exits, I found myself standing beside my dad. Just the two of us. I felt a glimmer of hope that he was about to bend and offer me the solace I needed.

'It's been a bad do has this, lad,' he remarked at length, staring into the distance. 'I hope it were nowt ter do with you.'

The glimmer of hope was extinguished in one short sentence.

'How d' yer mean?' I asked, hurt. 'Do yer think it was me who pushed him? Is that what yer think?'

'I'm not sayin' that, lad.' He still spoke without looking at me. 'All I'm saying is that you and him weren't beyond a bit of horseplay. Things like that can go too far. That's all I'm saying.'

'Well, there wasn't any horseplay, it was an accident – satisfied?'

His eyes were on me now, annoyed at my attitude. 'Just you watch your mouth when yer talking ter me, lad! I *am* yer father.'

'I thought fathers were supposed to be there when yer needed comforting,' I retorted, bitterly.

'No lad,' he said. 'That's mothers. You haven't got one of them – through no fault of mine.'

He walked off without another word, adding resentment to my brimming cup of emotions. That was the nearest he ever got to actually blaming me for Mam's death. He never said as much, but to his dying day I reckon he thought it was my fault that Utters fell out of that tree.

I stood for a long time, staring at the spot where my pal had died. I could take you there today, even after all these years. It wouldn't be too difficult. I found the conker that Utters had thrown at my head and planted it in the exact spot. I used one of the metal dowels to dig a hole with, then I hurled it and all the other dowels, with every ounce of my strength, in every direction. There's now a small but flourishing tree growing there. Utters' tree.

His mother cried when I told her about it years later and said what a nice way to remember her boy.

Not far away was a wooden bench on which all the Black Scorpions had carved their names and I sat there until the dying embers of that awful day's sun slipped over the fractured skyline of the Robertstown Estate. Needless to say, I became consumed with all the *if only* things you think about at such times. *If only* we'd gone straight home after Brick Road Feast. *If only* we hadn't met the girls. *If only* we hadn't played our daft tricks on the nurse and Bernard. How odd that I should remember his name. If only my pal Utters would jump out from behind a tree with that big daft silly stupid lopsided grin on his face and tell me how he'd tricked us all.

If only.

Henry and Jacky came and sat with me for a while. Well, Jacky sat with me. The news had flashed round the estate like wildfire. Henry just mooched around, hands thrust deep into his pockets, absent-mindedly kicking stones. They were pals of Utters as well, but not close to him, not like I'd been.

'We've only just heard,' said Jacky. 'We knew yer'd be a bit brassed off, so we came.' He looked at Henry. 'Didn't we, Henry?'

Henry nodded.

'Yer dad said yer'd still be here,' went on Jacky. He fished into his pocket and pulled out the remains of a bar of chocolate. 'He sent yer this.'

'Did he now?' I said. 'I reckon he's got a guilty conscience.'

The two of them looked at each other, not understanding my comment.

'He sent yer a full bar,' said Henry. 'But greedy bollocks had to have some!' He looked accusingly at Jacky. I broke the remaining piece in two and gave half to Henry. Jacky realized he wasn't about to get any more.

'I'm OK,' he said. 'I'm not all that hungry.'

'Good job,' said Henry. 'Yer weren't gonna get none.'

Jacky pulled a face and looked at me. 'If there's gonna be one o' them rectum mass things, d' yer think we'll be invited?'

I saw Henry turn round at the mention of the word *rectum*. He was about to take the piss out of Jacky. I looked up at him and shook my head. This wasn't the time nor the place.

Jacky really meant, 'Would they want *me* there?' He had a modest opinion of his status in society.

'I don't know about anyone else,' I assured him, 'but *Utters* would want us there. Blimey! We were his best pals.'

There was another period of silence, broken only by Henry's stone kicking. Then, wary of this intrusion on my grief, he stopped, then asked hesitantly, 'How, er . . . How did it happen?'

It took me a while to summon up enough composure to answer. 'Well, we took the girls up to the den . . .' I paused, anticipating some admonition for this serious breach of the Black Scorpions' code. But none came. The Black Scorpions had become a thing of the past that day. 'Anyway,' I continued, 'this nurse and a feller turned up . . .'

I described in detail the antics of the nurse and Bernard and felt myself smiling when I came to the bit about Utters and the whoopee cushion and me and the peashooter.

Henry furrowed his brow and gritted his teeth to suppress any untoward laughter. Jacky had no such inhibitions. He threw his head back and laughed out loud. Henry joined in, with a contorted look of apology on his face. It was okay. No one would have been laughing louder than Utters, had he been there.

'I knew it!' grinned Jacky, triumphantly. 'I knew when that bugger went, he'd go out in style.'

'Just one thing, Jacky,' I cautioned. The smile vanished from his face and he listened intently, with a serious frown. 'And this goes for all of us. Don't ever tell his mam and dad about that part of it. They wouldn't want to think *that* was the last thing he saw before he – yer know.'

Henry nodded his agreement. Jacky nodded because Henry had nodded. We all shook hands on it.

'Let that be the last secret of the Black Scorpions,' I said, knowing this would ensure that Jacky would carry the secret to his grave.

As they got up to go I asked them if they'd call in and tell my dad thanks for the chocolate and I'd be home later. I watched them trudge off into the gathering gloom and pondered over Utters' last day on this planet. All in all, it could have been worse.

After the assassination of Abraham Lincoln, there was a black joke going round Washington about a reporter who'd accosted Mrs Lincoln on the steps of the Ford Theatre after John Wilkes Booth had done his evil deed. 'Mrs Lincoln,' he'd asked, 'apart from that, did you enjoy the show?'

'Hey, Utters!' I shouted his name heavenwards, for that's where I assumed he'd be. 'Apart from that, did you enjoy your day?'

'I'm sure he did!'

It was a soft voice. I turned and smiled, happy to see her.

'Oh . . . ! Hiya,' I said. 'I didn't see you there.'

Helen smiled back. 'Sorry, I didn't mean to creep up on you.'

She sat beside me and unselfconsciously put her arm around me. We didn't speak at first, then a daft memory struck me. The first of many memories I'd have of Utters.

'He once told me he didn't want to go to heaven. He said he'd rather be with his friends.'

'Oh, I think he'll be up there all right,' smiled Helen. 'Mind you, I don't know what they'll make of him.'

'He was me best pal. When me mam died he was brilliant. It was like having a brother.'

'You've been lucky,' she said. 'I've never had a friend like that.'

'What about Fanny?'

I looked around at her and caught her smile. 'Fanny? Oh, Fanny's just Fanny. She's one of those people who just . . . tag along, and people don't mind, because she's such a good laugh. I'd hardly call her my best friend.'

I went quiet, because I didn't feel like talking any more and she understood. She was like that. My head dropped on to her shoulder and I must have nodded off. I awoke with a sudden jerk and she gave a quiet laugh. She had a pleasant smell about her and I didn't want her to go away.

'Do you fancy a walk?' I asked.

She took my hand and squeezed it, saying, 'I think a walk would be really nice.'

There was a warmth and charm about her that washed away the sadness of the day. I'd known her for half a day and for a lifetime and if I'd had any sense I'd have known that I was in love with her. But love was a word that didn't trip easily off the lips of unsophisticated Unsworth lads. We wondered if we had any right to feel so happy under the circumstances. It was the day before my sixteenth birthday.

'You're not from round here, are you?' I said. 'I'd have noticed you if you were.'

'Careful . . . that sounds suspiciously like a compliment.' She was smiling at me again. I liked that.

'Maybe it was. Where are you from?'

'I live on Harecroft Lane.'

I figured she lived somewhere like Harecroft Lane. A lot more upmarket than the council house I lived in. Maybe she wouldn't want to know me when she found out I lived in a council house.

'I live on the Robertstown Estate,' I said.

'I know.'

I looked at her, surprised she knew.

'When I got back home,' she explained, 'I told my brother

what had happened and I mentioned your name. Apparently you're his hero. So was Utters.'

'I suppose you think I'm an idiot? Everyone else does.'

She shook her head. 'I get the impression you're the type who acts first and thinks later. There's a lot to be said for that.'

'Do you know what Utters used to say about me?' I looked at her, she was waiting for me to continue. 'He said, "Foxy, you're always in the shit. The only thing that varies is the depth."'

She laughed and I asked her if she was still at school.

'I'm doing my first-year A levels at Notre Dame.'

'A fellow Catholic, eh?' I should have known this already with her brother being at Saint Iggy's.

'Sort of,' she said. 'But I'm not very devout.'

'Nor me.'

Our walk led us deep into the woods, to a place where the stream divides for a while, leaving a small, grassy island. The place was bathed in the pale light of a full moon, beaming down on us like a used-car salesman. I guided Helen across what we, the Black Scorpions, called the Secret Stepping Stones, although what was so secret about them beats me. We lay down together in the long, cool grass and gazed up at the stars, just holding hands, nothing more. Then she leaned over and kissed me on the mouth – and I realized I'd never been properly kissed before. As she pulled away I ran my fingers through her hair and drew her back down to me. It was a brief moment of innocent love between two young people. Although innocence tends to be short-lived under such circumstances.

About an hour before midnight we succeeded where Bernard and the nurse had failed. It was my first time and it was never like that again. Afterwards we lay side by side, both naked in the moonlight. I couldn't believe what I'd just done.

'Blimey!' I said. 'I never thought the day would end like this. Do you think it was a bit disrespectful?'

I propped myself up on one elbow and looked down at her, cushioned on a bed of soft grass. Her hands behind her head, smiling up at me. In all my life, even to this day, I've never seen anything so beautiful.

'I don't think you need to feel guilty about your pal,' she said, gently. 'I'm absolutely sure he'd have approved.'

I nodded. She was right. Utters would be as jealous as hell, but he would approve. I lay back down beside her.

'He never did it, you know.' I took her hand. '*You know*, what we've just done.'

'Well, I didn't think he had. It's the Catholic in us. Original sin and all that.'

Did this mean *she'd* never done it before? If not, she'd certainly got quite a knack for it. I looked at my watch. Eleven thirty.

'I'm not sixteen for another half hour,' I said. 'You could be locked up for what you've just done.'

She gasped in mock horror. 'What will it take to buy your silence, sir?'

'Sorry, miss, I cannot be bought. You must be punished, an eye for an eye, a tooth for a tooth!'

We lay in each other's arms until a distant clock struck midnight, heralding my birthday. She rolled over on top of me, then sat back on her haunches, straddling me. Her beautiful naked body illuminated by the scattered moonlight shining down through the sparse leaves of a nearby silver birch. She smiled down and took my breath away with her loveliness.

'Happy birthday, Billy,' she said. 'I'm ready for my punishment now.'

And so it went on for the rest of the summer.

You don't get too many days like that in a lifetime.

Five

U tters was buried in the cemetery beside the Church of Our Lady of Perpetual Succour.

'I suppose they're the perpetual suckers,' he'd once grinned, pointing at the graves. It was hard not to remember things like that, even as they were lowering him in. Utters the perpetual sucker, I think not. His mother came and stood beside me as I hung back afterwards to have a quiet last word with him.

'Our Martin was forever goin' on about you, Billy.' She smiled and put her arm around me. 'By 'eck! You got up to some stunts together, you and him. You couldn't have been closer if you'd been brothers.'

Then she linked arms with me and led me out of the cemetery. Mr Utterthwaite, walking in front beside Maggie, looked round to check that his wife was all right. On seeing she was with me, he gave a grey-faced smile of approval and walked on. It was an insignificant action but it gave me a little boost. Adults generally disapproved of me. I could never understand why.

Back at his house they had a funeral tea with ham sandwiches, pork pies and buns and things. I sat in the background with Henry and Jacky. Both of them went home at the earliest opportunity and I didn't blame them. People were standing round talking about everyday things, even to Mr and Mrs Utterthwaite. I suppose it was a cack-handed attempt to alleviate their distress. But I suspected they didn't want their distress alleviating, not yet anyway. I certainly didn't.

In the church the priest had said soothing words about Martin being in a better place. Taken before his time, but once we all accepted our loss, we should be happy for him, for he surely would be happy where he was.

It was the injustice of it all that angered me. Why should a potential world shaker like Utters be taken, when prats like Pisspot Perkins and Folly Berger were spared?

These were just two of the people who were determined to make my final year at school as uncomfortable as possible . . .

St Ignatius's College was a Catholic grammar school staffed half by Jesuits and half by lay teachers. Rumour had it that the Jesuits we got were the ones who'd been kicked out of the Gestapo for being too cruel. Discipline was strict. The standard punishment was the tolly, or the ferula, to give its proper title. Shaped like the sole of a gym shoe, it was made of gutta-percha, a barely pliable rubbery substance which, when properly administered to the hand, left no permanent marks. Tollies were ordered in multiples of three. The offender then had to deliver himself up for punishment to the tolly office and receive the punishment from whichever Jesuit was on duty. Failure to do this within twenty-four hours would result in the punishment being doubled. The psychological trauma thus inflicted on the boys was far worse than the punishment itself – and that was bad enough.

After receipt of the caning, you must remember to say a grateful *Thank you, Father* and walk nonchalantly out, past the usual gathering of boys, all keen to spot any sign of tears. It always helped to ease the pain if, in passing, you could manage to fetch at least one of these ghouls a casual but heavy clip around the ear, or perhaps a neat kick midst groin or buttock.

The worst torturer was 'Folly' Berger.

Although we kids referred to him as *Father*, he wasn't a fully fledged priest, he was a scholastic, a sort of trainee priest. He administered the tolly with great enthusiasm, *laying on*, as we called it. He was careful never to leave any tell-tale marks on his victims. I suppose there was a certain skill in this, although we didn't appreciate it at the time. In any case, who was going to complain? It was a great honour to win a scholarship to

St Ignatius's. Every raggy-arsed Catholic kid in and around Unsworth had had this drilled into them all through primary school. No, we knew we had to put up with the inconvenience of the odd torture session. It was unlikely any of our parents would be able to do anything about it, even if we told them. It was more likely they'd give us a clip round the ear for not behaving ourselves.

I had more than my fair share of the tolly. It wasn't that I was a bad kid, I just seemed to find trouble where others didn't. If I threw a stone, a window would get in the way. If I got into an argument, the other kid would take a swing at me and I would retaliate. Some kids are like that.

It started with a scrap. We were in the school chapel to confess our weekly sins, and I had a beauty to confess. It was two weeks since Utters had died and life around me was going on as normal. I'd been bracing myself to confess the ultimate carnal sin and had chosen Father Duffy as the man to give me absolution. There were always two confessionals in use. Father Smyth, who was terribly harsh on dirty boys who regularly practised self-abuse, had but a small queue of chaste, non self-abusers, awaiting his absolution. But Father Duffy, an understanding priest, ran a popular confessional and always handed out just two Hail Marys and a Glory Be, no matter what the sin. Errol Flynn would have been in and out in a couple of minutes, completely absolved of all carnal sin. Father Duffy had a long queue of regular customers snaking all round the chapel. This was known as the wankers queue.

As I knelt there I wondered if Helen was doing the same. In a way, confessing it to a priest devalued the love I felt for her. Absolution was given only if the penitent felt genuine remorse and made a genuine act of contrition. Just the thought of Helen brought a smile to my face. I certainly didn't feel very contrite. I would have to make a solemn vow not to sin again. How could I tell such a lie in confession? A battle with my Catholic conscience ensued. Like all the other boys, I'd had five years of religious lessons, which had revealed a lot of gaping holes in the logic of it all. We were supposed to patch over these holes with our faith. I remember Utters once wondering about the probability of five thousand people turning up to a long sermon with only five loaves and two fishes between them. 'Surely a few of them would have taken sandwiches,' he'd pointed out to Father Callaghan, who'd chastised him for his blasphemy.

Rather than add to my sins by making a false confession I decided to leave. Impatient to know if Helen had done the same.

The fight had started over nothing as usual. I spotted Blessed John McGilligan, as he was known, waiting outside Father Smyth's confessional, all holier-than-thou, as indeed he was.

'You're in the wrong queue,' I whispered.

'How do you mean, *the wrong queue*?' he asked, in all innocence.

I mimed my irreverent reply, indicating his probable hobby, which was a blasphemous thing to do in a place of worship – but I was only joking. McGilligan was an overtly pious, physically awkward and uncoordinated boy, who would probably have had trouble mastering the mechanics of this lonely but popular pursuit. He was annoyed at my implication.

Flying into a totally disproportionate rage, he dragged me out of the chapel and proceeded to pummel me hysterically, in that windmill way that non-fighters do. I fended him off for as long as I could, not wishing to add injury to insult, but eventually I had to give him a defensive crack on the jaw, just to calm him down. His jaw stood up surprisingly well, which is more than I can say for my fingers. I knew I'd broken a couple as soon as I hit him. If he doesn't give up, I thought to myself, instead of using my fists, I would use my head.

I would run away.

'Watch it, Foxy – Pisspot's comin'.' This warning came from one of the circle of fight fans surrounding us. A tall, pale youth pushed his way through. He had pale, insipid eyes, pale hair and pale eyebrows. (Uncle Stan said, 'Never trust a man with pale eyebrows.') His long bony nose was doing its best to burst through the flimsy tissue of spotty skin stretched across it. Austin Perkins was a school prefect. A title conferred on him as a result of a clerical error by the school secretary. His nickname, Pisspot Perkins, illustrated the esteem in which he was held by us younger kids.

'OK you two, I'm hauling you off to the beak!'

'Piss off, Pisspot, they only have beaks in Billy Bunter books!'

'Less of your cheek, Foxcroft – and don't call me Pisspot!' whined Pisspot. 'You'll probably get the sack this time.'

Expulsion was certainly a possibility. I'd recently been caught with the school shoplifting gang and escaped punishment by the skin of my teeth as I had no loot about my person. I'd dropped the packet of Camel cigarettes I'd nicked into Thick Harry's pocket. It didn't make any difference to him, his pockets were already full of stolen goods, an odd packet of fags wouldn't make much difference. Even he thought he'd nicked them. I'd been given the benefit of the doubt but warned as to my future conduct.

Folly Berger was tall and gaunt and in his mid twenties. He'd taken the cloth after his beautiful and wealthy fiancée had taken her hook. His sense of humour had also deserted him and his hair was seriously thinking about it. The milk of human kindness was not delivered to this man's door. It was not good news to find that he was duty tolly master. It boded ill, but I had a plan.

I eyed the upraised right arm of Folly Berger with apprehension and wondered if my scheme was going to work. It had seemed a good plan a little earlier when Folly had decided that nine strokes of the tolly to be administered there and then, followed by a visit to the rector of the college, Father O'Dea, would be adequate punishment. It was the second part of the punishment I was worried about. The rector was a god-like figure and to be sent to him was a very serious matter indeed. I was going to be expelled for sure. My dad would be livid.

'One!'

Christ that hurt! I'd held out my injured right hand first and was beginning to wonder at the wisdom of my plan.

41

'Two!'

The bastard was really laying on. He was smiling, but I couldn't see the joke! I figured I needed to take just one more to make my plan work.

'Three!'

I howled in agony and drew my hand away, genuine tears spurting from my eyes.

'Come on, Foxcroft!' snapped the smiling priest. 'Only six more to go and then we'll pay a little call on the rector.'

'You've broke me fingers, Father.' I said this almost gleefully, despite the pain throbbing through my hand.

'Don't be ridiculous, boy!' snarled the man who'd sent boys out of his office semi-conscious with pain but totally free of breaks and bruises.

I turned to leave his office, ignoring his hysterical demands that I stay for the remainder of my punishment. The fearfully waiting McGilligan, who had been awarded just three tollies, stared in amazement as I walked past him, blinking watering eyes and heading rapidly in the direction of the rector's study, closely followed by the berating Berger, now panicking as the implications of my injury began to dawn on him. We strode swiftly along the musty brown corridor in tandem. Our shoes tapping an ever-quickening duet on the worn oak parquet floor. Past many a gaping eye and open mouth. Using my good hand I knocked on the rector's door.

'*Come!*' boomed Father O'Dea.

I and my erstwhile torturer entered together. The study was regimentally tidy. There was dark, mahogany panelling on the walls. A colour photograph of Pope Pius XII hung beside a photo of a nun who looked to have made a wise career choice. Were it not for her wall eye and moustache you'd have sworn it was Rocky Marciano in a nun's habit. She could only have been a relative. Behind the rector's needlessly large desk stood a needlessly large bookcase full of learned books with obscure titles. On top of this stood a jar of Airwick, presumably to counteract the smell of stale Senior Service smoke and rectorial farts. Half hidden behind the air freshener was a picture of

Jane Russell, presumably to counteract the photo of the nun. I recognized the picture and knew that the air freshener obscured the interesting bits of Miss Russell. The rector was obviously putting his vow of chastity to a most rigorous test.

A shaft of dusty sunlight suddenly streamed through the window, illuminating the rector's bald and freckled head, to which there was attached a large, unexplained elastoplast. He was a small hawk of a man, who'd spent many years in Africa instilling the fear of the Devil into the heathen hordes. The rector could instil fear at a hundred yards and was a handy man to have on your side. Especially if you were God. All this fear was not enough to prevent his title being distorted into an obvious anal nickname.

Which we knew he knew about.

'What is it, boy?' The rector said this without looking up.

Folly's mouth opened and shut, when he realized the rector wasn't addressing him.

'Father Berger's broke me fingers, Father.'

The rector noticeably stiffened but still he didn't look up.

'Name?'

'Foxcroft, Father.'

'Show me the hand.'

I pushed my injured hand right under the rector's nose. It was bruised and swollen. He stared at it for ages. Not once did he look up at me.

'Get along to Miss Crigg, boy, and stop your whining!'

I wasn't whining. Maybe the rector thought a little bullying would stop me complaining too much. As I shut the door behind me I heard the rector say, 'You seem to have dropped a bit of a clanger here, Berger!'

Miss Crigg was the music teacher, who doubled as the school nurse. She was a tall woman with large breasts who figured in the sexual fantasies of most post-pubic pupils. As far as corporal punishment was concerned, she was the school's abolitionist.

I stood patiently at the back of the music room as she vainly tried to teach 3B the descant to 'A Lark in the Clear Air'. When she caught sight of me out of the corner of her eye, I held out my hand with a pathetic look on my face and said, 'Father Berger's broke me fingers with the ferula, Miss!'

She dropped her conductor's baton, let out a cry of triumph, then grabbed my hand to get a closer look.

'Are you sure they're broken?' she asked hopefully.

'I think so, miss.'

'Marvellous! Any witnesses?'

A word of sympathy wouldn't have gone amiss.

'Yes, miss.'

Miss Crigg was actively campaigning to have all forms of corporal punishment banned at St Ignatius's and my broken hand was just what she needed to alter the run of a losing battle.

'Sorry if I seem a bit a callous but you're like manna from heaven.'

'I thought I might be, miss.'

She gave me a sideways look and then smiled. 'Well, I think it's the hospital for you, my lad. The quicker the better.'

I had to agree with her. My hand was beginning to give me some real stick. I just hoped I hadn't been just a bit stupid and done some permanent damage. She left her class in the care of the class captain, who picked up the baton with great relish. Miss Crigg and I left the music room, leaving the choir singing 'Rock Around The Clock'.

She spent the rest of the day with me in hospital – she'd no need to. As I came out of the plaster room I saw Miss Crigg talking to Father McShane, the nearest thing to a human being amongst the St Ignatius Jesuits. He looked up as I arrived.

'Now then, young Foxcroft,' he smiled, flicking the last quarter inch of Woodbine reluctantly away and blowing a lazy smoke ring towards me. Celibacy releases the mind for all sorts of other skills.

'How's the hand?'

'It's broken, Father, and it hurts.'

'It's entitled to hurt considering what it's been through. It's a wonder you didn't break it on McGilligan's jaw. He's been sent here as well, you know. It's him I'm waiting for. He's in X-ray.'

McGilligan had complained to Berger about his jaw being possibly broken as a way of avoiding the tolly. The significance of this wouldn't have escaped Berger – or the rector. But I was the only one who really knew how my hand had come to be broken. Who was to say it wasn't Berger? Not me for a start. Only an idiot would hold out a broken hand for someone to hit with a tolly.

'The tollies came after the fight, Father.'

'I know,' agreed Father McShane. 'That's why they'll never be able to prove that you're lying. Miss Crigg's going to ask for Mr Berger's dismissal.'

'Do you think I'm lying, Father?' I asked curiously. It was a daft question, of course he knew.

'It doesn't matter what I think, does it? My only concern is for the school. Publicity like this won't do us any good at all.' The priest lit another cigarette.

'What about the boys, Father, don't you ever think of them?' I seemed to have joined Miss Crigg's crusade.

'There are some boys who never get into trouble, you know,' argued the priest. 'Some boys come to work, not fight and fool around.'

'I don't see how hitting me will make any difference. I don't fool around in your lessons and you've never had me punished once!' I felt I had him there.

'He's got you there!' interrupted Miss Crigg heatedly.

She'd been listening intently to our conversation. She'd seemed especially interested in the part about my fight with McGilligan. I was especially interested in the way her bosom heaved this way and that when she got excited.

'You know, Father,' she went on. 'If you could persuade the rector to ban that barbaric ferula, perhaps young Foxcroft here could tell a little white lie and say he broke his finger fighting. That way, the aptly named Folly Berger could keep his job,

45

unworthy though he is, and the school could avoid a lot of bad publicity.'

It was warm in the hospital and I was fascinated by a tiny bead of sweat travelling adventurously down from the front of her neck towards the exotic grotto between her open blouse and the delights that lay hidden within.

'Good heavens, I'm a man of the cloth!' replied Father McShane, who, I assumed, knew nothing about exotic grottoes. 'I couldn't possibly encourage the boy to tell lies, of any colour.' He grinned at me, flashing oddments of nicotine-stained Jesuit teeth and said, mischievously, 'Perhaps, under the circumstances, you'd better just say nothing and leave all the lying to me!'

Everything seemed to have got far more complicated than I'd intended. It had started out with me just trying to avoid getting expelled, it was never my intention to get involved in Miss Crigg's abolition crusade. How amazing that events seem to snowball with no effort from me at all.

Miss Crigg gave me a dazzling smile as we left the hospital, she seemed well pleased with the day's events. 'Billy,' she said, 'I know you've been through a lot of pain today but perhaps you'll think it worthwhile if you've helped rid the school of that barbaric instrument.'

'Yes, miss.'

She'd called me Billy! She must really fancy me, although I must say, she showed a lot of self-control. Of course, it would never do for a teacher to be seen lusting openly after a pupil, especially at a Jesuit school.

It would be our secret.

I went back to school a couple of days later. With my O Levels imminent I needed as much schooling as possible, although I couldn't do much work, as my writing hand was out of commission. With luck I'd be able to use it to take my exams, which were just over a week away. Halfway through the morning I was summoned to the rector's office.

'Come!' he boomed, in answer to my timid knock.

I shuffled in uncomfortably, not knowing what was in store. He was sitting with his back to me, reading something.

'Foxcroft?' he grunted.

'Yes, Father.'

'Tell me, boy, what is the eighth commandment?'

'Thou shalt not bear false witness against thy neighbour, Father.' Only a Catholic kid could rattle this off like a parrot.

'Thou shalt not tell lies!' interpreted the rector.

'Yes, Father.' I could see where this was leading.

'How did you damage your hand, boy?'

'Father Berger broke my fingers with the ferula, Father.' I found it easier lying to his back.

'If *Mister* Berger did this, then he must be punished, don't you agree?'

He seemed keen to correct me on Folly's proper title.

'There are those who say he should leave the college,' he went on. 'However, I have heard an alternative version of the story. I have heard that you damaged your hand fighting!'

He swivelled round in his chair and fixed me with a watery, grey-eyed glare that drilled through me.

'I want the *truth* here, Foxcroft. I'm not interested in a certain *arrangement*, which was presented to me by a well-meaning but misguided person, to cover up Mr Berger's alleged brutality in exchange for abolishing the ferula. If he did what you say he did, then I will have him dismissed and his teaching career within the Jesuit movement will be at an end. The ferula of course will remain, as a proven instrument of reprimand. However, I consider Mr Berger to be a devout, dedicated and compassionate man, with a good record as a teacher. One day he will make a fine priest.'

My plan had been contemptuously seen for what it was. I would no longer be Miss Crigg's hero. If I'd been older I might have stuck to my guns. I'd certainly have taken issue with him over his definition of *compassionate man*. Sad to say, I wasn't much of a liar and I knew I'd have to come clean. The rector clipped a pair of pince-nez to his nose, glared at me over the top of them, then boomed theatrically: 'Give me the boy at the age of seven and I will give you the man. Do you know who said that, Foxcroft?'

His question cut through my racing thoughts. Of course I knew, every kid in the school knew.

'St Ignatius, Father.'

'St Ignatius de Loyola,' confirmed the rector. 'Unfortunately, we don't get the boys until they are eleven. This presents us with something of a challenge. It is my opinion that the ferula helps redress the balance.'

I didn't agree with this but I thought it best not to mention it.

'I *might* have broke my hand fighting, Father,' I volunteered miserably.

'Might have?' he thundered. '*Might have*'s not good enough, boy! You are not a fool! I am not a fool! You will know the precise moment you broke your hand!'

'I *did* break it fighting, Father,' I confessed, resignedly.

A fleeting look of triumph flickered over his sharp face, disturbed only when his pince-nez sprang clear of his nose and bounced almost noiselessly on the parquet floor. He held me in a stony gaze and tapped his fingertips together, as though wondering what foul punishment he could inflict upon me.

'Your answer does not surprise me, boy. I do not consider you an asset to this college, so you will therefore leave. You will remove your belongings, your books and yourself. However . . . !' – he spun dramatically sideways in his chair and gazed up longingly at Jane Russell – 'the fact that you eventually saw fit to tell the truth goes in your favour, insofar as you will be allowed to return to take your O level examinations. It would be curmudgeonly of me to say otherwise. You will therefore be thankful for my generous and forgiving nature.'

I turned to leave, wondering if I should thank him for his generous and forgiving nature. Or perhaps I should thank Jane Russell. He called after me. 'What you did, boy, was dishonest – but it required an element of fortitude bordering on the foolhardy. This is a quality to be admired. Perhaps if you channel that quality in the right direction, you may become a man after all.'

'Thank you, Father.'

'Goodbye to you, Foxcroft.'

Did I detect a note of admiration in his voice? Perhaps not.

With all this and Utters' recent death on my mind, I didn't do as well as I ought to have done. My final exam was geography, which I shouldn't have failed but did. The fact that I had great difficulty writing didn't help. It was three o'clock on a Friday afternoon when I left the gates of St Iggy's for the last time. There were four of us marching down the road. Ceremoniously hurling our schoolcaps into the air as tradition dictated, never to be retrieved, except by more junior boys following in our wake in anticipation of such an occurrence. One of my pals looked round to see who'd got his cap. He grinned and nudged me.

'Pisspot's behind us,' he said.

I issued my instructions as we walked. A hundred yards from the school we turned to face him and within seconds we had him on the floor, yanking his trousers off. One of the other kids went a bit too far and pulled off his underpants and shoes. All of these were thrown over a nearby wall, beyond a locked gate. Irretrievable. He got to his feet in tears of shame, then, covering his privates with his hands, he ran back to the school through crowds of boys jeering and laughing at his bare backside. I watched, shocked at what I'd started. This wasn't revenge, this was cruelty. I was as bad as him – worse. Maybe Perkins learned a lesson that day. I know I did.

Six

O ur family consisted of me and my dad and Uncle Stan. My dad was forty-three years old, twenty years younger than Uncle Stan, who was actually my great uncle. In fact he was my grandad's younger brother, he who married my eskimo grandma. Uncle Stan came to live with us just after Mam died, he reasoned that we must have a spare bed, but short of taking my mam's place in Dad's bed, he was mistaken. Anyway, a bed was found and he came to sleep in my room. There was a good side and a bad side to this. The good side was all the amazing stories he used to tell me as we lay awake in bed at night. He'd been something of an adventurer. An airman during the war, he'd mined for coal in Featherstone, for gold in California, for diamonds in South Africa and for opals in Australia. He must have been a crap miner to finish up sharing a room in a council house, working as a club comic.

The down side was the nocturnal noises he made when asleep. Uncle Stan had a BSA Bantam motorbike that made less noise than he did when he was snoring. And when he wasn't snoring and farting, he was talking in his sleep. Oddly enough, I got used to it, but what I could never get used to was his awful habit of not using the bathroom when he needed a pee. He had a tin po, a chamber pot, a gazunda or whatever you choose to call it – a pisspot if you're Jacky McMahon. There was no need for it. When we'd lived in a terrace house with a cold and lonely outside lavatory it was a necessity, but not in our beautiful two-bedroom council house with indoor plumbing. Whenever he came in late, especially if he'd been out to the pub or been entertaining at a club, he'd sneak into our bedroom, ever so considerately not turning the light on, so as not to disturb me, then out would come the po. It was a tin po with annoying acoustics. A battered old receptacle that had travelled the world with him. He called it his carriage po. I'd hear him rustling about in the dark and then, if he was lucky and not too drunk, the first drop would score a direct hit. More often than not, he'd hit the lino first, eventually working his way into the po. It was the noise that got me. Tinkle tinkle silence. Tinkle tinkle bloody silence. As he was knocking on in years, he had something of a spasmodic bladder. Sometimes, when he'd had plenty to drink, he'd whistle to disguise the noise. It used to drive me mad, so I thought up a plan.

We had an alarm clock, one of those great loud things with a big bell on the top. There was something wrong with it, so we never used it. The slightest thing would set it off. Anyway, one night I wound it up and very carefully placed it in Uncle Stan's po. He'd been booked for just one spot at the East Unsworth Labour Club, so he wasn't going to be too late. About eleven o'clock he crept in. Rustle, rustle, tinkle . . . *Clang*!!!!!

On its own, the alarm clock was ear-splitting. When amplified many times by the po's amazing acoustics it was indescribable. Although Uncle Stan made a good stab at describing it later, using words rarely heard in respectable homes. He peed himself good and proper. He'd no idea what was happening. Dad dashed in and switched the light on. The clock was still at it, Uncle Stan was still at it.

'Daft young sod!' he yelled at me. 'Now look what yer've made me do!'

In his panic he'd put his willy back in his pyjamas, still in full flow, and he'd got a full bladder to empty, no tinkle tinkle stop this time. Well, plenty of tinkle but no stop. Dad wasn't much good at laughing. My mam dying had seen to that, but he nearly did that night. He was certainly entitled to – Uncle Stan was a comic, he was supposed to make people laugh.

My uncle gave up his po after that, so there's a moral in there somewhere.

*　　*　　*

It was about two weeks after I'd left school when Uncle Stan put his proposition to me. We were having breakfast one Saturday morning, the only morning the three of us got to sit round the breakfast table together.

'There's a job going down at Main Drainage,' announced my dad. 'Trainee site engineer. I've brought an application form home.'

'Main Drainage?' I enquired. 'What sort of a job's that, Dad?'

'It's a job wi' prospects, lad – and it's superannuated.'

Dad was a building inspector for Unsworth District Council and, to him, superannuation was the magic word. It meant security in old age. To a sixteen year old it meant next to nothing.

'Main Drainage?' said Uncle Stan. 'Sounds a bit smelly ter me. I'm not sure I want ter share a room wi' someone who works in Main Drainage.'

'It'll mebbe make up for all the snoring I have to put up with,' I retorted.

Dad ignored our banter. 'Yer need ter start work, lad. Take yer mind off what's been happening. Yer've got yer certificates, which was more than yer deserved under the circumstances.'

'I got four O Levels, Dad. For most decent jobs you need five. On top of which I was expelled.'

'Oh aye – and who's ter blame for that, I might ask? I've told yer about acting the goat till I'm blue in the face.' He signalled the end of the meal by lighting his pipe. 'I'll have a few words wi' a few people down at work. Mebbe I can swing it for yer. You bein' my lad should go in yer favour. I'll have yer working down the sewers afore yer know it.'

'Gee, thanks Dad.'

My attempt at sarcasm escaped him. I'd actually fancied going to art college but I knew what sort of reaction I'd get from him if I mentioned anything so airy-fairy. Painting pictures was for nancy boys and southerners. I was forced to smile as I remembered Utters' prophetic words. *The only thing that varies is the depth.*

Dad disappeared into the kitchen to make a fresh brew of tea and Uncle Stan leaned across to me. 'I've got a part-time job for yer, if yer interested.'

Considering the source of this offer, I had grounds for suspicion. 'What sort of part-time job?'

'An hour a night, two nights a week. Two quid a night.'

This was as much as I'd be getting for a forty-hour week as a trainee site engineer.

'I'll do it,' I said. 'What is it?'

'Stooge in my new double act.'

I knew it was too good to be true. 'You shouldn't get my hopes up like that, Uncle Stan. Save your jokes for the clubs.'

Uncle Stan looked genuinely offended. 'Joke? How d' yer mean, joke? Do I look as if I'm joking? There's nowt funny about comedy, lad. It's a deadly serious business.'

'You mean you want me to go on stage with you?'

'By 'eck! Yer a quick learner. You an' me'll get on famously.'

'Now then, what are you two plotting?' Dad returned from the kitchen with a fresh pot of tea, with which he topped up our empty cups.

'Uncle Stan says I can work part-time with him on the clubs . . .'

Uncle Stan jumped in before I said too much. 'Just helping me out backstage wi' props an' stuff. That sort o' thing.'

Dad pulled a face. 'Sounds like a lot o' foolishness ter me. It'd better not interfere wi' yer proper job.'

'I haven't got a proper job yet, Dad.'

'You will, lad. You mark my words.'

To be faced with such a daunting panel of interviewers was a bit much for a sixteen-year-old school leaver. I'd been waiting in a side room with other candidates for this and various other jobs. Some just looking for promotion within their own department.

There were three of us up for the Main Drainage job. Both the others looked far better prospects than me – especially Michael Murray from 5A at St Iggy's, who had twice as many O Levels as me. I glanced around and sensed a defeated demeanor about the ones already working there and seeking advancement. I'd seen this in my dad. As if they'd given up on the excitement of life and settled for something safe. Their talk was about salary scales and what other jobs they'd been turned down for and incremental increases – whatever they were. This was to be my life, my career. Did I want this? If the door hadn't opened at that precise moment I'd have walked out *and my life would have been so much easier.*

'Mr Foxcroft?'

This was the first time in my life I'd been called Mister. I felt unqualified for such a title. The man calling my name through the half-open door to the interview room gave me a short smile. I stood up nervously and followed him through.

Just one of the panel of interviewers smiled at me – a woman councillor. A young secretary taking notes at a side desk gave me a grin of encouragement. I smiled back at her and said good morning to the panel, prompting three male grunts and a polite good morning from the woman. My mind went back to my last encounter with Father O'Dea. Would I always feel intimidated by those in authority?

The interview was opened by councillor Jugg, one-time furnaceman and now chairman of the Highways and General Works Committee. He'd been one of the topics of discussion in the waiting room. *Thick as two short planks* was the general consensus of opinion.

'So, lad, yer've left school, have yer?' he asked.

'Yes, sir.'

'How many certificates did yer get, then?'

'Four, sir.'

He rubbed his hands. 'That's more like it. Some o' them other clever buggers have seven and eight. Didn't get none meself and it didn't do me no harm. University of life, that's where I went, lad. Finest schooling in t' world.'

'Yes, sir.'

Since then I've always harboured a mistrust of people who went to the university of life. It usually means they're a bit thick.

The borough engineer took over. 'I see you passed maths, both English subjects and art – but you failed your science subjects.'

'Yes, sir.' I'd got my excuse prepared. 'I'd been in an accident just before I took my exams and I wasn't feeling at my best.'

I'd half a mind to throw Utters' death in for good measure, but it didn't seem right somehow.

'What sort of accident?' enquired the woman councillor.

I was wondering if they knew – if they did I was sunk.

'I fell and broke two of my fingers.'

I held up my right hand by way of demonstration. She nodded sympathetically.

'I understand your father works for the council?' The question came from the fourth member of the panel.

'Yes, sir. He's a building inspector.'

'And a very good building inspector,' said the borough engineer.

And that was it. The first in-depth interview with William Foxcroft. I was asked to wait outside, then enjoyed a moment of pleasure when called back, to be offered the job. My two better-qualified rivals grudgingly shook my hand as I stood up to go back into the room. Somehow, being the son of Walter Foxcroft had swung it.

When my dad said he'd do something, it was as good as done, more's the pity. Mind you, I started work with Uncle Stan first.

Seven

'Won't the audience wonder about the age gap?'
I thought this was a reasonable query concerning
Uncle Stan's proposal to call our new double act the Fox
Twins. We were in a tiny dressing room at the Swillingfield
Labour Club, changing into our costumes. Uncle Stan had
been rehearsing me for three weeks, whilst Dad was at work.
It was a classic case of greed overcoming fear. I was prepared
to endure an hour's terror for two quid, but I knew full well
that I wouldn't be able to wing it for more than two or three
nights. Still, the money would come in handy.

'No one can fault yer for observation, Billy lad,' replied
Uncle Stan, 'but yer don't seem to have quite grasped the
basic idea of comedy.'

'Maybe not. Maybe I take after me dad.'

'Now then,' scolded my uncle. 'Don't go running yer dad
down. He's a good bloke is yer dad.'

'Oh, right! You *would* say that, wouldn't you? He gave you
somewhere to stay.'

'You an' me both, Billy. He looks after you as well . . . or
have yer forgotten?'

'He'll not be looking after me for much longer. It's like
living in a flipping morgue living in that house.'

He took mock offence at this. 'Oh well! Thanks very
much.'

'You know what I mean,' I said. 'You're hardly ever in. I
just wish he'd cheer himself up. It's been two years since me
mam died. He blames me for it, you know.'

Uncle Stan was genuinely shocked at this. 'Don't even think

56

such a thing, our Billy. Yer father's mourning the loss of a wife in a million. Yer can't put a time limit on such a thing. Unless, of course, you had no respect for yer mother!'

Uncle Stan had never spoken to me as sharply as that. I know there's right and wrong in everything and I hadn't exactly been an angel, but when my mam died, my dad wasn't there for me. He was too wrapped up in his own grief to notice.

'I loved me mam just as much as he did. We could have helped each other, but he wouldn't let me near him.'

He put his arm around me. Apart from Utters, no one had done that since my mam died. Not in that way, anyway. Helen was in another category.

'I'll have words wi' yer dad. See if I can't let him know what yer goin' through.'

It was too late for all that. I shook my head. 'I'd rather you didn't. I'm not going through it any more. I just wish he wasn't.'

'Good lad,' said Uncle Stan. 'Put it right out of yer head. Concentrate on the job in hand.' He stood in front of me and regarded me closely.

'How are yer feeling?'

'Nervous.'

This was an understatement, I'd been to the toilet half a dozen times. Uncle Stan nodded his understanding.

'I just want yer ter hang on ter one thing. Yer've got comic timing. That's why I asked yer ter come in wi' me. Yer can't teach comic timing, yer've either got it or yer haven't. It'll get yer through. Just mark my words.'

We were due to open with a short twenty-minute spot, just to warm 'em up. Then there was the 'spesh' act, a juggler and fire eater called the Great Zamboni. He was to be followed by Florrie Arnold (Songs from the Shows) and we were on last.

The Swillingfield Labour Club was a relatively new club. Formed just a few years previously by converting a row of pit cottages into a surprisingly spacious venue. The cottages had become available when the NCB had closed down the worked up Swillingfield Main and transferred the men to the Prince of Wales and other pits in the area.

At one end of the concert room was a bar with four hand pumps. Three selling Bootham's Bitter at a shilling a pint and the other selling Bootham's Mild at tenpence. Uncle Stan said there were only three types of beer in this world, good, bad and Bootham's. Lager had yet to infiltrate Yorkshire working men's clubs, the same with wine and other soft southern drinks. The women drank what they were bought, which was milk stout or, on a special occasion, Babycham. A wooden handrail channelled customers to and from the bar so there was never an argument about whose turn it was to be served. Uncle Stan said that, if it was raining, the men would always walk to the club with their flat caps tucked in their pockets, because no one likes sitting in a club in a wet cap. Between the bar and the stage were four rows of trestle tables, all well scrubbed and smelling faintly of stale beer and Domestos. These had been bought at a knock-down price from the now defunct colliery where they'd seen many years service in the pit canteen. Each row seated sixty and each row was occupied by sixty staunch socialist bottoms by eight o'clock on weekend nights.

Suspended from a red flock wallpapered wall, a faded photo of Bessie Braddock MP glared across at a poster on the wall opposite, which advertised a forthcoming men-only night. It was to be a darts, dominoes, pie and peas and 'Strip Teeze' night. A charity event to raise money to send Norris Pemberton and his arthritic legs to Lourdes. It was to be hoped that Saint Bernadette never found out about the 'Strip Teeze', or she might have been inclined to send Norris Pemberton straight back home with his tail between his arthritic legs, and maybe a complimentary dose of piles for his cheek.

To the left of the stage was the concert secretary's formica pulpit, from where Len Frampton, the current incumbent, conducted proceedings with all the charm and gaiety of the sergeant major he'd once been. Concert secretaries were all cast from the same mould. All had their own little confidence-inspiring introductions such as: 'Give good order *please*, for the next *turn*. He's not my cup o' *tea*, but the wife likes him . . . Thank you!'

The audience themselves would be good-humoured and appreciative, but keenly aware that the comic, who was always on the best money of all the turns, would be earning in one night what they'd be earning in a week. So bad comics didn't last too long.

It was a traditional proscenium stage with tiny dressing rooms either side, each with a cold water sink, a cracked mirror, a bucket and two pegs behind the door. They didn't like to spoil t' turns.

I was examining myself in the mirror when a small, bearded man squeezed around the back of me, a huge case under one arm and a unicycle under the other.

'Hey up, Wesley!' greeted Uncle Stan.

Wesley nodded, unscrewed the top off a whisky bottle and poured himself a decent measure.

'How do, Stan.'

'This is Wesley,' said Stan to me. 'Alias the Great Zamboni. Wesley, meet my nephew Billy. The other half of my new act.'

The Great Zamboni shook my hand, his own hand a little unsteady for a juggler.

'The wife buggered off this afternoon,' he said.

'Ah,' said Uncle Stan. 'So this is why you're celebratin', is it?'

'It's ter calm me nerves. She did her nut when I told her I were packing me job in to go full-time on the clubs.'

'Taken the plunge, eh? Good for you, Wesley lad. The man in the street – or the woman in the bungalow in your case – has no idea. The smell of the greasepaint and all that.' He looked at me. 'Talkin' of smells, when do you start yer new job?'

'Week on Monday.'

'I don't want you bringing any of yer work home.' He turned to Wesley. 'He's working down the sewers.'

Wesley pulled a face.

'I'm a trainee site engineer for Main Drainage,' I protested. 'I won't be working down the sewers. Not much, anyway.'

Len Frampton popped his head round the door. 'Two minutes, lads. I've just a couple of announcements ter make.'

'So long as yer don't announce any deaths,' cautioned Uncle Stan. He turned to me and inclined his head back at Len. 'He does that, yer know. Announces any deaths just before t' comic comes on. He thinks it's bloody hilarious. Then he'll have a collection tin going round during the act.' He turned back to Len, who was looking a bit sheepish. 'Well?' he enquired.

Len Frampton's face dropped, his plan had been foiled. One of the few pleasures of being a concert secretary.

'Old Monty Blamire popped off last Monday. I'll announce it during t' interval.'

He disappeared, Uncle Stan winked at me and tapped the side of his nose. 'Watch and learn, Billy boy.'

Uncle Stan wasn't a bad comedian on his own, with or without the help of my comic timing. Physically he was medium height and pear-shaped. I was the tall, skinny one. His permanently lugubrious expression was betrayed by a pair of twinkling blue eyes that shone out from behind a great purple conk of a nose, in the shadow of which flourished a fine moustache. His gravelly voice had been honed lovingly into shape by the dedicated smoking of fifty Players a day. During his travels he'd written a host of comic monologues and these formed the backbone of his act. I was to make my entrance at the end of his opening monologue about a boy called Freddie Fanshawe, who'd been tragically born without a hole in his bottom – a great favourite this, especially with the ladies. The lines leading up to my cue went:

> He wrote to the Prime Minister, 'Dear Sir,' the letter went.
> 'There's no hole inside my bottom, and it's inconveni-ent.'

'Dear Fred', came the P.M.'s reply, 'Best get down
  here quick.
'I've a cabinet full of arseholes, come and take your
  pick!'

I was visibly shaking with nerves when I made my entrance
– the audience were still laughing as I arrived centre stage.

'Wait for it,' whispered Uncle Stan from the corner of his
mouth. He had a golden rule about not interrupting a laughing
audience.

'I've come to tell yer that yer wife's badly. She's got
laryngitis.' This was my first line in show business and I
delivered it beautifully.

'Then I must go to her straight away!' exclaimed Uncle
Stan, with theatrical consternation.

'Why the rush?' I enquired.

He winked at the audience. 'Well, she's never had it
before . . . an' I don't want to miss it!'

My nerves disappeared the second they started laughing. I'd
got the bug. I stumbled over the odd feed but the audience
seemed to appreciate it even more when I quite obviously read
my lines from badly concealed notes. They thought it was part
of the act!

We went off to what I thought was thunderous applause,
with the concert secretary promising the audience that we'd
be back later. I couldn't wait. But I'd have to.

Had the Great Zamboni's wife not packed her bags and
left him that morning, my showbiz career would have continued without interruption. Wesley Simpson, alias the Great
Zamboni, had taken to drink to cushion the blow of his
wife's departure. When she'd married him he'd been assistant
manager at the Station Road Co-op in Cutsyke and had a
glittering career in retail in front of him. She'd got visions
of him becoming manager and them moving out of their tiny
bungalow and buying a three-bedroomed semi on the new
Rushton Park Estate. But these dreams were cruelly dashed
when Wesley, without consulting her, packed in his job in

order to tread the boards full-time. Such is the lure of show business.

The Great Zamboni's proud boast was that he was the only man on the northern club circuit who could juggle two eggs, a flat iron and a machete, whilst riding a unicycle. I suspected that no one else had thought of it. The juggling part of his act came to a premature end when his unicycle had a loud puncture, causing the machete to fly into the audience, pinning a packet of crisps to a nearby table. So he had to fall back on his fire eating, a new addition to his act which he hadn't quite perfected yet, but full-time spesh acts needed to be versatile.

The combination of Bootham's bitter and Bell's whisky tends to disturb a juggler's timing. A couple of handy golden rules for any fire eater would be to stay sober and clean-shaven. The Great Zamboni was neither. Nor was he altogether safety-conscious. The audience became increasingly restless. The Fox Twins had set a high standard that they expected to be maintained and the Great Zamboni was maintaining a very low standard.

Staring wildly at the wall with an ear cocked towards the stage was old Tinley Butterworth. He'd been blinded in a pit fall in 1946, the year they nationalized the pits. Tinley could tell the skill of any speciality act by the audience reaction and he knew as well as anyone that this act was not going well. He took it upon himself to register the audience's dissatisfaction.

'Gerroff, yer useless pillock!'

The audience cheered. Tinley waved his white stick in the air, then asked: 'Has he gone?'

To even louder cheers.

Florrie Arnold, in the meantime, was in the tiny ladies dressing room getting ready to change into a leotard and leather boots. Towards the end of her act she would strip down to this for her big finish, a rock-and-roll medley. In truth she was a bit old for such modern stuff but she liked to move with the times; although she knew as well as anyone in the business that all this rock-and-roll nonsense was just a flash in the pan and wouldn't last.

The Great Zamboni had ambitiously decided to do a bit of fire juggling. Combine his two skills as it were. As he picked up his fire sticks he inadvertently knocked over a can of paraffin that shouldn't have been there in the first place. To be fair, he was doing quite well. The audience had stopped their heckling, much to the disappointment of Tinley Butterworth. He then decided to combine his juggling with a bit of fire eating, all at the same time. This turned out to be a mistake. For this you need to be skilful and sober. One out of two's no good. First he burned off his beard to great cheers. Then he burned off his eyebrows, to further cheers. Then he failed to catch a flaming club, which flew over his shoulder and dropped into the puddle of spilt paraffin at the back of the stage.

Whooosh!!!!!!

The audience stopped their cheering. Setting fire to the place rarely merits applause. The curtains at the back went up in flames, with bits of burning curtain dropping on to the drums. The drummer, being of unsound mind as all drummers are, leapt on to the stage in a fatuous attempt to rescue his kit. The Great Zamboni left the stage and took refuge at the bar. Florrie Arnold emerged from her dressing room stage right, which was next to the seat of the fire. It was her only exit. She appeared dramatically through the flames at high speed and totally nude and she wasn't as young as she used to be, nor as slim. She travelled the full length of the club without breaking her stride, to the cheers of the crowd, pausing only to turn and hurl a stream of foul invective at the Great Zamboni, who was trying to order a pint.

'You great gormless arsehole!!!'

She wasn't from up north, she was a posh southerner. A posh, stark-naked southerner, who'd sung with all the greats. She'd sung for the Queen Mother at a Balmoral Christmas party, she'd sung at Covent Garden. In the fifties she'd made two gramophone records. This was not one of the high points of her career. She was a Conservative and it wasn't right for all these socialists to see her Conservative tits and things. The fire, which was raging out of control, was momentarily forgotten as Florrie, who was also raging out of control, aimed a fierce punch at the Great Zamboni, knocking him backwards into the cheering crowd. Then, with a defiant wiggle of what was a very shapely arse for her age, she marched into the ladies' toilets, from where she refused to budge, despite the advancing inferno, until she'd been brought something decent to wear and not just any old tat.

Show business, I felt, was just the job for me.

Eight

'**O**h, damn and blast – they're on flamin' strike again!'
Jigger Jackson, my immediate superior in the Main Drainage section of the Unsworth Municipal Engineer's Department, had taken me down to Bostrop Sewage Works to gain some site experience. His soft Scottish brogue made it sound like *shite experience*, which might have been more appropriate.

Jigger was the archetypal engineer. A wiry man of middle height and middle age. He wore Town and Country soled shoes, cavalry twills, thornproof tweed sports jacket and bright yellow waistcoat. Jigger despised architects, town planners, town councillors, folk singers and Frenchmen. There was a depressing liveliness about him which he did his best to inflict on those around him. It was this enthusiasm that fired me with a passing interest in sewage. But only passing.

The sewage works were situated on the southern edge of the town, in the lee of the prevailing wind, so that any untoward aromas would not trouble the delicate nostrils of the citizens of Unsworth. It covered about twenty acres and was surrounded by high walls and wire fences to keep out thieves. This was obviously very effective because it was an oft-quoted proud boast that in the sixty-year history of the sewage works, not a single turd had been stolen.

A crowd of donkey-jacketed, muttering men milled around the entrance gate. Muttering well-known phrases or sayings that strikers always mutter. *If yer pay peanuts, yer get monkeys*, was one that stuck in my memory. Mainly because it seemed so apt when considering the simian appearance of some of the strikers. In fact, for just a second a cold shiver ran through me as I thought I saw Skinner standing with them, but thankfully no, just a Skinner lookalike, only much, much bigger. Events would prove him to be a more evil prospect than Skinner. A huge hand-painted placard rose proudly from their midst like regimental colours:

IT MIGHT BE SHIT TO YOU,
BUT IT'S OUR BREAD AND BUTTER!

A traditional slogan used by English speaking sewage workers the world over. This was my fourth day at work. On my first day I'd been given a 'pitch'. This comprised a drawing board and a chest to put plans inside and a pot of tea on top. Jigger took me under his wing and gave me my first instructions: 'Don't try to justify your existence.'

I spent my first three days diligently carrying out these instructions. I joined the darts team, which met each lunchtime in the plan storage room and filled the rest of my day rearranging and cataloguing the extensive beer-mat collection which obscured the peeling walls of the Main Drainage office.

At the end of my third day, Bert Warburton, a senior draughtsman with startling ginger hair and a surgical boot, took me to one side and said, confidentially, 'We've been watching you, lad. You'll do all right here, you're the right type. Bone bloody idle!'

It's always nice to get off to a flying start.

My day release was Friday, when I went to the Unsworth College of Technology to study first-year Ordinary National Certificate in Building Construction, which would lead me, after five years, to Higher National Certificate in Civil Engineering, which would lead me, after several more years, to become an associate member of the Institute of Civil Engineers. I could scarcely contain my excitement.

The Skinner lookalike tapped on the car window, which Jigger cautiously wound down.

'Are yer forrus or agin us?' His belligerence rendered this question rhetorical.

'We're for yer, Lol,' lied Jigger. 'I've just popped down to tell you that the lads at Main Drainage are with you all the way.'

'Did yer hear that, lads?' yelled Lol. 'Them bastards in t' office is on our side.'

Jigger jabbed a thumb in my direction. 'My lad's dying for a Billy Wright and we're miles from a bog. Any chance of letting us through?'

'Lerrem through lads,' commanded Lol. 'T' young 'un wants a crap!'

The pickets stood aside. Sewage men understood more than most the urgency of bodily functions.

'That was Lol Bradley,' explained Jigger as he drove me into the sewage works. 'If he was a bit more intelligent he could pass himself off as a gorilla.'

He took me on a guided tour, introducing me to the filter beds and the primary and secondary sedimentation tanks, and spoke of them like they were old and valued friends.

'Lesson number one,' he said seriously. 'What's the difference between sewage and sewerage?' He sucked at his ancient and unlit meerschaum pipe like an old sage about to impart some ancient, well-guarded secret to a wide-eyed student sitting cross-legged at his knee.

'I've no idea.'

'Well, your sewage is your basic waste product, i.e. your shit. Whereas your sewerage is your pipes and tanks etcetera, with which your sewage is dealt with, as it were. This is often a source of great confusion to your average man in the street, your layman, as it were.'

Offhand I couldn't think of any layman who'd given the matter much thought but I didn't say as much to Jigger as I thought he might be hurt by such sacrilege.

'Best job in the world, lad,' he said, in answer to my unspoken question, 'and we're not subject to market forces. Folk might stop buying this and that, and folk who make this and that'll go out of business. But *we'll* never be out of business, if you get my drift.'

The sewage works were situated by the Aire and Calder Navigation and on this canal was moored an unusually long – maybe a hundred feet or so – barge. It was about twelve feet across the beam and had been recently painted in a handsome blue and white livery. For reasons I never found out she was called the *Mavis Greenwood*. She was not a passenger-carrying vessel as, apart from a small wooden wheelhouse at the stern, the rest of her was a tanker. A middle-aged man threaded his way between the maze of pipes and valves and nozzles protruding from its deck. He had corrugated, seafaring skin, a greasy cap and a wooden leg. He greeted Jigger with a cheery hello and went back to his work. Jigger waved back and shouted, 'What's tha gorron on board, George?'

'Two hundred tons o' finest Yorkshire shit,' replied George.

This apparently was a traditional exchange which normally passed between lock keepers and the bargee. Jigger and George were giving me a demonstration of this witty banter, for my personal amusement, which of course was jolly decent of them. The barge, with its cheerful paintwork, belied its unusual cargo.

'What's it really carry?' I asked in my innocence.

'Shit!' said Jigger.

I looked at my boss, wondering what had prompted this uncharacteristic expletive.

'It's disrespectfully called the *Shitboat*,' he explained, 'because that's what it carries. Two hundred tons of it twice a week, from here to the North Sea. It helps us with sewage disposal.'

This explained many things about the holidays I'd spent in Cleethorpes. We stayed and chatted to George for a while as a gulping pump filled the barge with its unwholesome cargo.

As a local government officer and a fully paid-up member of NALGO, I had decided to keep my other job a secret. This was not going to be easy. As we left, Lol stood in front of the car and walked round to my side, motioning me to wind down my window. He was joined by one of his colleagues.

'I told thee it were him! That's a bob yer owe me,' said Lol.

'Nah! It dun't look a bit like him! He were older an' he had black hair!' the argument continued.

'If it's not him, I'll show my arse in Woolworth's winder for a week!'

'Well ask him!'

'Ask him what?' enquired Jigger.

'Were thee one o' the comics on at t' Bostrop Workin' Men's Club last Sat'day neet?' The enquiry was addressed to me.

'Don't talk daft,' said Jigger dismissively. 'He's one of our new engineers.' He drove on, leaving the confused picket to fork out a shilling he'd unjustly lost.

'I don't know what they want more money for,' he said, once we'd cleared the sewage works. 'They're only paid from the neck down! Fancy thinking you're a comic. Dozy bugger!'

'Fancy!' I muttered.

'I mean, what's the soft bugger thinking of, you've only got to look at you. You're engineering material, you. You stick at it an' you'll make a first-class sewage man. There's security in sewage, lad. It's like undertaking. Folk'll never stop dying . . . and they'll never stop shitting!'

I knew this to be true.

On his retirement, Jigger became the first man in the country to be awarded the OBE for *Services to Sewerage* (or was it sewage?) On receipt of his honour he unthinkingly repeated this piece of philosophy in answer to a polite question from Her Majesty, who moved graciously but swiftly on, with his final word still ringing in her royal ears.

Nine

I'd always envisaged that my first faltering steps into adult-hood would be taken in the company of Utters. We'd planned our first parent-free holiday together – a week in Blackpool. What a time we'd have. Me and Utters and Henry. Jacky was a bit too young; although I suspect his mother would have been glad to get rid of him for a week. Of course, it wasn't to be.

Jacky was a Protestant, a Proddy dog like Henry, as opposed to a cat like – like me and Utters. Henry, who was a very talented footballer, had trials with Oldham Athletic but was told to try again next year when he looked less like a stick insect. In the meantime he took a temporary job in the post office and concentrated on putting on weight. So hard did Henry concentrate that when he finally left he was thirty-five years old and weighed eighteen stone. Oldham Athletic had completely lost interest in him.

We still knocked about together, but gradually drifted in different directions. I drifted in the direction of Helen, who seemed as struck on me as I was on her and I was very happy about this. She'd had many boyfriends before me and I'd had many fictitious girlfriends before her. My pride wouldn't allow me to tell her that she was my first and it said a lot for her that she pretended to believe me. Helen had stayed on at school to take her A levels. She'd got nine O levels and she was destined for university and a bright future.

I was destined for a future either in sewage or on the stage. Utters' prophetic words about me always being in the shit were beginning to have a ring to them.

The autumn of 1956 saw the Fox Twins become a polished and popular act. We were working three nights a week and Uncle Stan put my money up to two pounds ten a night, leaving a fiver for him, which was only fair. I could afford to give my dad all my wages from my proper job and still be a man of means. Uncle Stan gave dad ten bob a night for the loan of the Austin, so all in all the Foxcroft household was not without a few quid.

I'd learnt to waltz, foxtrot and quickstep at Olive Shearer's School of Modern Dance. Well, I'd been four times with Henry and picked up enough to get by with. I could already bop with the best of them. Two years of Wednesday nights at the Alderwoods Road Methodist Youth Club had seen to that. I'd been Methodist on a Wednesday, C of E on Friday (table tennis) and Jewish on Sunday (five-a-side football). In fact I was in the team that won the Unsworth Judean Inter-Youth-Club Five-a-Side Championship in 1955, along with Protestant Henry, two members of the St Ignatius's under-fifteens and a Jewish kid.

Every Tuesday, Helen and I would dance the night away, right up to half past eleven, at the Royalty Ballroom in Blenheim Square. Then we'd catch the last bus home to her house. Every Tuesday at midnight, we'd sneak into her dad's garage and do naughty carnal things squashed between a 1933 lawnmower and a 1954 Ford Popular. Every Tuesday at 1 a.m. I'd walk the three miles back to number fifty-seven Elmtree Bank, the Foxcroft family seat, with joy in my heart and relief in my loins.

The Fox Twins would invariably be booked on Friday, Saturday and Sunday nights. Helen had been along a couple of times and said we were very funny, but I could tell she'd never be a fan. This, I thought, was good, because it meant she wanted me for myself, and not simply to bask in the reflected glory of my impending stardom. You can see how my mind worked in those days.

'Have yer got nothing less?' enquired Mostyn, as I proffered a ten-bob note for my ninepenny Saturday lunch.

Those five words heralded a new era in my life. An era of wealth. I'd never been asked for anything *less* before. Normally I'd be coppering up, unsticking a molten jelly baby from my last penny or maybe offering to pay the balance next time around.

I shook my head. 'Sorry, Mostyn, it's all I've got.'

'Where is it ternight?' he called over his shoulder. 'London Palladium?'

'Ackersfield Liberal Club.'

'How's the proper job goin'?'

'Oh, it's OK. Pretty good, in fact.'

I tried to sound enthusiastic. The job *was* OK. It didn't offer the same excitement as walking out on stage and hearing people laugh at your comedy, but it was mainly outdoors and it was interesting. Jigger had promised to let me loose setting out a line of drains the following Thursday and I was actually looking forward to it.

He had devoted a lot of time to teaching me how to use a theodolite and a dumpy level, as well as offloading much fascinating information about the wonderful world of sewage. I was Jigger's protégé and such was his confidence in me that he left me on my own to set out a surface water drainage outfall. This outfall was to be my downfall.

Basically it was a simple, earthenware pipe, which took all the rain water off the roofs and roads of the Bostrop Sewage Works and deposited it into the Aire and Calder Canal. I went there on that fateful Thursday, armed with tape measure and dumpy level and accompanied by 'General' Herbert the chain man. Herbert was a bombastic little chap who'd once made the mistake of claiming he'd been an army officer during the war. His less exalted role in life was to hold the other end of my tape, or to hold the staff at which I looked through my dumpy level.

The Bostrop sewage workers' strike was entering its ninth week and the strikers, under Lol Bradley, were becoming more militant. Lol was apparently short for Laurence. He'd had a chequered career, having played rugby league for Hunslet and football for the Armley Jail Inmates first team. He took up burglary when Hunslet dispensed with his services after he'd been suspended sine die for breaking a referee's nose in a match against St Helens. His ineptitude at burglary had landed him in various prisons up and down the country, so he made what he thought was an inspired career move and switched to bank robbery. With one of his many brothers waiting outside in the family getaway car, a 1948 Morris Eight, he'd entered the Stourton Road branch of the Yorkshire Penny Bank, carrying a shotgun and wearing a tea towel as a mask. The robbery would have gone well with a little more forward planning. The getaway driver, 'Our Eric', had absent-mindedly turned the engine off, so when Lol made his hurried exit from the bank with his bag of loot, he was confronted by the sight of his none too bright brother desperately trying to start the getaway car with a starting handle; with a helpful policeman standing over him, offering well-meaning advice.

Lol wisely chose this moment to turn over a new leaf and end his life of crime. Resigned to his impending capture, he kicked his bending brother up the backside with all the vim and vigour of a man who'd kicked a fifty-five yard penalty at Odsal. Then he handed his bag of swag to a somewhat surprised policeman, who hoped his single-handed capture of two desperate bank robbers would lead to promotion.

All this experience led to Lol Bradley becoming a labourer at the Bostrop Sewage Works and shop steward of the union.

Had the workers elected a marginally more intelligent man as their representative, the dispute would have been over long since. But Lol was a bully and he was enjoying his moment of power as bullies do, or in this case, his nine weeks of power. He'd bullied his way into the shop steward's job and he was trying to bully his employers into a 45 per cent wage rise to keep in line with inflation. I suspected that Lol hadn't got as far as percentages at school and had misplaced a decimal point somewhere, but his pride was at stake and he wouldn't be told. He'd surrounded himself with a small band of like-minded villains, who guarded the gates to the sewage works.

Bostrop Sewage Works were out of sight of the entrance gates and, unknown to Lol and his heavies, work was going on pretty much as normal. This was down to Jigger's clever little ruse of bringing in contract workers by boat, down the canal from a wharf near Ackersfield Bridge, and disembarking them round the back of the sewage works. This had been going on for weeks and it was amazing that Lol's intelligence network hadn't picked it up. Or was it?

I was on board this very boat, with General Herbert and half a dozen contract workers that fateful December morning. It was a motor launch we'd hired from the Marine Cadets, who were stationed below Ackersfield Bridge. The morning was fine and clear with a real December nip in the air. The boatman was singing a melodious 'Unchained Melody', the romantic mood broken by some of the lads, who were having an early-morning farting contest. A coal barge was noisily offloading its grimy cargo alongside Hargreaves' coal depot. Two optimistic anglers cast their lines into the still, black water, in which only a most desperately lost fish would stray. A couple of youngsters on their reluctant way to school took time off to wave us a cheery hello, then tried to sink us by hurling a couple of bricks in our direction. Our captain broke off from his serenade and told them to *bugger off to school yer little tossers*. I had money in my pocket, two jobs I enjoyed and a girl I loved. Life, for Billy Foxcroft, was good.

But not for long.

A smaller boat was tied up to a concrete jetty, sitting quietly above its own dismal reflection beside a derelict, windowless warehouse about half a mile from where we had set off. It left its mooring as we came into view round a bend, then headed towards us on a converging course, its bow slicing cleanly through the oily skin of the canal as its angry outboard motor thrust it noisily towards us. Our captain hailed the other boat.

'Watch where yer goin', yer barmy bugger!'

The barmy bugger remained on his collision course. I counted that there were six barmy buggers altogether in the boat, including Lol Bradley, who waved at us and gave us a dangerous and scarred grin. He was a far more daunting prospect than any Skinner. His unwashed greying hair was cropped very short, like an old tennis ball. His neck was about the size of my waist, he had two cauliflower ears and a cauliflower nose, if there is such a thing, and he weighed in at about nineteen stone. He grinned again as their boat drew alongside, he had brown and yellow broken teeth and a habit of lolling his tongue out as he grinned. Perhaps he was well named. It was a demented grin that said, *I've got you now, you bastards.* There were six of them and only nine of us, so we were vastly outnumbered, mainly due to the fact that they wanted a fight and were physically equipped for one. We didn't and we weren't.

One of them jumped on to our boat holding a rope and wordlessly but efficiently tied the two craft together. We, in turn, didn't have a lot to say. There was an atmosphere of menace about the whole situation. A splash behind me told me that our boatman had jumped into the canal, no doubt on the grounds that this had nothing to do with him. He was one captain who wasn't going down with his ship.

Lol Bradley climbed purposefully on board, armed with a pickaxe handle, with which he gave old Herbert a demonstration whack across his shoulders.

'Right, yer shower o' blackleg bastards. Yer can go for a swim or yer can have some o' this!'

He emphasized the choices on offer by slapping the pickaxe handle noisily into the leathery palm of his free hand. A swim in the icy canal had never seemed more tempting. There were more splashes as two of the contractors abandoned ship. There were now six of us left, including Herbert, who bravely but foolishly grabbed Lol's legs, trying to throw him off balance. Lol laughed and showered a hail of vicious blows and obscene invective on the foolhardy old chap, leaving him slumped and bloody in the bottom of the boat, rapidly losing consciousness. I felt I was witnessing a murder. My heart was racing with fear as Lol raised the pickaxe handle for one final blow.

'Leave him alone, he's an old man!'

The words were out before I realized it was me doing the talking. It stopped Lol in his tracks. Later, General Herbert would insist that my intervention had saved his life. Lol turned his attention to me.

'I've seen you before, yer long piece o' shit!'

There was a slow look of recognition, as his brain scanned its sparsely filled memory section.

'It *were* you, weren't it? In that club that night.'

I nodded dismally, licking my dry lips. Perhaps opening a dialogue might defuse the situation. No harm in giving it a try.

'I never said it wasn't me!'

I tried a disarming smile, but my upper lip stuck to my teeth. I was wrong about this defusing the situation – it seemed to make matters worse. He effortlessly shoved me backwards, snarling, 'Yer cost me a bleedin' shillin', yer lyin' bastard!'

I tripped over one of the slatted seats and banged my head on the hull. Dragging me to my feet by the scruff of the neck, he stood me on a seat near the side of the boat.

'Right, yer lyin' little twat, in yer go!'

He drew the pick handle back, signalling his intention to swipe me into the river. I ducked under the swinging weapon and instinctively threw a left jab on to the end of his shapeless nose. Although I got plenty of weight behind it, I don't suppose it hurt him, but it did throw him off balance. He took a clumsy step back, tripped over the now unconscious General Herbert and, with a loud, venomous curse, fell clean over the side.

'I'm arresting you for manslaughter, you do not have to say anything . . .'

I didn't hear the rest, I was in a bit of a daze. The policeman looked sympathetic and not much older than me. He gave me one of those I'm-only-doing-my-job looks. It didn't stop him slapping a pair of handcuffs on me and bundling me unceremoniously into the back of the police car. There was much curtain-twitching up Elmtree Bank that morning. Uncle Stan followed us to the car, protesting loudly about the stupidity of it all. Jigger stood there gobsmacked. He'd just brought me home from Unsworth General Hospital after they'd checked me over and found nothing wrong, apart from a bruise at the back of my head where I'd struck it in the boat. My dad wasn't around. Perhaps he hadn't heard.

Apparently, Lol's cronies had all seen me knock him clean out of the boat to his watery, non-swimmers' grave. Their version conflicted with my version and the contractors' version. General Herbert didn't have a version as he was unconscious when the blow was struck. So, to be on the safe side, they'd decided to arrest me.

Of course, there was no logical reason for me to feel any sense of guilt or remorse over Lol's death, but I did. Perhaps it was just shock. Whatever it was, the police couldn't get much sense out of me when they tried to interview me at first, so they locked me up in a cell to give me time to collect my thoughts. I was there all night, locked up with a plastic mattress and a tin bucket with better acoustics than Uncle Stan's po. In the cell next to me I could hear a drunk who was alternately weeping pathetically, then singing 'Heartbreak Hotel'. Apparently his baby had left him and he'd found a new place to dwell. His baby had made a good move. I would have liked a new place to dwell myself, although the cell was much nicer than some of the dressing rooms I'd been in.

A middle-aged, slack-jawed lawyer called Sidney Fozzard came to see me the following morning. He had a cheap pinstripe suit, a soup-stained tie, bad breath and badly fitting false teeth which didn't help his diction.

'I shouldn't worry too mucsh lad. I'm sure it'sh all a mishtake,' he said.

This made me worry. Sidney Fozzard didn't inspire confidence, an aura of abject failure enveloped him.

'How do you mean, *a mistake*? Lol Bradley *is* dead, isn't he?'

'Well, technically, yesh. But that's not necessharily your fault.'

'Whose fault is it then?'

'Of coursh, I'm not privy to all witnessh shtatementsh at

thish moment in time but I undershtand from one of them that Mr Bradley might have tripped over, er . . .' He fished a fag packet from his pocket and read a note scrawled on the inner leaf. '. . . over – General? – Herbert.'

'That's right, he tripped over Gen— over Herbert. He's not really a general, but you can hardly blame him, he was unconscious, thanks to Lol Bradley.'

'Well, there you have it! Mr Bradley had only himself to blame. I also undershtand that he'd been drinking and wash a non-shwimmer. All these factsh are in our favour, should I shee fit to enter a plea in mitigation.'

He made it sound as though I might get off lightly with maybe five or six years.

'There'sh a hearing in Magishtrates' Court in a couple of hoursh. I'll apply for bail.'

He gave me a loose-toothed grin which told me my situation was hopeless.

'Are you a solicitor or a barrister?' I asked out of curiosity.

'I'm a sholishiter.'

I just wanted to hear him say it.

As it happened I was granted bail, not because of Mr Fozzard's eloquence, but because the police didn't contest the application. I left the court with Uncle Stan and was met on the steps of Unsworth Town Hall, where the courts were located, by a solemn-looking Jigger, nervously chewing his dormant meerschaum.

He put his arm around my shoulder and said confidentially, 'I've been asked to tell you not to come back to the office until this thing's sorted out. I know it's a bit unfair, lad, but that's the way things work in local government. Everything's got to be whiter than white, if you get my drift.'

'Does this mean they're going to sack me?' I was only sixteen and I didn't get his drift.

'Oh no, lad! There'll be a specially convened council meeting later on this week and you'll be suspended on full pay pending the outcome.'

*   *   *

'Remember Billy, *the show must go on*,' said Uncle Stan.

I didn't feel very funny, but it was Friday and we had a booking. Helen was there and, oddly enough, she agreed with him. She volunteered to come and watch and I said no thanks, because I didn't want her to see me show myself up, things were bad enough. She'd taken a day off school so she could be there, if and when I got back.

We'd been for a walk in Wyke Valley Woods, where we'd spent many a happy and promiscuous hour the previous summer and autumn. She tried to reassure me that all would be well. But what did she know? If she'd met Sidney Fozzard, she might have changed her tune. How would a long stretch on the Moor affect my show business career? Would my public wait for me? Would the Main Drainage Department wait for me? These and many other questions meandered through my mind as Helen and I meandered through the woods. It must have been obvious to her that I was feeling sorry for myself, because she spun me round and confronted me with a look that said, *Pull yourself together, Billy Foxcroft*! Then she kissed me, shamelessly and passionately, right in front of an old lady who tut-tutted her way past us, shielding her curious old husband from such naughty goings-on, lest he get any foolish ideas himself. And at his age too!

It was a kiss that put things into perspective. It was a kiss that set the world to rights. It was one of those *one thing leads to another* kisses. At least it did with us.

We returned home happy, even jovial, considering the circumstances. Uncle Stan put a friendly arm round Helen, saying, 'I don't know what magic you've worked on him, lass, but I wouldn't mind some meself!'

Helen, being one of life's gigglers, did very well to control herself. Perhaps Uncle Stan had arrived at an age when he'd forgotten about the sort of magic that Helen had worked on me. Dad gave me an old-fashioned look that devout Catholic dads give to their lapsed Catholic sons. I have to say he hadn't been much help to me throughout all this. He didn't condemn me for what had happened, because he had no justification for doing so, but I could tell he was wondering why I was such a walking disaster.

I agreed to do the show that evening and Helen agreed not to come with us. I wish she *had* come.

We were Bostrop bound once again. This time to the Bostrop Conservative Club, although I wouldn't have thought Conservatives would be too thick on the ground in such an area. Apart from the sewage works there was much heavy industry here. South Unsworth Foundry, The Greenham Engine Company, Coleridge Iron and Steel Works and much more. The houses were all grim, brown and terraced, covered with a coating of grime from the myriad chimneys which pointed up to the sky like mucky fingers, belching out smoke and soot and steam night and day, as they had since the industrial revolution. A revolution which was to create health and wealth for the few but rasping coughs and breadline wages for the many. From these houses that night there emerged over two hundred staunch trilby-hatted Conservative men who made their way to their club – their politics determined by the fact that the steward at the Con Club kept a better cellar than his counterpart at the Bostrop Labour Club and the barmaid had nice tits. A measure of the capricious voting habits of the British working man. They took their seats in happy anticipation of seeing Danny Angel, the Fox Twins and Voluptuous Vicki.

We were the stars of the Bostrop Conservative Club Men-Only All-Star Night. The running order was to be as follows: Danny Angel; Pie and Peas; the Fox Twins and Voluptuous Vicki. We'd been working on a little innovation to our act. This involved me dressing up as a tramp. It had a good comedy effect and effectively disguised my youth, which, in Uncle Stan's opinion, didn't lend itself to comedy.

In a roundabout way this change was to have a devastating effect on my career. If I could have had my pie and peas at the same time as everybody else, we'd have picked up our money and been halfway home in the Ford Popular before Voluptuous Vicki had taken her spangled knickers off. Uncle Stan wasn't bothered about strippers. I suspected he'd seen more than his fair share in his time.

Danny Angel went on first. He had an unusual voice for a man, a bit like Eve Boswell. Danny wasn't as young as he used to be, so to compensate for his lost youth he wore a very obvious jet-black wig, which always seemed to move fractionally after his head did. The audience became fascinated by this and bets were made as to whether or not it would remain in place throughout his set. Uncle Stan, having faith in the professionalism of his fellow artists, bet me half a crown it *would* stay on. It was Danny's grand finale that won me my two and six. His version of Bill Hayley's 'Rock Around The Clock'. The clock was just striking 'five, six, seven o'clock', when Danny's wig deserted him in style and landed on the snare drum, to great cheers from me and all the other winners in the audience.

I spent all the pie-and-pea interval in the dressing room putting my tramp outfit and make-up on. Uncle Stan went on first and did a self-penned monologue entitled The Elephant's Trunk. A touching piece about a young footballer who'd mistakenly suffered an unfortunate amputation whilst under anaesthetic. Thinking they'd chopped his leg off . . .

> 'I'll never play centre half no more,' said 't lad with
>   some emotion,
> 'Cut off in me prime, just when we'd got promotion.'
> 'Don't worry lad,' the doctor said, 'you'll be there for
>   t' kick off.
> It's not yer leg what's missin', they've gone an' chopped
>   yer dick off!'
> When he heard this dreadful news, poor Billy's spir-
>   its sank,
> 'Whatever will I do?' thought he, 'next time I want to
>   have a – wee!'

We could always tell what sort of an audience we'd got by their reaction to these lines. If they laughed at this, they'd laugh like drains when they heard how the doctors transplanted an elephant's trunk to replace his lost appendage. The Bostrop Conservatives reacted well, it was going to be a good night. The monologue goes on to relate how Billy Brown and his elephant's trunk becomes a celebrity. It ends with him at a posh dinner with the Lord Mayor and town clerk, the latter being a bit brassed-off when the elephant's trunk keeps snaking out from under the table, pinching potatoes and bread buns and the like, so he complains bitterly to the mayor, who says,

> 'This is a very important do, and I'm not havin' you
>   muckin' it up.'
> Town Clerk said, 'It's all right for you, it's not your arse
>   it's shovin' 'em up!'

The Bostrop Conservatives were obviously poetry lovers, for I'd been standing centre stage with Uncle Stan for fully a minute before their laughter subsided sufficiently for me to get my first line out.

'I've had to tek me wife to the doctor's, she got women's troubles.'

Uncle Stan nodded in sympathetic agreement then I added, 'She doesn't look like one!'

He had generously given me some comic lines of my own. He fed me the next line.

'An' what did the doctor say?'

'He told her she were too fat!'

'An' what did she say?'

'She said, "I'd like a second opinion."'

'An' what did the doctor say?'

'He said, "Yer ugly as well!"'

Our humour was delivered absolutely deadpan, not the trace of a smile from either of us. We'd gone up a notch, the audience loved us. All my troubles of the last couple of days were forgotten. We had the audience in the palm of our hands, we were in command, and there's not a feeling like it in the world. It was in the days when some club stages still had curtains and we even took a couple of curtain calls. When they shouted *more* we politely shook our heads. We didn't have any more.

'We're goin' to need more material,' said Uncle Stan, back in the dressing room. 'Me an' you are goin' places.' How right he was!

He left me to take off my tramp's outfit and make-up, then reappeared a couple of minutes later with a plate of steaming pie and peas.

'I got 'em to save you a plate. You'd best stay in here and eat it while the stripper's on. I'm off for a pint . . . See you!'

He left through the door to the stage – the only door – walked across the stage and through the curtains just as the three piece band struck up with 'Fever'.

I didn't see her dance, I was too full of pie, peas and euphoria to be interested. Even if I had, it would have been unprofessional of me to peep round my dressing-room door at the back of the stage. I saw her make her entrance – her door was opposite mine. She winked at me as I ate my pie and peas. The audience thought she was great, although some of their comments were a bit lewd for Conservatives.

Voluptuous Vicki was out there for a full twenty minutes, which is a long time for a stripper. She came off to whistles, catcalls, laughter and raucous applause. The curtain came down and she appeared at my dressing-room door wearing tassels and a G string. Complete nudity being very much frowned upon by the watch committee in those days. The concert chairman called her back to take a bow, 'An' give us one last look at the biggest pair o' tits we've seen at Bostrop Con Club since Neville Cocker's missis got drunk last New Year's Eve!'

'And what has Neville's wife got between her tits?' enquired a loud voice from the back.

'*Her belly button!*' replied two hundred voices in well-rehearsed unison.

A raucous debate followed as to the relative merits of the bosoms of the two ladies.

'Vicki's got the biggest tits!' commented Reg Hewitt, a

self-taught bosom expert who'd seen all four contestants and whose opinion on such matters carried a lot of weight, as did all four contestants.

'Vicki's might be bigger!' retorted an indignant Neville, 'but my Hilda's are longer!'

There was a murmur of agreement at this compromise, which converted to a loud cheer as the curtain went back up for Vicki to take a naked bow and retrieve her scattered clothing, which she brought with her to my dressing room as the band struck up with 'In the Mood'. I heard the concert chairman ask for best of order while the band played a few closing numbers and did anyone fancy getting up and giving us a song?

So there we were, in my dressing room, with the band unconsciously standing guard. I could have made my excuses and left, but I didn't. Voluptuous Vicki was well named. I'd have backed her against Neville Cocker's wife any day. She had closed the door behind her, away from prying drummer's eyes. Smiling cheerfully, she removed her tassels and flicked off her G-string, making no attempt to conceal her spectacular nudity from my gawping gaze.

'I seem to have come into the wrong dressing room.'

'Er . . . no problem,' I said.

'I can't leave until the band's finished,' she added, although this was not strictly true. 'So . . . what do you think?'

'Think about what?' I was incredibly naïve in those days.

'I just wondered if yer fancied a shag while we're waiting.'

She asked so nicely that somehow it seemed ungallant to turn her down. The disturbance within my trousers told her my answer. I just stood there dumbly as she removed all the clothing I'd just recently donned and more, saying, 'I wouldn't like you to think I do this all the time. It's just that I've got a thing about comedians. The trouble is, most of 'em are ugly old sods. So with you I thought I'd better strike while the iron is hot, so to speak.'

The iron was certainly hot, I'd never known it hotter. I noticed for the first time just how pretty she was. It just shows you where my mind had been for the past few minutes! A drunk in the audience had got up to sing 'Secret Love'. He didn't last long.

But he lasted longer than me!

If Vicki was disappointed she was good enough not to say so. She just lay beneath me as I caught my breath, perhaps she was waiting for me to go again. We were still lying there, naked and sweaty, on the dressing-room floor – me with my head nestling comfortably between Neville Cocker's wife's two main competitors and her trying to light a Hamlet behind my head – when I heard footsteps.

It was her shoes I recognized first. She'd been wearing them that afternoon in Wyke Valley Woods. My eyes travelled reluctantly up to the face of the girl I loved most in all the world. Helen just stood there, dumbstruck, a bright bubble of tears welling up in each eye. Then she turned and walked out of my life. All because of a plate of pie and peas.

I've never eaten them since.

Vicki had the good sense to realize that something very bad had happened. She even apologized as she picked up her clothes and went across the stage to her own dressing room. I'd hurriedly dressed by the time Uncle Stan came dashing in. He looked round, surprised that Helen wasn't here, then dismissed it from his mind, saying, 'We're in trouble! Lol Bradley's brothers are in the club. The concert chairman's tryin' to fob 'em off, but you can't go out through the door. Yer'll have to get through that winder! I'll meet you outside.'

There was a small window in the dressing room, no more than a foot by eighteen inches, but under the circumstances it was more than big enough. I shot through it like a rat up a drainpipe, leaving my tramp outfit behind. The Austin Ten was parked right next to the front door, so I waited until I saw Uncle Stan leave the club before darting out of the shadows towards him. A frightening shout rent the crisp night air.

'That's the murderin' bastard! Don't lerrim gerrin that car!'

It sounded just like a reincarnated Lol. Apparently all six

brothers sounded the same. They were also all built the same and had the same outlook on life. Which was bad news for me!

One of the things that really surprised me that night was the speed at which Uncle Stan, a portly man of sixty-three, could run. The five surviving Bradley brothers had followed him out of the club door and had spotted me almost immediately. I turned and ran for my life – Uncle Stan was not far behind me. He was still with me when I jumped over a wall into someone's back yard – in fact he landed on top of me. We crouched, in breathless silence, between the bins and the outside lavatory. You could smell the fear. Well, you could smell something. We lay there, huddled together, terrified for our lives, for they would surely have killed us had they found us. Such was their mentality.

'How did they know where I was?' I whispered.

'Somebody at the club spotted you and sent word out to the Bradleys.'

'What? A Conservative did a trick like that? I'll report him to bloody Churchill!'

'It'll have been a socialist infiltrator,' whispered Uncle Stan.

Several minutes passed and the Bradleys seemed to be everywhere, shouting to each other obscenely.

We lay there for over an hour before we decided the coast was clear. Fortunately it was a moonless night so there were plenty of dark places through which to flit. Going back to the car was a bad idea. Even the brainless Bradleys would know to leave a man guarding it. They were still about, we could hear them shouting and effing to each other. A bedroom window scraped open and a harridan voice screamed at them.

'Pipe down yer bastards and watch yer bleedin' language at this time of night!'

It was going to be difficult to avoid them. But I had a plan. There was a gap in the fence at Bostrop Sewage Works. Jigger and I had purposely made one for the odd occasion when we might need to get into the place without the inconvenience of going in by boat. I led Uncle Stan there, along cobbled streets, through the flickering shadows the street lamps couldn't reach. We got in without a problem and sat behind a hut, breathing easily for the first time in a couple of hours. Then we wandered around, safe from discovery, looking for a place to bed down for the night. I noticed the barge moored quietly by the concrete jetty, the dark water lapping gently against its hull. A light shone from inside its wheelhouse. I knocked on the window and said in a low, but hopefully audible voice, 'Ahoy there!'

Uncle Stan said something about it being a barge not the Queen bloody Mary, but I thought the bargee might appreciate my being a bit nautical. George greeted us at the wheelhouse door dressed in his greasy captain's cap and off-white long johns, with torn knees and sagging crutch.

'Piss off!'

'I thought he was a pal of yours,' whispered Uncle Stan.

'Oh, it's you!' said George, shining a torch in my face. 'Yer'd best come in, it's bloody freezin' out here.'

Ten

W hen we didn't come home that night my dad wasn't immediately concerned, apart from wanting his car back. At lunchtime he rang the Bostrop Conservative Club to see who we'd spent the night with. It wasn't uncommon for Uncle Stan to get too legless to drive after a good night. When the steward answered and told him about the previous night's events my dad put the phone down, then picked it straight back up and rang the police.

Within an hour the five surviving Bradley brothers were safely locked up in Unsworth Bridewell and within three hours police frogmen were searching the canal for the second time in forty-eight hours. The Fox Twins were missing.

There were many witnesses to the start of the previous night's chase. Some would testify that they'd heard the Bradley brothers mention that they intended 'drownin' the bastard like he did to our kid'. It was an open-and-shut case, at least it would be once they found our bloated bodies.

Meanwhile, our bloated bodies were basking in the bleak winter sunshine on board the *Mavis Greenwood* as she made her pungent way to the North Sea. I didn't pay the accompanying stink much heed, anyway George said he couldn't smell anything. Uncle Stan tied a handkerchief around his mouth like a Wild West bandit but it didn't do much good. Irish Linen could filter out many things but not nasty smells. I didn't pay the Bradley brothers much heed either, although Uncle Stan couldn't stop talking about them. I was consumed with self-pity over the loss of my lovely Helen. For lost she certainly was. Even Uncle Stan agreed with me that this was an affair beyond redemption. My mind raced with one useless excuse after another. I was drunk. I'd been raped. Vicki had come into the wrong dressing room by mistake and accidently knocked me over as I was getting changed and we were both unconscious and just coming round when she walked in. This didn't explain Vicki smoking a cigar.

Keep thinking, Foxcroft.

It was my idea not to tell anybody of our whereabouts, because I figured that Helen would be so devastated at my disappearance she'd forgive me anything once she found out I was alive. Uncle Stan went along with this idea despite it meaning us losing our Saturday night gig. His motives were different from mine. He didn't know the Bradley brothers were safely behind bars, or he would have insisted that the show must go on.

We'd spent a cramped but warm enough night on board the barge. For my part it was a sleepless night. Due partly to Uncle Stan's nocturnal noises, which were in much too close proximity to ignore, partly due to George, whose body odour could strip pine, and mainly to the sudden loss of Helen. There was a grinding emptiness inside me, akin to losing my pal Utters. At first light George had gone out for a *Yorkshire Post*. I'd made the front-page headlines, nudging aside the Suez crisis, which had dominated the headlines all week. Maybe I was just being used as a diversion from the other canal battle.

YORKSHIRE COMIC ON MANSLAUGHTER CHARGE

I wondered what Jigger would have made of this. There was no mention at all of my being a junior engineer for the Unsworth Municipal Engineers' Main Drainage Department. In fact the reporter didn't seem to be at all clear as to what I'd been doing on the boat in the first place.

Former schoolboy boxing champion and half of the famous Fox Twins comedy team, Billy Foxcroft, twenty-two, was arrested yesterday for the manslaughter of former rugby league star Laurence (Lol) Bradley, thirty-eight.

A fierce fight on board an Unsworth canal boat led to Lol Bradley, a non-swimmer, being allegedly knocked overboard by a single punch from the above-named comedian. Mr Bradley's body was later recovered by police frogmen. Also on board and now in intensive care in St Luke's Hospital, was war hero Captain Herbert Flatley MC, sixty-seven.

The last bit was a turn up for the books. Fancy General Herbert being a war hero, and a genuine officer! The report went on to record how Herbert had risked his life rescuing wounded men under heavy enemy fire at Ypres, earning himself the MC. I've no idea where they'd got the schoolboy boxing champion thing from, probably the same source as my age. It made me sound like something I wasn't. This would do my case no good at all. Uncle Stan loved the bit about the *famous Fox Twins*.

'It's all good publicity, lad. There'll be no stoppin' us once all this has blown over. Hey – an' fancy you bein' a boxin' champion!'

He asked me if I knew the name of the boxer who won a British Championship then shit in the ring. I was a bit too concerned about the newspaper report to be even vaguely interested, but George fell for it.

'I've no idea, who was it?'

'Black Bob . . . Crufts 1965!'

The grim, industrial, river-bank scenery gave way to more greenery and pleasantness as our noxious voyage progressed. A couple of hardy Yorkshire sparrows cadged a lift and ate a stale ham sandwich discarded by George, then thanked him by crapping on his cap. It was a good idea to sit at the front of the barge, upwind as it were. So there I sat, feet dangling over the bow of the barge, with Utters' words in the forefront of my mind. *The only thing that varies is the depth.*

I occupied myself helping Uncle Stan with the lock gates. From time to time a lock keeper would appear and do us out of a job. They all knew George and they all shouted down the same question, just to brighten up their day.

'What's tha gorron board, George?'

'Two hundred tons o' shit and t' Fox Twins.' George had altered his script to accommodate his additional cargo. This performance had been repeated three times before Uncle Stan tapped George on the shoulder.

'George,' he asked, patiently. 'When we get to the next lock, d' yer think yer could give us top billing?'

It was late afternoon and the watery winter sun was low in the sky when we pulled in for the night next to the Navigation Inn, 'One of Tetley's Houses'. Uncle Stan and I decided to stay there overnight, and to repay George for his hospitality we offered to stand him a slap-up meal and as much beer as he could drink. Of course, we now know this was a mistake, but at the time it seemed no more than a grateful gesture.

Minutes before we docked at the pub we'd passed an extraordinarily pretty cottage. Set back fifty yards or so from the canal bank with its garden running right up to the towpath. The walls were a brilliant white, latticed with black Tudor beams under a beautifully thatched roof. In summer there would have been roses round the door and no doubt trails of flowers draping from the hanging baskets suspended from various wrought-iron wall brackets. A spiral of lazy blue smoke drifted from a crooked stone chimney stack. In the middle of the manicured lawn was a fountain in the shape of a peeing boy. This was the home of someone with fastidious taste. Beside the fountain a bad-tempered duck quacked disapprovingly at the passing barge.

George stood animatedly on the cabin roof, shaking an angry fist at the innocent-looking dwelling.

'One day! One bloody day!' was all he said.

A shit-boat captain's life is a lonely life. A lonely, friendless and odiferous life. Many's the solo voyage he'd completed. Many a canal he'd navigated. Many a pungent cargo he'd delivered to the ungrateful fish of the cold North Sea.

During the war he'd risen to the rank of first officer on the frigate *Neptune*, and was on the brink of being posted to a command of his own when his vessel had run aground off the south Cornish coast. A court martial had placed the blame unfairly and squarely on George's shoulders and exonerated his captain of all blame. This was largely due to the fact that, at the time of the incident, the captain of the frigate, Captain Battersby-Blunt, was sharing a bunk with the other chief witness, the second officer, who was supposed to have been the officer on watch at the time in question. George was then posted to a motor torpedo boat which was blown up in the Channel, along with George's leg and naval career. The *Neptune*'s captain went on to become a knight of the realm and a rear admiral, which George said was very appropriate. He was now living out a comfortable retirement on his admiral's pension in the pretty white cottage. George had passed it twice a week for ten years, and for the five years it had been occupied by Rear Admiral Battersby-Blunt, he had been planning a spectacular revenge.

Anyway, that was George's version of the story, which he related in vivid and increasingly dramatic detail over several pints of Tetley's Exhibition, which was a much stronger beer than George was used to. At sixteen I was apparently too young to drink strong beer, so Uncle Stan insisted I stuck to Tetley's Mild. Uncle Stan being a responsible adult.

Saturday night at the Navigation was Free and Easy Night. Piano and drums, jokes from the landlord/compère and a prize of four free pints for the best volunteer turn. George was sworn to secrecy about the presence of the famous Fox Twins. Tonight was a night for relaxation. We'd dined well on home-made steak and mushroom pie. George and Uncle Stan were giving me the benefit of their advice as to what to do about Helen.

'You're sixteen, lad, you've got your whole life ahead of you, don't tie yourself down. *We* didn't, did we, Stan? We bloody did not! Women? Who needs 'em? We don't need 'em, do we, Stan? We bloody do not!' The more they drank, the less they bloody well didn't need women. I got the impression that they both thought sixteen was a bit too young for me to be losing my virginity.

'How old were you, George?' enquired my uncle, his inquisitiveness fuelled by drink.

'How old was I when what?'

'When you had your first –' Uncle Stan searched for a genteel word – 'shag.' He couldn't find one.

'Nineteen,' said George without having to give the question any thought. 'It was me nineteenth birthday present from the lads on the ship. They all clubbed together and bought me half an hour with a big mucky Frenchwoman in a Marseilles brothel. To be honest it were a bit embarrassin' – me bein' a Barnsley lad, I'd no experience of such things. The buggers took her to t' bar afterwards and asked her what she thought o' me performance.' He sipped his pint and smiled as his memory took him back across the years.

'I remember what she said ter this very day.'

We both looked questioningly at him, as curious as his shipmates.

'She said I were *pathetique*, which I thought was a bit harsh. I mean, how could she make such a snap judgement in twenty seconds?'

'Absolutely uncalled-for,' sympathized Uncle Stan.

Four eyes were now on him, waiting for him to reveal his first sexual conquest.

'What about you?' asked George. 'How old before yer first made love to a woman?'

I was impressed by the genteel phrasing of his question.

'First made love?' queried Uncle Stan. 'As opposed to just having a shag, you mean?'

George nodded, not having a clue what my uncle was on about.

Uncle Stan's eyes dimmed. 'I first made love to a French girl called Yvette on Armistice night. November the eleventh, 1918. I was twenty-five years old and loved her more than my life. We planned ter get married . . .'

George looked at me, we both decided not to press him any further. There was unhappiness in this story. It took him a long time before he explained himself. Before he revealed a secret he'd kept locked up in his heart for thirty-seven years.

'On November the thirtieth, she died of influenza . . . and I knew I'd never marry anyone else.'

He scratched his nose and I could have sworn he was close to tears. 'Thousands died of flu around that time. They reckon more people died of flu than got killed in the war.' He turned to me and smiled. 'Did yer know that, Billy, lad?'

'I didn't, actually.' In those days 1918 was too recent to be covered by history lessons.

'Well it's true,' he assured me.

George nodded his concurrence.

'And my Yvette just had ter be one of 'em,' continued Uncle Stan. His smile was still there, but it was a sad smile. 'There'd have been more justice to it if it'd been me. You'd have liked her, Billy. She spoke English better than me and she laughed at me jokes.' He shook his head at his own naïvety. 'What am I talkin' about? She laughed because she knew it pleased me. She were like that.'

'Dad never told me,' I said.

'Yer dad never knew, nobody knew.' He looked at George and gave a half smile. 'I had it all planned. We were going ter get married over there, then I'd bring me beautiful bride home ter Featherstone ter meet me family, then we were set ter go to America ter start a new life. But it never happened and I didn't want people mitherin' over me, so I said nowt. It were t' best road.'

George nodded his agreement. 'Aye,' he said. 'Sometimes sayin' nowt's t' best road.'

I didn't feel qualified to add anything.

* * *

A young man had taken the microphone and embarked on an excruciatingly bad impersonation of Johnny Ray singing 'Little White Cloud That Cried', complete with heartbroken tears. The four free pints of beer were not heading his way. He was crap.

'Gerroff! Yer crap!' called out a critic.

Johnny Ray, oblivious to all abuse, was *Walking down by the river, feelin' very sad inside.* I knew how he felt.

'Leave him alone, he's doin' his best!' bawled a large woman who'd been sitting with Johnny Ray, obviously a fan.

'He sings the same soddin' song every soddin' week! Dun't he know nowt else?' This was a different critic.

'He's singin' it cos it were soddin' requested! An' I'm requestin' you to shut yer cake 'ole before I shut it for yer!' This a different fan.

'Gerrim off! He's mekkin' me piggin' beer go flat!'

'I'll mek yer piggin' nose go flat if yer don't shut yer piggin' face!'

There were obviously two large opposing camps in the audience. We were inadvertently sitting in an area of no-man's-land between them both. Insults of increasing vehemence were passing to and fro, it seemed a good time for us to leave. As I stood up a heavy glass ashtray whistled past me and caught George just above the eye. He indignantly hurled it back whence it came, his action marking the commencement of hostilities. Uncle Stan, with great presence of mind, shouted, 'You stay outa trouble, Billy. Remember yer on bail!'

This advice was of no avail, because glasses, bottles, chairs and fists were now flying. Many of them into our neutral territory. The Fox Twins and the Shit-Boat Captain fought a brave but retreating battle towards the exit. George was the busiest of the three of us. With blood streaming from his cut head, he howled like a hooligan, laying low anyone of any camp who came within arm's length. His wooden leg a lethal weapon which he could swiftly swing to crutch height with tear-jerking precision. Captain George was a brave and formidable warrior. He took some persuading, but amidst all

95

the rampant chaos, we eventually got him outside, pausing long enough to ask the weeping landlord to cancel our room reservation.

George had drunk more than was good for him. He himself didn't think he'd drunk enough, so he looted a bottle of Johnny Walker while the bar staff were otherwise engaged.

Back on the barge, Uncle Stan and I found a couple of blankets and huddled together for warmth and a second night on board. As I nodded off, I heard the motor throb to life beneath me and I sleepily thought George was doing a wise and sober thing in moving away from the Navigation Inn and all its rowdiness. It seemed barely a couple of minutes before George was cuffing us awake, with a note of cheerful urgency in his voice.

'Wake up lads, it's mornin' and time to abandon ship!'

George had had the wherewithal to carry out his master plan for many a moon. All he needed was the courage, the audacity, and the drunkenness to see it through. Many's the night he'd dropped off to sleep with a smile on his cracked, seafaring lips, as he visualized his plan coming to fruition. Then many a morning he'd woken up to the cold light of day to realize the stupidity of it all. Perhaps it was just the *possibility* of it happening that kept him going. George was a man with a chip on his shoulder, a man with a grudge. George was a man who'd had too much to drink. It was not a good time to be Rear Admiral Sir Norman Battersby-Blunt (retd).

We must draw a veil over the sexual proclivities of the rear admiral on the grounds that they're nobody's business but his. However, he did have a manservant called Clive, who was young, brown and beautiful. Not at all like you'd expect a manservant to be, certainly not in the Jeeves mould. It had taken the admiral quite a while to work out who the mad bargee was who shook his fist and howled abuse in his direction twice a week. Even when George revealed his identity, the admiral couldn't understand why he was so upset, it had all happened such a long time ago. How childish to bear a grudge for so long.

Clive had just brought his master his early-morning tea, *Sunday Times* and *News of the World* and was hovering next to the bed in his green silk dressing gown – with a yellow dragon on the back – when he heard a noise from the bottom of the garden.

'See what all the row is, Number One,' ordered the admiral, who still liked to use naval terminology.

Number One, who had no objection at all to the title, minced across to the window and poked his elegant brown head around the chintz curtains that he himself had chosen.

'It's that awful barge person!'

'Blast his eyes! What the devil does he want at this time on a morning!'

'Excuse me,' lisped Clive through the open window. 'The admiral wants to know what you want. Oh dear! He's showing me his bottom! Shall I tell him to go away?'

'No, leave him to me, I know how to deal with his sort!' The rear admiral donned a blue velvet smoking jacket and strode purposefully to the window.

'You there, you bloody oik! Get off my property or I'll call the police . . . and stop pissing on my duck, you vile fucker!'

George gave a final display of his pale, deflated buttocks, then he staggered off, singing, up the canal towpath, leaving the malodorous *Mavis Greenwood* moored at the end of the admiral's garden. This enraged the admiral, who knew only too well what the barge was carrying, and he was just on his way out to cast it adrift when the thunderous explosion came.

And the world went dark.

It was a professional job, not too much, not too little. George had prepared it all, in a sober but vengeful moment, some weeks previously; all he needed to do was light the fuse. There was enough explosive to blow off the top of the barge and send its fermenting cargo two hundred feet in the air, before scattering itself over a good wide area, which easily included the admiral, his manservant and his dwelling.

Two hundred tons of sewage is a lot of shit, and when

it lands on you, your manservant and your beautiful white cottage, much discolouration occurs, not to mention foul and unacceptable odours. These will occur to you, to your smoking jacket, to your white walls and, worst of all, to your newly thatched roof in which a fetid and unsociable stink will lurk for many years to come. Admiral Sir Norman Battersby-Blunt (retd) was most put out; but George was well avenged.

Despite being bargeless and therefore jobless, he was a very happy man. He would soon be a very wanted man. We took him, still deeply drunk, by bus to Goole, which is an inland port on the Humber, and signed him on as a deckhand on a vessel leaving on the ten o'clock tide for some unpronounceable Scandinavian port to bring back timber. It didn't bring George back.

But we never forgot him.

We were well clear when we heard the bang. George had told us what he'd done, so we didn't hang about, nor did we waste our time trying to dissuade him from committing such a folly, the fuse had already been lit. Anyway, it seemed such an entertaining idea that it would have been a shame to spoil it by expressing our disapproval. Some months previously he'd been transporting several boxes of high explosive to a limestone quarry in East Yorkshire and one of them had been inexplicably left on board. This, coupled with George's wartime explosives training, had sown the seeds of his daring plan. A night polishing off his plundered whisky had given him all the resolve he needed.

The three of us sneaked back, like errant schoolboys, on the other side of the canal to see what damage had been wreaked. This was revenge worthy of the highest commendation. It was an image that will dwell in my mind for ever. A scatological spectacular. The twisted hull of the *Mavis Greenwood* was listing aimlessly in the recently polluted waters. Its steel lid ripped and curled open like the top of a sardine tin. The wooden wheelhouse loitered precariously on top of a leafless, shit-spattered sycamore tree. Odd bits of nautical wood and metal littered the towpath, floated untidily in the canal and were generally scattered over a surprisingly wide area. The erstwhile cargo had dramatically altered the landscape. It hung, festooned, from the trees, from the hedges and the bushes. It dripped down the walls of the cottage and totally covered the lawn and the duck, now flapping in slow motion and quacking in disgust. There was a lot of it. The admiral and his manservant were standing motionless in the middle of what used to be the lawn. Now cloaked in moist effluent and glittering cheerfully in the early-morning sun. Rear Admiral Sir Norman Battersby-Blunt (retd) let out a great howl of anguish and slowly lifted his arms heavenwards, as if imploring the Almighty to remove this foul visitation to whence it came. As he did so, between the end of his outstretched arms and his body, he grew gossamer wings, giving him the appearance of a brown angel. It was enough to make any watching atheist think again.

Eleven

'If ever God wanted to give the world an enema,' said Uncle Stan, 'he'd stick the tube in Goole!'

This was just a preliminary observation, based on what we'd seen walking to and from the docks, where we'd seen George off. Goole may be called many things, but pretty isn't one of them. We found lodgings in a pub called the Pack Horse. It was very affordable and when we saw our room we understood why. It had a concave double bed which occupied 80 per cent of the floor space. A cheap and chipped chest of drawers, supported on three legs and five telephone directories. A cracked porcelain po under the bed and two pegs on the back of the door. A single 40-watt bulb swung unadorned from the nicotine-brown ceiling. A cracked, unwashed window looked out on to a cracked, unwashed back alley. There were no en suite facilities. There were no off-suite facilities. It was either the po, a daring dick out of the window, or an icy, moonlit, cross-legged journey to the outside bog.

The telephone directories served a purpose in reminding me that I really ought to ring my dad. I supposed he must have been wondering where we'd been for the last couple of days, but I *had* been a bit preoccupied. Anyway, our ominous absence could well win me back into the arms of my Helen.

I rang Mr Rosenberg next door. He went quiet when I told him who it was, then I heard him say to Mrs Rosenberg, 'Go fetch Walter, it's their Billy . . . he's *alive*!'

I froze when I heard the last bit. *Alive*? Why wouldn't I be alive? Surely he knew we'd be OK! I heard a banging of doors and shouting outside, which I couldn't make out. Then my dad came on the phone.

'Billy! Is . . . is that you?' His voice sounded gruff. What had I done now?

''Course it's me, Dad, who did you think it was?'

'Well, to tell the truth . . . we thought you were . . . we thought you'd been drowned when you didn't come home on Friday night!' It took him a while to get just these few words out, I felt two feet tall. It never occurred to me that he might actually worry about me.

'Sorry, Dad.'

There was a long pause, then he said, 'Sorry's not good enough, lad, for what yer've just put me through.'

I didn't know what to say.

'Is Uncle Stan all right?' he asked at last.

'Uncle Stan's fine, Dad.'

'Is he lookin' after yer?'

'We're lookin' after each other, Dad.'

'Where are you?'

'We're in Goole, Dad.' I fully expected him to insist on me coming straight home, but he didn't.

'The police have been draggin' the canal. They thought them Bradleys had got you!'

'Blimey! Who told 'em that, Dad?'

'I did, who d' yer think? When I heard what had happened on Friday night, I put two an' two together . . .'

'An' made five!'

'Don't you dare go blamin' me, my lad!'

'Sorry, Dad.'

'Anyway, they've been locked up on suspicion of murder!'

'I know how it feels, Dad. They're goin' to be mad when they get out. Are you going to tell the police we've rung?'

'Not unless they ask me. I reckon if yer can manage it, yer should stay clear of Unsworth for a bit just in case they get let out . . . they're a vicious lot are them Bradleys.'

'I know, Dad.'

'Billy?'

'What, Dad?'

'You take care, an' keep in tou—'

At this point the pips went and I had no more money so I yelled down the phone that I'd keep in touch, and the phone went dead.

During the war my dad had been in the RAF. He ended up as flight sergeant, which, had he stayed in, would have provided him with a secure and varied career. He'd flown as a gunner in Lancasters and been a bit put out that the pilot and navigator, both officers, had been awarded the DFC simply, as far as Walter Foxcroft could see, for completing the same tour of duty as the rest of the crew who weren't commissioned officers. They'd got nothing. He never mentioned anything else about the war.

He went back to being a joiner and ended up taking a secure job with Unsworth District Council as a building inspector. Why I was an only child I'll never know. Mam was a Catholic and Dad became a convert to the religion. If it was good enough for Mam it was good enough for him. Grandma Mabel followed suit because she'd spent her whole life trying to fit in. The two converts became religious maniacs, whereas Mam could be quite blasphemous at times. It seems I take after her.

Looking back, I sometimes wonder if I hadn't judged my dad too harshly. Apparently he'd had a tricky time in the war, having been shot down in 1944. Being brought up in Featherstone without a dad and with an eskimo for a mother was probably quite tricky as well. Then his mother had been killed in a road accident and two years later his beloved wife suffered a similar fate. If there's one thing to be said in my dad's favour it's that he loved my mam. Judging from that phone call, maybe he loved me as well.

That was the story as I'd been told it by my mam and various relatives. My dad never talked about the war.

'Me dad seemed all right with me over the phone,' I said to Uncle Stan after we'd climbed into bed together. We must have looked like Laurel and Hardy.

'Why shouldn't he be all right?'

102

'Oh . . . you know. I don't want to go through all that again.'

He lit a cigarette and settled back, staring at the cracked ceiling.

'Have you ever heard the term *shell shock*, Billy?'

Of course I had. Most kids my age had an interest in the war, having lived through part of it. My earliest recollections were of having to suffer the ignominy of being given a Mickey Mouse gas mask when all the bigger kids had proper ones. I remembered air-raid sirens, barrage balloons, my dad not being there and the VE Day street party.

'It's when you get a nervous breakdown because of bombs and stuff,' I said.

Uncle Stan nodded. 'I've heard it described more technically, but that just about sums it up. Anyway, from what I can gather, yer dad flew his last two missions suffering from shell shock, or something very much like it. He should have been invalided out, but he wasn't. The gallant bloody captain of his aircraft didn't believe in it. He thought he could work through it. So yer dad stuck it out. Mind you, he had no option.'

This was news to me. Neither Mam nor Dad had ever mentioned it.

'The officer came out with a DFC.' Uncle Stan almost spat the words out. 'If anyone deserved a medal it was yer dad. What he did took real guts.'

'This shell shock,' I asked, 'when did that happen?'

'When he got shot down. He was a rear gunner in Lancasters. They shot the complete arse end off his plane and him sitting in it. Imagine that if yer can.'

'I don't think I can. Why do you think he never mentioned it?'

'Who knows? Maybe it was his way of coping with it. It must have been a right bloody shock, dropping through the air, spinning like buggery, knowing you were going ter die any second.'

'What happened? Did he tell yer that?'

'He never spoke about it to anyone. Some of the crew got

103

out. One of 'em saw yer dad's bit of the plane below him, then all of a sudden a parachute opened. They reckon he must have been sucked out and managed ter pull his ripcord.'

'Was he OK . . . injured or anything?'

'Not a scratch . . . He just didn't talk to anyone. Did as he was told, spoke only when spoken to by an officer. It was as if he'd gone on some sort of work to rule. The bastards made him fly two more missions to complete his tour. Apparently he just sat there staring out into space. Never fired a shot in anger. They took him off aircrew and gave him a job on the ground. Never sent him to a doctor or nowt.'

'Are you saying he'd gone a bit potty?'

Uncle Stan laughed. 'By heck, Billy, yer've got a way wi' words!' He shook his head. 'No, he didn't go potty. I reckon his nerves were shot ter bits, just like that plane he were in. He were no use ter the RAF . . . They should've sent him home, but this were 1944 and they had better things ter think about.'

'I suppose so,' I accepted.

'Anyway,' continued Uncle Stan. 'Him comin' home ter yer mam were the best tonic anyone could have prescribed for him. I've never known a man love a woman as much as he did her. As soon as he got home he were as right as rain.'

'I remember him before me mam died. I thought he was great.'

'He was, lad. When yer mam died, a lot of him went with her. Had it not been for you, I reckon he might have topped himself.'

'Give over!' I wasn't having this. 'He never had any time for me after Mam died. I reckon he thought it was my fault.'

'I'm just telling it as I see it, lad. There's stuff going off in yer dad's mind that no one can fathom. You're the only bit of yer mam he's got left. He might not show it but he thinks a lot about yer.'

'You're right about him not showing it.'

Uncle Stan laughed. 'I'm just telling it as I see it, lad. We're a funny family, us.'

I made up my mind to be a bit more tolerant of my dad's ways. Uncle Stan changed the subject and I fell asleep listening to one of his many show business tales.

'Now me cousin Tilly Titterington from Todmorden could dance a bit. Ballet, tap, you name it. But she were thwarted in love by pianna player from Eccles so she decided to end it all. She laid her head across t' railway line and waited for London ter Glasgow express ter come end it all for her. Unfortunately the Glasgow ter London express arrived first and chopped one of her legs off.'

'Just one? Why not both of 'em?'

'Well, according to her, she were paintin' her toenails, cos she wanted ter look her best when they found her.'

I nodded, that would explain it. It didn't explain why I was listening to such rubbish.

'What happened to her?'

'War broke out, so she got a job in a knicker factory in Todmorden making knickers wi' reinforced gussets for lady parachutists. This was ter stop 'em whistling on the way down.'

Despite the situation he had me laughing. Thus encouraged he went on. 'Then she met this bloke called Albert Crapper who were a sapper in the Royal Engineers. Tappin' Sapper Crapper he called hisself. He took one look at our Tilly and swept her off her foot.'

'I hope you're not just making this all up, Uncle Stan.'

'Would I lie ter you?' he protested. 'Anyroad, he persuaded her ter take up tap-dancing again.'

'What? With only one leg?'

'That were her gimmick, yer see. They used ter bill her as Tilly Titterington, the Todmorden Tapper. She used ter dance 'Knee Up Mother Brown'. I tell yer lad, she only had one leg but she went down well!'

He could keep this nonsense up for hours. A bit like Utters in a way, only he'd lived a lot longer so he had more lies to tell.

I dropped off to sleep, completely oblivious to his snoring

and intermittent peeing in the cracked porcelain pot beneath the bed. Until I was awakened by one loud, rasping, staccato snore, which woke us both up. He leaned over the side of the bed to examine the level to which he'd filled the po before deciding he'd risk another bladderful. So I ventured out, before first light, into the cold miserable street and bought a *Hull Daily Mail* from a cold miserable man in a cold miserable paper shop. It was Monday morning and I was not warm and I was not happy. I was even less happy when I read the headlines. I shared the front page with the trouble in Hungary, which looked to be coming to a head.

MISSING FOX TWINS IN BARGE EXPLOSION MYSTERY.

It was George's ritual exchanges with the lock keepers that had given us away. The report described in graphic and waggish detail all the devastation the explosion had caused.

> Billy Foxcroft, twenty-five, and Stanley Foxcroft, fifty-eight (I'd aged many years in the last few days, but why was Uncle Stan getting younger?), were being hunted by the East Riding Constabulary in connection with an explosion on board a barge carrying sewage to the North Sea.

The reporter, an environmentalist before the word was invented, devoted much of his report to the revelation that such a cargo was being regularly dumped in the sea without public knowledge. The report did go on to mention that I was already on bail for manslaughter on that very same canal and gave the reader the strong impression that I was a modern-day Captain Kidd, the scourge of the Aire and Calder Canal. All the article needed was a picture of me with a patch over my eye and a parrot on my shoulder. George wasn't even mentioned!

'We'll be world famous when all this blows over,' chortled Uncle Stan, who thought the article was informative and well written. 'I'll tell you what, lad, yer bloody good for publicity!'

'Uncle Stan, it was nowt to do with me! It was George, and he never even got a mention!'

'I know, lad, but he was *your* mate, not mine. Ee Billy! All this publicity's worth a fortune. We'll be on double money once we get back on the clubs.'

'Double money won't be much good once them Bradleys get hold of me!'

'Aye lad! You've a point there and no mistake. It's gonna take a bit of thinkin' about is that one.'

I'd already thought about it on the way back from the paper shop. 'We'll have to change our name, an' stay clear of Unsworth for a while,' I said.

Uncle Stan hated the idea, as I knew he would, but he could see the sense in it. While ever the Bradleys were around, at least half of the famous Fox Twins was in mortal danger.

We spent the next six hours in a dismal police station in dismal Goole telling and re-telling our story, which we'd rehearsed, like the troupers we were, before giving ourselves up.

'What was the name of the ship that this here George went on board?'

'I've no idea, we just dropped him off at the docks,' I lied.

'I've no idea, we just dropped him off at the docks,' lied Uncle Stan, in the next room.

As this was the only fictitious part of our story it was easy to stand up to their interrogation. Especially as they found it hard to keep a straight face when we went over the aftermath of the explosion. Apparently the admiral was a well-known pain in the arse in those parts. In more ways than one.

The good thing that came out of our visit to the police was the news that the manslaughter charges against me had been dropped. Some of Lol's cronies had altered their statements and corroborated my story. It was with enormous relief that I walked out of the Goole cop shop into the wintry drizzle.

Twelve

The coroner's court was full to bursting at the Lol Bradley inquest. Unlike Utters' inquest, where a verdict of accidental death had been announced to less than a dozen of us. Death had been instantaneous – he'd broken his neck as soon as he hit the ground. Utters' mother wept throughout, so did his sister, so did Helen and Fanny. We all faltered our way through our evidence, once again leaving out the part about the nurse and her beau. Utters' mother wouldn't have liked that.

I'd never seen the Bradley brothers in daylight. Lol had been the oldest, but he was by no means the biggest. There was also a Bradley mother. Today was a very special day for them. It was the first day in many years that they'd all been out of jail at the same time. Hilda Bradley, the fifteen-stone matriarch of the family had been released that very day after serving six months for actual bodily harm to the landlord of the Horse and Groom, who'd refused to serve after-hours drinks at her sixtieth birthday party. He'd added to her annoyance by telling her to 'fuck off home'. Now, sexual swear words of this nature were anathema to Hilda, who'd been brought up as a lapsed Methodist. If her sons weren't allowed to use the forbidden word, she wasn't going to take it from that bastard of a landlord. There had been a touching reunion outside the coroner's court, where she'd kissed or cuffed her various offspring in accordance with whether or not she considered their mode of dress suitable for such an occasion.

Gary Bradley, the youngest, suffered the most. Gary was a Teddy boy. Purple drape jacket with a black velvet collar, and black drainpipe trousers leading into red suede beetle-crushers the size of violin cases. He wore a bootlace tie with a death's head emblem. His well-oiled mousy hair was combed into a DA (duck's arse) at the back and a quiff at the front that cantilevered, with the aid of half a cup of egg white, a good four inches beyond his spotty forehead.

'What have you come as? Coco the bleedin' Clown?' Hilda fetched him a savage blow. 'Have yer no respect for yer dead brother, yer big brainless shitehawk?'

Gary mumbled his apologies as she kicked him quite violently through the doors of the courtroom. A court usher stood aghast as she grabbed him by his gown, saying apologetically, 'Sorry about this, cocker. The little pillock's got no respect for these places but don't you worry, as soon as I get him home I'll tan his little arse for him. Now then, there's about thirty of us including them piss artists from the 'Orse and Groom so where do you want us?' The non-use of the F word didn't seem to inhibit Hilda's vocabulary.

The usher wisely took them to the upstairs gallery, away from the main action, much to my relief and to the relief of the four nervous policemen who had been assigned to protect me.

One by one, we witnesses gave our evidence, under the menacing stares and mutterings from the gallery. I told my story without looking up, but I could sense the silent hatred being directed at me. The last of us was the best of us. General Herbert commanded the instant respect of the coroner by wearing the ribbon of the Military Cross on his donkey jacket. He told about the unprovoked attack on the boat, he poured scorn on the men who'd jumped overboard to safety, which I thought was a bit unfair. Then he pointed at me and said, 'Had it not been for that young feller, I wouldn't be here to tell the story. It was he who stopped that animal Bradley from beating me to death.'

'I'll beat yer to death meself, yer lyin' old bastard!'

Hilda was on her feet, shaking a scarred fist at Herbert, who looked scornfully up at her, saying, 'Madam, your son was a loud-mouthed cowardly bully. He was an idiot – and looking at you it's easy to see where he got it from!'

I could see how a man like that would win an MC.

Hilda came over the top first, amazingly agile for a woman of such size and advancing years. Her fall was broken by the court usher, who was now regretting taking them all upstairs. She was followed by Gary, who was eager to get back into his mother's good books. The rest followed. They poured straight down from the gallery into the well of the court like lemmings, fists flying at anything and anyone who got in their way. I made myself scarce, but they ignored me anyway, Herbert being the object of their immediate affections. He was standing in the dock normally used by miscreants. Directly behind him were the steps to the cells, down which he beat a tactical retreat accompanied by two policemen. The Bradley bunch unwisely followed, their obscene threats dying away into distant subterranean echoes as they disappeared, all thirty-odd of them, down to the cells. A grinning policeman smartly jumped down the first few steps and slammed a heavy door shut on the last of the howling pursuers.

It took less than three minutes for Herbert to reappear, with the two policemen. All three were standing like beaming schoolboys at the door to the courtroom.

'Can we say that there'll be no more unpleasantness now, Constable?' enquired the coroner.

'Yes, sir. They're all in custody, awaiting charge.'

'Very good, can we continue?'

The verdict was *death by misadventure*, whatever that means. No fault was assigned to me, in fact I came out of it rather well, with a commendation by the coroner for my 'courageous action, which saved Captain Flatley from serious injury or worse'.

As I left with my dad and Uncle Stan, a police sergeant took me on one side.

'I've just come up from the cells, lad,' he said, 'and I think it's only fair to warn you that they're coming after you when they get out. There's nothing we can do about it until they actually commit a crime. It might be as well if you lie low until they cool off.'

This was enough to seal the immediate future of the Fox Twins.

Thirteen

I turned up the collar of my coat against the icy December chill and moved to the lee side of the telephone box, where I absently read the graffitti etched into the red paintwork, shaking my head, more at the pathetic spelling than the obscene content. The day was as grey as my mood. The Main Drainage Department had, on police advice, offered me temporary unpaid leave until my problems with the Bradleys had been resolved. As these problems were directly caused by my job, I thought this was a bit mean of them and NALGO, my union, had promised to take up the cudgels on my behalf but I'd been told not to expect too much. Somehow I had to earn a living and I couldn't do it as one of the Fox twins. Uncle Stan came out of the telephone box with a suspicious grin on his face. He'd been talking to Mickey Boothroyd, an agent he knew in Hull.

'Right, Billy lad. I've fixed us up with a couple o' weeks' work in Hull. We'll be working under different names so the Bradleys'll be no wiser.'

'Sounds OK,' I said. 'What names are we working under?'

My uncle didn't answer straight away as we walked back to our digs in Leeds. Unsworth was no place for a Foxcroft. My dad had already had one confrontation with Hilda Bradley, who'd turned up on our doorstep looking for me. Fortunately my dad can give as good as he gets in the verbal confrontation department and he was doing just that when the police, having been alerted by Mr Rosenberg from next door, rolled up and sent her on her way.

'Well?' I enquired once again.

'Now, yer must remember, Billy lad, it's only until Christmas – and it's not bad money. Four quid a day between the two of us for only six hours work.'

'That's two quid each then?' I calculated, hopefully.

'Well, being as I play the starring role, so ter speak, I think one pound ten for you and two pound ten fer me. They're paying us top whack cos we're performers who'll be able to attract the customers. At least that's how Mickey's sold us.'

It sounded like a pantomime. I'd always fancied being in pantomime. My grey mood began to lift. 'What names are we working under?' I asked once again.

'Well – I'm Father Christmas . . .' He looked at me, warily.

My heart sank again. I was to be an elf. If there was one job I didn't want to do it was to be one of Santa's bloody elves. I dug my heels in.

'I'm not going to be an elf.'

'No,' he agreed. 'You're going to be a fairy!'

He strode out, deaf to my protestations, waving a dismissive hand.

'Billy, lad. We need the money. You're a good-lookin' lad. A bit o' make-up an' no one'll know the difference.'

Atherstone's was Hull's biggest department store and Atherstone's Santa was the biggest Santa job in the whole of the East Riding. I've done many things in my life, but this was among the most terrifying. My role was to stand behind Santa and hand the children their presents. No words were necessary, which was just as well, as my voice was many octaves deeper than any fairy I'd ever heard.

A girl from the make-up counter had been enlisted to spend half an hour with me every day and I'm almost ashamed to say that I made a very pretty fairy.

'I'd swap you legs any day of the week,' said the make-up girl, who had fat legs, so it was no compliment. Certainly not to a young man who had always envied the chunky bronzed legs of a pro footballer just back from Majorca after the summer break. Mine were more your Betty Grables, albeit quite hairy. I had to wear a sort of tutu, white tights and plenty of bosom-enhancing cotton wool. On top of my blonde wig was a glittering tiara and, at the other end, my size-nine feet were jammed into a pair of size-eight silver satin high heels.

Uncle Stan, on the other hand, fitted into the Santa costume without an ounce of padding. His wig and beard enhanced his nose and he was the most realistic looking Santa I'd ever seen.

'It's all right fer you, our Billy,' he grumbled, 'I'm sweating cobs under this lot.' Maybe he had a point but I had no sympathy.

Santa's Den was the highlight of the grotto, that year's theme being Snow White and the Seven Dwarfs. Our first day was a Monday, a quiet day which enabled us to get used to things before the Saturday rush. Uncle Stan, who had done it before, quickly established a routine.

'I never promise 'em nowt fer Christmas,' he told me. 'Their mams and dads might not have a tanner ter scratch their arses with. Never sit the little buggers on yer knee, that's asking fer trouble. Yer never know what they've just done. Ask 'em their name, make 'em laugh, wish 'em Merry Christmas and get rid of 'em.'

'What do *I* do?'

'Say nowt, smile and give 'em their present.'

It sounded easy.

Johnnie, one of the window dressers, came in to put the finishing touches to Santa's Den. He looked at me and grinned.

'You look delightful, dear.'

I smiled, blew him a kiss and lifted a coy shoulder. 'You men say the nicest things.'

If you can't beat 'em, join 'em is always the best defence against people who take the mickey. This is a sound philosophy provided you know exactly who it is you're joining. In many ways I was a very naïve sixteen year old. But in 1956 we all were.

Johnnie tipped his hand to his mouth, miming the drinking of a pint. 'I'm off at five, fancy a quickie?' he asked.

'I think we'll both fancy a quickie by then,' said Uncle Stan.

'Right,' said Johnnie, with reduced enthusiasm. 'See you both in the Angel.'

The kids were many and varied. But whether they were tearful, cheeky, charming, spoiled, shy or noisy, they all stood before Santa with the same look of awe upon their faces. Uncle Stan sent them out with a smile and a cheap present clutched in their hands. He was good at his job and word went round. Atherstone's Santa was the best in town. Consequently Saturday was bedlam.

A long queue of harrassed parents and impatient children snaked through the grotto and out into the toy department. Business was good but my feet were killing me and there were another five days to go. Five days of listening to the tapping of dwarf picks and shovels down the gold mine and listening to an interminable 'Hi-Ho, Hi-Ho', interspersed with 'Some Day My Prince Will Come', which Uncle Stan made rude jokes about to any mother he thought might like a vulgar laugh at Snow White's expense. Most did. The flatulence of young children has an eye-watering virulence, especially within the confines of Santa's grotto. If the money was good we were certainly earning it.

I'd grown to like Johnnie. We'd been for a drink every night after work. He was about the same skinny build as me but had a delicate manner about him which I found pleasing. Hindsight tells me it was my feminine side reaching out to him. At least that's how my wife read the situation when I told her about it many years later. I was still only sixteen, but my height belied my age, which was never questioned in the pub. Not even Johnnie thought I was under age.

'Two pints maximum,' cautioned Uncle Stan when he decided not to join us after the first couple of nights. He'd promised Dad he wouldn't lead me into bad ways. He was working on the premise that you can't lead if you're not there.

With just me to talk to, Johnnie seemed more animated and

funny. He was a couple of years older than me, but to all intents and purposes we were the same age. It had been a long time since I'd enjoyed male company of my own age. Johnnie wasn't exactly Jack the Lad, but he was intelligent and amusing.

By late afternoon on Saturday I was ready for a sit down and a cuppa, and Uncle Stan's bladder was causing him some discomfort. We had no relief Santa to take over when we took a break, so we had to shut up shop for half an hour for a tea and comfort break, as Uncle Stan called it. Johnnie had been deputized to inform the queue that Santa had to go and feed his reindeer, whereupon he closed the door to Santa's Grotto. During the week, this had been no problem, but on Saturday when people had already been queueing for an hour it caused a lot of bad feeling. Such was the layout of the grotto that the entrance was just beyond a wooden partition wall, a few feet away from where we were situated. We could hear everything that was going on. At the head of the queue was a woman with a coarse mouth and three equally coarse children.

'Feedin' his reindeer?' she exclaimed. 'How d' yer mean, feeding his reindeer?'

Johnnie tried to explain the obvious euphemism, but his voice lacked authority. 'Santa hasn't had a *comfort break* since twelve o'clock.'

'Did yer hear that, kids? Santa hasn't had a break since twelve o'clock. Oh dear, oh bleedin' dear!'

Her voice rose to a threatening crescendo. Uncle Stan was chatting to the tail end of the queue already in the grotto. He cocked an ear towards the noise. The coarse woman was getting into her stride.

'I haven't had a break since ten o'clock this mornin' and I've got ter pick me turkey up in half an hour other-wise it'll be sold off an' I'll lose me deposit. So yer can go tell Father Christmas ter feed his bloody reindeer some other time!'

There was a strong murmur of support from other people in the queue. A rumble of increasing annoyance was travelling from mouth to mouth. A security man arrived to ask what the problem was.

'I was just telling them that Santa needed a comfort break,' explained Johnnie.

'I'll give him a break. I'll break his bleedin' nose if he dun't frame his bleedin' self!' cursed the coarse woman. Falsetto profanities came from what presumably were her children.

'Now look, missis,' insisted the security man, tersely. 'No one goes into this grotto unless I say so.'

'Oh – is that bloody right?'

'Yes – now stand away from the door.'

There was a loud bang as the door burst open and dozens of loud, angry voices echoed through the grotto. We could hear people rampaging through the tableaux. Sounds of destruction.

'Bollocks ter this!'

Uncle Stan had his Santa suit off in an instant, all bundled up and thrown behind his throne. He had his ordinary clothes on underneath and, still bearded, ran out of the exit as the coarse woman arrived in Santa's Den at speed, brandishing a papier-mâché Grumpy by one of his short legs. She was very large, dark-haired and angry. A black gaberdine raincoat stretched across her stomach like a ship's sail bent forward in the wind. Her face was red and blotchy from some skin illness, as though she'd been ducking for apples in a chip pan. Three runny-nosed children, clinging to her coat, seemed to have inherited many of her coarse ways. A second, equally belligerent woman followed, waving Dopey in the air. Within seconds the place was full of angry people carrying assorted dwarfs, all demanding to see Santa.

'Where is the little red-nosed bastard?' screamed the coarse woman, spitting bile in my face.

Sounds of mayhem and destruction came from within the grotto, I sensed our employment coming to an end. The coarse woman pushed me backwards.

'Tell me where he is or I'll bash yer bleedin' head in!'

She drew back Grumpy to carry out her threat. I struck back

in self-defence at the only woman I've ever hit in my life. She staggered back into the throng, giving me enough time to make my own escape.

Johnnie was hovering by the exit. He grabbed me and hurried me through the crowded store and through a door marked *Staff Only*. A police whistle shrilled across the toy department as I cowered behind the door in my tutu. Johnnie opened the door partially to report seeing the coarse woman being led away in handcuffs, blood pouring from her face, followed by three small but obscene children. I could hear her shouting something about being assaulted by a fairy, but I figured the police might not believe this.

'It can't all be me,' I said to Johnnie as he brought me my first pint in the Angel. He'd been back and rescued my clothes from the grotto, which was totally destroyed. Six arrests had apparently been made and a hard lesson learned. Never close a Christmas grotto on the Saturday afternoon before Christmas.

'Everywhere I go, trouble seems to break out. It's as though I'm jinxed. I ask you – was that my fault?'

Johnnie shook his head and smiled. 'You know, some people have an aura around them which creates certain . . . vibrations.'

'So, you think I give off violent vibrations, do you?'

'It's just a theory. I could never prove it.'

'I think I might be walking proof. Did you see where Uncle Stan got to? He deserted his post quick enough.'

'Do you blame him?' laughed Johnnie. His blue eyes bore into mine, making me feel slightly uncomfortable. The last person to look at me like that was Helen. I stared into my drink.

'No, I don't suppose so. They'd have lynched him if they'd caught him.'

I normally left after two drinks, but as this was probably our last time together, I stretched it to three.

The talk ebbed and flowed from subject to subject. My conversations with Uncle Stan were mainly him talking and me listening, but with Johnnie it was fifty-fifty. I stayed clear of Utters and Helen, both touchy subjects, but it still left much to discuss, especially my relationship with my dad. He knew the problem.

'My mum and dad were divorced years ago. Dad thinks I should have followed him into the building trade. He's a general foreman, whatever that is. I think he's a bit ashamed of me.'

'Well,' I said. 'If everyone had their proper job, I'd be in the building trade.'

I'd never mentioned the Bradleys to him. Uncle Stan and I had decided it was to be a taboo subject, just to be on the safe side. But I couldn't see how Johnnie could be a risk. Oddly enough, he knew all about it when I told him, but he hadn't realized it was me and Uncle Stan. No one at Atherstone's had associated the name Foxcroft with the Fabulous Fox Twins.

'And you were on that barge that blew up,' he recalled. 'That made the front page in the *Hull Daily Mail*.'

'I know,' I admitted ruefully, 'but it was nothing to do with me.'

'And that club that burnt down. That was you as well, wasn't it?'

'The juggler caused that, I just happened to be there.'

'They should have sent you to Germany when war broke out. You and your uncle would have flattened the place in a fortnight.' He sat back and looked all around my head, then grinned. 'Can't see it.'

'What?'

'Your violent aura.'

'I've never been a violent person,' I said. 'That's what's so strange.'

'You don't have to tell me that, Billy. You're one of the nicest people I've ever come across.'

Suddenly his mood changed, as if he'd arrived at a point where he needed to get something off his chest.

'Is there . . . is there anyone in your life at the moment?'

119

I grinned, embarrassed at being asked the question in such a way by a bloke.

'Not really,' I replied, truthfully. 'There was someone, but . . .' I shrugged and shook my head. Talking about Helen still wasn't easy.

'Were you very much in love?'

I nodded, glumly. 'I suppose I was.'

Johnnie nodded. 'Your uncle told me about that. He said you didn't like to talk about it.'

I was surprised that Uncle Stan could be so sensitive about my love life.

'Uncle Stan said that? I'm amazed.'

'I think your uncle's got your interests at heart, more than you know.'

'Really?' I wasn't at all convinced.

'The reason I asked,' he said, earnestly, 'is that I'd like to be the one to step into his shoes.'

He placed his hand on top of mine and looked into my eyes again. I was confused.

'Shoes? Whose shoes?' I enquired, naïvely.

'Oh dear, I feel I'm jumping in too quickly,' he said, apologetically.

I didn't have a clue what he was on about. 'I'm not with you, Johnnie. Whose shoes are you talking about?'

It was Johnnie's turn to be confused now. 'I believe his name was . . .' He hesitated, perhaps worried that the very mention of the name might upset me. 'I believe your name for him was Utters.'

'Utters!' I exclaimed. 'Utters was my mate . . . He's dead!'

Johnnie took my hand and squeezed it tightly. 'I know, Billy,' he said, 'but life has to go on.'

The reality began to dawn on me. God, I was thick! Things were falling into place. Odd remarks he'd made were beginning to make sense. Jesus! Johnnie was a queer!

I silently chastized myself for allowing such a hurtful word to cross my mind, if only for a second. Up until then, the very thought of homosexuality had disgusted me, but

Johnnie was such a nice bloke. How the hell did I get out of this?

Quickly and tactfully were the words that sprang to mind. I released my hand from his grip.

'What exactly did Uncle Stan say about Utters?' I asked, defensively.

Johnnie thought for a minute until he had the right words. 'He said you were very close. To quote him, he said, "Our Billy loved that lad more than anyone or anything in the world."'

I nodded. Johnnie had obviously translated Uncle Stan's words to suit himself.

'Uncle Stan was right,' I said. 'I loved him like the brother I never had.'

I smiled in an attempt to ameliorate Johnnie's growing disappointment and embarrassment. He was shaking his head in disbelief, nervously running his hands through his thick brown hair.

'But when I just asked you if you were very much in love, you said you were. Being *in love* isn't very brotherly.'

I was going red by now, sure that everyone in the pub could hear us. In a voice just loud enough for him to hear, I said, 'I wasn't talking about Utters. I was talking about a girl. A girl called Helen Ash.'

'Ah . . .' Johnnie's head dropped. 'I seem to have been reading signs that weren't there. I apologize.'

He looked up, but not at me. There were tears in his eyes but I wasn't sure what had caused them. Disappointment, sadness, anger at himself? Who knows? I sure didn't. It never occurred to me that he'd actually fallen in love with me, just like I had with Helen. With his eyes still focused somewhere to the side of me, he got to his feet.

'Look . . . I've obviously made a complete fool of myself,' he said quickly, and before I could stop him, he was gone. I watched him disappear from my life through the pub door and wondered if I was in any way to blame.

The headlines in Monday's *Hull Daily Mail* read:

Ken McCoy

LATEST FOX TWINS RIOT
The Fox twins have turned up as Santa and his fairy in
a Hull department store, causing the inevitable riot . . .
Santa's Grotto was completely destroyed and six people
arrested . . .

The reporter neglected to mention that we weren't amongst
those arrested. Uncle Stan couldn't figure out who'd leaked
our identity to the papers. I could have made a good guess.
Hell hath no fury . . .

Fourteen

'I had it ter pay for, tha knows!' muttered the stranger in the club. 'Half a crown a bloody week for three years!'

Uncle Stan and I were having an evening drink before our show started in a couple of hours time. The stranger had been staring at us for quite some time before he finally came over and spoke. Uncle Stan gave me one of those eye messages that said, *We've got a nutter here.*

'What was it you had to pay for?' asked Uncle Stan.

'Tha knows very well what!'

'Pretend I don't and give me a clue!'

'Tha's forgotten me, haven't thee? Think back thirty years to that silly stupid race thee organized, then tell me thee dun't know what I had to pay for!'

My uncle stared hard at the man, then realization dawned. 'Toke bloody Barraclough!'

The man gave a thin smile that lacked any hint of warmth. He was in his late forties but could have been twenty years older. Toke was a very long man whose all-enveloping overcoat was a tribute to his tailor, if only for the way it matched the length of its inhabitant. He wore the permanent expression of a man who has just stuck his finger through the toilet paper.

'Aye, Toke Barraclough . . . an' tha's Stan Foxcroft. I knew it were thee when I saw thee picture outside.'

We were in Bridlington. Since the Santa's Grotto disaster, we'd wintered up and down the east coast of Yorkshire, taking the odd club job as and when they turned up. We'd called in to see my dad at Christmas, but the threat from the Bradleys was very

123

real and the general opinion from everyone who knew them was for me to make myself unavailable. The Fox Twins had gone to ground, but were secretly operating under the highly original name of Chalk 'n' Cheeze and had been taken on to Mickey Boothroyd's books as a managed act. He knew our secret and we were in fact doing very well. My job at the Main Drainage Department was still on ice but life wasn't too bad, although living under the constant threat of being discovered by the mad Bradleys was a bit disquieting. All in all though, my life had become fairly uneventful, which made a welcome change. I missed Helen, she hadn't been in touch once, even when I was missing. I missed my dad and my pals. I even missed Jigger Jackson and the Main Drainage Department. There were, however, many compensations. These compensations had, in recent weeks, begun to arrive by coach and train every Saturday lunchtime. Saturday afternoon would see them parading themselves around town wearing wide, red and white smiles, thick woolly jumpers, daring, above-the-knee skirts and kiss-me-quick hats. Saturday night would see many of them in whatever venue Chalk 'n' Cheeze happened to be appearing in. The more discerning of these would be attracted to handsome young Charlie Cheeze and the reflected glamour of show business. It was a tiring time but I was not yet seventeen and lack of stamina was not a problem. Even Uncle Stan, or Chesney Chalk as he was better known, had a following among the women of a certain age. What's more, the money was good. Uncle Stan and I were splitting sixty-forty, no need to say who was getting the sixty, but it was more than fair.

'It's bothered me for thirty years,' continued Toke.

Everything about this man was long. He was bald, apart from a wiry fringe. Encircling his skull from ear to ear, it looked more like a circumcision than a haircut. He had a long chin, long ears and a long hair growing out of his long nose.

'I don't remember a thing about the bloody race,' he said, in a mournful voice. 'But I do remember borrowin' me uncle's hoss an' cart. We searched for it for a week. Me uncle put an advert in the paper. I'm told I started the race and I were last seen neck-and-neck with thee, but nobody saw nowt after that and thee left to go to Australia or somewhere afore I could get hold of thee to ask thee owt.'

He drained his pint and set it down in front of Uncle Stan, with a rheumy-eyed look that said, *I wouldn't mind another if tha's buying.*

Even *I* could have set his mind at rest. The Great Pit Hill Race was one of Uncle Stan's favourite stories. I'd always thought it was something of an exaggeration, but Toke turning up added a touch of authenticity to it. I can only tell it as Uncle Stan told it to me . . .

The General Strike of 1926 lasted for just nine days. For the miners it lasted six months. For many it was the end of their working life. The term *lions led by donkeys* had been coined to describe the common soldiers in the Great War. But it could have been just as easily applied to the miners. They'd been out for four months when Stanley Foxcroft, younger brother of my grandad, Billy Foxcroft (of grizzly bear fame), returned home that September from his great gold-mining adventure. Striding triumphantly into the back yard, he signalled his arrival by banging with a cheerfully clenched fist the galvanized tin bath that hung on a hook against the scullery wall. He stepped across the single scoured step and entered the house through the back door, front doors being reserved for special occasions, such as weddings, funerals and police raids. Not even a bailiff would have the temerity to knock on anyone's *front* door. Uncle Stan was burdened with two cases, one of whisky, one of clap, both of which he'd picked up whilst panhandling in California, about seventy years after all the other panhandlers had left. He'd left school on his fourteenth birthday and had spent two years down the pit before reading an article in the *Castleford and Airedale Argus* that much gold was still to be had in sunny California, for a man with *patience* and *endurance*. Had Uncle Stan been an educated man, he'd have fully understood the meaning of these two words and realized that panhandling was not for him. Eighteen months of his two-year American odyssey had been spent working his passage there and back. The other six months had seen him panning for gold in the company of a half-crazed homosexual Dutchman who kept making unnatural demands on Uncle Stan's body. Such activities were frowned upon by Featherstone lads of that era and Uncle Stan finally lost his temper, laid his partner out, nicked what bit of gold they had and buggered off back to Featherstone – his words not mine.

But he was alive and was greeted with tears of welcome by his sister-in-law (my grandma Mabel, whose Inuit name was too complicated to pronounce) and a grunt of acknowledgement from his father. Both of these relatives were striking in their different ways. His mother was out on the pit hills picking out coal from amongst all the discarded pit waste. This was technically illegal and apparently too demeaning for her colliery-deputy husband. Grandma Mabel had also been making slurry balls, fashioned from the contents of the slurry ponds at Fryston Pit. Although very dirty and smoky, these would give out an intense heat, ideal for the oncoming winter. The family was living on nine and six a week parish relief so anything to supplement the family income was welcome.

Uncle Stan made himself immediately useful by going out to the pit hills and giving them the advantage of his vast gold-mining experience. Many a fierce fight had broken out in the past between coal pickers who figured they had a right of ownership of a certain part of the hill.

'You must all stake your own claim,' he advised them, 'then from here on in that'll belong to you and yours, in perpetuity, until the strike's finished!'

This obvious legal jargon impressed all the coal pickers, who unanimously elected him to work out the best way of staking a claim.

'The way they did it in California,' explained my uncle, 'was to have a race. First come, first served. Plant your stake in the pit hill an' that's your patch. We'll have them all squared-off before yer start, so they'll all be the same size.'

This fired the imagination of the coal pickers, whose lives had been miserably devoid of any kind of fun and games since the strike began. A route was plotted. A race date fixed – it was to be a Saturday so all the kids could be there, either to cheer on their racing relatives or to compete themselves.

There were few rules to be broken, any means of transport was allowed. This really meant bike or horse and cart. Car ownership was not for the likes of the miners of Featherstone. The route ran from the Hippodrome Picture Palace, past Featherstone Rovers rugby ground, across various recently picked pea fields, through a carefully selected maze of back streets, into the pit yard and on to the pit hills. This route was only provisional, if any contestant thought of a quicker route there was no rule that said they couldn't take it. The race would be about two miles, with many obstacles en route. Fifty-two contestants entered for the race and fifty-two plots were duly staked out. Excitement mounted in the town. Illegal bets were placed with illegal bookies who'd been operating as a public service for many years. The pit owners weren't too pleased but were advised by the police to leave well alone. It wouldn't be worth the trouble if they tried to put a stop to it.

Secret training went on after dark. Shadowy figures on bikes and horse and carts urged on by rough-tongued female trainers. The contestants were being trained to a hair under threat of either withdrawal of sexual favours or renewal of sexual demands. Whichever threat was the greater.

A pit hill was a mound of shale and slag, with scatterings of coal that had somehow missed the screens. There was one area that everyone knew about, which for some reason had a much higher percentage of coal. This, as Uncle Stan called it, was *The Mother Lode*. Anyone staking a claim on or near it would have plenty of coal for the winter.

A hot favourite emerged as the bookies laid the odds. Young Toke Barraclough, who was racing his uncle's pony and trap. A speedy combination, which would be slowed down only by the uneven ground of the recently picked pea fields. Uncle Stan was the Foxcroft family representative. Starting off by bike, then on foot, then by bike again. They'd borrowed a second bike from cousin Sefton in Airedale. This was to be hidden at a prearranged spot en route.

'But isn't that cheating, Uncle Stan?' asked my thirteen-year-old dad, who'd always had an annoying sense of fair play.

'Of course it's not cheatin', young 'un,' explained Uncle Stan. 'Blimey! I should know, I made the rules up.'

'What are the rules?'

'The rules are, that there aren't any rules, so there's no argument!'

The cold and drizzly race day arrived. So did the fifty-two cold and drizzly contestants. So did the Salvation Army Band and spectators by the hundred. Nozzer Aycliffe had a German pistol he'd brought home from the Great War. It was still loaded with the one bullet which would start the race. If it didn't fire, the contingency plan was for Nozzer to shout *Ready, steady, go!*

Nothing was left to chance.

Nozzer stood proudly on the top step of the Hippodrome Picture Palace with his pistol held aloft, waiting for his pocket watch to tell him it was twelve noon. He gave the captain (and conductor) of the Sally Army Band an official nod that said it was time to start the race. The captain brought 'Onward Christian Soldiers' to a damp and premature end; then led the musicians and spectators in a short prayer for a successful and safe race for all those involved. Nozzer closed his eyes and squeezed the trigger. The loud, smoky explosion was followed by a muffled clang as down the end of the Salvation Army euphonium went Nozzer's hand, still gripping the pistol, but no longer an integral part of Nozzer Aycliffe, who lived out the remainder of his life with just the one hand and not much faith in the power of prayer.

But the race was on.

Benny Robinson had rustled a Clydesdale that very morning from Marden's farm and it was he who led the field in the charge up Station Road. This provoked comments such as, *Hey up! It's Kit bloody Carson!*

The massive horse had a lead of several lengths as they all

turned right towards the rugby ground. But Kit bloody Carson had yet to master the art of turning a nineteen-hands Clydesdale and it continued its happy, crapping, clodhopping journey straight up the road, scattering and injuring spectators on its way. The first quarter of a mile saw many casualties. Freddie Whatmough ran his bike into the chip-shop wall, buckling both his front wheel and his skull. Arthur Inkpen, the lone unicyclist, got his lone wheel stuck in a gulley grate just as he was nicely picking up speed. His unicycle remained upright and quivering where it had stopped and Arthur Inkpen catapulted forward in a graceful arc, his fall being luckily broken by Bert Pinkney, who broke his nose on the cobbled road. He took this badly and sought retribution by breaking Arthur Inkpen's nose. Quite contrary to the spirit of the race.

The turn towards the rugby ground saw minor chaos, leaving a half dozen contestants lying on the ground in varying states of unconsciousness. Toke Barraclough, as expected, was out in the lead as they arrived at the pea fields. Uncle Stan and other assorted cyclists were not far behind and closing up on them were the swiftest of the footracers. Toke, standing up like Ben Hur at the chariot races and whipping his horse unnecessarily, made a mud-splattering detour towards an open gate, which allowed the cyclists to make up lost ground. They all shouldered their bikes, all except Uncle Stan, who abandoned bicycle number one, climbed over the low fence and set off running across the glutinous fields. The mud slowed Toke down sufficiently for Uncle Stan to keep pace with him. All the cycle-carrying contestants were dropping far behind but the dogged footracers were hard on Uncle Stan's heels. This, of course, was no problem to a man who had a second bicycle to look forward to. The hawthorn hedge which marked the boundary of the fields grew near. Behind this was secreted the bicycle that would carry Uncle Stan to victory. Or was it? Toke looked across at my panting uncle. He had a suspicious grin on his face. He pointed to the hedge where the bike was no longer hidden, shouting, 'Hey up, Stan! Our Maurice says to thank thee for lending him tha bike!'

'You thievin' pillock!' shouted my thwarted uncle.

'Nay! He's only borrowed it. Tha can have it back in half an hour.'

With a final surge of energy, born out of anger and frustration, Uncle Stan hurled himself on to the back of Toke's cart and snatched the reins out of his hands. The horse, already brassed off at having to trot through the muddy pea field, took the bit between its teeth and, midst clouds of steam emitting from body, nostrils and rectum, it took control of its own destiny. Toke and Uncle Stan were too preoccupied with the business of trying to knock the crap out of each other to notice that the horse had set a course for the Fryston slurry pond.

Not a pond you could do much swimming in.

Toke, in his ignorance, never showed much gratitude for what followed, but Uncle Stan, to this day, maintains he saved Toke's life by knocking him clean off the cart, seconds before it plunged into the pond. Fortunately, Uncle Stan spotted the danger just in time and hurled himself clear. The horse galloped headlong into the gluey grey lake. In a couple of gulps and a bubbly belch the hapless combination sank without trace into the pond's unfathomable depths.

Toke was still unconscious when Uncle Stan heard the train whistle. The pit was still keeping marginally busy, with the help of the management. Uncle Stan had heard the narrow-gauge colliery train, rattling empty to the pit hills.

The footracers were winning the day. The crowd of soaking spectators standing in the sludge at the foot of the pit hill gave a damp cheer as they came into sight. On and on they splattered, red-faced and heavy-booted, beside the rail track. Sleeves rolled tightly up pale, hard-muscled arms. Tortured lungs pumping out clouds of hot breath into the cold, miserable day. Braces dangling against thighs in true Corinthian fashion. The train clanked sootily past them, totally ignored by the excited crowd.

No one saw the smoke-obscured figure that leapt from it as it passed between the crowd and the pit hill. All they saw was my blood-and-grime-streaked Uncle Stan, triumphantly planting his stake in the Mother Lode after the train had spluttered on out of sight.

He was rewarded with a somewhat grudging and piecemeal cheer; his victory had taken the crowd by surprise. Within minutes all the good claims had been staked. The Foxcroft family would be warm that winter.

The last person to arrive on the scene was a bruised and bewildered Toke Barraclough. His uncle ran over to him.

'Well?'

'Well what?'

'Where's me bloody hoss an' cart? That's what!'

Toke's uncle was a big man who didn't realize that Toke had already suffered enough. He emphasized his question with a clip round Toke's ear, which sent him spinning to the ground.

'What did tha do that for? I haven't got thi bloody hoss an' cart!'

'I can see that, thi great sackless pillock! *Where is it*?'

Toke, in his ignorance of the situation, took to his heels, with his loud and violent uncle hard on them.

Toke Barraclough had woken up lying by the slurry pond to find several things missing. Two of his teeth, his uncle's horse and cart and his memory. This was handy as he was totally unaware that he had a horse and cart to lose. He did wonder about his missing teeth and his general dishevelled appearance, but as there were no witnesses to tell him what had happened, the mystery would remain unsolved. Uncle Stan was backward in coming forward to fill him in on the gaps in his memory.

Toke's memory of the race remained a blank page in his life, although he always harboured a suspicion that Uncle Stan knew more than he was telling. Mysteries such as this leave a nagging emptiness inside, which needs filling. Even after thirty years.

Uncle Stan took Toke's glass. 'Can I buy you a pint, Toke, while I try an' remember?'

Toke gave a nod that flicked an unsavoury looking drip off the end of his nose. He looked at me.

'Who are thee then?' he sniffed, as though he had every right to know. The *thees* and *thas* in his vocabulary are only to be found in certain parts of Yorkshire and in the Bible. But there was nothing biblical about Toke Barraclough. I'd already taken a dislike to him and no longer felt the pity for him that I had when Uncle Stan had related the story of the race.

'Billy Foxcroft, Stan's nephew,' I answered, with a politeness his manner didn't merit.

'What's all this Chalk an' Cheeze crap then? Why dun't thee go by thy own names?'

'We just thought it'd be a catchy name. You need that in our business.'

He gave me a sly look, as though some distant penny had dropped in his cumbersome brain. 'I reckon I know why. I reckon it's to do with them Bradleys not findin' thee.'

Uncle Stan arrived with the drinks. 'What's that about them Bradleys?' he asked, pointedly.

Toke picked up his pint without a word of thanks and swilled half of it straight down, much of it dribbling down his blue, unshaven chin.

'I've bin readin' about thee in t' papers. Only thee called thysens the Fox Twins, so I were askin' t' young 'un why thee changed thy names.'

Uncle Stan was immediately on his guard. 'We had to change it for our Equity membership,' he lied. 'There's another set of Fox Twins down south somewhere.'

'That's not what t' young 'un said,' sniggered this obnoxious man. 'I reckon tha changed thee name 'cos tha's shit scared o' them Bradleys. I read in the paper that they're after thi. Mad bastards, them Bradleys!'

'No, that's all over and forgotten,' laughed my uncle, unconvincingly. 'Even them Bradleys know it weren't our Billy's fault that Lol got drowned. Anyway,' he asked, swiftly changing the subject, 'what were you sayin' about an horse an' cart?'

'I was sayin' how I thought thee knew more about it than thee ever let on. I looked out for thee for years, but tha were never in the bloody country. Then, after all this time, I read about thee in the papers an' I figured it were the same feller, but nobody knew where tha were. An' then, bugger me! I come on the Wakes-Week outin' with our lass an' I see thi picture grinnin' at me. Large as life an' twice as bloody ugly.'

'It's a small world,' said Uncle Stan cheerfully.

'It were a big bloody hoss an' cart!' said Toke meaningfully. 'Come on,' he continued, slyly, 'I bear no grudges. Tha knows what happened to it, dun't thee? Just tell us an' it'll be a weight off me mind.'

'It'll be a weight *on* my mind if he ever finds out the truth,' I thought. He looked a very mean and spiteful man.

Uncle Stan took a contemplative sip of beer. 'Do you know, Toke, I think I do remember.'

My heart sank.

'It were a pony an' trap, weren't it?' he went on. 'Quite a nice rig if I remember rightly . . . an' you say you didn't get it back?'

He took another sip, I was willing him not to tell the truth.

'Well, it's a long time ago but I seem to remember your horse takin' fright at summat. I think it might of been a dog. That's right, it were a dog, one of them little yappin' buggers. I remember your horse rearin' up. I jumped outa the road, made meself bloody scarce like. I think you must of fallen off, cos the next thing I knew were your horse an' cart rushin' past me and swingin' off towards Fryston slurry ponds. Don't you remember fallin' off?'

'The first thing I remember were me wanderin' round in a bloody daze, wonderin' what were happenin' like.' Toke seemed satisfied with Uncle Stan's fictitious but plausible explanation, but then added suspiciously. 'Didn't tha bother stoppin' to see if I were hurt?'

'Nay, Toke!' ad-libbed Uncle Stan brilliantly, 'There were dozens chasing me. They'd have stopped if they thought you were hurt.'

'None of 'em bloody stopped,' whined an aggrieved Toke. 'I could have been lyin' there dead for all they cared. They must have run straight over me.'

'Lousy sods!' sympathized Uncle Stan.

'I never saw t' hoss an' cart again, tha knows. Biggest mystery of my life. It disappeared off the face of the bloody earth.'

Both Uncle Stan and I thought it must have been blindingly obvious what had happened to it, even in the new version of the story. Then Toke had a flash of inspiration, his watery eyes displayed a passing semblance of intelligent life within.

'Where did tha say it were headin' when it passed thee?'

'When what passed me?' asked Uncle Stan, with deliberate stupidity.

'T' hoss an' cart. Tha said it were headin' towards Fryston slurry pond. Tha did, I bloody heard thee.'

'Did I say that?' said my uncle, maintaining his ignorance of the obvious. 'That's right, I did. It were headin' for the slurry ponds. What's that got to do with owt?'

Toke looked at me and tapped his finger against the side of his forehead with a sideways, despairing glance at Uncle Stan.

'Well, it's a bit bloody obvious what happened to me horse an' cart now,' he said, as though he'd just cleared up the mystery of the century.

'It's not obvious to me!' confessed Uncle Stan, feigning stupidity to the end.

Toke looked at me with a gap-toothed grin. 'Tell him!' he urged.

I gave Uncle Stan that disparaging look that Winky Binks, our old latin teacher, used to give to me when I stumbled over my conjugation.

'I don't know what a slurry pond is,' I lied, 'but I reckon Toke thinks that's where the horse and cart finished up.'

'That's it!' exclaimed Uncle Stan. 'Why didn't I think of that. The slurry pond. Aye, that'd do it all right. You'd never see it again if it went in the slurry pond. Bloody Hell! You could lose the Queen Mary in that slurry pond. Well Toke, this calls for another drink, what are you havin'? Poor bloody horse though, what a way to go!'

Toke had fallen for Uncle Stan's elaborate lie, hook, line and sinker; but not enough to volunteer to pay for another round.

Fifteen

All this happened in the Bridlington Cocoa Cabana Club. It was actually no more than a big pub with a stage and a kitchen that sold fish and chips, making it into a restaurant and thus avoiding the ten o'clock closing time imposed by the local watch committee. It was Saturday and our last night there before we moved on to Scarborough. Next week would be the beginning of May and the resorts were showing signs of life. Mickey Boothroyd was negotiating a short summer season for us in a new holiday complex and caravan park near Filey, called Paradise Valley.

Toke went off to fetch *our lass*, as he called his wife. He never once mentioned her real name – if he had, Uncle Stan would have been on his guard. About half an hour before we were due on stage, he returned, booted and suited, with a reluctant wife in tow.

Ethel Barraclough looked too good for Toke. This was something she had in common with 99 per cent of the female population. She'd married him to avoid having their child out of wedlock, which would have seen her ostracized from Featherstone society, such as it was. Ethel was Toke's first and last sexual conquest. It happened one drunken night about two months after the Great Pit Hill Race. The miners had gone back to work in sad defeat. Uncle Stan had gone off to Australia because he'd read in the *Castleford and Airedale Argus* that there were opals out there for anyone who could be bothered to bend down and pick them up; and Toke had gone out to the Crown and Mitre to celebrate his re-employment. It was there that he met Ethel. She was with Minnie Pocock and her

135

hen-night party. Sixteen-year-old Ethel could drink beer with the best of them and seventeen-year-old Toke foolishly tried to match her pint for pint. He became devastatingly drunk and woke up the following morning in Ethel's bed, with her lying naked by his side and him remembering nothing as usual. She was a girl with a reputation. Few mothers would want her as a daughter-in-law. Toke didn't have a mother – he lived with his uncle, who thought their Toke was a brainless prat and a waste of space who had lost him his horse and cart. So when Ethel revealed her pregnancy, Toke's uncle jumped at the chance of getting rid of him, even if it meant setting him up in a house of his own. Toke, incidentally, had lied about paying half a crown a week to his uncle for the horse and cart. Toke never paid for anything if he could avoid it. They were married in Maude Street Primitive Methodist Chapel and, seven months after his night out at the Crown and Mitre, he became the father of a full-term, ten-pound bouncing baby Desmond. Toke was ever so proud because he thought Desmond was the image of his dad and Toke was right.

But he knew little about gestation periods.

Uncle Stan did a theatrical double take when she walked in. 'As I live and breathe,' he said, 'Ethel Nesbitt!'

'Ethel Nesbitt as was,' smiled Ethel. 'I'm Ethel Barraclough now, God help me . . . and have been for nearly thirty piggin' years.'

She had a brassy look about her. Hair was bright yellowy blonde in the popular beehive fashion. Her lipstick heavily enlarged her normally thin lips, giving her a common look. Her figure, once apparently eye-catching, was in surprisingly good shape for a woman in her late forties. Perhaps if her life had taken a different path she might by now have become a lady of well-preserved but fading beauty. Unfortunately, Ethel's life path had been littered with potholes, puddles and Toke Barraclough.

'How are you, Stanley?' she asked, with a knowing gleam in her eye.

'I'm doin' fine,' answered Uncle Stan, 'and you're not lookin' a day older than when I last saw you.'

I was thinking unkind thoughts about how rough she must have looked all those years ago when Uncle Stan introduced me.

'This is me nephew, Billy. Our Walter's lad.'

'Pleased to meet you, Billy,' twinkled Ethel. 'By heck! He's a bonny lookin' bugger. Are you sure he's a Foxcroft?'

'Less o' yer bloody cheek, us Foxcrofts are a desirable breed o' men.'

'I'll not argue with you there,' laughed Ethel, to whom I'd taken an instant liking.

'I gather you've set buggerlugs' mind at rest about his bloody horse an' cart. Do you know, there's hardly a day gone by over the last thirty years when he hasn't mentioned it.'

Then she whispered something in Uncle Stan's ear, to which he smiled secretively. Toke had gone to the bar and came back with a pint and nothing for his wife.

'Can I get you a drink, Ethel?' asked Uncle Stan.

Toke grinned the grin of a man whose ploy had worked.

'Thanks very much, I'll have a gin an' tonic. It doesn't look as though buggerlugs is buyin' tonight.'

It occurred to me that theirs was not a marriage made in heaven. Toke perched on his chair in the stiff pose of the working-class man unused to suits and smart surroundings. His face was freshly shaven, smattered with dots of bloodied talcum powder betraying the hand of a man unused to regular razor use. I watched with fascination as a dewdrop formed on the end of his elongated nose and built up to form a shimmering stalactite before plunging into his beer. Toke had his own method of making a pint go a long way.

Chalk 'n' Cheeze did two half-hour spots, sandwiching a forty-five minute slot when the four-piece band played background music while the customers had a good natter. After our last spot they'd step up the volume and the tempo and persuade the tiny dance floor to fill up with gyrating inebriates. No inebriate gyrated more than Toke Barraclough.

They were playing an old-time set and it was the charleston that drew Toke to the floor like a magnet. He'd been a young man in the roaring twenties and the charleston was Toke's speciality. His was a solo performance, as it had been all his life. Toke never attracted willing partners, not even in marriage – especially in marriage. The drink had taken its toll of Toke's bladder and it was his final trip to the gents that proved to be his undoing. It certainly proved to be his trousers' undoing, for Toke had overlooked the rebuttoning of his flies. This, coupled with Toke's unwholesome disregard for the wearing of undergarments, led to a seldom-seen display of collier's genitalia bouncing enthusiastically in time with Toke's ungainly steps. As his long rubbery legs danced their uncoordinated way round the floor, he became aware of his clapping audience. He was blissfully *unaware* of the reason why they were clapping. A smile creased his long face. He looked like a happy horse. Urged on by his drunken supporters he lumbered on to the stage, where the band, never ones to look a gift horse in the mouth, or anywhere else, played on.

'Chalk an' bloody Cheeze!' he shouted disdainfully across to us. 'I'll show yer how to entertain. Yer know bloody nowt, you two!'

We nodded our acknowledgement of his superior talent to entertain and urged him on. A lady in the audience seemed highly critical of his equipment. 'The last time I saw one like that, luv, it had a hook in it!'

'That reminds me, it's meat an' two veg for tomorrow's dinner!'

These and other ancient gems were much in abundance, but Toke was not universally popular. Complaints were made. The constabulary were summoned and arrived to find Toke in the midst of a frenzied scissor-legs movement that enhanced the wobbling of his wedding tackle, of which he was still drunkenly unaware. His arrest was made easier by him taking an unwelcome step back into the saxophone player, who pushed him away, only for Toke to fall into an unconscious heap amid the drums. He was carried out by the policemen between two files of applauding spectators, his offending bits concealed beneath a policeman's helmet. Toke awoke briefly and gave a semi-conscious wave of acknowledgement to his adoring fans. Uncle Stan leapt on to the stage in his role as master of ceremonies.

'Thank you, ladies and gentlemen. If you'd like to give the band a round of applause to show your appreciation of their new dance, which is to be called, The Dance of Barraclough's Bollocks. As our demonstrator has been unexpectedly called away, are there any volunteers to take his place?'

Uncle Stan could get the most out of any situation. There were no takers. I'd watched all this from the dressing-room door. Stepping out on to the stage, I looked around the room to see if anyone there was daft enough or drunk enough to take Uncle Stan seriously; what I saw made my blood run cold.

Hilda Bradley stood there with two of the surviving Bradley brothers. The impromptu floor show didn't appear to have amused them.

The granite-faced Hilda (whose name means *warrior maiden*), issued a string of stentorian, expletive-ridden directives to her two sons. They were to remove me from the face of the earth in an undignified fashion. I, in turn, removed myself from the club in an undignified fashion. Still dressed in my tramp's outfit, I made my exit by bounding across the table tops, cheered on by the audience, who'd all made up their minds to come again to this wonderful place and bring their friends.

The older and larger of my two pursuers was Tommy Bradley. He'd successfully channelled his limited talents into becoming a professional wrestler and was known on the wrestling circuit as Tommy the Troglodyte. This was one of the most apt names I've ever come across in wrestling circles, or any other circle, come to think of it. I therefore need describe him no further. Eric Bradley was much smaller than Tommy, in fact he probably weighed little more than sixteen stone. He'd spent some time in prison, being the late Lol's failed getaway driver. Eric hadn't lived up to his early promise, having left borstal with glowing references.

139

Perhaps murdering me was his big chance to make something of himself.

I ran swiftly through the bustling Saturday-night streets towards the harbour, formulating a plan as I weaved through the late-night revellers. My exit via the table tops had given me a valuable lead of maybe half a minute, but the Bradleys were on my trail like baying bloodhounds, only not as cheerful-looking. It was approaching midnight and I knew that a certain fishing coble would be leaving around this time to take a party of fishermen on a *Moonlight Fishing Trip*. I knew this because the skipper of the coble, who I knew only as Barry, had that very day been trying to persuade me and Uncle Stan to join them.

A circle of donkey-jacketed men stood quietly talking fishing talk on the high wooden jetty as I hurtled towards them, my hobnailed tramp boots echoing loudly on the slatted floor.

'Hey up! It's Charlie Cheeze!' shouted Barry. 'I knew you wouldn't be able to resist our luxury cruise. Hold on! What are doin', yer daft bugger? We're not ready to go yet, there's still—'

'Sorry, Barry!' I interrupted as I jumped the six feet or so from the jetty into the coble *Our Dolly*. I'll explain later.'

As it happened, no explanations would be necessary. I undid the painter, cast the boat adrift, tugged the motor to life and steered towards the harbour entrance and safety. Or so I thought. The Bradleys had arrived and were busy persuading Barry to start up another boat for them. Their methods of persuasion led to three of the prospective fishermen being thrown into the icy harbour. Barry was soon convinced and started up *Our Dolly*'s sister ship, the *Our Elsie*.

Barry was instructed to *Follow that bleedin' boat, yer little twat!* Barry followed that bleedin' boat until the coble chugged clear of the harbour, then he did a wise and courageous thing. He jumped ship.

Eric Bradley, the failed getaway driver, took over the tiller and, unfortunately, soon got the hang of it. For my part I thought I was free and clear. I'd left the harbour and was heading for Flamborough Head, slumped darkly on the horizon like a sleeping puppy. Aiming the pointed end of *Our Dolly* towards the flashing Flamborough lighthouse I settled down for a trouble-free journey to Filey, which lay just around the corner in the next bay. It was a beautiful night. A bright new moon hung in the distant sky. *Shining like a tanner on a sweep's arse* (as Uncle Stan would say) and reflecting itself many times over on the dark, dancing sea. Lolling in the back of the boat with the tiller in the crook of my arm, I stared up at the twinkling night sky, remembering that night up our tree with Utters. He'd wet himself with laughing if he could see me now, I thought. How I wished he could be there so I could tell him my story, nobody liked a good laugh more than Utters. Then I thought of Helen and *our* night under the stars. There'd been plenty of girls in the last couple of months but there hadn't been any Helens. If only I could think of a way to make it up with her. I suspected her parents disapproved. My much-publicized part in the great shit-boat explosion wouldn't have helped, they were a bit straight-laced were Helen's parents. If I could get my job back at the Main Drainage Department, it might help. No, it wouldn't, she'd be at university in a few months and I'd never see her. Better to forget Helen. This wasn't possible. I thought of Uncle Stan and how he'd never got over Yvette. At least Helen was still alive and where there's life there's hope. That's what they say.

My thoughts switched to Voluptuous Vicki, who'd caused all my problems with Helen. Wasn't it a bit unreasonable to expect a sixteen-year-old boy not to succumb to the advances of a beautiful naked lady? Surely Helen could see I was the innocent party in all this. Maybe if I got Vicki to admit her guilt – perhaps throw in a white lie about how I did my best to resist on the grounds that I was in love with my girlfriend. That's it! Job's a good 'un, as Uncle Stan would say. I'd convinced myself of my innocence, all I had to do was convince Helen. Why hadn't I thought of this before?

With the towering cliffs of Flamborough Head to my left, I headed towards the north star, winking at me from below the

Great Bear. There was a deep, unfathomable infinity up there that makes a lad in a small boat seem a bit insignificant in the greater scheme of things. When something's unfathomable it gives us an excuse to become religious and make up the parts we can't fathom, usually to our own advantage. That's the way me and Utters worked it out. The human race is a bit greedy when you come to think of it. Greedy in assuming that there must be more to life than what's around us; as if life isn't enough for us. I suppose for people who are having it tough there's some excuse for this kind of thinking. Maybe they're right. I hope so, for Utters' sake.

Utters reckoned we should keep our options open, believe in everything and believe in nothing. He'd know now, one way or the other, surely if there was something out there he'd find a way of letting me know. I searched the night sky for signs. As Filey Bay came into view I remembered a story Utters once told me about a priest asking a dying Irishman if he'd renounce the devil and all his works and pomps – whatever pomps are. Paddy refused to do this on the grounds that it was a bad time to start making enemies.

In the distance I could see the lights of a large ship heading east and I wondered if George might be on board. I smiled at the thought of him. It turned out that the barge wasn't his, so he'd lost nothing from a financial point of view. The revenge that had been festering inside him for ten years had been exacted in great style. A powerful emotion, revenge. I shuddered as I remembered the reason for me being out there on the high seas in a stolen boat, dressed as a tramp.

When I first noticed *Our Elsie* behind me, it didn't immediately occur to me that the Bradleys were on board. It was the erratic steering and the occasional expletive, drifting towards me on the cold night wind, that alerted me to the danger. Even then I wasn't desperately anxious. I knew it was *Our Elsie* from the single mast, which none of the other cobles had, and I knew it was one of the slowest boats in the harbour. Barry had chosen well. By the time I beached *Our Dolly* on Coble Landing in Filey, I'd be twenty minutes clear of the Bradleys.

I wrapped my Army and Navy Stores patched tramp overcoat round me to keep out the biting breeze and settled down for the hour's ride ahead of me.

It wasn't by any means the first time I'd steered this boat. Barry had taken me and Uncle Stan out many times to the fertile fishing grounds above the Flamborough wrecks. It was a great way to fill the day between gigs. I even considered casting out a line that very night then marvelled at myself for my coolness under fire. The rods were all there in the bottom of the boat alongside a big tub of mussels for bait. The sea in that area was rich in cod, plaice, dab and mackerel. *Our Elsie* was dropping away in my wake. Foxy Foxcroft was home and dry. Then the motor spluttered to a stop, which correctly told me it was out of fuel. I was in it again, deep this time. *The only thing that varies is the depth.*

I had two options. One was to swim to shore. It looked very tempting, Flamborough cliffs towering above me made it look no more than a couple of hundred yards to dry land. Unfortunately past experience told me it was nearer a mile and I'd probably die of hypothermia before I got there. Besides, I'd most likely be swept further out to sea by the tricky currents in that area. Perhaps in a few weeks someone would come across a body washed up on that pencil-thin peninsula of land called Spurn Point, half-eaten by fish and totally unrecognizable except that, by the look of his clothing, he was obviously a tramp. To save the authorities trouble I'd be buried below Spurn Point lighthouse in an unmarked grave. So sod that for an idea.

My mind was adrift, as was my boat. *Our Dolly* was drifting away from land, bobbing about dangerously in the increasingly choppy sea. It was bad enough being adrift in a powerless boat without having the mad Bradleys heading towards you. For once in his life Foxy Foxcroft couldn't think of a single plan. I just sat there in the bobbing boat awaiting my doom and dying to go to the toilet for a sit-down one. Fear plays havoc with my bowels, I was like that the first time I went on stage. *Our Elsie* was not easy to spot. It was only when both boats were on the crests of waves at the same time that I could see her, less than quarter of a mile away. Perhaps the Bradleys couldn't see me. Maybe they'd think I'd outrun them and it was useless to keep up the chase. Optimism is a strong Foxcroft characteristic.

Our Elsie seemed to come from nowhere. The sea had grown to what Barry would call a ten-footer and I was upwind of and, if anything, drifting towards the Bradleys. I don't know whether or not they actually saw me – if they did they behaved with unbelievable stupidity. Then again the Bradleys *were* unbelievably stupid, so I'll never know.

Our Dolly was broadside on to them, in the trough of a deep swell, when they appeared out of the moonlit sky and plunged down on top of me, with a great splintering crash, flinging me backwards into the water. This was one hell of a shock to the system, I can tell you. I felt myself heading down and deeper down towards the Flamborough wrecks, no amount of kicking could stop me sinking. Panic gripped me in its dead hand. Then, just in time, common sense set in. I wriggled out of the army greatcoat, pulled off my hobnailed boots and with lung-bursting gratitude I kicked back up to the surface.

It was a while before I stopped coughing and spluttering long enough to have a look round. One boat was upside down about fifty yards away. There was no sign of the other. There was no sign of the Bradleys either. The ten minutes it took me to get to the boat, which was forever drifting out of reach, nearly did for me. It was *Our Elsie* and had old rubber tyres all along its hull to protect it from collision with the dock, and/or other boats. One of these saved my life. To this day it commands pride of place on my living-room wall. Much to the displeasure of my darling wife, who says she'd rather have the Monarch of the Glen.

I had no strength to climb up on to the hull. It took everything I had just to climb inside the tyre, which had become partially unfastened. I then lapsed into unconsciousness.

As soon as Barry clambered ashore he made his way back to the jetty to check on the welfare of his customers, who were standing there shivering and soaking and asking for their money back on the grounds that this hadn't turned out to be the exciting moonlit adventure they'd been promised. He then turned his attention to *my* welfare and turned out the Bridlington Lifeboat. It was all he could think of. It was all he needed to think of. He knew *Our Dolly* was down on fuel, he'd been about to attend to that when I'd arrived. So he had a fair idea as to how far I'd get and a fair idea of what the Bradleys would do once they got to me. His heart apparently sank when he saw the single upturned hull bobbing about. He recognized it as *Our Elsie* and knew that his own boat and me in it had probably joined the rest of the Flamborough wrecks. It wasn't until they steered around *Our Elsie* looking for a good place to attach a line that they spotted me. I was three parts dead but they revived me, God bless 'em.

The Bradley brothers were never seen alive again and I knew Hilda would be annoyed.

Sixteen

I awoke in hospital. Staring down at me were Uncle Stan, Ethel Nesbitt as was, a bulbous-nosed hospital porter and a policeman. The porter leaned over me. He had an abundance of blackheads on his face and looked like an Eccles cake. A nurse would have been nice.

'He's awake!' sniffed the porter, breathing last night's stale beer fumes into my face and nearly sending me back to sleep again.

He was overheard by a nurse, who shooed everyone away while she leaned over and had a good look at me. 'Good afternoon, Billy,' she said cheerfully. 'You're in Bridlington Hospital. When you feel well enough there's a policeman who wants to talk to you.'

'I don't feel well enough.'

'I'll tell him to go away and come back later.'

'Thank you, nurse . . . Nurse?' I whispered the last bit. 'Would you ask Uncle Stan to pop back when the others have gone?'

'OK, Billy, but only because it's you.'

She had a lovely face but I couldn't see the rest of her. She drew the curtains around my bed and after a few minutes Uncle Stan reappeared.

'By heck, our Billy! You've cracked it with that nurse.'

'What's happening, Uncle? What did that copper want?'

'Them Bradleys are still missin'. He wants to know what happened.'

'Blimey, Uncle. How should I know? The last time I saw 'em, they were chasing me through the streets!'

'That's exactly what I need to know.'

The voice came from behind Uncle Stan. It was the policeman, who'd followed my uncle back to my bed. My nurse was hard on his heels.

'It's all right, nurse, he seems fit enough to talk now. Isn't that right, son?'

I nodded reluctantly. My nurse hovered in the background, very displeased with the policeman.

'All right, son, in your own time, just tell me what happened.'

He was a sergeant with a black moustache and snow-white hair, which I thought looked most unusual. But he was a friendly chap and jotted a few notes down in a small black book using a short stubby pencil with a rubber on the end which spent most of its time inside his mouth.

My time in the sea had blurred my memory of events – they say it's nature's way of protecting us from such trauma. I told him all I could about the chase and my short sea voyage; but my memory of the actual collision was very sketchy. All I could remember vividly was running out of fuel and panicking. The sergeant snapped his notebook officially shut.

'I think that's all we need for the time being,' he said. 'We'll want to talk to you again when you're feeling better. By the way, I've just heard, there's two less Bradleys in the world. They were found washed up on Filey Brig about half an hour ago. Seems like you're wiping out the whole Bradley clan single-handed.'

'Now then, Sergeant! He can do without silly talk like that.'

My nurse insinuated what turned out to be a slender body between the policeman and me, indicating who was in charge here, and it was not the sergeant. She wore a pleasant perfume that easily overpowered the ubiquitous hospital smell. The policeman gave me a friendly wink and disappeared. Uncle Stan sat on the chair beside the bed. I looked up at the nurse and asked, 'How long will you be keeping me in?'

Nurse Pauline Stokes (according to her badge) gave me a

dazzling smile and said, 'What's the rush? You don't have a show tonight, do you? It's Sunday.'

'Ah, I suppose you've seen our act.'

I always found it mildly embarrassing meeting people in the cold light of day who'd seen our act. Some people thought we were a bit rude.

'Yes, I've seen your act!' she said, thrusting a thermometer into my mouth.

'Well?'

'I thought you were a bit too clean for my taste. But you're very funny.'

She was trying to humour me, but I'd fallen in love with her, so she could humour me all she wanted.

'We're actually doing a charity show in Scarborough tonight,' chipped in Uncle Stan. 'Why don't you come? Bring a friend for me. Someone more my age, you know, mid to late thirties.'

'I don't think I know anyone that old,' laughed nurse Pauline Stokes, 'but I'll try my best. It all depends on whether the doctor gives him the all-clear.'

'It's a concert for the Friends of St Thomas's Hospital in Scarborough, so this doctor of yours had better have a good excuse to keep him in.'

It was the first I'd heard of it. Apparently Uncle Stan had set the whole thing up as a kind of insurance to get me out quickly once I woke up. The gig was genuine enough, he'd seen a poster on the hospital wall and rung up to offer our services. His offer had been gratefully received.

The plan worked. The doctor gave me the all-clear on condition that nurse Pauline Stokes came along to the concert to keep an eye on me. I reluctantly bowed to his request. Unfortunately Pauline couldn't find an escort for Uncle Stan.

'Not to worry,' said Uncle Stan in the taxi that took us back to our digs, 'I've made my own arrangements.'

We'd all arranged to meet in the lounge bar of the Crown Hotel, from where we'd take a taxi to Scarborough, paid for by the Friends of St Thomas's. Uncle Stan didn't throw money away. Pauline arrived about five minutes after us. She was nineteen, blonde and looked very classy. Not what I'd got used to over the last couple of months. For a start she didn't have a lipstick-stained fag dangling from her mouth and she didn't giggle inanely when I said Hello. I did wonder for a minute just what she saw in me, but only for a minute. Uncle Stan was sworn to secrecy about my age.

'If the subject comes up, I'm eighteen.'

'It'll cost you a few pints,' he said.

I was now six feet tall and practically acne free. I looked older than my age, so why take a chance?

Shortly afterwards Uncle Stan's date turned up – Ethel Barraclough. She wasn't the same Ethel Barraclough I'd seen the night before. Her beehive was missing, her hair was short and fair, her lipstick was more subtle. She wore a matching dark-blue jacket and skirt, and dark-blue, very high heels.

'My God, it's Grace Kelly!' said Uncle Stan. 'What's happened to that bird's-nest you had on top of your head?'

'I've left that back at the digs. I only wear it when I'm out with buggerlugs.'

'Why? Does Toke like it?'

'No, he hates it. But I make a special point of dressin' to displease him. I'd throw up if ever he started fancyin' me!'

I brought Pauline up to date on the events of the previous night with a brief breakdown of the events leading up to it. Ethel leaned across to her and said in a loud stage whisper, 'Think twice before you get mixed up with a Foxcroft. It's a dangerous pastime!'

She was joking, but I knew it to be true.

Pauline laughed. 'I *do* read the papers you know, but I've never been fussy about what company I keep!'

'Was it Toke who told the Bradleys?' Uncle Stan asked Ethel pointedly.

'I think it probably was.' Ethel sounded embarrassed. 'I heard him talkin' to someone on the phone just before we came out last night. I thought it was a bit unusual, the only person Toke ever talks to on the phone is his bookie!'

'Where is he now?' asked Pauline.

'He's in clink. Locked up for . . . indecent exposure!'

Ethel just managed to get the last couple of words out before breaking down into a fit of giggling. This set me and Uncle Stan off and it was a while before we all regained sufficient composure to explain to Pauline what it was all about.

Uncle Stan chuckled. 'If they lock him up a week for every inch he should be out in a fortnight!'

'Ten days, if it's a bit cold in them cells!' added Ethel.

This started us all off again. Uncle Stan described Toke's dance to Pauline, in graphic detail, right up to the point where Toke was carried out with the policeman's helmet covering his naughty bits. By the time he'd finished his story, practically everyone in the hotel bar was laughing, Uncle Stan was never off-stage.

'But why did he tell the Bradleys?' I asked. 'Uncle Stan explained to him about the horse and cart.'

'He told him *his* version, you mean,' said Ethel. 'Me an' Stan know what happened to that pony an' trap and have done these past thirty years. No, Toke believed Stan – mind you he were always a bit limp under t' cap were Toke – but there was another reason Toke had a grudge against Stan. A livin', breathin' reason.'

A man had entered the bar. Thirtyish, not a tall man; dark-haired, slightly plump and familiar-looking. He stopped to look round, gave a broad grin when he saw Ethel and walked over to our group.

'Hello, Mam!' he called. 'Can I get anyone a drink?'

He addressed the last question to us all. We were gobsmacked by his appearance. Ethel waved him away to get one for himself as we were all OK, thank you.

'You can see he hasn't inherited his father's generosity,' she said, when he was out of earshot. Then added with a twinkle, 'Or has he?'

Desmond Barraclough was the absolute spitting image of his father. I could see it. Uncle Stan, sitting there, white-faced, could see it. Even Pauline could see it, and she'd never met Toke. Ethel looked at Uncle Stan and said, by way of explanation, 'You can see why Toke carries a grudge against you.'

Uncle Stan nodded, speechless.

'Uncle Stan, he's the spitting image of you!'

'I know, our Billy. Christ, even I can see that!'

'So can Toke!' said Ethel. 'He's never said anything, but even *he*'s not that bloody thick. It became more an' more obvious as he grew up. It hasn't helped with you havin' your picture in the papers so often with all your bloody daft antics!'

'I'm sorry about that, Ethel,' said Uncle Stan awkwardly. 'I didn't realize. Why didn't you tell me?'

Ethel looked down at her shoes and fidgeted with her patent-leather handbag.

'To be honest, I wasn't sure whose he was at first. I was a bit of a girl, if you remember. The only thing I *was* sure of was that it wasn't Toke's. *He* couldn't father a bleedin' ferret. I tricked him into thinkin' it was his, it wasn't difficult. If his brains were dynamite, he wouldn't have enough to blow his cap off, wouldn't Toke.'

'But why pick on him? What was wrong with me? Or anyone else for that matter – you were a good-lookin' lass. I don't reckon *I*'d have said no.'

'You weren't around to say yes, and the rest weren't much better than Toke. I picked him because he was the daftest; easier to fool than anyone else. I had to marry *someone* – you know what it was like in them days.'

'So Desmond's my . . . er . . . my son then?' This type of instant parenthood was not easy for Uncle Stan to take in.

Ethel smiled and nodded, slowly, taking Uncle Stan's hand. 'Desmond's your son. When you went off digging for opals in Australia you left me with a dose and a Desmond.'

'Ah! Sorry about that.'

'Sorry about what? The dose or the Desmond? Toke never found out about the dose, I never let him near enough to see.'

'I don't think I'm sorry about the Desmond. He looks a decent bloke.'

'He *is* a decent bloke, and there was no one happier than me when I realized who his dad was.'

'Does Desmond know who I am?'

'At the moment all Desmond knows is that Toke isn't his dad. He reckons it was the happiest moment of his life when I told him that.'

Desmond arrived back with a tray full of drinks. He politely handed them round then sat down in a chair Uncle Stan had brought across for him. Our group fell silent. Ethel took Desmond's hand and said gently, 'There's someone here you might recognize.'

Desmond smiled and gave an embarrassed shake of his head as he looked over at me and Pauline. Uncle Stan was sitting next to him so he couldn't get a full-facial view of his father. Then my uncle turned to face his son. Desmond stared at him for what seemed like an age, then he looked across at his mother, who gave an apologetic shrug and a tearful nod. Desmond looked back at Uncle Stan.

'Jesus Christ! Are you . . . are you who I think you are?' His voice was wavering.

Uncle Stan's eyes half closed, trying to keep control of himself. Normally he'd have made a joke about his name being Stan and not Jesus Christ. But this was no time for humour.

'So I've, er . . . so I've just been told.'

Desmond looked back at Ethel, who wore an apprehensive smile, hoping for the best. Then he returned his attention to Stan. 'Well – of course, I knew you'd be out there somewhere,' he said. 'Me mam, er – she said you were still alive and kicking.'

'I didn't know about you at all until just now.'

'So . . . I've come as a bit of a shock then.'

Uncle Stan nodded. There was an atmosphere of something ready to explode, the calm before the storm. As if neither of them wanted to commit themselves to any emotion before they knew the absolute truth of the situation. Ethel broke the deadlock.

'I'm being a bit rude here. I haven't introduced you. Desmond, this is your dad . . . Stan, this is Desmond, your son!'

It was the first time in my life I'd ever seen Uncle Stan in tears. The two men reached out and clung to each other, like lost children, oblivious to everything around. I looked at Pauline, her eye make-up was running down her face. Even I felt myself filling up. The other people in the room were staring at us in amazement. Five minutes ago we'd had them all in fits of laughter, now we were all roaring our eyes out.

Seventeen

A comedy act has two main ingredients. The comic (or comics) and the audience. A good act and a bad audience equals a bad act. This is why comedy is the hardest job in show business. Audiences put up with bad singers, but not with bad comics. Uncle Stan and I had often performed identical routines to different audiences on consecutive nights and been a roaring success one night and died a death the other. This is one of the reasons why we turns always like to do the occasional charity show. The audiences are unfailingly on our side, knowing that we're forsaking our vast fees for the sake of their favourite charity. This is good for our ego; and a turn is nothing without an outsize ego. It reinforces your belief in yourself, especially if you've been going through a thin time. Not that we'd been going through a thin time, not professionally anyway.

The Friends of St Thomas's Hospital charity concert was a great success. The only cloud on the horizon being Mrs Rona Fitzgibbons of the Scarborough Amateur Operatic Society. She'd been star of the show since its inception six years previously and wasn't happy to see her stardom threatened by a *vulgar vaudeville act* at the eleventh hour. The organizer, Mrs Olive O'Toole, would have been more than pleased to see us close the show in Rona's final spot, but Uncle Stan said a diplomatic no.

The show was held in the Sir Harold Ovington Memorial Hall near Peaseholme Park. A makeshift stage had been erected, beside which was a small function room that served as a communal dressing room for both men and women. Amateur

154

theatricals seem to prefer mixed dressing rooms, they say it's more professional. I think there's a much ruder reason.

The night went well. Alec Armitage, a retired bus driver suffering from a cold, managed to sniff his way through most of 'Albert and the Lion', before dissolving into a bout of sneezing. He wisely decided to make the most of the ensuing laughter and applause by making a premature exit. A small, precocious ten-year-old girl lisped a tuneless 'Somewhere Over the Rainbow' to polite clapping and lots of *aahs*. The inevitable Andrews Sisters appeared, as did Al Jolson, W C Fields and Johnnie Ray. To my mind the star of the show was a junior doctor who bounced on stage in a huge, cardboard top hat which covered the whole upper half of his body, right down to his waist. His nether regions were covered by a cheap wig. Two small false arms sprouted out from either side of a cleverly made costume which made it look as if he was a very short man with a huge head. His face was his bare bottom. On each rosy cheek was stuck a cheeky paper eye. He had big floppy ears and a big floppy nose. From beneath a bushy black moustache protruded a cigar of Churchillian size. This had been inserted in the only place which could possibly act as a mouth. He stood in a single spotlight in centre stage and sang 'She was a Bird in a Gilded Cage' in a tremulous falsetto voice. I was jealous of his thunderous applause. Uncle Stan and I made a mental note to steal this idea. I thought Uncle Stan could do it, he thought I could do it. In the event neither of us did it. Uncle Stan said he didn't have the cheek to carry it off.

We were well received, the audience hanging on to our every word. Laughing at punchlines a second before they were delivered. I could hear Rona warming up in the dressing room. Unfortunately for Rona, so could Uncle Stan. He unhooked his microphone from its stand and took it with him to the half-open dressing-room door, through which he disappeared, leaving me on my own. At the back of the stage Rona's diminutive, long-suffering husband Rex was sitting at the piano. In his foolish youth he'd made the cardinal error of marrying for lust. Rex liked big women and Rona fitted the bill. Rona had married him for the status of being a doctor's wife. They were ill-matched, physically, temperamentally and intellectually. Rona was the type who wasn't bright enough to realize how stupid she was. I asked Rex to shove up and sat beside him on the piano stool. This got an undeserved titter from the audience. Uncle Stan's voice came over the speakers: 'Rona, love, you'd best get a move on. You're on in five minutes an' you're not even dressed yet!'

This drew loud laughter from the audience, who all knew Rona. And therefore knew just how annoyed and embarrassed she would be. The laughter increased in volume as the voice continued: 'Yes . . . I can see you've got your shoes on! But that's *all* you've got on! And what are you doin' with that young doctor under that table? And why hasn't *he* got any clothes on? What would your Rex say if he could see you now? What do you think you're doing? And do you mind not doing it while I'm talking to you?'

This last comment seemed to appeal to Rex, who laughed himself off his stool. I've rarely seen a man so animated. Tears were rolling down his cheeks. He was indeed a happy man; but God help him if the redoubtable Rona saw him. The more Rex laughed the more the audience laughed. Uncle Stan, who'd finished his unseen ad-libbing, came back on stage to see what all the commotion was about and it was he who spotted that Rex was in fact in the throes of a terminal heart-attack.

Despite an audience full of medical people there was nothing that could be done to save him. Rex passed away there and then. Would that everyone could end their days in such a fashion.

The Foxcrofts had struck again!

We returned to Bridlington that night in a subdued taxi. Ethel had gone off with Desmond with a promise to see Uncle Stan the following day. Rona had taken full advantage of the situation with a startling display of histrionics rarely seen on the amateur stage. Rex, who was well into his sixties, had been pronounced dead by three doctors, two nurses and the caretaker of the Sir Harold Ovington Memorial Hall, who considered he'd be neglecting his duty not to do so. Rona's tears dried up almost as soon as Rex was carried off stage into the dressing room. It transpired that she'd got him well backed with the Prudential and she wouldn't be short of a bob or two. In the spirit of *the show must go on* she even offered to go out on stage and close the show with a tearful 'You'll Never Walk Alone', but Olive O'Toole declined her brave offer, much to Rona's obvious disappointment.

Financially it had been the best concert they'd ever had and Mrs O'Toole thanked Uncle Stan and me quite profusely for our contribution and said not to feel guilty about old Rex because he'd been suffering with his ticker for years and it was a nice way to go. I dropped Uncle Stan off at our digs and went on in the taxi to where Pauline lived.

Any carnal expectations I might have had were nipped in the bud when she pecked me on the cheek as the car pulled up outside the nurses quarters.

'Billy,' she smiled, 'I can't remember when I've had a more interesting and enjoyable evening. You'll be pleased to know that I can now pronounce you fully recovered from your ordeal in the sea.'

'What about my ordeal in the show tonight?'

'That will of course require a further course of treatment.'

'Will it be a long job?'

'It all depends on the patient.'

'I'm not a very good patient.'

'In that case it could be a very long job. I'll be holding a clinic in the Crown at eight o'clock tomorrow evening. We could start the treatment then.'

'If you say so, nurse.' I kissed her lightly on her lips.

Billy Foxcroft was a happy man, well, a happy lad. What would she do if she found out how old I was?

Toke Barraclough pleaded guilty to the charge of indecent exposure and threw himself on the mercy of the court, a risky thing to do when you're Toke Barraclough. The magistrate found him as attractive a personality as everyone else did and was no doubt sorely tempted to lock him up for the maximum time allowed, and then some. He was, in fact, fined ten pounds and bound over to keep the peace, much to Ethel's disappointment. Uncle Stan, in a very last gesture of goodwill towards Toke, paid his fine for him. Toke reckoned it was the least Uncle Stan could do, considering all the trouble he'd caused him, and in a roundabout way I suppose he had a point.

There was a very nice pub opposite the courthouse, as is often the case. Our lawmakers and breakers always like to operate within ordering distance of a decent glass of something or other. Toke, the convicted indecent exposer, leaned against the bar displaying neither a hint of shame nor a hint of willingness to pay for a drink. Desmond cheerfully *got 'em in.*

I was feeling badly disposed towards Toke, who'd nearly got me killed.

'Was it you that told the Bradleys where I was?' I asked, not expecting a straight answer for a minute.

''Course it were me!' sniggered Toke, giving me a straight answer.

Uncle Stan stepped between us. Toke's long, moist nose was simply asking to be hit.

'If it hadn't been for me, Toke,' said Uncle Stan, 'you'd have been at the bottom of Fryston slurry pond with that horse an' cart. You didn't *fall* off that cart, you thick sod. *I* knocked you off.'

Uncle Stan made this confession as he held tightly on to the lapels of Toke's voluminous overcoat. The head and shoulders height discrepancy was well compensated for by my uncle's belligerence.

'Leave him alone, Dad! He's not worth it.' Desmond pointedly addressed his request to Uncle Stan.

'Have you met my son?' teased Uncle Stan, with uncharacteristic cruelty. 'Oh! Of course you have, you're the one he keeps referring to as "That useless old pillock"!'

Toke, who generated little compassion from his fellow man, or from his fellow woman for that matter, said nothing.

'Oh! By the way, Toke,' announced Ethel, matter-of-factly, 'I'm leaving you!'

Toke stared at his beer. The place went quiet. It was as if everyone in the pub had heard. He picked up his pint, drained it in one and curled a disdainful lip at Ethel.

'Why didn't tha tell me that thirty years ago? I only wed thee cos no bugger else'd touch thee wi' a barge-pole. You bein' a whore an all that.'

He turned to Stan. 'Just in case tha's thinkin' o' givin' her one, I should have her checked out at the clinic. She were riddled wi' clap when we got wed. As far as I know, she's still gorrit!'

He banged his empty glass down on the bar and left. I, for one, never saw him again and I shed no tears over *that*.

'I suppose you could say that went quite well,' observed Uncle Stan.

'Well, it wasn't one of his longer conversations,' admitted Ethel. She regarded Desmond, who grinned at her and shook his head. 'In case you're wondering, I didn't believe a word he said.'

'Good. You've just saved yerself a clip around the ear.'

'There *is* something that bothers me, though,' said Desmond, looking from Ethel to Uncle Stan.

'Who gets custody of me?'

Eighteen

The inquest on Tommy and Eric Bradley was my third inquest in nine months. I was beginning to attract quite a following. My last inquest, which had ended in thirty people being locked up for seven days for contempt of court, had not gone unnoticed by the press and they turned up in droves, hoping for a repeat performance. The Fox Twins' cover, as Chalk 'n' Cheeze, had been well and truly blown, so we reverted to our original name, except that Uncle Stan preferred the word fabulous to famous.

'*Famous* can mean owt, lad,' he explained. 'Adolf Hitler were famous but no one ever accused him of bein' fabulous.'

I was forced to agree with him. We were famous for all the wrong reasons, in fact we were one of the best known double acts in the country, which of course pleased Uncle Stan no end. He and Mickey Boothroyd were making hasty arrangements to make hay while the sun shines. I was hoping to survive long enough to enjoy some of this hay.

Hilda Bradley's face was a mask of white hatred when she entered the coroner's court. Her three surviving sons shuffled obediently in her wake. She fixed me with a glare which I could feel boring into me as I studiously looked the other way. I knew just how Perseus felt when he tried to avoid catching Medusa's eye. Although I'm sure Perseus would have much preferred tackling the gorgon to tackling Hilda Bradley. The rest of the Bradley supporters had failed to make the journey to Bridlington, perhaps wisely, in view of their previous incarceration. There were many policemen about, to forestall any repeat of such trouble. The proceedings went without incident and a verdict of death by misadventure was recorded. The Bradleys were ushered out of the court ahead of everyone else, so it was a mystery to me who had put the note in my pocket. It had obviously happened in the crush outside the courthouse. The place was swarming with reporters.

'Mr Foxcroft!'

I automatically turned my head in the direction of the reporter.

'Could you give us a statement about your relationship with the Bradley family?' he asked.

'What?'

'Have you received any threats from the Bradleys?'

The questions came thick and fast from all directions.

'Isn't it more than just a coincidence that you're involved in so many deaths? Could you tell us something about the death of Rex Fitzgibbons, the pianist? Weren't you sitting beside him when he died?'

'I should be careful, young man!' Uncle Stan warned this particular reporter. 'You may or may not have noticed, but Mr Foxcroft is standing beside *you* at this very moment! So if you don't want to be next on his list, I suggest you clear off!' Uncle Stan had a way with the press.

I'm not sure what prompted me to put my hand in my pocket at that particular moment. Perhaps I'd unconsciously felt someone put something there. If so, my sixth sense was working well. I pulled out a piece of paper on which was written a short message. It was a bit like being given the black spot by Blind Pew.

YOU MERDERING BASTAD. YOU ARE AS GOOD AS DED.

I gave it to Uncle Stan, who barely had time to read it before it was whipped out of his hand by a reporter. Within the space of two minutes every reporter in the vicinity of the courthouse knew that I was *as good as ded*.

The local papers printed a reasonably factual account of my last two encounters with the Bradleys, all of them included a picture of my threatening note. Though none of them took the risk of pinning its authorship on the Bradleys. It was the national newspapers who made a meal of it. The *Daily Sketch* sent a reporter up to Unsworth, who, through a combination of bribery and creative detective work, wrote a two-page story on the hapless history of Billy Foxcroft. Apart from my problems with the Bradleys, he chose to dig up the story of the shit-boat explosion, which had little to do with me. He found out about the fire which totally destroyed the Swillingfield Labour Club, the night the Fox Twins were appearing; once again not my fault. Then in an orgy of callous journalism he wrote about the death of my pal Utters and how he'd fallen out of the same tree that I just happened to be at the top of. He made me sound like a walking disaster area. It was inevitable that he would find out about the incident with Harry the carthorse. Everyone in and around Unsworth knew about that and I suppose I must shoulder at least some of the blame, but the real culprit was Raymond Sprunt.

Along with me and Utters, Sprunty was a founder member of the Black Scorpions. Even after all these years I can remember that day vividly. It was a cold Saturday in February 1953. It was a big day for Unsworth Town FC, then languishing in the bottom half of the Third Division North. They'd reached a fifth-round replay in the FA Cup, a feat unprecedented in the inglorious sixty-five-year history of the club. It was widely accepted that their success was largely due to the shrewd purchase of Denis O'Leary, a Northern Ireland international in the twilight of a famous career. At the age of thirty-two he was enjoying a renaissance, having dropped back from his old position at centre forward to a more creative role as centre half. Unsworth Town were playing away against Aylingford Athletic, currently languishing in the bottom half of the second division. The prize for the winners was a lucrative away tie against mighty Newcastle United, so there was great excitement in the town. Unsworth Town could and should have won the home tie, had it not been for a blatantly unfair last-minute penalty awarded against them when the Aylingford left winger had tripped over his own boot outside the Unsworth penalty area and dived into the box. The replay should therefore have been a mere formality, a hiccup in Unsworth Town's unstoppable march towards immortality. At least that's what Geoff Dimmock, the sports reporter on the *Unsworth Observer*, thought. But Geoff Dimmock failed to make allowances for Harry the carthorse.

He was an eighteen-hands white horse, well, technically a grey. He was very handsome, or so we thought, but we were inner-city migrants, so what did we know? The three of us, Utters and Sprunty and I, used to go and feed it most Saturday mornings in the field where it had been left by its owner to spend the winter. We always took a bag of apples from the back of Jack Sizer's greengrocers. They were what Jack called *past their best* and were fit for either the pigswill man or us. For many weeks we'd been daring each other to climb on to the horse and ride it up and down the field. That Saturday was the day that Utters and I had vowed to carry out the *duff*. Sprunty had been non-committal, wisely reserving his decision until he'd seen how we got on.

Harry was a big docile creature who'd recently lost his regular job to a Massey Ferguson tractor. His lifetime of hard work and loyalty was shortly to be rewarded by a trip to the knacker's yard. Harry enjoyed our weekly visits. He was waiting for us when we arrived, his great head nuzzling towards us over the fence as the sweet smell of apples drifted around his steam-snorting nostrils. Utters climbed on board first, tentatively gripping Harry's unruly mane as he stepped from the top rung of the fence on to Harry's strong, wide back. He sat there, very still, waiting for something to happen, his twelve-year-old legs almost doing the splits as they straddled the enormous creature. Harry appeared not to notice, too busy munching the apples that Sprunty and I were feeding him in order to distract his attention away from his new passenger.

'Come on Foxy,' urged Utters, 'this is great. There's loads of room for all three of us.'

'I'll keep feeding him apples while you get on.'

Sprunty said this as though he was doing me a great favour. I sensed that he himself was a reluctant equestrian. I'd never been on a horse before, or since for that matter, and the subsequent events will explain why. I climbed up behind Utters, my wellington-booted legs very much akimbo across Harry's hard, wide back. I held quite tightly on to Utters, who in turn was holding on to Harry's mane. Harry had finished the apples and took it upon himself to take us for a walk, which, I have to say, both Utters and I found quite enjoyable. The big, friendly beast wandered carefully along, parallel to the fence, as if not wishing to unseat his cargo of benefactors. At the other side of the fence walked Sprunty, who was shouting words of encouragement such as *Ride 'em cowboy!*

To this day I don't know why he did it, it was just one of those things daft lads do without thinking of the consequences. In fact, at first it seemed not to be a problem. We'd have preferred to stay in the field and we both told Sprunty this when he stupidly opened the gate, but we weren't unduly worried when Harry sauntered through it on to the wide grass verge beside the road. There wasn't much traffic about, just a lone cyclist in a belted, fawn raincoat and shapeless brown trilby, slowly wobbling up the incline on a creaking old bike which didn't appear to have a low enough gear for him.

Lester Buttershaw, the cyclist, had two ambitions in his cloistered life. He taught Latin at Unsworth Secondary Modern School, an unlikely subject for such an establishment, whose students usually graduated into bricklayers or burglars – or sometimes both. He harboured a wild and foolish ambition to have one of his pupils pass a Latin O Level. His other, more attainable ambition was to ride up Cenotaph Hill without taking his shiny corduroy-clad backside off the comfortable ladies' saddle of his J.T. Rogers Tourer. His excitement mounted as the second of his dreams approached realization.

Harry stopped to have a noisy munch at the longer grass at this side of the fence. We were contemplating dismounting and guiding him back into the field when we heard the coach coming. Harry twitched his ears and lifted up his head.

Sprunty recognized the coach. He was a keen Unsworth Town fan, desperately disappointed at not being able to get a ticket for the replay. He was one of Town's faithful 500 supporters; but very few of the five thousand or so available tickets found their way into such deserving hands. It was a special day in the history of the town, so most of the tickets went to Unsworth's leading citizens, who'd never been to a match in their lives.

'It's the team bus!' shouted Sprunty.

He took off his red and white Unsworth Town scarf and waved it wildly in the air as the red and white team coach droned up the hill towards us.

'Up the Town!' he yelled, dancing like a maniac in the middle of the road.

Harry, who was not an Unsworth Town fan, snorted a steamy raspberry of disapproval through his rubbery nostrils. Utters and I were mildly amused at this, but this quickly turned to terror as Harry broke into a canter. We could tell by the clatter of his hooves that we were on the road; other than that, I had my eyes shut, so did Utters. I can only relate the subsequent events as they were told to us, because Harry didn't hang around long enough for us to witness the aftermath of this part of our disastrous ride. As I mentioned in a previous chapter, if I throw a stone a window gets in the way. By the same token, if I cross a road on a runaway carthorse, the Unsworth Town team bus gets in the way.

It can't all be my fault.

Harry galloped down the middle of the road like the original dashing white charger, with us bouncing up and down on his back like a couple of badly coordinated trampolinists. The Unsworth Town team coach had picked up speed as the hill began to level out. It was just overtaking the indomitable Lester Buttershaw when the driver, seeing the oncoming Harry, blasted his horn. Our mount swerved off at the last second. So did the coach, both thankfully choosing different directions. Harry set off up a side road towards St Silas's Church as the coach drove into an unforgiving oak tree. Lester Buttershaw, head down and grimly determined to conquer this hill without lifting his bum from the saddle, continued his creaking, wavering way, oblivious to the mayhem surrounding him. Had his chain not snapped just yards from the crest of the hill, Lester Buttershaw would have had a happy Saturday.

Denis O' Leary, in his chosen role as team morale booster, was leading the lads in song as they began their three-hour drive down to Aylingford. Had he been sitting in his seat, he wouldn't have been thrown the full length of the coach, knocking himself out and breaking a radius, an ulna and Jimmy Widdowson's collar bone. As Jimmy Widdowson was the goalie, it left them a bit short-handed. Fortunately, apart from a few cuts and bruises and the odd concussion, these were the only serious injuries sustained by the team. They took to the field without their two key players and lost seven nil. Utters and I carried the blame for this on our twelve-year-old shoulders and Sprunty, who was the real culprit, got off scot free.

At the time, we were unaware of the trouble we had caused because our eyes were still closed, although we'd heard the horn and the crash, so I suppose we knew something was amiss. I opened mine as Harry slowed down to a canter and his hooves began a welcome thudding on soft earth. The lychgate of St Silas's came into view and Harry obviously liked the look of it because he lurched off to the right and took his two sore-arsed passengers through its rotting wooden arch. This doubled as the roof over the head of St Silas's resident drunk, who, rudely aroused from her meths-induced slumber, instinctively threw an empty bottle at Harry's departing hind-quarters, to which Harry retaliated with a cheerful burst of equine flatulence.

Ahead of us I could see a procession of black-suited people emerging from the crumbling Gothic doorway of this ancient place of worship. You could tell it wasn't Catholic because of its antiquity. The C of E commandeered most of the good churches. The leading members of the procession were carrying a coffin. We seemed to have chanced upon a funeral. The Foxcroft timing was once again exquisite.

Mrs Alice Moon was being buried that day. She'd lived a full and miserable life, dying at the age of seventy-three from God knows what. Alice had survived three husbands, who'd all died on her out of spite and it was her intention to follow them so they didn't get away with it. She was a large woman who'd challenged the expertise of Messrs Poskitt, Potts and Pocock, the local undertakers. By a miracle of economical carpentry they'd managed to squeeze eight cubic feet of Mrs Moon into seven and a half cubic feet of pine coffin. This had been carried out strictly in accordance with her final instructions. Fat Alice, as she was called, but never to her face, carried her vanity with her to the grave, not wishing to encourage any sniggering comments about the size of her coffin.

The pall-bearers paused at the top of the twelve steps that would take them down to the graveyard and glanced nervously at Harry, who, along with his two desperate passengers, was cantering happily up the path that led to the foot of the steps. An air of uncertainty overcame these four out-of-breath coffin carriers as our mount began clattering up the steps towards them. In less than the blink of an eye they came to a mutual and cowardly decision. They dropped Mrs Moon and her tight-fitting pine coffin at the top of the stone steps, sending it tobogganing down towards the ascending Harry. It met him halfway down and it was perhaps he who kicked the lid off in passing. By the time it came to a rest at the bottom of the steps, Mrs Moon was no longer in residence. She was lying in her blue and green Marshall and Snelgrove's frock on the gravel path. Her wig was tilted over one eye and her nylon tights severely laddered. On top of this she'd been dead for nearly a week and was going off a bit.

Utters and I dismounted from Harry and took cover behind the headstone of Egbert George Ovenden, solicitor, who'd been tragically taken from his wife Emily in 1842 at the tender age of thirty-seven. Happily, they were reunited in 1843.

There was a rush of bowler-hatted undertakers to the empty

box and its erstwhile inhabitant. It was obvious that Mrs Moon was not going to spring back into her coffin as eagerly as she'd sprung out. It seemed that inflation had set in and the best the undertakers could manage was a make-do-and-mend job. This involved wedging as much of her in as they could and strapping the lid on with a piece of coffin rope.

Utters and I peeped out from behind Mr and Mrs Ovenden's gravestone as they lowered the late Mrs Moon down to her final resting place with as much dignity as they could muster under the circumstances. As the coffin clumped to its final halt the pressure of the tightly roped-down lid on the gaseous corpse took its inevitable toll, resulting in what Utters later described as a requiem fart booming up from the depths of the grave. Mrs Moon was bidding her final farewell to a world she hated so much.

'I think that's what's known as being *interred*,' whispered one irreverent mourner to his equally irreverent wife, who'd been giggling disgracefully throughout the solemnities.

There was a familiar whinny and a clatter of hooves from the direction of the church and we turned to see Harry the condemned horse emerging from within. Perhaps he'd popped in to make his peace with his Maker. He was followed by an irate young curate, wearing a black frock and white running shoes.

'What's the problem, Thomas?' shouted the vicar, who'd just conducted Mrs Moon's burial wearing a black frock and wellington boots.

'It's that awful horse, Reverend!' screamed Thomas, who for a man of the cloth lacked a lot of self-control. 'It wouldn't have been so bad if it had been a small horse! But look at the size of the thing!'

'Yes, Thomas, he *is* a big horse,' agreed the vicar soothingly. 'I can *see* he's a big horse. And he's messed up Mrs Moon's funeral, but there's no need to get upset. After all, he's one of God's wonderful creatures, just like us.'

Thomas gave his boss a mournful look. 'It's all right you saying that,' he grumbled. 'But I've got a wedding in an hour and God's wonderful creature's just shit all up the aisle.'

Utters reckoned this was a sign that Harry was a good Christian horse who gave what he could to the Church. A week later he departed this mortal coil via the knacker's yard and I'm sure God would have been mightily impressed by his new equine angel. I'm not sure what sort of welcome Harry would have got from Mrs Moon.

This, and many other Foxy Foxcroft misadventures were grossly exaggerated by the *Daily Sketch*.

Unlike me, Raymond Sprunt sailed through life completely unscathed by the mayhem he left in his wake. In the late swinging sixties he made his fortune when he patented Sprunt's Luminous Snot, a popular novelty item that sold all over the world until the fad wore off in the sophisticated seventies.

Nineteen

E rnest Haddock was a plasterer's labourer by profession. It
was a calling that stretched his intellect to the full. There
were many bad things about Ernest: his manners; his temper;
his attitude; his language; his teeth and his breath. The one
good thing about him, which was by no means all-redeeming
to those who knew him well, was his voice. Ernest Haddock
could sing like Mario Lanza. He'd worked the northern clubs
in the forties and early fifties, impressing all the women, right
up to the moment he opened his mouth to speak. He had an
uneducated Hull accent and a single-figure vocabulary,
although if swear words were included it would rise easily
into three figures. Spoken links between songs were wisely
kept to a minimum on the advice of his agent/manager,
Mickey Boothroyd, who fixed him up with a new name,
Tommy Tempest, and new teeth.

In 1955 his record, 'You're my First and Only Love', was
in the top twenty for seven weeks. This took him out of the
working men's clubs and into the theatres, where he played
to packed houses. Tommy Tempest's career was on the wane
when we appeared as one of his supporting acts at the Leeds
Empire in July 1957, but he could still fill a theatre. He was
Grimsby's answer to Frankie Vaughan.

Uncle Stan had worked with him before and didn't like him.
'He's a bad-tempered big-head,' was his considered opinion.
We'd been working in Paradise Valley Holiday Camp and
enjoying life. The fear of the Bradleys' revenge was receding
into the background. Unsworth police were keeping what they
called a *weather eye* on the Bradleys' movements and the staff

at the holiday camp had all been given pictures of the surviving family members to memorize and warn us about if they were spotted. Such pictures being surprisingly easy to obtain from the Unsworth police photo album.

Our three months at Paradise Valley had been more or less incident free if you don't include the time when a holidaymaker's wife, a brassy type who'd been pestering me all week, paid a late-night visit to the chalet I shared with Uncle Stan. Fortunately for me, I was out at the time, making a social visit to another chalet, strictly in the line of duty as a camp entertainer.

My lady visitor, who'd had plenty to drink, climbed into my farting, snoring uncle's bed with the intention of seducing me. On finding herself in bed with the wrong Fox Twin she decided to make the best of a bad job and proceeded to seduce Uncle Stan, who, being a Foxcroft, was very accommodating.

The following morning I was summoned to the camp commandant's office, where the seductress's fuming but unprepossessing husband was being placated by Gerald 'Cock-up' Cockcroft, the camp manager.

'That's him!' spluttered the cuckolded husband.

If his voice had been any higher it would have been audible only to cocker spaniels. I could see why his wife sought sexual solace outside the marital bed.

'That's the dirty sod what took advantage of my wife!'

I took a step back in case an irate finger was followed by an irate fist – he wasn't a big man but he was very cross.

'What's he talking about?' I protested, with genuine innocence. 'I've never been near his wife!'

'You had her in your chalet last night, don't you bloody deny it! She were seen comin' out!'

Up to this point I'd been very much in the dark. Uncle Stan had still been asleep when my summons arrived, and I now knew why! I knew whose husband this man was and I felt like telling him I wouldn't touch his gruesome wife with a bargepole but I didn't think that would help the situation.

'Sorry, mister,' I retorted, 'I think you must 'ave got the wrong chalet.'

'No mistake, lad!' he squeaked bitterly. 'She were seen comin' out of your chalet at one o'clock this mornin'!'

'Not *my* chalet, mister. It was turned two when I got back to *my* chalet.'

'Can you *prove* that?' asked Cock-up Cockroft.

'I suppose so.'

'Well yer'd better *had* just prove it – 'cos I for one don't bloody believe yer!' shrieked the helium-voiced husband.

'I was in E26 chatting to two young ladies!'

'Good!' said Cock-up, in a conciliatory tone. 'This should be easy to clear up.'

As our small posse advanced on E26, the flimsy morning sun bounced off the flimsy yellow and white prefab chalets, built just after the war so that families could take a holiday they could afford after all the dismal years of fighting Hitler. Dare-Devil Stumpy, the bald-headed, one-legged, middle-aged, pot-bellied high diver, hopped up the steps to the fifty-foot high board for his ten o'clock dive. He'd been a young and promising acrobat just before the war. In 1945 he'd had his leg removed by a German grenade. For the past five years he'd been diving off the high board twice a day, six days a week during the holiday season for ten pounds a week. During the off season he strapped his wooden leg on and became assistant caretaker for eight quid a week.

There's no business like show business.

The occupants of E26 had already missed the early-morning breakfast call. It was a while before a sleepy-eyed, scantily clad young lady peeped round the door, blinking in the bright sunlight. She saw me, grinned and shouted back into the chalet.

'Casa-bloody-nova's back and he's brought a couple of friends. I don't fancy your two, Beryl!'

Cock-up blushed. 'This young man,' he said, pointing at me, 'claims he was in your chalet last night, er – *talking to you* until two o'clock this morning. Could you vouch for that?'

172

As the second scantily clad girl arrived in the doorway, the two of them broke into fits of giggles.

'Talking to us?' said Beryl. 'Is that what he was doing? Well, yes. I have to say he gave us both a right good talking to!'

'In fact, I think he shouted at us a couple of times, do you remember, Marjory?'

'It might have been three!' said Marjory. 'Or were you just pretending to shout the third time, Billy?'

'Well thank you, ladies,' said a duly embarrassed Cock-up. 'I think that clears the matter up,' he said politely to the unconvinced irate husband.

'We enjoyed our little talk!' shouted Marjory.

Needless to say, Uncle Stan came out of all this smelling of roses.

'Keep an eye on that nephew of yours,' advised Cock-up. 'He's at a funny age, his hormones are running bloody riot and the campers will be running bloody riot if he keeps this up!'

'I've been asked to tell yer to keep yer hormones under control,' advised a strict Uncle Stan.

'Don't you bloody push it!' I advised Uncle Stan.

Tommy Tempest was on a tour of the Moss Empires and his regular support comic, Charlie Sweeney, had broken his leg in Leicester during an after-show drinking session. Mickey Boothroyd, who was booking the whole tour, brought us in as last-minute substitutes. It was a travelling variety show with a full cast, headed by Tommy. Our spot at Paradise Valley had been taken over by Barrington Barrymore: Magic, Mirth, Mayhem and Music.

The Fox Twins were quite happy about the arrangement as it meant more money for a lot less work. We had two fifteen-minute spots, before and after the interval. One show a night, six nights a week. This all added up to a total of three hours work a week, for which we were being paid seventy-five pounds. After Uncle Stan and Mickey had taken their cut, I was left with twenty-seven pounds week, or nine pounds an hour, which I reckoned was more per hour than the prime minister was earning. Perhaps the country could afford to fork out for a better man.

'Long time no see!' greeted Uncle Stan cheerfully as he walked across the stage to where Tommy had just finished taking his band call.

Tommy pretended not to recognize Uncle Stan at first, which I thought was a bit far-fetched. Uncle Stan wasn't someone you forgot in a hurry.

'How're ya doin', Sam?' grunted Tommy in a phony Hull/Texan accent.

'I'm doin' jest great, Ernie!' drawled Uncle Stan in a more genuine Texan accent. 'This here's ma sidekick, Billy. Say howdy to Ernie, Billy.'

'Hello,' I said.

Tommy/Ernie chose not to acknowledge me and walked over to the pianist to discuss a middle eight, which, apparently, he knew as much about as I did.

Uncle Stan had successfully got up the nose of the star of the show and we'd only been in the place two minutes. I wasn't best pleased with him.

'What did you have to go and upset him like that for?' I complained. 'We've got to work with him!'

'Start as you mean to go on, Billy lad. Just you watch the way he bullies all the other acts – but he'll not bully us. Ernie's a thick sod and he can't stand having the piss taken out of him, so he'll leave you an' me alone.'

Tommy Tempest *was* a bully. He didn't particularly scare me – I'd been scared by much scarier people than Tommy Tempest. But he was a pain in the neck who endeared himself to no one, least of all the dancers, who suffered from his obscene advances. The man had little time for the supporting cast and even less for the staff. He appeared to thrive on unpopularity among his show-business colleagues. As long as his public loved him, no one else mattered. But the public are fickle bedfellows.

The most annoying thing about him was his voice. It was stupendous. He smoked, drank, took no singing lessons, used no throat spray, took no throat-soothing honey. He just sang like a sodding angel. When the Good Lord dished out voices, He made a right cock-up giving that one to Tommy Tempest. That was one voice that went to the wrong man! It sent shivers up my spine just standing there in the wings listening to that fabulous sound come out of such a coarse mouth.

I sometimes wondered what I was doing there among all these well-practised show-business experts. There was a roller-skating juggler called Alec Bowness. It's hard enough roller-skating round a tiny stage without having to juggle five Indian clubs as you go. This could only be achieved after years of dedication and self-denial. But why would anyone wish to set out on such a journey?

The same with Freddie Ferentino the magician, who produced an Alsatian dog from beneath his cape. A miniature French poodle would have been amazing but no, he had to show off, it had to be an Alsatian. I was surrounded by dancers, musicians, singers and speciality acts, all of whom knew so much more about the business than I did and yet, along with Uncle Stan, I was next to top of the bill!

Our first night was something special for me. I'd never played a big theatre before. It was Monday night and the place was full. I'd done Monday nights before and played to a dozen people who were more interested in playing dominoes than listening to us. We were to close the first half. Freddie Ferentino had come off to great applause and the stage lights had dimmed. Uncle Stan and I stood behind the curtains, waiting for the compère to introduce us. My uncle was wearing bright-blue top hat and tails and I was in my tramp suit. I concentrated on my breathing and ran my opening line over and over in my head. They say you have to be nervous to perform well – I was nervous all right.

'Ladies and gentlemen . . . You've heard about them! You've read about them! Here they are in the flesh! Welcome on stage *the Fabulous Fox Twins*!

Out of the corner of my eye I saw the bored-looking stagehand stick a half-smoked fag into the corner of his mouth, pull on a rope and, with a loud rustle, the great gold curtains swept open on to a sea of faces and flapping, applauding hands. Two powerful spotlights picked us out, blinding the audience from our vision. The welcoming applause died down and an expectant hush descended on the old theatre. We walked side by side down the stage towards the dimmed footlights.

'Watch out! There's a Bradley about!' shouted a lone joker from the gods.

The audience gave a nervous titter.

'Good evening, ladies and gentlemen,' breezed Uncle Stan. 'I was about to begin by doing my impersonation of the village idiot . . . but that gentleman in the gods has just beaten me to it!'

The audience exploded. The Fabulous Fox Twins were up and running and we were in charge.

'Are you all right up there!' shouted Uncle Stan to the lone joker. 'I've just recognized your voice. I hope your wife's bringing my kids up properly!'

He gave me a double take as I stood there with what I hoped was a gormless grin on my face.

'You've been in that pub again, haven't you?' he said. 'I've told you about goin' to them places. What have you been drinking?'

'I haven't been drinkin'. I were asked to leave.'

'Asked ter leave? Yer a disgrace to the family! Why were you asked to leave?'

'I asked for a glass of water with a little dash of lemonade in it – and the landlord just looked at me stupid.'

'Well I can't understand why,' said Uncle Stan, to titters from the audience. 'And what did you say to him then?'

'I told him straight. I said *you*'d be drinkin' that, if you'd got what I've got.'

'Yer did right,' said Uncle Stan. 'An' what did the landlord say to that?'

'Well . . . he asked me what I'd got.'

'What? He came straight out with it? Just like that? The cheeky monkey!'

176

'He did.'

'And what did you say to that? I hope yer gave him a piece of your mind.' He looked at the audience and added, 'P'raps not.'

'I, er . . . I told him what I'd got . . . and that's when he threw me out.'

Uncle Stan looked to the audience for help. 'I don't like askin' him,' he said. Turning to me, he asked, 'And, er – what had yer got?'

'Tuppence,' I said.

In Tuesday night's *Yorkshire Evening Post* we got great reviews. The reporter pretty much glossed over Tommy Tempest's performance, we were the lads in the news.

> After all the publicity surrounding the Fabulous Fox Twins in the past few months, I got to see their *proper* act last night and I have to say that for my money they were the stars of the show. An early heckler was slapped down to great applause by the veteran half of the act, which went on to give an hilarious and polished performance. Remarkable, considering the fact that, despite ill-informed newspaper reports, young Billy is only seventeen years old!

There were two down sides to this. One was that Tommy Tempest wouldn't take too kindly to us being called the stars of the show, and the other was that Pauline would now know just how old I was. It was the latter that bothered me most. We'd been going out for over three months, on and off, and I was still madly in love with her. With her being in Bridlington and me now being on tour, we weren't going to see much of one another for a while. In the meantime there was at least one dancer who would help me overcome my loneliness. In fact, as things turned out, there were several. I think it was this that turned Tommy Tempest against me.

Twenty

A part from the incident of the irate husband, our time at Paradise Valley had gone well and I'd be excused for thinking that the Foxcroft jinx was a thing of the past. Tommy Tempest was to prove me wrong.

The first three weeks of the tour was a memorable time in the life of Billy Foxcroft. It would have suited me never to do anything else. Tommy Tempest was becoming increasingly obnoxious but Uncle Stan's constant mickey-taking kept him well clear of us. Freddie Ferentino was of Italian parentage, he'd inherited his act from his father, Franco, and even watching him rehearse I couldn't figure out how he got that Alsatian out from under his cape. Tommy referred to him dismissively as *that Eyetie conjuror*. Alec Bowness, on one occasion in Liverpool, skated straight into the band after being shoved in that direction when Tommy thought Alec's rehearsal was eating into his band-call time. Alec narrowly missed the drummer, who was just setting up.

The drummer, being a drummer, said, 'What did you do that for, Tempest, you big thick Yorkshire pillock?'

Tommy Tempest insisted that the drummer be sacked or he wouldn't do the show.

'You can't do the show without me,' pointed out the drummer.

Then to illustrate his point he walked out, indicating that he'd be in the Three Horse Shoes if the big thick Yorkshire pillock changed his mind.

'I've got a mouth organ if it's any help!' offered Uncle Stan.

Tommy declined Uncle Stan's kind offer and stormed off to his dressing room, followed by the theatre manager and Tommy's musical director/pianist. A compromise was eventually reached, which involved the drummer being lured out of the pub and Tommy coaxed, petulantly, out of his dressing room. This was followed by a quick, insincere shaking of hands and the band call continued. All this without a word of apology to Alec Bowness, who that day wished his late dad had bought him a drum kit instead of a pair of roller skates.

The girls suffered worst – they had even less clout than a roller-skating juggler. Tommy's obscene remarks and gestures reduced a couple of them to tears. Back in his building-site days Tommy had plodded along, blissfully unfettered by the burdens of intelligence. This had marked him out as the butt of every known building-site practical joke; which are many and varied and wonderfully cruel. Now, finding himself in a position of some power, he was exacting a form of revenge on the society that had devoted itself to poking such fun at him. Uncle Stan and I, being professional mickey-takers, were exempt from that revenge. Looking back, I think we might have been the cause of it, reminding him of his bad old days. Uncle Stan, however, felt it his bounden duty to bring Tommy down to size at every opportunity.

The fourth week was the worst. Tommy was fed up because his recently released record, 'Time's the Greatest Healer', looked unlikely to make the top twenty. He was up against the likes of Elvis, the Everly Brothers and Lonnie Donegan. Tommy's career had passed its peak and even he knew it. We were playing Manchester and the houses were pretty good – sold out for Friday and Saturday. It was on the Saturday that Tommy went right over the top.

The dancers were badly paid. Once they'd paid for their digs and meals there wasn't much left over for the luxuries of life. There was no way they could afford to eat in decent restaurants, unlike Foxy Foxcroft. I'd like to think it was my personal charm that attracted them to me but I couldn't be absolutely certain. It may have been that they were taking advantage of me, but the rewards were such that I decided to put up with it. We Foxcrofts are an uncomplaining lot.

During the past four weeks I'd taken four of the six girls out for an after-show drink or for a meal or for whatever else was on the menu. Never a pushy chap, I always let an evening take its natural course, with the girls making all the running. With the exception of Mary, they were all older than me and liked to mother me, although they did seem to mother me in a most unusual way.

Mary was much the same age as me and I took her out to celebrate her seventeenth birthday. She didn't have the sophistication of Pauline or Helen and I suspected she didn't understand much of my humour, but Mary and I got along very well. Pauline *would* have come but she was working that night. I'd strongly, but wrongly, suspected that she had cooled towards me somewhat since she'd found out how old I was.

'I've known all along, you dope,' she'd tell me later. 'It was on your medical records!'

Foxy Foxcroft had never thought of that one – perhaps I wasn't so Foxy after all. Maybe there was someone else over in Bridlington who was even more sophisticated than me. I would have been heartbroken if I'd ever found out Pauline was two-timing me, I loved her nearly as much as I loved Helen. Mary didn't know about any of this and I didn't feel it right to burden her with my emotional turmoil. After the show we went to a restaurant, where we ate steak, drank wine and laughed a lot. I thought back to my sixteenth birthday and what had happened in my life since then. I told her bits of it, she laughed like a drain at the exploding barge story and cried when I told her about Utters. Then she took my hand and asked if I could keep a secret.

I had many faults, but gossiping wasn't one of them. 'What is it?' I asked.

'Promise you won't tell anyone. I'll lose my job if you do.'

'Scouts honour.'

'Alec Bowness is my dad.'

It didn't seem much of a secret – having a roller-skating juggler for a dad; but Micky Boothroyd had this stupid rule about not having close family members in the show as separate acts. He'd apparently been let down when three family members, all separate acts, had left the show high and dry to go to their mother's funeral.

'How come you've got different names?'

It was a daft question to ask anyone connected with show business. Her name was Mary Guinness.

'Guinness is our real name. Dad had to change his because there was already someone else—'

'Point taken.' I'd already worked it out.

'You don't look like him. I reckon your mother must have had all the looks in your family.'

'Mum died last year.'

'Sorry.'

'That's okay. Anyway, that's why I'm on the road with Dad. He sort of looks after me.'

I almost volunteered to look after her myself, she was that sort of girl. Vulnerable and nice with short dark hair, a small, cheerful face and a cheeky smile – and, like all girl dancers, she had a great body. I liked Mary very much.

She came from Bowness on Lake Windermere, that's where her dad got his stage name from when he realized some up-and-coming actor was already using Alec's real name.

We took our time walking back to the digs, it was a fine night and we laughed and giggled, both unused to wine, especially a bottle each. She slipped her arm around my waist and squeezed me to her. We kissed out there in the street under the disapproving stare of a patrolling policeman.

'All right, you two, enough of that.'

We laughed and moved on, both of us knowing how the night would end.

She and the other girls occupied two rooms on the top floor. I had my own room, which I considered a luxury, not having to put up with Uncle Stan's nocturnal noises. He always took a double room, which was convenient for the occasional visits he had from Ethel Nesbitt as was. In fact she was Ethel Nesbitt as *is* now, having reverted to her maiden name. At sixty-three, Uncle Stan's lifetime of bachelorhood looked in grave danger.

Hand in hand, we walked up the stairs. My room was on the first floor. She stood patiently as I turned the key.

'Coffee?' I asked.

She shook her head. 'I just want to come in.'

'Be my guest.'

I took my coat off and went to hang it in the wardrobe. She was humming happily to herself, dancing round the room. Suddenly her blouse was unbuttoned, sliding off down her arms, then dangling from an outstretched hand, brushing naughtily against my face. I recognized the tune she was humming, having heard it many times when we'd shared the billing with a stripper.

Most strippers are pretty much self-taught. So to see a trained dancer performing a striptease, which had apparently been choreographed by her and her dancer friends, was something to behold. I sat on the bed and enjoyed the show. Her routine lasted about three of the most sensual minutes I've ever experienced. At the end of her dance she elegantly removed her knickers, threw them across the room at me, twirled and did a bow. I applauded her brilliant performance with her knickers on my head and the most urgent erection I'd ever had. She'd have caused a riot at the Bostrop Con Club.

Mary stood in front of me, her body lithe and long-legged and beautifully formed. 'I've never actually done it before,' she said, almost apologetically.

I took her in my arms and allowed her to undress me. Looking back I've no doubt the wine had something to do with her lack of inhibition and, had I been stone cold sober myself, I hope I wouldn't have taken advantage. We Foxcrofts do have certain principles in that respect. However, I wasn't sober, so that was that. She was the first one to spend the night in my room. The first girl I'd actually slept with. All my other dalliances with dancers had been of an al fresco nature.

Mary and I celebrated her birthday in some style. What she lacked in experience, she made up for in enthusiasm and energy. The following morning I woke up totally exhausted and madly in love with her. She woke up and dashed madly

182

up to her room, hoping in vain that the other girls wouldn't suspect anything. But girls have a built-in radar where such things are concerned. One of them foolishly mentioned it to Tommy Tempest.

That night's performance started well enough. We followed Vera Delmare, a coloured blues singer, who Mickey had brought in on a week's trial. There was quite a lot of heckling, which suited Uncle Stan down to the ground.

'Last night,' he began, 'the place was full of drunks and pimps and jailbirds. How nice it is, to see so many familiar faces back again tonight! A word of friendly advice, sir – never drink on an empty head!'

I, in my tramp suit, turned my back on the audience and gazed gormlessly up at the ancient red curtains which formed our backdrop. Uncle Stan did a theatrical double take, then looked back at the audience.

'I daren't ask 'im!' he said, puffing frantically at a cigarette.

'Do you know what?' I announced.

'Well, I don't, but I've a feelin' you're goin' to tell me.'

'The last time I saw a pair of curtains like that, I never saw me grandad again!'

The Manchester crowd loved the Fabulous Fox Twins. The girls went out to open the second half with their three-minute spot and Uncle Stan and I relaxed in our first-floor dressing room. We wouldn't be on for another thirty minutes. Andy Dale, the compère, was to sing a couple of numbers, then Freddie Ferentino, then us, then Tommy. We had a loudspeaker which, unusually for dressing-room speakers, actually worked, so we knew when our time on stage was approaching. I sat back in my chair, opened up a paper I'd found lying around and began to read about Jacky Stewart winning the Grand Prix at Monza. Uncle Stan was running through some lines in front of the mirror and practising his facial expressions.

I heard the girls clattering noisily up the uncarpeted stairs to their dressing room at the end of the corridor from us, but was surprised to hear Tommy's voice just outside our door.

He had his own dressing room downstairs and never ventured up to consort with us lesser mortals.

'Geroff, Tommy!' The voice was unmistakeably Mary's.

'Come on, yer little tart! Give yer uncle Tommy a big wet kiss!'

Uncle Stan was out of the door first, I was not far behind. To my left I saw the girls standing with a combination of fear and rage as they watched what was going on. Their red and blue second-half costumes were a bit on the revealing side but not as revealing as Mary's, whose top had been pulled down to her waist by Tommy, who was roughly mauling her.

'Come on, try it with a real man. Not that long streak o' piss yer had it off wi' last night.'

I could smell the drink on his breath; he'd been at it all afternoon. As Uncle Stan approached, he threw Mary, weeping, to the floor and aimed a heavy punch at my uncle, who fell back on to me. Tommy then lurched unsteadily towards me as I manoeuvred Uncle Stan into the care of the girls. The sight of Mary sitting weeping and half naked on the floor filled me with a rage unbecoming a Foxcroft. My first punch broke both Tommy's nose and the same fingers I'd broken on McGilligan's jaw only a year and a bit ago. Fortunately, further punches from me wouldn't be required. Alec Bowness rushed past me and laid into Tommy like a whirlwind. He was only a little bloke but he had much uncontained fury foaming inside him, which was very bad news indeed for Tommy Tempest.

Tommy and Alec fell back down the stairs, Alec punching wildly as they went. I picked Mary up, still crying. As the girls helped her away she turned to me with a frightened look on her drained face.

'Make sure Alec's all right,' she sobbed. 'Make sure he doesn't say anything about – you know . . .'

'OK,' I assured her, but the secret was out, blurted out by Alec, who with every blow he struck was telling Tommy and anyone who cared to listen that no one molested his daughter like that and got away with it.

The compère, who wrongly fancied himself as a singer, was

in the meantime crooning away, centre stage. The audience were impatiently listening to him, waiting for a proper turn to come on, when their attention was happily diverted by the sight of Tommy Tempest appearing backwards stage left, with a bloodied nose, frantically fending off violent blows from that little bow-legged juggler they'd seen in the first half. The battling twosome worked their flailing way across the stage behind the crooning compère, who was oblivious to all this. Andy Dale's curiosity was aroused by the audience's laughter and he turned round to see what was going on a split second after the combatants had disappeared from view, stage right. A piece of theatrical timing that seemed to further amuse the audience, which howled even louder. As Andy Dale bowed and accepted a round of wild but undeserved applause, the theatre manager strode out on to the stage and took the mike from him.

'Ladies and Gentlemen,' he said, with great aplomb. 'Is there a doctor in the house?'

The house lights went up as the manager waited patiently for the raucous element in the audience to calm down. Eventually an elderly gentleman who'd been hanging back to see if there were any other volunteers, climbed reluctantly up the steps to the stage. Dr Clifford Fletcher turned and gave a stiff bow to loud cheers, then disappeared into the wings with the manager. Uncle Stan and I were sitting in the green room just behind the stage. Tommy had retired to his dressing room, away from the still-vengeful Alec.

I heard the compère introduce *The Fantastic Freddie Ferentino*, who walked out with managerial instructions to *Stay out there until I give you the bloody word*!

Then the manager, referring to us, said to the doctor, 'I just want them two barmy buggers patched up so they can finish the show.' He didn't ask us how we felt about it. Uncle Stan had no broken bones, just a black eye, which was coming on a treat.

'This lad really needs to get to hospital,' said the doctor, who didn't understand showbiz necessities.

'I'll be OK,' I volunteered bravely. If I could stand three

tollies from Folly Berger on a broken hand, I could stand on a stage for fifteen minutes.

'Too bloody right you'll be OK,' said the manager, who didn't seem all that sympathetic. He disappeared into Tommy's dressing room with the doctor in tow. It cheered me up no end to hear a pained *Ow! That hurts, yer bathtard!*

The *bathtard* reappeared at the dressing-room door with an indignant expression on his whisky-red face. Doctor Fletcher hadn't paid good money to be insulted by this ill-mannered oaf.

'He doesn't mean it, Doctor, he's sorry – aren't you, Tommy?' The manager spoke to Tommy as if he was a naughty child.

'Thorry!' shouted Tommy from within.

'He's ever tho thorry, Doctor!' mimicked Uncle Stan.

'I can't find me teeth,' complained Tommy. 'Where'th me thuckin' teeth? Oh bollockth!'

After a marginally prolonged set from Freddie Ferentino, Uncle Stan and I stood apprehensively behind the curtains. Me with my hand bandaged and my arm in a sling and Uncle Stan with a brilliant black eye that he'd been advised by the doctor *not* to try and cover with make-up. I alleviated my apprehension by jiggling Tommy Tempest's false teeth around in my pocket.

The curtains shuffled open to great laughter and applause from an audience we'd already softened up in the first half. Uncle Stan stepped forward on his own. I followed a couple of seconds later. He gave my bandaged hand one of his double takes.

'Have you been pickin' your nose again, Billy?'

'No! I've broke me arm in two places!'

'You shouldn't go to them places!'

'How did you get that black eye, Stan?'

'Did you see Vera's husband walk into her dressing room?'

'Yes, I did.'

'Well I didn't!'

We'd worked this short routine out backstage, it wasn't hysterically funny but it explained our patched-up appearance.

Our set went well – enough for a curtain call. Uncle Stan took advantage of the situation to make an impromptu announcement, to the annoyance of the compère.

'Ladies an' Gennermen. It gives me great pleasure to announce the star of our show. The only singer to have a soup named after him, Thick Yorkshire Vegetable. Put your hands together for Tommy Tempest!'

'Follow that, pervert!' I hissed, as we passed the star of the show in the wings.

'Get thtuffed,' replied a slowly sobering Tommy, who thought he'd done little wrong.

The audience gave an audible gasp as the curtains went up to reveal their hero with a black eye, no teeth and huge elastoplast across his nose. Many singers would have considered it unwise to venture out on to the stage in such a state, but Tommy's attributes were few, and wisdom was not one of them. His broken nose had an adverse effect on his diction.

His opening number was probably ill-chosen: 'You're thuch a thweet thexy girl, my thweet thexy pearl.'

His ardent fans were horrified, the neutrals highly amused. He sounded more like Violet Elizabeth Bott than Mario Lanza. It was his rendition of 'Thixteen Tons' that drove the ardent fans across to join the neutrals. There was now a splinter group who were in hysterics.

'Thmile, though your heart is aching, thmile even though itth breaking . . .'

The splinter group was acquiring new recruits by the second.

'Thummertime, an' the living ith eathy . . .' he sang.

Would that the Fabulous Fox Twins could do this to an audience.

'Thing thomething thimple,' called out a former fan from the upper circle.

'Thing thomething from thongs for thwinging lovers,' came from the back stalls.

Tommy Tempest retired defeated, his act in tatters. The audience retired happy, to tell their friends that they'd been there on that night and what a night it had been.

Twenty-One

'I want you to keep your mouths shut about this or we'll have to cancel the rest of the tour,' warned Mickey Boothroyd.

There was a hard edge to his voice that I'd never heard before.

'Surely you can't let him get away with it?' I said. 'He molested Mary!'

'Look Billy, I'm not stupid. I know there's something going on between you and Mary, but this is a big tour for all of us. You're making plenty out of it, an' rest assured, Tommy won't go within a mile of them girls again. He knows what's at stake.'

'Don't worry Mickey, we'll keep quiet, but if that bastard puts a foot wrong!'

'He won't, Stan. You've got my word on that. He'll be as good as gold from now on. OK Billy?'

'I suppose so,' I shrugged.

I wasn't convinced. It seemed to me as though Tommy was getting away with it. 'What about all the newspaper reports about Tommy's performance?' I pointed out. 'He was a bit of a laughing stock.'

'You know what they say. There's no such thing as bad publicity. We sold out this week's show this morning, within three hours of the papers hitting the streets. I'm putting your money up to a hundred a week. Oh, by the way – I'm having to let Mary go.'

'You can't do that! She was the victim in all this. You can't punish her!' I said angrily.

'She knew the rules, so did her dad. I don't want any related people working for me, it always creates problems. That's why they kept me in the dark.'

'What about us? We're related!'

'You're the same act. I'm talking about different acts. Come on, you know what I mean!'

'I think you could have kept her on till the end of the tour, under the circumstances,' I argued, hotly. 'It was Tempest who created the problem, not Mary!'

Mickey's calm indifference to Mary's ordeal was really beginning to annoy me. He shrugged and walked out of the room. It was the following Monday afternoon and we were in Sheffield, in the manager's office.

'Don't do anything stupid, Billy! This is our livelihood, remember,' warned Uncle Stan after Mickey had left.

'Don't worry, Uncle Stan, I won't do anything stupid.' Then off I went to do something stupid.

I didn't intend to go back on my word to my uncle. It was just the way things turned out. Mary was sitting quietly by the stage, her knees hunched under her chin as only dancers can, watching her friends go through their paces. Apparently Mickey had just given her the news.

'It's what I expected,' she sighed philosophically. 'He was right, I knew the rules. He could have been a bit nicer though, he warned me not to tell anyone. He's told the girls not to breathe a word or they'll be out of a job, so if I did say anything it would be my word against that pig Tempest.'

Tommy walked out on to the stage at that very moment and gave her a leering sneer. The plaster had come off his nose. Fortunately for him, his face was never a pretty one at the best of times, so his swollen nose didn't look too much out of place. I knew I couldn't work with this man.

'Come on, Mary, I'll walk you to your bus or train or whatever it is you're catching.'

'That's just it,' she said. 'I've got nowhere to go, my dad will have to look after me.'

'You won't be able to work for Mickey again.'

'There's other agents without his silly rules.'

'Do you want to try some?'

'I've got nothing else to do!'

We caught a taxi to our Sheffield digs. A large Victorian pile of grimestone about a mile from the centre of town. Uncle Stan had stayed there before.

When we'd all arrived at her door earlier that morning, bags in hand, Mrs Nellie Flaxington had stood before us, arms sternly folded. A multitude of holes in her thick brown stockings betrayed thick, white, varicose-veined legs planted sturdily akimbo on the top step. A menacing woman. Did I really want to spend a week under her jurisdiction?

'Good day to you, madam,' greeted Uncle Stan, doffing his flat cap with a sweeping bow. 'Do you have any special terms for theatricals?'

'Aye – bugger off!' said Mrs Flaxington, slamming the door. She opened it again a second later and rushed out to give Uncle Stan a huge bear hug. 'Come in, yer daft old sod, an' bring the rest of 'em in with yer!'

It was to this Mrs Flaxington's house that Mary and I returned later that day. I explained Mary's predicament to her and asked if we could use her phone to ring up a few agents. True to our word we said nothing about Tommy Tempest's attack on Mary.

'Hello, is that Al Beanland? Hello Al, it's Billy Foxcroft here . . . fine thanks . . . No, I haven't heard from them since Bridlington. I was wondering, have you got anything for a dancer? She's just been laid off halfway through a tour and she's at a bit of a loose end . . . She's brilliant . . . you've got my word for it . . . Mary Guinness . . . That's right. Her dad's Alec Bowness, the juggler.'

There was a silence at the other end, which I took to be Al racking his brains on our behalf.

'Billy,' he said in a confidential tone, 'this didn't come from me. I'm only telling you because you're a mate, at least, your uncle is, but Mickey Boothroyd's been ringing round putting the block on her.'

'How do you mean, the block?'

'It's just a way we have of stopping acts taking one agent for a ride then switching to another. He's put a block on her dad as well!'

Al was the first person I told about Tommy Tempest. But he wasn't the last.

'There's not much I can do, Billy,' he said sympathetically. 'If I were you, I'd tell her to go to the police.'

Even as I put the phone down I knew exactly what I *was* going to do. Mary was already booked into Mrs Flaxington's for the week and, as Mickey had grudgingly paid her up to the end of the week, she could afford the rent. If not, any one of the rest of us would have paid. Uncle Stan arrived back with Alec later in the afternoon. Alec, like his daughter, had philosophically accepted Mickey's decision, he'd even thanked Mickey for his generosity in paying his daughter up to the end of the week.

'Did you know that Mickey's put the block on Mary?' I asked Uncle Stan.

'Don't be daft, our Billy, why would he do a thing like that?'

'I've no idea, unless Tommy Tempest put him up to it, he's put a block on Alec as well! If you don't believe me, ask Al Beanland!'

Uncle Stan knew then that I was telling the truth.

'Why would he want to put a block on me?' asked Alec, who could see unemployment staring him in the face.

'It was you that gave Tommy Tempest that pasting!' explained Uncle Stan.

'What about your Billy? He broke his nose.'

'Well, we're not as easy a target as you, he knows we could kick up a fuss.'

I could see Uncle Stan was slowly coming round to my way of thinking. 'We've got two choices,' I suggested. 'We can either go to the police or we can go to the papers.'

'Police,' decided Mary and Alec.

'Papers,' decided the Fabulous Fox Twins.

'Papers,' agreed Mary and Alec.

191

So it was decided upon. It turned out to be a fateful decision. There was money at the back of Uncle Stan's mind when I suggested the papers. The Fabulous Fox Twins had already sold a lot of newspapers in this country and it was about time someone paid us for it. Split four ways, we'd still pick up a tidy sum. Uncle Stan was unanimously elected as financial negotiator. By the time we left for the theatre he'd done a deal with the *News of the World*.

'They said they wouldn't sensationalize it,' he explained.

'Who offered the most money?' I enquired.

'Funny you should ask that.'

'How much?'

'Two grand. Two thousand pounds. Five hundred quid each apiece all round.'

'They can sensationalize it all they like,' I said.

'That's what I thought.'

The three of us who were still gainfully employed left for the theatre. Uncle Stan pointed out that, as the papers wouldn't be published until Sunday, there was no point missing a week's work. When I walked in and saw Tommy Tempest, my stomach turned. Mickey Boothroyd had gone back to Hull, best place for him. Our act went down OK. It had to, we only knew one way to work. As soon as we walked on stage, we entered our own little world, nothing else existed but us and our audience. They were the other half of our act. Within a couple of days Tommy was back to his odious old self. None of the acts spoke to him. The band didn't seem surprised at this, they only had him for a week and that was a week too long. He kept making snide remarks to Alec, asking him what he'd do when he was out of a job next week. A few similar remarks were aimed at us, making me wonder just what Mickey was planning. It stood to reason he'd take Tommy's side in all this. Tommy was his creation. Mickey was Tommy's Svengali. He'd taken a singing rectum and made him a star. Quite an achievement, when you come to think of it

The reporter and photographer had been and gone. Arrived Tuesday, left Wednesday, the money duly paid and split four ways. We awaited Sunday's *News of the World* with a certain apprehension.

Hilda Bradley was possibly Tommy Tempest's greatest fan. He'd been with her in prison, grinning down at her from the walls of her grim Holloway cell. He was now in her grim Unsworth bedroom. Every night she fantasized about him being with her in her grim Unsworth bed. It was Tommy Tempest who, unknowingly, persuaded her to give up her grudge against Billy Foxcroft. She'd watched him adoringly every night, during the week he was in Leeds. Her initial fury at seeing the Fabulous Fox Twins instead of Charlie Sweeney soon mellowed when she realized that Tommy must like them, or they wouldn't be in his show. Hard as it was to understand, she had to go along with Tommy's judgement and she'd given strict instructions to the remaining Bradley brothers to break off hostilities against Billy Foxcroft. If I'd only known.

When the *News of the World* broke the story, our part in the revelation was made clear. There were pictures of me, Uncle Stan, Mary, Alec and of course Tommy Tempest. The front page headline read.

TOMMY TEMPEST TRIED TO RAPE ME
Had it not been for the intervention of the Fabulous Fox Twins, I would have been raped.

Tearful Mary Guinness, dancer with the Tommy Tempest Show, told a *News of the World* reporter that singer Tommy Tempest subjected her to a drunken backstage sexual assault. He was hauled off her by Stan and Billy Fox, the Fabulous Fox Twins, resulting in Tempest having to finish the show with a broken nose. Billy Fox went on stage with a broken hand and Stan with a black eye.

No mention was made of Alec's part in this. It was lurid stuff. They'd uncovered all sorts of skeletons in Tommy's cupboard. Other dancers from other shows who'd suffered at his hands had been unearthed and told similar stories, some of them suffering far worse than Mary. It was reasonable to assume that Tommy Tempest's career was finished. It was also reasonable to assume that Mickey Boothroyd would not be feeling well disposed towards us. What we didn't know was that Hilda Bradley's feelings towards us had changed again.

It was a short television interview that sealed our fate. A camera team had tracked Tommy down to his hotel and encamped outside to await his appearance. It didn't take long. The television camera attracted Tommy like a magnet.

'Do you have anything to say about the report in the *News of the World*, Tommy?'

'It's a load o' f***ing crap,' explained Tommy.

'Is the girl telling lies?'

'It's them f***ing Fox Twins, they're behind it all. They're f***ing jealous that I'm a f***ing star an' they're not.'

Despite the ill-disguised bleeped-out taboo words, this was all Hilda Bradley needed to recommence hostilities.

Oddly enough, Mickey didn't drop us like the hot potatoes I thought we were. He rang Uncle Stan up at Mrs Flaxington's late that Sunday morning. We were all sitting round waiting for the dreaded call. It arrived just as our hostess was about to serve Sunday lunch.

'It's that bugger Boothroyd for you, Stan!' she called from the hallway, loud enough for that bugger Boothroyd to hear.

Uncle Stan picked up the receiver, prepared for the worst and ready to give as good as he got.

'Why didn't you tell me what was going on?' asked an oddly subdued Mickey.

'You brought it on yourself when you put the block on Mary and Alec, there was no need for that, Mickey, no need at all!'

'Tommy's finished!'

'Tommy's a pillock!'

'You know there's no show without him!'

'I know there's no *Tommy Tempest* Show.'

'That's what I said.'

194

'Bring someone else in!'

'How can I get a big name in time for tomorrow? No, I'll just have to ring Newcastle up and cancel. It'll cost me a bloody fortune.'

'Ask 'em if they fancy havin' the Fabulous Fox Twins Show instead.'

'You've got cheek, Stan, I'll say that for you! I'll ring you back!'

We all heard him, and just like Mickey, we all thought he'd got cheek, apart from Freddie Ferentino, who put us all straight on a few facts.

'I think they'll go for it. You two have had more to do with filling those theatres than Tempest had. Mickey knew that, I'd heard him say as much to Tommy once when Tommy wanted him to sack you. That's the only reason you got away with taking the piss out of him so much. He's not the big star he used to be. You've been in the papers more than he has this past year.'

This was the longest speech I'd ever heard from Freddie, who, like most magicians I'd met, was something of an introvert. Uncle Stan looked at me and winked cheerfully.

We'd all settled back after lunch in Mrs Flaxington's comfortable sitting room, when the phone rang.

'Tell Stan it's that bugger Boothroyd!' said the caller.

'It's that bugger Boothroyd!' shouted Nellie.

Uncle Stan took his time strolling to the phone. He picked up the receiver, took a deep drag on a Player, and said casually, 'Yes?'

'They're going for it,' said Mickey. 'I had to do a bit of fast talking but they're going for it. Naturally, I've offered to do it for a bit less money.'

Uncle Stan jumped in very quickly. 'I hope you haven't overdone that part of it, Mickey. I mean, we'll be wanting more money if we're topping the bill.'

I cringed when I heard him say that and expected the phone to be blasted out of his hand.

'Don't be greedy, Stan,' said Mickey. 'I'll have to fork out on another male vocalist to balance the show out.'

'We'll settle for one fifty, that's less than half of what Tommy was getting.'

'One twenty five, and you're putting me out of pocket.'

'What about Mary and Alec, are they still in?'

'Is there anything else you want, you blackmailing old sod? Yes, 'course they're still in.'

'You're both back in the show,' Uncle Stan told Mary and Alec.

'Thanks, Mickey!' Alec shouted down the phone.

'Don't thank him, thank me!' said Uncle Stan, loud enough for Mickey to hear.

In the space of less than a year, we'd risen from a newly formed club act to top of the bill. I suppose in a roundabout way the Bradleys had had a hand in our success, helping us with our publicity. At least that's what Uncle Stan said. He'd have changed his tune if he'd known what they were plotting.

Tommy Tempest's fall from grace had affected Hilda far more than the deaths of her three sons. To avenge their deaths was simply a matter of family honour and only to be carried out if convenient. Taking revenge for Tommy Tempest was an affair of the heart. Hilda put her three surviving sons on the train to Newcastle the minute she heard we were taking over the show from her beloved Tommy.

We opened at the Newcastle Empire the following night as top of the bill. Mickey brought in a young singer called Danny Dream. He had looks, charm, a sense of humour and youth, but he couldn't sing like Tommy Tempest. Just as well or we wouldn't have stayed top of the bill for long. As things turned out, we didn't.

Twenty-Two

'Yankee Whisky Downwind. Over . . .'

Malcolm Pritchard pressed the button on the radio, waiting for the tower to acknowledge his call.

'Yankee Whis— continue do— ind until advised. Over.'

Malcolm looked down to his left and saw an incoming aircraft, which took priority over a learner pilot doing circuits. He'd saved up for these lessons for two years. His job as a draughtsman at Conley's Sheet Metal Works left him little spare cash, but every penny went on his flying lessons. One day he hoped to become a commercial pilot. His Private Pilot's Licence would be the passport he needed to get him away from his humdrum existence.

'Yan— sky, clear for crosswi— Over,' crackled over his radio.

Malcolm was at last getting used to the bad reception over the radio and was able to fill in the gaps. He banked the Cessna over to the left until he was straight and level. He could see the small commercial aircraft in front of him, just about to touch down.

'Yankee Whisky. Downwind. Over.'

'Yankee Whis— Clear for finals . . . over,' crackled back.

This was the fourth circuit he'd done that afternoon. One more and his hour was up. He dropped to 500 feet and lined his aircraft up with the runway. Had he not needed to concentrate so much on trying to land without bouncing down the runway like a Barnes Wallace bomb, he might have noticed the five figures running across the field beneath him.

'Yankee Whisky on finals. Over,' he called.

197

'— clear to lan— Ov—' was the only bit of the tower's message he actually made out, but it was enough. He angled the plane into the wind, pulled the flaps up another notch and floated down on to the runway with scarcely a bump. He was euphoric. Alec Bradford, his instructor, would be watching and cringing lest his aircraft suffered untold damage. Instructors always worried more about the aircraft than about the pupil. Pupils were easy to replace. As his aircraft slowed down, Malcolm stabbed his foot on the left brake pedal and slewed into a taxiway which would lead him back to his take-off position. Fifty yards short of the runway he stopped, turned off the engine and jumped out to do his pre-flight checks, prior to another circuit. A discipline instilled into all pupil pilots to a point where it becomes second nature. As usual, he'd forgotten to release the flaps – they were still down at forty degrees. He waved across to Alec Bradford, who'd come to the door of the Tyneside Flying Club to give Malcolm the thumbs up for his first ever bump-free landing. He called something out but, being a hundred yards or so away, Malcolm couldn't hear him properly. He gave a wave back.

From round the back of the Cessna appeared an out of breath but desperate-looking oldish man, who barged into him, pushing him to the ground.

'Quick Billy! Get in,' the man gasped.

A tall gangly youth appeared, equally out of breath, and climbed quickly into the cockpit. As he did so, Malcolm got to his feet and made a dive for the old man, who was about to follow his young companion into the plane.

His adversary proved amazingly strong and agile for some-one of advancing years.

'Sorry, lad!' he apologized, and with his last ounce of strength he hit Malcolm squarely on the jaw with the punch of a much younger man, planting him back on the tarmac.

Malcolm came round in time to see the Cessna taxiing down the runway. Standing over him were three of the most frightening-looking individuals he'd ever seen in his life. Alec and a few of the club members had arrived.

'Who the hell was that?' exclaimed Alec, his ex-RAF moustache quivering with indignation.

One of the rough-looking newcomers grabbed him unnecessarily by his shirt collar.

'I'll tell yer who that were!' he snarled. 'That were the Fabulous Bastard Fox Twins, only they'll be the Fabulous *Dead* Bastard Fox Twins when we get hold of 'em!'

Alec shook himself contemptuously free of Jim Bradley's grip and stared with great concern at the departing aircraft, still on the runway despite having reached its take-off speed of seventy miles an hour.

'Christ! The flaps are still down. He's trying to take off with the flaps down! He'll never make it! Come on, you stupid sod, get the flaps up! Bloody Hell! He's going to hit the fence!

Our first night in Newcastle was our best ever. With no Tommy Tempest to get up our noses, we had a happy company. Vera Delmare was signed on for the rest of the tour and closed the first half with her spine-tingling Billie Holiday-style blues. Alec Bowness did two short spots in each half. He'd been a street entertainer for many years and, adapting his old patter, he had the audience eating out of his hand. Danny Dream came on after the dancers in each half, and in each half he had the teenage girls screaming. How I wished that *I* could sing. Freddie moved up to next to top of the bill and we closed the show with a single thirty-minute spot we could do standing on our heads. I had found my one true love in Mary Guinness and things couldn't get better.

We chose not to act the big-time stars as far as digs were concerned, we mucked in with everybody else. This was partly due to Uncle Stan's inherent frugality and my wanting to be near Mary. Our only luxury was a car that Uncle Stan had bought very cheaply in Manchester. A 1951 Ford Popular, it rekindled fond memories of my nights of fumbling passion in Helen's garage. It all seemed such a long time ago, in the days when I was a callow youth of sixteen. It was odd that, despite Pauline and Mary, I still couldn't get Helen out of my mind.

On the Tuesday, Uncle Stan and I called in to the Fell-monger's Arms for a quiet lunchtime drink with Alec and Freddie, while the singers and dancers went on to the theatre for a two o'clock band call.

It was Gary Bradley's Teddy boy outfit I recognized – without it I wouldn't have known him from Adam. I'd have recognized his two brothers, though, from the inquests. Jim Bradley was the biggest Bradley of all and the ingeniously named Bradley Bradley was probably the ugliest man I've ever seen in my life. Whereas Toke Barraclough's nose was long, Bradley Bradley's nose was wide. It inhabited most of his face, which was as well because the rest of him was a misshapen mess. A result of the many personal attacks he'd encountered throughout his life from his enemies, his friends and his family. Bradley Bradley was an annoyingly aggressive man with total lack of coordination twixt brain and limb. This resulted in him being almost completely defenceless against anyone who chose to put up a serious fight against him. Cosmetically, he made Skinner look like Clark Gable. Jim Bradley on the other hand was a dangerous thug, who, apart from his mother, was the only genuine psychopath left in the family.

'We've got yer now, yer murderin' bastard!' rang out across the smoky taproom of the Fellmonger's, alerting the lunchtime drinkers to the imminent spectacle of one of the Fabulous Fox Twins being brutally chastised by experts.

Drinks were herded out of harm's way as the customers stepped back, not wishing to cause impediment to such large, determined individuals. As the Fabulous Fox Twins made their ignominious exit through the back door, Freddie Ferentino, with admirable presence of mind, slowed the Bradleys down by waving a fiver tantalizingly under Jim's nose. As Jim made a grab for it, Freddie screwed it up in his hand and tossed it over his shoulder. Jim, figuring he had ample time to retrieve the fiver *and* the Fox Twins, pushed Freddie roughly out of the way and dived under the table to where he could see the note, still crumpled up.

'That's to be shared between the three of us,' grunted Bradley Bradley.

'Aye, two quid each,' agreed Gary.

'Bastard!' howled a furious Jim. 'It's a piece o' bog paper!'

He looked round, intending chastising Freddie for such mean deceit, but Freddie and Alec were long gone, as were the Fox Twins.

Uncle Stan's car was parked at the front. We hurtled up the alley at the side of the pub and were just getting into the car when Jim burst out through the front door. Fortunately the engine was still warm and the Popular started first time. This was unusual for a car that more often than not ran on only three of its four cylinders. Uncle Stan didn't understand the need for car maintenance. Jim had his hand on the door handle, and us dragging him twenty yards down the road did little to improve his temper.

'Bastards!' he yelled.

The Bradleys were not an eloquent family. Without the word *bastard*, their conversational English would have been severely limited, especially as the only other adjectives they knew were strictly forbidden. Fortunately they had other talents. Not the least of which was breaking into and starting motor vehicles. A corporation dustbin wagon, parked behind where we had parked, was scarcely a challenge, as the keys had been left in the ignition. The driver and his gang were illicitly wetting their dusty throats in the Fellmonger's, not dreaming for a second that anyone would want to steal a wagonload of crap. It became apparent that the Bradleys had taken up the pursuit when the dustbin wagon rammed our Ford Popular from behind, jerking my head back almost on to the back seat. Uncle Stan, having at first nearly driven off the road, regained control with some composure. He put his foot hard down and slammed the car through the usable gears up into top. As there were only three forward gears, this didn't take long. We tore through the Newcastle suburbs, touching forty-five miles an hour at times, with the bin wagon nudging us along from behind. Things were looking bad. As we left the suburbs and found ourselves on clear country roads, we discovered, to our relief, that a three-cylinder Ford Pop is marginally faster than a fully loaded bin wagon, which we were gradually leaving behind. My thoughts went back to my time in the boat off Flamborough Head and how I was outpacing *Our Elsie* when my boat ran out of fuel. Needless to say, the car ran out of fuel.

'Dammit!' cursed Uncle Stan. 'We're out of petrol!'

'Let's get out of the car!' I suggested.

Uncle Stan was out before I'd finished. So was I. We left the car where it had stopped, doors wide open and key still in the ignition. There was a fence beside the road. We were over it in a flash, looking round as the bin wagon screeched to a crashing halt when it hit the stationary car.

'Head for them buildings,' yelled my uncle, pointing towards a group of low buildings about half a mile away.

The sun glinted off a much higher glass-windowed building that towered above the others. I saw a small plane taking off.

'It's some sort of an airport!' I yelled.

We ran without any sort of plan in mind. The Bradleys were two hundred yards behind and easily keeping pace with us. I couldn't think of an immediate plan. But Uncle Stan could. He was watching the small plane as he ran. It circled the airport and looked to be coming back in to land.

'Circuits and bumps!' wheezed Uncle Stan, pointing up at the plane. 'He's doing circuits. Practising his landings!'

I wasn't really interested. 'What's that got to do with . . . ?'

'Just keep yer eye on that plane,' he panted. 'Head for where it lands!'

I couldn't think of anything better myself, so I did as I was told. I looked round. The Bradleys had cut into our lead and Uncle Stan was slowing down. The airport had a perimeter fence with more holes in it than Nellie Flaxington's stockings. We dived through one of these and headed to where the plane was taxing to a halt. The pilot got out and was walking round it, kicking the tyres, running his hands along the fuselage and waggling the tailplane.

As we approached, he waved to someone in the low building

opposite, then he disappeared round the other side of his aircraft and we followed him. Uncle Stan led the way, I had absolutely no idea what he had in mind. With the Bradleys hot on our heels I had enough to think about. I arrived round the other side of the plane just in time to see my uncle push the pilot to the ground.

'Get in, Billy!' he shouted.

I got in without thinking. Through the open door I saw the pilot make a lunge at Uncle Stan, who walloped him on the jaw. 'Good God!' I thought. 'We'll get locked up for this!'

Uncle Stan jumped in beside me, turned the key, which the pilot had left in the ignition. The propeller spun a couple of times then whirred into action. My uncle pulled a brass lever that was apparently the throttle and the plane moved off. I was gobsmacked.

'What the hell are you doing?'

He was too out of breath to reply. Instead, he indicated that I should fasten my safety belt. As he taxied out on to the runway his breathing slowed down enough for him to talk.

'It'll be all right, Billy,' he wheezed.

He then picked up the hand-held radio. 'This is, er . . .' he looked around the tiny cockpit to see what we were called. 'This is Stan Foxcroft in a borrowed aeroplane. Taking off . . . er, over.'

'Request denied!' crackled the voice from the tower.

'Sorry, pal!' said Uncle Stan. 'We're takin' off anyway.'

Pulling out the throttle as far as it would go, we picked up speed. I looked at the air-speed indicator – forty, fifty, sixty, seventy miles an hour. Stan pulled the control column back. A worried look came over him.

'Is there a problem?' I asked.

'There's a bloody big problem! We should have taken off by now!'

An inaudible voice crackled over the radio. Stan picked it up and shouted an exasperated *Not now*! into the mouthpiece.

There was a twelve-foot high fence at the end of the runway and we were heading for it at seventy-five miles an hour.

'Yan— Whisky!' the voice came over slightly clearer. 'Yo— laps are still down! Over.'

'Bloody *hell*!' shouted Uncle Stan.

He reached down by his side, grabbed a lever that looked like a handbrake and released it. As he did so my stomach lurched up through my mouth as the aircraft lurched into the air like a paper kite on a sudden gust of wind; even so, we only managed to clear the fence by inches. I looked through my side window and saw the ground dropping away below us.

'Silly sod!' complained Uncle Stan. 'The first thing you do when you've landed is bring your flaps back up again. How did he expect me to take off with the flaps down?'

'Yankee Whis— ankee Whisky . . .' the crackling voice was getting very persistent. 'You are m—ing an illegal flight . . . Please bring the aircra— in on yo— next circuit! Over.'

'Sorry,' apologized Uncle Stan, 'but this is a life and death emergency. There are three madmen down there who wish to kill us, so we won't be landing there. Over!'

'Are y— qualified pilot?' asked the tower. I was interested to hear the answer to this myself.

'Not really!' answered my pilot, blithely.

The reaction from the tower was lost in a deafening crackle of interference. Uncle Stan picked up the handset.

'I don't know if you can hear me but we can't hear you. We are not stealing this aircraft, we are just borrowing it. I'll leave it somewhere safe for you.' He shrugged and looked at me. 'We're on our own, Billy.'

'Can you land it?' To me this was the all-important question.

'Well, I've never actually landed one myself before, but I know all the theory. I spent some time a few years ago helping a pal of mine in America with his crop dusting. Mind you, all I had to do then was pull a lever – but he *did* teach me how to take off – and I've watched him land often enough. Blimey, how hard can it be?'

He took Yankee Whisky up to two thousand feet. We could

see the Northumberland coastline down on our left as we flew south.

'There's one good thing about it,' said Uncle Stan, looking at the instruments. 'We won't run out of fuel.'

'Well, that's a blessing,' I said.

Optimism is a wonderful quality and we Foxcrofts have it in abundance. There are those, however, who might mistake it for stupidity. It was a beautiful afternoon and under other circumstances I might have enjoyed this, my maiden flight, even more.

'Uncle Stan,' I said to my whistling relative, 'one or two problems spring to mind.'

'Oh yes, our Billy, what are they?' He sounded like an agony aunt about to answer all my embarrassing questions about puberty.

'Well, apart from a worry I have about landing, I was wondering what the attitude of the police might be to aeroplane thieves.'

'We haven't stolen it, our Billy. I've already told 'em that. We've just borrowed it.'

'They might do you for assault!'

'Nay! Billy – I'm an old man. How can they accuse an old man like me of assaulting a young feller like that? I only tapped him. Good God! You're such a worrier! Look, enjoy yerself. We'll muck about for a bit then I'll find a nice field to land in and we'll ring for a taxi.'

'Can I have a go at flying it then?' I asked.

'It's all yours, Billy. Just watch that line on that dial, that's called an artificial horizon. Keep that level with the line in the middle an' that keeps us flyin' straight an' level.'

We flew around for half an hour. Studiously ignoring urgent demands over the radio for us to give ourselves up. It seemed that everyone knew exactly where we were except us. I was enjoying myself. It was the spur that would make me take up flying later in life. The weather was perfect, a brilliant blue sky broken only by the odd bit of cotton-wool cumulus. I took it out over the sea, dropping down to a couple of hundred feet to wave to a trawler crew cheerfully chugging out to the fishing grounds. Then we climbed to five thousand feet, above what clouds there were. The sky above was as blue as an Unsworth Corporation bus.

'To hell with show business!' I thought. 'This is the life for me!'

'OK Biggles!' chuckled Uncle Stan. 'I'm taking over. I think it's about time we landed before they send someone to shoot us down.'

'Roger!' I replied.

'Don't you roger me!'

'I wouldn't dream of it, besides, it's illegal. You're my uncle!'

We dropped down to fifteen hundred feet again and looked around for a decent place to land. Uncle Stan pointed down at a stream of white smoke drifting across a field.

'That'll be a farmer, burning off his stubble. It tells us the wind direction. Sort o' south-westerly.'

'Why don't we land in *that* field?' I asked logically.

'Fields that's been ploughed are no good,' explained Uncle Stan. 'The wheels'll get caught in a furrow. We'll flip over as soon as we land.'

This seemed a good enough reason to me.

'What about down there?' I suggested, pointing to a group of playing fields down on our right.

'That's the place,' nodded my uncle. 'You can't get much flatter than that.'

He lit up a cigarette and positioned Yankee Whisky for a landing into the south-westerly wind he'd so scientifically worked out.

We'd chosen to land on the playing fields of St John Boscoe's Catholic Boarding School for Boys, an exclusive school run by Jesuits. The annual inter-house cricket match was in progress between Fisher and More. The square-leg umpire had just taken off his dog collar in the afternoon heat. He squinted up at the circling aeroplane.

'He's a bit low, Father!' called his colleague, umpiring behind the wicket at the school end.

'I think he might be in trouble, Father!' replied square-leg umpire. 'He's looking for somewhere to land.'

'Well, he can't land here!'

'I don't see how we can stop him. OK boys!' he shouted. 'Clear the field! Back to the pavilion!'

The white-clad cricketers trotted, unconcerned, back to the pavilion; as if having an aeroplane land on their pitch was an everyday occurrence. The stiff upper lip had been ruthlessly implanted into these boys at an early age. The green and white colonial-style wooden building emptied as the occupants, with languid curiosity, came out to see what was going on.

The small, single-engined plane came buzzing in to land. It swooped down on to the second eleven pitch like a hungry kestrel on a fieldmouse, bounced a lively fifty feet into the air, landed at deep midwicket on the first-eleven pitch, then with a roar took off again for another circuit.

'I think I've got the hang of it now!' my uncle assured me, flicking his half-smoked fag out of the window. 'I came in a bit too fast. I must cut the engine just as I'm about to touch down. I remember now. It's all coming back.'

So was my lunch. We came in for a second attempt. I knew that once Uncle Stan cut the engines there'd be no coming back for another try. He put me in charge of the flaps and unconsciously lit another Player. Perhaps he thought that giving me something to do would take my mind off the prospect of dying. He was wrong. There was a dial above my head to show me what angle I'd put the flaps at.

'OK . . . ten degrees,' he said calmly. 'Twenty, thirty, right . . . full flaps! Here we go, Billy lad! Put yer 'ead between yer legs an' kiss yer bum goodbye!'

I chose not to take advantage of this safety tip. I preferred my own method of just closing my eyes, as I had done on Harry the carthorse all those years ago. I heard Uncle Stan cut the engines and braced myself, fearing the worst. The inevitable bump came, but it wasn't as bad as last time. I opened an optimistic but cautious eye. We were on the ground. No we weren't, we were in the air . . . no, we were back on the ground again. No! Wrong again! This up-and-down kind of existence continued all the way to the pavilion, where Uncle Stan managed to slew the aircraft to a halt at the last minute to avoid demolishing the place. The cricketers burst into spontaneous applause, as true sportsmen do when witnessing an event of great skill and/or daring. They noisily surrounded the plane, yanking open the doors. Uncle Stan and I climbed out of our respective sides to be congratulated by back-slapping boys, some a year or two older than me. The square-leg umpire stood back and shook his head in disbelief.

'William Foxcroft, as I live and breathe!'

'Good afternoon, Father!' I called out. 'I was just passing and wondered if there was any chance of a game?'

'Any more cheek from you, young Foxcroft, and I might have to think about ordering a few tollies,' grinned Father McShane. 'By the way, do you mind moving your aeroplane off our square-leg boundary?'

'I wouldn't have a clue how to start, Father,' I admitted.

'Neither would your friend, judging from his landing!'

'He's no friend of mine, Father, he's my uncle Stan. Uncle Stan, meet Father McShane. The only human being ever to teach at St Ignatius's.'

Uncle Stan touched a forelock in a genuine mark of respect for the priest. 'I'm very pleased to meet you, Father.' I thought he was genuflecting until I realized he was grinding out his fag beneath his heel. 'Take no notice of our Billy, Father, he's just had a bit of a shock.'

'We've all had a bit of a shock. I'm just pleased to see our pavilion's still in one piece. I take it that flying isn't your profession?'

'Er . . . no, Father. Actually I'm . . . well we, me and our Billy, that is, we're . . .'

'Comedians, I know. I haven't seen you myself, but I understand you're quite good.' He looked at me. 'It's nice to know that your five years at St Ignatius's wasn't entirely wasted.' He glanced at my hand, which was still bandaged after the Tommy Tempest affair. 'I assume that's a new injury, not a reoccurrence of the old one.'

'It's a bit of both, I suppose, Father. Same fingers, different target.'

'Ah! Would that target have been the nose of a certain Mr Tempest?' He *had* been following our exploits. 'You know, you really should have worked more on the left jab, it was always a weakness of yours.'

'I'll bear that in mind, Father.'

'Look, I'll just move the aeroplane out of your way and we'll be off,' put in Uncle Stan.

'Surely you'll stay for tea? I'd love to hear the story of how you got here in that thing. I can add it to all the other stories I've been reading about you. You're a pair of celebrities, in more ways than one!'

We stayed to watch Fisher bowl out More for a hundred and fifteen, then sat on the grass to eat our crab sandwiches and scones, surrounded by what appeared to be a fan club of well-spoken, well brought-up teenage boys. Under other circumstances, I could well have been one of them, had the Foxcroft family been a family of bankers instead of the rhyming alternative.

It appeared that Father McShane had openly boasted, if that's the right word, of his association with me at St Ignatius's. The exploits of the Foxcroft twins had been avidly followed by the boys ever since Father McShane had told them the story of my broken fingers and how it had precipitated his transfer to St John Boscoe's. It was, by all accounts, not an unpopular transfer, as he'd brought the same touch of humanity to this school as he'd brought to St Ignatius's. The regime at his new school was equally as strict, but the Jesuits had, by and large, got the boys at the age of seven, so the end product was of a higher quality. The tolly was used much less frequently and the boys around me looked a bright and cheerful bunch. Despite our similarity in age, though, I felt years beyond them in experience. In another way there was a certain maturity about them that I would never have, nor would Uncle Stan.

The thing I envied most was their obvious camaraderie. There looked to be a brightness inside them all that was getting ready to explode upon the world. Unfortunately this would be later dulled and distorted by a few years at university.

But you can't have everything.

Today, however, I was the object of *their* envy. An excited buzz ran through them as the story of our latest flight from the Bradleys was passed around.

'I think a phone call to the police wouldn't be a bad thing,' said Father McShane, coming out of the pavilion carrying a couple of beakers of lemonade. 'It seems you're back in the news again. According to the radio, you were last seen heading out to sea – after that you disappeared from the local radar screens.'

There was a rush of boys into the pavilion to catch the tail end of the Home Service news bulletin.

'That'll be when you dropped down to wave to that trawler,' said Uncle Stan. 'We'll have gone under the radar and they can't have picked us up again.'

'If they don't know where you are, you could fly to Southern Ireland,' suggested one of the younger boys. 'I've got an aerial map in my study. There's no extradition treaty with Southern Ireland.'

'You're a dope, young Bovington,' said Fisher's fast bowler (at St Ignatius's he'd have been called much worse). 'Of course there's an extradition treaty with Eire. Father McShane's quite right, they must give themselves up.'

He looked questioningly at Uncle Stan. 'Any chance of a spin in her, sir, before you give the old crate back to its rightful owner? I know a bit about them, my father was a wing commander during the war.'

'Me an' your dad have a lot in common then,' said Uncle Stan. 'Next time you see him, tell him you've met Corporal Stanley Foxcroft. Happen he'll have heard of me!'

Now, why did this not surprise me?

It was now mid-afternoon and we needed to be at the theatre for seven. We said goodbye to Father McShane, into whose hand Uncle Stan stuck one of the many complimentary tickets he'd conned out of the box-office girl. In return, Father McShane said he'd report the location of the aeroplane to the Tyneside Flying Club and sent the wing commander's son, who was also Fisher's fast bowler, to accompany us to the school office, where we could phone for a taxi.

'Bloody Hell! It's the fugitives,' exclaimed the driver as we climbed into the back of his cab. 'There's a big reward out for you two, dead or alive – seven and fourpence ha' penny.'

'Get stuffed!' said Uncle Stan. 'Just take us to my car, it's parked somewhere near the Tyneside Flying Club. Yer'll be able to recognize it. It's the one with the corporation bin wagon rammed up its arse!'

'It's not much to go on, sir, but I'll do me best!'

Even if Uncle Stan's car had been driveable we couldn't have driven it, because, as soon as we arrived, we were accosted by a bored and lonely, sweet-sucking policeman, who promptly arrested us; then, by way of compensation, offered us each a Nuttall's Minto. He then tried to arrest our taxi driver for harbouring wanted criminals. When the driver pointed out that we were all miles from anywhere and his was the only transport, the policeman settled for a taxi ride back to the local nick, where he had a further argument about who should pay for our bit of the journey.

'Nay the heck!' moaned Uncle Stan. 'Whoever heard of folk bein' arrested, then havin' ter pay their own taxi fare to the nick?'

'But you weren't arrested for the first part of your journey. So you should pay for that bit,' argued the policeman logically.

Stan handed the taxi driver a couple of complimentary tickets. 'There,' he said, 'will that cover our bit?'

The driver gave an unhappy nod. Uncle Stan offered the policeman one, but he reluctantly declined on the grounds that it could be construed as bribery. 'Besides,' he reasoned, 'how can you do a show when you're locked up?'

As we walked in, we passed Malcolm Pritchard coming out.

He flinched as he saw my uncle, who, to be fair, was a much smaller man. Uncle Stan's hand shot out as his face beamed an apology. Malcolm Pritchard's face was swathed in bandages, supporting his dislocated jaw. He unenthusiastically shook the proffered hand.

'Sorry about that, lad! Does it hurt much? No, I can't have hit yer all that hard, can I? Me bein' an old feller. Here's a couple a tickets for tonight's show. No, take four, bring yer family. I've left yer aeroplane safe an' sound. If there's any expense, send yer bill to me!'

We left Malcolm Pritchard standing there gobsmacked in more ways than one, four tickets in his hand and a baffled expression on his face.

Our phone call to the theatre brought the manager and a solicitor hurrying to our aid. Apparently both the Flying Club and Malcolm Pritchard were pressing charges, which, if they weren't dropped, would be quite serious. A custodial sentence loomed for the second time in a year. I could hear familiar threatening voices coming from the cells, the Bradleys had picked up our scent.

'We can 'ear yer Foxcroft, yer bastard! Yer a dead man! Yer bastard!'

They'd all been arrested at the flying club by pursuing police who'd arrived only minutes after we'd made our dramatic exit. But those minutes could have been very vital to our existence. The furious fight they'd put up had landed them in the cells with no chance of being bailed. Our welfare, it seemed, was being taken into consideration. The police-van journey between the flying club and the nick had been punctuated by the most terrifying of threats on my life. The police couldn't in all conscience set them free. Besides, two out of three of them were still on parole from prison, which didn't bode well for them when they appeared in court. Hilda, however, was still at large.

Our solicitor, a sharp-suited young man, who looked more like a used-car salesman, secured our temporary release. Whether or not this had anything to do with Uncle Stan handing out the rest of his complimentaries, I couldn't say. We were released on police bail, to appear before magistrates at a time and date to be notified.

Twenty-Three

The saga of the fleeing Foxcrofts had been broadcast to the nation on both radio and television. We were becoming true celebrities, but for all the wrong reasons. A clutch of reporters and a BBC TV camera crew were waiting for us outside the theatre when we eventually arrived with the manager.

'You'd better speak to the pilot!' I shouted, in answer to a dozen inane questions, hurled simultaneously from all sides.

'Are you being offered police protection?' was one of the more sensible offerings.

'Police? I think we might have to call the flippin' army in!' replied Uncle Stan. 'Look, why don't you all step into my office and we'll have a right good natter about it all over a cup of tea?'

The theatre manager was overjoyed at all this free publicity, as no doubt were the managers of all the other theatres we were due to visit over the next few weeks. A couple of bottles of Scotch and a crate of Newcastle Brown were produced, seemingly out of thin air, and we all sat around on the stage, this being the only part of the theatre big enough to accommodate us. After a bit of back of the hand coaching from Uncle Stan, I opened the proceedings.

'Ladies and gentlemen,' I began. I couldn't have done this a year ago, but my year treading the boards had given me so much skill and confidence. 'I would like to introduce you to the senior half of the Fabulous Fox Twins. Adventurer, traveller, Yorkshire farting champion 1922. Miner, gardener, drains cleared at reasonable rates, still having sex six times a week at sixty-three – Mister Stanley Foxcroft!'

A thrusting young lady waved her hand in the air, indicating that she was to be first to ask a question and would everyone else shut up.

'Mr Foxcroft' – she addressed her question to my uncle – 'Is it true?'

'Is what true, love?'

'Is it true that you're still having sex six times a week at sixty-three?'

Her colleagues went quiet, leaning forward on their seats.

'True as I'm talking to you, Miss,' said Uncle Stan. 'Mind you, my wife's not best pleased about it.'

'Why's that, Mr Foxcroft?'

'We live at sixty-two!'

The thrusting young lady sat back red-faced and deflated. All the other reporters were immediately on their guard. The TV reporter made a note to cut the bit about the farting champion and to check on the sex at sixty-three bit. Half an hour, two bottles of Scotch and two dozen bottles of Newcastle Brown later, they all went away in a happy haze to file their various reports. The band had arrived and were grumbling about there being no drinks left for them. Uncle Stan, totally out of character, magnanimously promised to stump up for an after-show party that night.

'Send out for whatever you think we'll need, lads, and the management will pay.'

That last bit was more like my dear old uncle.

The theatre that night was packed. Ethel Nesbitt turned up, so did Desmond, so did Father McShane and every other beneficiary of Uncle Stan's largesse. During the interval a Granada TV man called Reg Davison dropped into the dressing room to ask if we could do a spot on a TV show next Sunday called Holiday Town Spectacular, over in Morecambe. As Sunday was our day off, we said there'd be no problem.

'We're on our way, lad,' chortled Uncle Stan. 'Once you've been on telly, your money goes sky high!'

215

I have to say, he was a mercenary old sod.

As soon as the curtains swished open on the dapper man-about-town and the tall skinny tramp, the audience were on their feet, cheering us. We walked forward together to take a bow as our amazing reception died slowly away. I stole a quick glance at my uncle. The sentimental old sod had a tear in his eye. It wasn't there for long. Uncle Stan doffed his top hat to a well-proportioned lady of advancing years sitting in a stageside box.

'I took my mother-in-law to the doctor's last week,' he said. 'She's got women's problems . . . She doesn't look like one.'

The lady in the box laughed, with body-bouncing abandon.

'Good evening, madam,' said Uncle Stan, doffing his topper once again, this time with a great sweeping bow. 'I see you're on the peanut and melon diet. I don't think the peanuts are working but the melons . . .'

Laughter drowned the remainder of his line. The woman herself laughing the loudest.

'Did you know that when you laugh your bosoms bounce up and down like jelly trifles?' I was relieved he said *bosoms*.

The woman tearfully shook her head, the spotlight cruelly swung on to her and her male companion.

'Good evening, sir. Is the good lady your wife?'

The man gave a nervous nod.

'Do you mind if I ask how long you've been married?'

'Twenty-five years today!' came the nervous answer.

Of course, we already knew this. The audience gave them a spontaneous round of applause. Uncle Stan looked at me.

'Now there's a coincidence!'

'What sort of coincidence?' I enquired.

'It's twenty-five years tonight since I proposed to my Mildred. Twenty-five years since I said them four magic little words . . . *You're not, are you?*'

I knew Father McShane was there, but I couldn't see him for the spotlight. God knows what he was making of our routine, which Uncle Stan called 'Cheerful Vulgarity'. We went off to thunderous applause and, for the first time ever, Uncle Stan responded to the shouts of *More*! by going back on his own to recite the monologue of the Elephant's Trunk. I went back on stage to take a final bow with him. Up to now this had been the best night of my life. I was still taking off my make-up when a tap came on the dressing-room door.

'Come in, it's a shop!' Uncle Stan yelled out his usual greeting. 'Oh! Sorry Father, I thought it were someone else!'

Father McShane's smiling face appeared in the doorway. He was wearing a tailored tweed sports jacket that had been tailored for someone a couple of sizes bigger than him and shiny corduroy trousers. His dog collar was still in place, though, above a black shirt.

'I just popped in to congratulate you, I haven't laughed as much in years!'

'Oh! We're glad you enjoyed it, Father,' I said cautiously. 'Uncle Stan's to blame for anything you think might be a bit, er, tasteless. He's our scriptwriter!'

'No, no! Well, you did skirt the boundaries of decency once or twice. But I understand comedy is a difficult art and like all artists you must use whatever material you handle best.'

I'd never heard it put like this and made up my mind to write it down as soon as he'd left, it might come in handy one day as an off-the-cuff quote.

'Just remember,' he continued, 'the talent for making people laugh is among the most precious of all God's gifts, so you must never abuse it.' He shook our hands warmly and left as Ethel and Desmond walked in.

'Toke's asked for a divorce,' she said cheerfully. 'I know it's hard to believe, but he's found another woman.'

'Does that put you back on the market then?' asked Uncle Stan.

'Hey, you! I'm not a sack o' spuds, you know, I'm a very desirable young lady.'

'Well, you're younger than me, I'll grant you that.' Uncle Stan turned to Desmond. 'Would you have any objections if I took your mother's hand in marriage?'

217

'I most certainly would!' objected Desmond. 'You take the lot or you take nothing!'

'I'm surrounded by bloody comedians. Don't I get a say in this?' demanded Ethel, her eyes sparkling with a light that probably hadn't been there for thirty years.

'No!' said Uncle Stan. 'This has got nothing to do with you. This is man's talk!'

'Sorry!' muttered an apologetic Ethel.

'I should think so!' admonished my uncle as he gathered Ethel up in his arms. 'Right! Me and the lad have settled it, we're going to get wed.'

'You can't!' said Ethel. 'Desmond's already spoken for!'

'Bugger! I'll have to settle for *you* then.'

Ethel looked at me. 'You heard all that, Billy! He wants to marry me on the rebound. What should I do?'

'Play hard to get. Teach him a lesson.'

Ethel looked hard at Uncle Stan.

'No!' she said. 'No, I won't marry you! No, no, no, no.'

'No, are you sure?'

'Oh, go on then.'

It was as romantic a betrothal as ever I've seen. Desmond and I shook Uncle Stan's hand and kissed a tearful Ethel.

'When you two get married,' inquired Desmond thoughtfully, 'does that mean I won't be a bastard any more?'

'I wouldn't go as far as that!' said his loving mother.

Eddie the saxophone player poked his bald head round the door. 'Five minutes to booze-up time!'

I'd never been drunk in my life before. Mainly because I didn't particularly like the taste of beer. I'd given up cigarettes, which I'd only ever smoked for bravado. It was still a smart thing to do in the fifties. So, all in all, at seventeen I'd acquired few of the social graces. Eddie the drummer set about my alcoholic education with some enthusiasm. He found me a willing and able student. He was a studiously unconventional, middle-aged teenager, who played drums, darts and fast-and-loose with whatever women fell for his amoral charms.

218

There were maybe two dozen of us at this impromptu party: all the acts, the theatre staff, Ethel, Desmond and of course the band. As midnight approached, the dancing started. Uncle Stan and Ethel gave their wild, flapping version of the charleston, soon to be joined by the girls, who showed us all the difference between amateurs and professionals. Not that any of us cared. I had a go on the drums, Mary tried her hand at the trombone and Uncle Stan surprised us all by his singing and banjo playing. He took centre stage, banjo in hand, a little the worse for drink, wearing a lady's music-hall hat he'd found backstage and sang 'I'm going back to Himazaz' in a roisterous, rasping, music-hall voice, which told me instantly that we should put it in the act. Nine choruses later, it appeared to be the only tune he could play, so I decided to take it out of the act. It had been in long enough.

I don't know whose idea it was to start a conga line but it was a popular one. The theatre manager led the way, on the grounds that he knew his way round the theatre better than anyone.

I was behind Alec Bowness, who was behind a dancer, who was behind Uncle Stan. Behind me was Mary, who was singing louder than anyone. She wasn't exactly legless, but like me she was very merry. We started dancing in a surprisingly well-choreographed circle round the stage, then down the steps into the auditorium, up one aisle, down the other, back up on to the stage, back down again. Then, pleased with the obvious professionalism of his troupe, the manager became more adventurous. He took us through to the box office and up the stairs to the circle. We paid a visit to the gents' toilet as requested by the ladies and to the ladies' toilet as requested by the gentlemen. Drinks were being drunk en-route and the disciplined line of dancers became distinctly rowdy and unruly. Casualties were incurred as conga dancers fell and were trampled underfoot, staggering to their feet unhurt as only drunks can and rushing to join the back of the line. The dance had become increasingly loud and frenzied as we set off down the stepped aisle running down the centre of the dress circle. The manager lurched to the right at the bottom and took his followers between the front seats and the low balcony. One by one we stumbled down the shallow steps, still kicking out wild, dangerous legs and still breathlessly chanting *Aye Yi Yi Yi Conga!* as we went. One by one the line lurched to the right at the bottom and followed our leader, who was by now on his way back up the side aisle. Uncle Stan momentarily lost touch with whoever was in front of him and quickened his drunken step to re-establish contact. As the person in front of him lurched to the right Uncle Stan carried straight on and disappeared over the balcony. The girl behind him just managed to stop herself from going over as well, as we all piled up, concertina fashion, behind her. I remember looking up, wondering why we'd stopped. The front of the line had reached the top of the side aisle and were bumping through the double doors that led to the upper circle, still singing, still kicking, still drinking.

Uncle Stan was just still.

I looked down over the balcony. It wasn't a huge drop, maybe twelve or fifteen feet. I could just see the barely scuffed soles of Uncle Stan's brand-new-on-today patent-leather shoes looking back at me. His head was buried out of sight beneath the seats. Mary and Alec ran back down the stairs to the stalls. I climbed over the balcony and dropped heavily into the aisle just beside where my uncle had fallen. The girl dancer went after the others to tell them what had happened.

'Uncle Stan, are you OK?'

I was kneeling beside him. He obviously wasn't OK. It was just over a year ago since my pal Utters had fallen to his death. Surely it hadn't happened again.

'Let's have a look at him, Billy.' It was Alec Bowness, who'd arrived out of nowhere. He seemed to have some rudimentary knowledge of first aid. 'Somebody ring for an ambulance. Tell them it's an emergency!'

'Is he all right? What happened?' asked a shocked Ethel.

Desmond, looking equally shocked, was standing with his arm around her.

'I don't know,' said Alec. 'I think we'd better get him out from under that seat and have a good look at him.'

Whether or not moving an injured man was a wise thing to do, I don't know. It certainly didn't seem very dignified to leave him hanging upside down until an ambulance arrived. Why we carried him all the way up to the stage, I can't explain. We laid him gently down on the boards. His eyes flickered. He was still alive.

'Oh, thank God!' sobbed Ethel. 'Stanley Foxcroft, you daft old sod, what have you done now?'

I knelt down at the side of him as his eyes opened. He gazed up at all the concerned faces looking back at him. Then he turned and grinned at me and said hoarsely, 'Me mother said there'd be days like this, Billy!' Then he died.

Twenty-Four

It was all so shockingly sudden. He always said he'd like to go out with a bang, preferably being shot by a jealous husband at the age of ninety-eight. But not this way. There was too much life in him, too much going for him. It all seemed like a big mistake. There was no mistake – he was gone, and with him went Ethel's dreams, Desmond's new found dad. And my best pal.

I stood up and backed away from him, not wanting to see him like this. I walked away from the scene and back to my dressing room, where I sat for a while surrounded by Uncle Stan's things. Alive and then not alive, just like Utters. It didn't seem possible that he wasn't here any more. Mary followed me, but I waved her away, almost rudely.

'I want to be left on my own,' I said.

She left, slightly chastened, saying, 'I'm here if you need me.'

An ambulance bell disturbed my thoughts and I picked up my coat and found myself out in the street, walking amongst late-night people who knew nothing of the tragedy that had just befallen me.

I strode through the city-centre streets, aimlessly heading towards the southern suburbs. Shocked at the thought of another death somehow involving me. Shocked at the thought of losing not only my uncle but my future, which was inextricably linked with him. Was I being selfish, thinking of myself at a time like this? My life had suddenly collapsed. All my eggs had been in Uncle Stan's basket. He'd been the act, not me. If I'd died instead of him, he'd have hired another stooge – ten a penny in our business. I began to realise my actual worth. Which wasn't much. Tears of sorrow and self pity misted my eyes as I trudged south, towards Helen, who would make everything right for me.

A leg stretched out from a shop doorway, sending me sprawling painfully to the pavement; banging my head just above my eye. I sat up, dizzy and perhaps a bit scared of what was to come next.

'Sorry, pal, ah didn't see yer there, man.'

The voice sounded friendly, apologetic even. A young man, no older than me, got up from the shop doorway and held out a hand to pull me up.

'Are yer all right, like?' The accent was Geordie.

'Not really.'

'Ah well, that'll be mah fault.'

I wasn't going to argue. The daft sod had tripped me up.

'Why don't yer come an' sit beside us, while yer feel better,' he invited.

I didn't feel as if I had much option. The knock had sent me groggy. We sat together for a while until he introduced himself.

'Ah' m Arthur,' he said, holding out a hand for me to shake.

'Billy.'

'Pleased ter meet yer, Billy. Ah bet yer wonderin' why ah'm sat here?'

It actually hadn't crossed my mind. I had other things to think about. 'Why *are* you sitting here?' I couldn't have cared less. I only asked out of politeness. We Foxcrofts are polite to a fault.

'Ah'm thinkin' o' robbin' that shop over there, man!'

He now had my vague attention. The shop in question was a jeweller's. Holden's Jewellers, the only illuminated window in the street. There were bars at the window to prevent such eventualities.

'How are you going to get past the bars?' I asked, curiously. Oddly, I hadn't said a word to warn him against such foolishness. It was like George and the barge. Somehow, robbing a jeweller's seemed a worthwhile undertaking for someone other than me. Either that or my mind was too full of remorse to worry about the law of the land. He turned to me and grinned.

'Ah can get us arm through far enough ter grab a tray o' rings. They usually take all the ones within reach out of the winder before they shut up shop, but they didn't ternight, like.'

'That was a bit daft of them.'

'It were us what were daft, man. Ah work there, like. It were us what didn't take all the stuff out, like. In fact, ah moved a tray o' the most expensive rings where ah could reach 'em.'

'But won't they suspect you if you work there?'

'Why should they suspect us? All they can do is give us a bollockin' fer not doin' us job properly.'

'They could give you the sack.'

'They've already done that, man. Sacked us terday. Given us a week's notice. Ah've done nowt wrong, man, but the manager wants ter bring his own lad in, which ah think is all wrong, like. Ah've worked there since ah left school, never had a day off, man. Wor mam went mad when ah told her. Wor dad's been laid off for six months an' there's little enough money comin' in without all this.'

He'd justified his proposed actions and who was I to argue? There was little enough justice in this world, Uncle Stan dying was proof of that. I was happy that my new pal Arthur was redressing the balance a little.

'How much are the rings worth?'

'There's sixteen rings on the tray wi' a retail value of just over two grand, man. If ah can sell 'em for a quarter o' that, it's us wages for over a year, like.'

'Do you know someone who'll buy them?'

'I haven't thought that far ahead.'

He wasn't a proper criminal, just an angry amateur. I should have done more to dissuade him, but I wasn't in that sort of mood.

'D' yer fancy keepin' a look out for us, like?' he asked.

'Yeah, why not?'

I'd allowed myself to become an unpaid accomplice. Why? I've no idea to this day. We got to our feet, Arthur had a brick in his hand. The road was deserted.

'What d' yer think?' he asked.

'Looks all-clear to me.'

He was across the road in a flash. The smashing of the window seemed incredibly loud, but the robbery was all over in a second. We set off running together, an alarm bell clanging behind us. He led me through a zig-zag of streets until I was completely lost. What the hell I was following him for, I've no idea. Putting my hand on his shoulder I brought him to a halt.

'Look, I'm leaving you now,' I said breathlessly. 'I hope everything's OK.'

'Thanks, man,' he grinned. Before I could protest he thrust half a dozen rings into my hand and set off running again. I watched him disappear into the night and continued on my way.

It was almost half an hour before I saw a sign pointing towards the Great North Road. As good a direction as any. My thoughts were a million miles away when a black Wolseley slid to a halt beside me. A uniformed policeman got out and stood in front of me, another sat in the driver's seat listening to a crackling police radio.

'Do you mind telling me where you're going, sir?' he enquired.

Had I not been recently involved in a jewel theft, I might have taken exception to being questioned like this for no reason. My heart started thumping.

'I'm not actually going anywhere,' I answered nervously. 'Just walking.'

Normally I might have added something sarcastic like walking not being a crime. You're cheeky like that when you're seventeen.

'Do you usually go walking at this time of night, sir?'

'My uncle died a couple of hours ago, it's thrown me a bit,' I explained.

'You seem to have had an accident, sir. How did that happen?'

'I fell.'

'Too much to drink, eh? People do daft things when they've been drinking.'

'I'm not drunk.'

'Could I have your name, sir?'

'Billy Foxcroft. My uncle's Stan Foxcroft. But he died a couple of hours ago.'

The policeman nodded. 'Sorry to hear that, sir.' He managed to say this without a trace of sorrow. 'Do you mind showing me the contents of your pockets, sir?'

My heart sank. This was one of my blacker moments. I'd already identified myself, so running away would be no use. They'd soon put two and two together. He took my hands and examined them, like my mam used to do before a meal, usually as a preface to frogmarching me and my mucky hands to the kitchen sink.

'Place your hands on the side of the car, sir.'

He leaned into the car. 'Give us a hand here, Alan.'

The driver got out and stood beside me, presumably to make sure I didn't do a runner. By this time the rings were out of my trouser pocket and in my left hand. I was wearing an overcoat, which they asked me to remove before examining it minutely. As they handed it back to me I slipped the rings into the side pocket. Freddie Ferentino had taught me bits of slight of hand such as this. I laid the overcoat on the bonnet of the car as they proceeded to search the rest of me.

'There seems to be a lot of money in this wallet, sir.'

'I earn a lot of money.'

'Young feller like you? I don't think so.'

'Look, don't you need a warrant or something for this?'

'Only if you've got something to hide, sir. We can always do this down at the station.'

They were becoming frustrated at not finding anything. So sure they were of having caught the culprit. The driver picked up my overcoat, perhaps to have another look through the pockets.

'You don't know who I am, do you?' I said, quickly.

'Yes sir, your name is Billy Foxcroft.'

'And doesn't the name ring a bell?'

The driver was the first to realize. Over the past few months I'd scarcely been out of the news.

'You're the one who stole the plane? You're one of the Fox Twins.'

'Borrowed it, officer. To escape *real* villains.' I accentuated the word *real* to emphasize the fact that I personally wasn't one. Their attention was now distracted from the search.

'And it was my uncle who borrowed it, not me.' I added.

'The one who's dead?'

'He died just after the show tonight. That's why I'm wandering around in a bit of a daze. We were very close.'

'Oh, I am sorry, sir,' said the first policeman, genuine sorrow in his voice now. 'You see, there's been a robbery and you fit the description of one of two men running away.'

'I'm on my own,' I pointed out. 'Could I have my coat please? I'm freezing.'

Before either of them could respond, I picked it up and slipped it on.

'Right, sir,' said the driver. 'I can see we've made a mistake. Perhaps we can give you a lift somewhere?'

'No thank you, officer, I just wanted some time on my own.'

'Sorry about that, sir. Just doing our job.'

'That's OK,' I said magnanimously.

'Goodnight, sir.'

I waited until the police car had turned a corner then doubled back into a street I'd recently walked down. A light went on in one of the bedrooms of the tiny terraced dwellings. Sounds of a baby crying from upstairs. I dropped all six rings through the letter box. Perhaps a young mother would find a use for half a dozen valuable rings. She'd know where they came from soon enough, the rest was up to her. It all depended how honest – or desperate – she was.

Trying to second guess her reaction to this occupied my thoughts for a while until I found myself on the Great North Road passing a sign saying Durham twelve miles. Helen was only twelve miles away. Helen would repair all the damage the last few hours had inflicted on me. My relief at escaping arrest was still very much tempered with sadness at the loss of Uncle Stan.

There was a damp fog in the air that suited my mood. My thoughts were disturbed by occasional rumbling wagons, about their nocturnal business. A bus slowed, wondering if I was a potential passenger, but I waved him on. Buses had destinations. I wasn't in the mood for destinations.

Seven miles outside Durham I stopped at an all-night transport café. The only place open at three in the morning. I was tired and fed up, but beginning to think clearly at last. I didn't know where Helen was staying. I had no phone number for her and no means of obtaining one. Her parents wouldn't be in a hurry to help if I rang them, certainly not at three in the morning. Besides, Helen didn't want to know me. The futility of everything hit me as I sat in front of a cooling mug of tea, tears streaming down my face.

'You all right, love?'

I'd been joined by a woman I should have recognized as a prostitute, but I don't think I'd actually seen one before. Apart from her exposed cleavage she seemed a decent sort. Well built, mid-thirties, bottle blonde and pleasant enough. I looked up and attempted a smile.

'Yeah. I'm OK, thanks. Just feeling a bit sorry for myself.'

She placed her hand on mine and looked sympathetically at my bruised forehead. 'Been in the wars by the look of it. Whatever it is, I could make you feel better if you like.'

Even then I didn't twig. 'Thanks, you're very kind,' I said.

'Come in a car, have yer?' she enquired.

I shook my head. 'No, I've just walked down from Newcastle.'

I didn't say why. It was no business of hers.

228

'Bloody hell! Yer must be worn out, pet.' Her Geordie accent had a sympathetic lilt to it.

'I am, actually.'

'Look, I only live five minutes away. Business is a bit slack ternight. Why don't yer come back wi' us?'

I didn't know what business she was talking about, nor did I give it any thought. Suddenly the thought of a warm bed and a good night's sleep seemed irresistible. I stood up and followed her like a lost sheep.

She lived in a single room, or perhaps that's just where she operated from, I never did find out. Once inside, she patted the double bed.

'Settle yerself in there, pet,' she smiled, and went over to a sink in the corner, where she proceeded to undress and wash herself.

I was on the verge of making a complete fool of myself and asking where she was going to sleep, when I realized what she was – and what I was expected to do! Well done, Foxcroft! Back in it again. I fumbled in my wallet, not knowing how much her services would cost. She looked across and smiled as she removed her bra, allowing her pendulous breasts to tumble gratefully out.

'We can sort all that out later, love. I've got different prices for different services. Us name's Pandora, by the way.'

I'd never come across a less likely looking Pandora in my life.

'Look,' I said. 'I'm willing to pay the going rate for whatever you have on offer. But all I want is a good night's sleep.'

She shrugged and took off the rest of her clothes. 'To be honest, I'm a bit knackered meself. Why don't I jump in wi' yer and we'll call it two quid. That way, if yer fancy a shag later on, it'll not cost yer extra.'

This seemed reasonable enough. I stripped down to my underpants and slid under the sheets. She climbed in beside me, stark naked and pulled me into her arms.

'Might as well cuddle up tergether pet, and keep worsens

nice an' warm – and if yer dicky starts ter misbehave itself, yer won't have far ter come.'

She exuded a blend of stale Newcastle Brown and cheap perfume, but I still had the best night's sleep I'd had in a long time. It was eleven o'clock when I woke up. For a few seconds I had no idea where I was; then I remembered Uncle Stan and the gloom descended. Pandora opened her eyes, questioningly.

'Well?' she asked.

'Well what?'

'D' yer fancy one before I put us knickers on?'

It was nice of her but I chose to decline. 'I've already had the best two quid's worth in town,' I said. 'Let's not spoil our friendship.'

She laughed uproariously. 'I can do yer a sausage sandwich if yer like?'

'I'd like that.'

'You wait there, pet. I'll bring yer breakfast in bed.'

She got up and reached into a drawer for a pinafore, which she tied around the front of her naked body, leaving her ample rear in full view. Pausing in front of the wardrobe mirror she gave herself a nod of approval.

'Us tits might have dropped a bit but us arse is still firm. D' yer not think so, pet?'

'Very nice,' I said, as complimentary as I could. Actually it was huge, but she was right about it being firm. Lighting the gas stove and a cigarette, she went to get the bread and sausages from a low cupboard, farting as she bent over.

'That'll be the Newkie Brown I had last night,' she explained, shamelessly. 'It allus makes us fart. I hope yer don't mind, like.'

My minding wasn't going to make a difference, so I said nothing. I've had my breakfast cooked by more appetizing chefs.

'There's a phone downstairs,' she said, as she watched the sausages sizzling in the pan, the sound drowning any further flatulent squeaks. 'Yer can ring for a taxi after this. I don't suppose yer fancy walking back ter Newcastle or wherever yer headed.'

Back to Newcastle sounded like a sensible idea. Being turned down by Helen, even if I found her, was a bit more than I could cope with, given the circumstances.

When I left, Pandora reckoned she had no change for my fiver, so she wrote me out a credit note for a shag and a sausage sandwich when I was next passing. I'd have preferred her not to have come to the door in her pinny, then turn round and waggle her bare backside at the taxi driver. It made the journey back to Newcastle a bit embarrassing.

'She's me auntie, she's a bit odd,' I explained. But I don't think he believed me.

Twenty-Five

The day before we buried Uncle Stan we held a wake. He'd often talked of having a proper send-off with all his friends around him so we had the undertaker lay him out in the front room of number fifty-seven Elmtree Bank in his best blue stage suit and we provided refreshments. Some brought their own. Mostyn and Marion Mallinson parked their chip van outside and offered *Free fish and chips to them as wants them*, which my dad said was very good of them. Uncle Stan had been very partial to fruitcake and, lo and behold, there seemed to be fruitcakes galore, provide by some unsung benefactor. How unusual it tasted – but how popular it was. Unknown to us, the benevolent baker had sought to alleviate our gloom by including an illegal ingredient, very popular with students and show-business people. Mary seemed to like it more than most.

Guests turned up from all four corners of Uncle Stan's rich and varied life. Old air-force buddies, miners, musicians, dancers, comics, strippers, agents, Father McShane and the Fisher fast bowler – whose dad most definitely remembered the legendary Corporal Stanley Foxcroft. Uncle Stan apparently ran the quartermaster's stores like a personal business and only escaped court martial due to an aerodrome bombing raid which wiped out all the evidence. During the raid Uncle Stan had committed an uncharacteristic act of bravery, pulling a young pilot out of a burning Hurricane. Apparently the pilot owed him one pound seven and six. Anyone else would have been decorated, but the powers that be took a swings-and-roundabouts view of things, which Uncle Stan wouldn't have complained about.

I learned all this from the pilot himself, who turned up, now in his thirties and holding the rank of squadron leader. He stood by Uncle Stan's open coffin and saluted, which made everyone in the room go quiet. It didn't stay quiet long when he told us the tale of Uncle Stan's selfless heroism and how he'd charged him an extra ten bob for *collection fees*. When he finished he bent over my uncle's body and pinned something on him.

'It's my DFC,' he explained. 'I always meant to give it to him, never got round to it, dammit. Still, better late than never. Don't take it off, I'd like to think the mercenary old bugger took something of value with him.' He saluted again, bade his farewell and left, as did others, including Father McShane, Desmond and a tearful Ethel, leaving just a hard core of old friends.

By this time I was feeling dizzy. Mary had thrown up in the toilet and had left with her dad.

Perhaps the events of the past few days were taking their toll. I sat down in a chair with a glass of beer and another piece of funny fruitcake. Marion Mallinson, another big cake lover, began to sing – which was most unusual for her. She was normally quite shy, but that afternoon she sang. She was out of tune, but no one cared. In fact, many people joined in. Despite the sad occasion I was greatly amused, everyone was.

But we didn't know why.

Marion Mallinson stood on a chair and loosened her hair, allowing it to cascade sensuously over her drip-white, bony shoulders. Then she began to strip, urged on by her husband, no less, who then decided to join her in this lewd exhibition. Thankfully they both stopped at the underwear stage, but they were not alone. Others had taken their lead and many mourners were now dancing round the room in various stages of nudity.

Mostyn suggested a visit to his Fish Emporium, so out we all went. Two of Uncle Stan's old miner pals brought him along too. After all, it was his party. We all piled in, some in the front, most in the back and Mostyn drove us off to the Red Lion just in time for opening. Ignoring the landlord's protests regarding breach of dress code, we lined up at the bar. Mr Rosenberg from next door, who, to the best of my knowledge, didn't drink, placed the order in his wonderful Jewish accent.

'Fourteen pints of kosher bitter, you truculent little twat.'

The truculent little twat began to pull the pints while his truculent little wife went to ring the police. Had they turned up a bit sooner they might have prevented Mrs Mallinson from removing her last vestiges of decency by doing the dance of the two veils on top of the bar.

I noticed my dad had fallen asleep in a corner with a rare smile on his face. Uncle Stan's two miner pals sat in a corner, singing loudly, with Uncle Stan between them, head on one side, a pint of beer clutched in his hand. Uncle Stan would have enjoyed that. By the time the police arrived we had five dancing nudes among us and others behaving in a manner unbecoming respectable mourners. The police decided to arrest the lot of us, including Uncle Stan, but excluding my sleeping parent. I tried to explain that Uncle Stan was an innocent party in all this, but the bobbies didn't believe me and even made the two miners do their job for them and carry my deceased uncle into the police van.

'Empty your pockets,' demanded a sergeant when we arrived.

'I haven't got any pockets, you naughty little man,' smiled a nude Mrs Mallinson.

'Bang 'em all up,' ordered the exasperated sergeant. 'We'll sort 'em out later. Best put all the women together in one cell, and find some clothes for them that's without. It's like a flamin' nudist colony in here. I wouldn't mind if there was owt decent to look at.'

'Would you like a piece of cake, officer?' I said, having found a bit in my pocket. I put it on his desk by way of a peace offering. He picked it up and was about to drop it in a waste bin when he had second thoughts and put it to his nose.

'Where'd you get this?' he asked very sternly.

'It was in me pocket.'

'Don't you mess me about, this stuff's laced with cannabis! Where did you get it?'

Apparently I just smiled and passed out. I awoke several hours later. They'd put me in a cell with a comedian, the two miners and Uncle Stan. He was the only one who didn't look ill. I felt terrible and I couldn't understand for the life of me what I was doing there. All the others were dead to the world, especially Uncle Stan. I banged on the cell door. I knew it was a cell, having been in one before.

'Hello!' I yelled. I couldn't think of anything else to shout. A hatch in the door slid open and a grinning mouth said, 'Room service.'

'Could you tell me why you've locked me up, please?'

'Because you've been a naughty boy.'

'Oh! Could I have a cup of tea, please?'

'Would that be with or without the cake, sir? The cake with the mystery ingredient.'

'What? Just a cup of tea, please.' I could have done without his flippancy.

'Mouth like the bottom of a parrot's cage, sir?'

The cell door opened and a constable walked in to survey the scene. He smirked and said sarcastically, 'Will your four sleepy friends want cups of tea as well?'

'Well, three of them might, the other one's dead.'

The policeman blanched. 'Dead?'

'As a doornail.' I assured him, gazing down at my uncle's peaceful face.

'Sergeant!' The constable backed out of the doorway as his superior arrived.

'I was just telling the constable that my uncle's dead,' I said. The sergeant leaned over and touched Uncle Stan's cheek, which had been refrigerated until the previous afternoon. And corpses don't thaw out in a hurry.

'Damn!' he said. 'Just what I need. A death in custody. Get a doctor down here – *now!*'

The constable sprang into action.

I was still feeling dizzy and disorientated or I might have

explained the situation a little more fully to the sergeant. He shook the others awake.

'Right, you lot, outa this cell, and don't touch *him*.'

The four of us trudged, dizzily, into an interview room, where we promptly fell asleep again. In his confusion our constable had left the door open, so when I awoke a while later I was able to hear the doctor give his verdict.

'He's dead all right. Died of a severe blow to the head.'

'Oh heck!' groaned the sergeant. 'This could put us in something of a bad light.'

'I can see you're not a sergeant for nothing,' observed the doctor, who didn't like being called out at two in the morning to look at five-day-old corpses.

'Do you have a time of death?' asked the sergeant, desperately hoping the doctor could pinpoint death to a time before the police became involved, otherwise . . .

'I couldn't say precisely, but I would estimate four, maybe five . . . days ago!' The doctor deliberately hesitated before the last two words. I went to the door to see the look on the sergeant's face.

'You mean four or five *hours*,' corrected the sergeant.

'I mean what I say, Sergeant. You appear to have arrested a cadaver. I hope he didn't put up too much of a struggle.'

The doctor left, having amused himself at his clever little joke. The sergeant looked up and saw me gazing at him with what no doubt was a very glazed expression. Banging from the cells told me that the other mourners were waking up. The sergeant's beckoning finger ordered me to stand before his desk.

'Explain!' he demanded.

'I can't explain,' I explained. 'I don't know what happened and I don't know what I'm doing here – and I feel sick.'

I threw up in his waste-paper basket, which left me feeling much better.

'Get him out of here!' yelled the exasperated sergeant. The constable put me back in the interview room. Having a corpse in custody presented the sergeant with a dilemma. This was more of an inspector's problem. The inspector came and had a look at Uncle Stan.

'It's my uncle Stan!' I shouted helpfully. 'He's a comedian. At least he was.'

The inspector emerged from Uncle Stan's cell and walked purposefully towards me. 'So, you all thought you'd get popped up on cannabis to celebrate his passing, did you?'

I didn't know what he was talking about. 'Cannabis?' I said. 'Really? What's cannabis?' I'd heard the word but I couldn't place it, my brain wasn't functioning as well as it might.

'Don't come the innocent with me, young man. You know exactly what I'm talking about. Marijuana, hashish – illegal drugs.

Marijuana struck a chord. I'd heard of that. It was a rarity in those days. I vaguely remembered what the desk sergeant had said about the cake.

'I've never had marijuana before. I can't say as I like it. It made the cake taste funny.'

'Didn't stop you eating the cake though, did it, sir? I reckon you've eaten enough to paralyse an elephant.'

'We were having a wake for my uncle Stan,' I explained. 'He's the dead body you arrested.'

The inspector stiffened. Arresting a dead body wasn't a good move. The words *stock* and *laughing* sprang to his mind.

'And how come you brought the deceased to the pub with you? Was it his round or something?' The inspector was attempting sarcasm, but it fell on deaf ears.

'It was you lot who arrested him, he wasn't doing any harm. If he wasn't dead he could sue you for wrongful arrest. It's not very nice for a dead person to have to spend his last night above ground locked up in a cell. We're burying him this morning, so you'd better release him on bail.'

Behind the inspector I recognized a sleepy-eyed reporter from the *Unsworth Observer*, who wrote a column under the name Ben Bull. He was taking all this down with great relish.

'Listen, you comical craphouse!' bellowed the inspector,

who hadn't seen the reporter yet. 'Who brought the bloody cake to the wake?'

'I've no idea. Can I go home?'

'No, you bloody well can not go home until I've got to the bottom of this. Oh bollocks! You're all I need.'

This last remark was made as he spotted the reporter, who had stopped grumbling to himself about being woken up at two in the morning to find out what was happening at Unsworth nick. This was front-page stuff, another Billy Foxcroft sensation.

The inspector never did get to the bottom of it, nor did I. Whoever did it had their own secret motives, although it did jolly the wake in its own way. Uncle Stan would have liked that. The police grilled us all as best they could but we were very poor interviewees, so they let us all go. I like to think the DFC pinned to Uncle Stan's stage suit impressed the inspector. They wouldn't want it too widely known that they'd arrested a dead war hero. Needless to say, the *Unsworth Observer* made a meal out of it as usual and grossly exaggerated the story.

Uncle Stan was buried later that morning. We invited the inspector and the sergeant. But they didn't come.

Twenty-Six

I t was an embarrassed Jigger who came to the phone when
I rang him a few weeks later to ask about getting my old
job back.

'I don't think it's going to be as straightforward as I thought,
lad. They held your job open for a few months but it's been
taken now and there doesn't seem to be any vacancies coming
up this side of Christmas.'

The show had folded with the death of Uncle Stan. Mickey
Boothroyd was insured against such an eventuality, so he came
out of it OK. The other acts went their separate ways, as they
would have anyway at the end of the tour. It was no great
hardship to them, only to me and Ethel – and Desmond.

I said goodbye to a tearful Mary, who would have come
home with me at the drop of a hat, but I had nothing to offer
her. And at the back of my mind there was always Helen.

I booked myself a driving test. With the help of half a dozen
lessons from the Douglas Rigby (Unsworth) Limited Driving
Academy I passed first time. It helped to fill the great vacuum
in my life. It also helped when, acting on no one's advice but
my own, I spent most of my savings on a second-hand Humber
Hawk, the dream car of my childhood. This was a rash purchase
that can only be put down to the impetuosity of youth. Dad said
I was barmy.

'Blimey, Mister Jackson!' I groaned. 'I've just bought a car.
I've got hardly any money left!'

'I'll see what I can do,' said Jigger helpfully. 'I think I
might know someone who can fix you up with a temporary job.'

'That'd be great. Thanks, Mr Jackson!' I wasn't high enough up the sewage ladder to call him Jigger to his face.

It took me a long time to accept that my show-business career was at an end. I'd had a remarkable year or so but, without Uncle Stan, I hadn't an act. Standing up solo in front of a club audience didn't appeal to me one bit. Gradually I accepted the inevitability of an ordinary job, earning ordinary wages. This was to be my life.

Jigger eventually fixed me up with a small, Irish civil engineering contractor. Actually the contractor was quite big but his firm was small. Jimmy Docherty had the roadworks contract for all Barden Homes sites, which at that time numbered around seven or eight in and around Yorkshire. Paul Barden was an ex-bricklayer. He wasn't a particularly intelligent man. What he had was initiative, ambition, greed and ruthlessness. In business these qualities far outweigh brains, which are for teachers and professional people. Intellectuals have no place in business. *Bullshit baffles brains* is a saying with a lot going for it. When I eventually met him I found I didn't much like him, but I wasn't working directly for him. I was to work as a setting-out engineer for Jimmy, who only had Jigger's word that I could do the job.

Jigger Jackson saw himself as my guide and mentor. This job was to be but a temporary interlude before I was restored to my rightful place at the Main Drainage Department. During the week before I went to work for Jimmy, Jigger gave me many free hours of intensive coaching in the art of setting out roads and sewers. I probably learned more in that week than I would in a year at night school. Jigger was a knowledgeable and enthusiastic teacher, who thought nearly as much of me as he did his beloved sewage. This of course was an honour indeed.

J. P. Docherty (Engineers) Ltd consisted of Jimmy Docherty, Mick Docherty (brother), Danny Lavelle, John O'Donnell, Martin Carroll, Old Sean Mooney and me. They all originated from Mayo in the west of Ireland. All of them came from farming families and when the farm, which was rarely more than a smallholding, passed on to the eldest son, the rest of the sons would head for either America or England, depending on which way they were facing when they made their decision.

Any time Jimmy needed to work two sites at once he promoted his younger brother Mick to ganger, and brought in extra sub-contract labour and hired in plant. He had a ten-ton truck, a Drott and a Priestmann Cub excavator. He knew about these newfangled JCB things but wasn't impressed. My first job with them was in Netherton, a large market town in East Yorkshire. It was a big site and we expected to be there throughout the winter – Jimmy had also picked up the contract for doing the groundworks for all the houses, which made it quite a lucrative job for him. This was reflected in my wages, which Jimmy had set at ten pounds a week. These were *man's* wages and I knew then that I would have serious second thoughts about returning to work under Jigger's wing.

Danny Lavelle, at nineteen, was the youngest. He was not a handsome youth, he was not an educated youth, but he *was* a wild youth. He was generous-natured, hard-working, funny, quick-witted and friendly and he took it upon himself to show me what drinking was all about. If I had a best pal at J. P. Docherty (Engineers) Ltd, it had to be Danny. I seemed to have an affinity with the building-site Irishman, perhaps it's the Eskimo in me. They're a special breed of man. Rarely involving themselves in bricklaying or joinery or any of the namby pamby trades, that was women's work. The Irishman likes the big work: laying miles of kerbs, shifting thousands of tons of muck, laying hundreds of tons of tarmac and digging sewers twenty feet deep. This was *man's* work, and it was a lot less boring. This work required ingenuity rather than skill; brute strength rather than the craftsman's delicate touch. The Irishman likes to spend his working day on or below ground level, as God intended.

Danny liked a practical joke but rarely knew where to draw the line. Me joining forces with him would eventually end my employment with Jimmy Docherty, but it's always been my lot in life to be drawn like a magnet to the jokers of this world. It brightens up the day, but it had its drawbacks.

Old Sean Mooney was a bit of a loner. He'd taken over a derelict caravan that had been on the site since before we got there. This became his home. At a quarter to twelve every Thursday he'd ask Jimmy if he could put his stew on. Stew was Sean's Thursday treat. He'd go to his caravan and place a pot of water on a calor gas stove, into which he'd throw whatever ingredients he'd gathered during the week. No one ever asked to share Sean's stew with him, nor were they ever invited. He was a man of few words, none of them obscene. Sean was a religious man, as we could tell by the crucifix on the inside of his caravan door. But he was a good worker and Jimmy Docherty had issued countless warnings, especially to Danny, not to upset him. Sean's stew had been the topic of many a dinner-time conversation. The smell which wafted across the site was never appetizing and the lads reckoned it was made from dogmuck and nettles.

Then the day came when Danny found a dehydrated dog turd on the site and wondered if Sean would notice if he added it to the stew. The deed had been done before it was brought to anyone's notice. We were sitting in the cabin having our dinner when Danny mentioned it.

'I put a dog turd in yer man's stew.'

'Jesus, Danny!' said a shocked Mick. 'A ting like dat could kill him! It's poison fer sure.'

'Not at all,' said Danny, grinning widely. 'Yer should see der shite he puts in himself. Yer man'll nivver know der difference.'

All eyes turned to look through the cabin window at Sean's caravan, from where the old man emerged with a large brick-layer's trowel in his hand and marched towards our cabin. He stood in the doorway – his face was frozen with rage as he held out the trowel for our examination. The dog turd, or part of it, was there, covered in gravy with an onion or two stuck to it.

Danny leaned forward and sniffed at it. 'Needs more seasoning, what yer tink, lads?'

Danny's smart comment didn't help the situation. Sean threw the contents of the trowel at him, along with the first obscenity I'd ever heard him come out with.

'Danny Lavelle, yer dirty little bastard. I've had ter throw away nearly half me fuckin' stew!'

Had it not been for Ben Bull, the all-seeing eye of the *Unsworth Observer*, my employment with Jimmy Docherty would have gone unnoticed by Hilda Bradley. By the end of October, Jim and Bradley Bradley had been released after serving ten weeks of their four-month prison sentences for stealing a bin wagon, dangerous driving and assaulting a police officer. A sentence I considered unduly lenient under the circumstances. Just two weeks after their release the article appeared. It was not much more than a snippet really, just something to fill up page four. If only these reporters would think before they printed such life-threatening information.

BILLY FOXCROFT QUITS SHOW BUSINESS

After the death of his uncle, Stan Foxcroft, the junior half of the Fabulous Fox Twins has decided to give up show business and go back to the construction industry, from where he originally rose from obscurity to stardom. Billy Foxcroft (twenty-one) is now working as a bricklayer on a Barden Homes site in Harrogate.

The inaccuracy of the reporting probably bought me a couple of weeks grace while the Bradleys tracked me down. Being a bricklayer for Barden Homes was fast becoming one of the least sought after jobs in the industry. Using a process of elimination they were being systematically beaten up just in case I was using a disguise. A five-foot-two brickie in Bradford was threatened to reveal his true identity. The Bradleys obviously thought I'd disguised my height. Ben Bull had a lot to answer for and they hadn't even got to *me* yet. Strange to say that no word of all this reached our site. Although I knew about the article, I wasn't unduly troubled. As soon as the Bradleys realized I wasn't a bricklayer in Harrogate they'd give up looking. Foxy Foxcroft knew these things.

It was Friday dinner time, about half past twelve. We were all sitting in the cabin, having the crack. Medical problems were the topic of conversation.

'I got der piles!' said Sean Mooney.

'Yer a pain in de arse!' observed Mick Docherty.

'I *got* a pain in de arse!' corrected Sean, finding a more comfortable sitting position on his personal bag of cement. 'I wonder if yer could look into it for me?'

'It's der lime in dat cement, it infiltrates der rectum. If yer kep yer arse away from dat cement yer'd nivver get dem pile tings!' advised Martin Carroll, the self-styled medical expert. The lads always went to him with their complaints.

'Dere's a quick way to get rid o' dem!' he added importantly. 'Sit in a bucket o' Jeyes' Fluid!'

I didn't know for sure, but I suspected this would do the trick.

'D' ye know anything about dat sugar diabetes?' inquired John O'Donnell.

He'd not been feeling well that morning and had made his own drastic diagnosis. My diagnosis put it down to the fifteen pints of bitter he'd drunk the previous evening. Martin thought long and hard about this one.

'Sugar diabetes . . .' he said sagely, 'was der finest bantam-weight dat ever came out of Wales.'

I was writing all this down just in case I ever changed my mind about going back on the stage. The door of the cabin burst open.

Bradley Bradley stood there, his very face enough to strike dread into most men. Behind him were his two brothers. Danny was next to the door, he looked at Bradley Bradley and then grinned at me.

'I tink it's de Avon lady.'

Bradley Bradley didn't understand humour. He reached inside the cabin with an abnormally long arm and dragged me out. His brothers stood there, grinning in triumph.

'Right, yer murderin' bastard, we've got yer now!'

He aimed a punch at my face, which, had it connected and had I been lucky, would have put me to sleep for a fortnight. Fortunately I could see it coming and ducked very easily underneath it. There was obviously some family pride at stake here because the other Bradleys didn't lift a finger to help. They stood, one at either side of us, to cut off any escape route. I was long and gangling. Six feet tall and maybe eleven and a half stone. My opponent was maybe six feet three and eighteen stone, so I was at a disadvantage. I was also terrified. I noticed the rest of the lads emerge from the cabin and couldn't understand why they didn't immediately spring to my aid. Bradley Bradley came at me again and missed me again. I'd never seen a man so uncoordinated, but he only had to catch me once and *I'd* be uncoordinated. The lads started laughing at him, which annoyed me. If they didn't want to help they shouldn't be antagonizing him. Jim Bradley and Gary didn't look too pleased either.

As he swung at me a third time I risked a jab to his face, feeling I had nothing to lose. He was such an easy target, and such a big one. I became conscious of my suspect fingers on my right hand, so I concentrated on jabbing him with my left. His reach was at least a foot longer than mine but I was getting through to him with unbelievable ease. Even my puny blows would take their toll eventually. I began to realize why his face was such a mess. One of my punches drew blood – and applause from my supporters.

'Give him a belt in der gut!' advised one expert.

Bradley Bradley was breathing very heavily, we'd been at it for several minutes and he was out of condition. There'd been no keep-fit facilities at his recent prison. I launched into a two-fisted attack, throwing caution to the winds. He had no defence against me. Had he not been a Bradley, I'd have felt sorry for him. Lumbering backwards, he fell heavily into a pile of bricks. I winced when I saw him bang his head. There was a lot of blood gushing down his face, my argument with Bradley Bradley was over. Out of the corner of my eye I saw Jim Bradley step forward, only to be restrained by Jimmy and Mick Docherty. Bradley shook himself free.

'Don't bleedin' panic!' he rasped angrily. 'I'm not goin' ter touch the little bastard! I just want ter tell our kid summat.'

He walked towards his defeated brother with a look of disgust on his face. 'I knew it were a bad idea o' me mam's ter let you sort him out. Our lass coulda done a better job than you, yer big useless monkey turd!'

Bradley Bradley was barely conscious and in need of hospital treatment but his brothers turned their backs on him and walked off the site.

And out of my life.

It had evidently been Hilda Bradley's instruction that my punishment be carried out by Bradley Bradley to make up for all the shame he'd brought on the family by constantly being beaten up. Surely he couldn't fail against a weakling such as me. Had I died, her useless son would then have restored both his own and the family pride by serving life imprisonment. His failure would now bring unbelievable shame on the family name, and I was to blame for all this. It was something I'd have to learn to live with.

An ambulance was called for to transport the injured man away to hospital. I didn't realize it but I'd damaged my hands again. There was nothing broken, but Martin, our medical man, took it upon himself to bandage me up. I was offered not one word of congratulation by the lads on my famous victory against all odds, nor one word of explanation why they didn't immediately come to my help. The reason became apparent later in the day.

Paul Barden had a very strict rule against fighting on the site, dating back to a manslaughter charge he'd had levelled against him when he'd been attacked by a sub-contract plumber. The resulting fight had ended with the plumber dying of a brain haemorrhage. It wasn't through remorse that he'd imposed this rule – it was simply bad for business. Barden's site foreman had witnessed every blow of my scrap with Bradley Bradley and within minutes of the fight ending he was on the phone to his boss.

Our bollocking duly arrived at eight o'clock the following morning in the shape of Mr Paul Barden, who was nasty, arrogant and foul-mouthed. Never having met me before he dismissed me with, 'I suppose you're the brainless twat who caused the trouble. Just get out from under me feet before I show yer what fightin's all about!' He then proceeded to give Jimmy a verbal lashing.

My boss couldn't afford to cross him. Jimmy, unwisely, had all his eggs in the Barden basket. It was the incident that happened a week later that invoked real displeasure from Paul Barden. Danny Lavelle was the instigator but I was his happy accomplice. I suppose the drink played a major part in the affair as well.

Twenty-Seven

O ur week finished on Saturday lunch time and we'd all trooped down to the King's Arms to start the weekend. The centre of the town was crowded, it was the annual winter horse fair. The place had been invaded by gypsies, genuine and imitation, horse dealers and stealers; and those here for the simple expedient of extracting unwise money from gullible drunks. A bigger gathering of rogues and ne'er-do-wells would be hard to find.

It was a dull, damp day, brightened by the lively crowds. There were stalls selling horse stuff: saddlery, leather straps and things that horse people like to wrap round their animals. There were horse brasses, horse blankets, lucky horseshoes, jodhpurs, riding boots and riding hats. The air was alive with the sound of dealers dealing, horses making horse noises and people making people noises – talking, laughing, cursing, shouting, singing. There was a smell of horses, hot dogs, roast chestnuts and body odour. A kiddie's funfair jangled cheerfully away in the background.

Horse-related items were everywhere, particularly under-foot. I was not a horse person, so I decided to stay in the pub after most of the lads had left to have a look round. Danny stayed to keep me company.

'I wouldn't mind a horse meself,' he mused, over his eighth pint. 'Den I could become a cowboy like dat John Wayne feller.'

'I don't like 'em,' I announced, over my seventh pint. 'I once had a funny experience on a horse.'

I told him about my adventure on Harry the carthorse. Danny

found it amusing, so did I after all these years. We giggled into our beer as drunks do. He made me repeat the part where Mrs Moon farted her way down to her last resting place.

'Dat has ter be der greatest way ter say goodbye.' He closed his eyes and squeezed out a demonstration of his own proposed flatulent farewell to this world, which I have to say would rank alongside Mrs Moon's.

'But can you do that when you're dead?' I said. 'That's the trick.'

'Not widout an assistant. Yer'd need an assistant ter set it all up for yer. I bet der's lots o' people who'd like to go out like dat. We could start a business, arrangin' fer people to fart their way outa dis life. I bet it'd please God no end. Get rid of all der wind before yer go through der pearly gates. Der last ting He would want is fer der new arrivals ter enter der kingdom of heaven and start fartin' all over der joint. Yer don't need dat sort o' behaviour in paradise! Upsettin' all dem angels!'

'We could call it Final Fart Ltd!'

Three pints later we'd liquidated this promising company and I allowed myself to be convinced that being a cowboy was the only job for me. We unanimously decided to leave the pub immediately and seek our fortunes on horseback.

There was a field nearby populated by a large herd of Friesians. They totally ignored our unsteady, but stealthy approach, being preoccupied with filling their bellies from the fodder-filled mangers. We had already acquired our mount, a vintage delivery bicycle, left unloved and unattended outside the pub. There was no sign of human life. The cattlemen had unwisely posted no guards to protect the herd against rustlers.

'John Wayne would have left guards. Can yer see if dere's any brands on dere arses?' said my sidekick at the top of his voice.

Leaving my trusty, rusty steed to graze quietly beside the fence, I examined the nearest black and white set of crap-encrusted hindquarters and loudly but confidentially informed my fellow rustler that I couldn't see a brand. Danny laid a brotherly arm around my shoulder and whispered earnestly into my ear, in a voice you could have heard back in Unsworth, 'In dat case, dere's no way anyone can prove dat dese cattle don't belong to us.'

I was in total agreement with him. Our plan was completely foolproof. After searching for a while at the hinge side of the gate for a way to open it, we eventually spotted our mistake and pushed it ajar. We swung it open and shut several times, enjoying the exciting ride it provided us two happy drunks. The cows wandered disdainfully past us into the road with absolutely no encouragement from the rustlers. We marvelled at our cowpunching expertise.

I was put in charge of the mount as Danny was the only adult I'd ever come across who couldn't ride a bike. He perched in the front panier as we wobbled behind our herd ringing the bell to encourage them to pick up speed.

We had apparently chosen to head our newly acquired herd into town. I don't remember being aware of this at the time but it didn't seem a bad idea. In response to our bell-ringing and yells of 'Yipee-Yi-Yo-Ki-Yay' the cows broke into a nervous trot. Behind us a car sounded an impatient horn. The cattle picked up speed as we arrived at the end of the High Street and were going along at a steady gallop by the time they reached Market Square, where all the horse activity was taking place.

I was told later that there were nearly a hundred cattle in all, which is a lot of cows to be running flat out through your market square at the best of times. But for this to happen on winter horse fair day can lead to trouble. Needless to say, the *Yorkshire Post* sensationalized it.

CATTLE STAMPEDE AT NETHERTON WINTER HORSE FAIR BILLY FOXCROFT ARRESTED

They'd added the last bit as though I was the automatic suspect.

The Market Square in Netherton was a scene of devastation on Saturday afternoon, when a herd of cows stampeded through it whilst the winter horse fair was in full swing. Damage to stalls and property was estimated to run into thousands of pounds. Many horses broke loose and fled into the surrounding countryside. The Mayor of Netherton, Councillor Derek Butterbowl, who was in the process of crowning Miss Bernice McCrombie (twenty-two) as Winter Horse Fair Queen when the stampede occurred, said last night that this was the worst tragedy to hit the town since the whisky still explosion of 1879, which destroyed the Market Tavern and part of the town hall. An emergency fund has been set up to provide for those worst hit by the tragedy. Billy Foxcroft, surviving member of the Fabulous Fox Twins, was being held in police custody last night pending investigations.

Danny and I shared a cell that night. The other cells being occupied by all the other winter horse fair drunks. The police had wisely segregated us, as we were not popular people. The other incarcerated drunks didn't appear to like us. They hurled threats and insults along the corridor outside our cell. It was as well we were fast asleep or we would have been dreadfully worried. The following morning Danny was the only person in the police station not to have a hangover. Even the sergeant was drinking Alka Seltzer. He showed great compassion for a fellow sufferer and made one up for me. This was my maiden hangover and it's not a memory I treasure. As my head cleared I formulated a plan.

No one had seen us open the gate so we would deny it was us. Simple as that. All we'd done, your worship, was follow the cows on a bike we had found to make sure they came to no harm. Then a car came along and sounded his horn, which panicked the cows and, try as we might, we couldn't stop them. Yes, we'd had a couple of drinks, but who hadn't? After all, it was winter horse fair day. We couldn't understand why anyone should want to blame *us* for it. Farmers should keep a better eye on their cattle and not neglect their herds in such a fashion.

251

We didn't even have to go to court. The police sergeant listened disbelievingly to our story then called his inspector, who rang his superintendent. After he'd put the phone down, the inspector shrugged his shoulders and said, rather nastily, 'I don't believe a word you've said, but we've got absolutely nothing to prove you caused it, so you can both bugger off. Just don't think for one minute that I haven't got my eye on you. By the way, Foxcroft . . . !'

I was on my way out of the door when he called after me.

'I saw you at the Empire in Leeds. I thought you were crap!'

'I agree with you, Inspector, but who are we against the thousands who thought the Fox Twins were brilliant?'

Danny hadn't a clue what I was talking about. We left the cop shop and threaded our way through the broken remnants of the Netherton Winter Horse Fair.

'That's them!'

A shopkeeper, supervising the reglazing of his front window, hurled an accusing yell across the square at us.

'They're the ones what caused it all!'

I was about to set off running when Danny took charge of the situation.

'I hope you're not de feller dat told der police all dem lies about us!'

He approached the man, with a threat in his Irish voice. The shopkeeper backed off into his shop doorway.

'When der police found out dat someone had been lyin' about us, dey weren't too pleased. Dey let us go when dey found we were der only ones what tried ter stop dem cows. Iverybody else ran away. Did you run away, mister? I bet yer did!'

He turned to face the apprehensive crowd that had gathered a safe distance away from this mad Irishman.

'What about der rest of yer? I didn't see any acts of great bravery from any o' you snivellin' lot!'

He fired a great gob of Irish spit on the ground and walked back over to me in mock disgust. We strolled off together full of self-righteous indignation.

'Sorry, lads! We didn't know!' The repentant shopkeeper called out his grovelling apology.

Without turning round I waved a hand in magnanimous absolution. Some you win. But some you lose.

The second part of this equation proved true the very next day, when Paul Barden came to visit. He'd apparently choked over his breakfast as he read the *Yorkshire Post* account of our mishap. His eggs and bacon was going down well, up to the moment it was revealed that Billy Foxcroft worked for Barden Homes as a bricklayer. This last bit was obviously plagiarized from the *Unsworth Observer*.

Barden arrived on site mid-afternoon, his Jaguar ploughing to a halt in the mud well short of his site cabin. By the time he arrived, his blue suit had much splattering on it.

'Get Docherty an' that idiot engineer of his!' he instructed his site agent as he kicked his way through the cabin door.

Jimmy and I were at the far end of the site, setting out a kerb line. Snow was beginning to fall quite heavily and we were thinking of calling the lads off. I say *we* because Jimmy was beginning to treat me as an equal in many ways. The more I learned about the job the more I felt my future lay with this man rather than with Jigger. He'd said little about my weekend escapade, which was more than can be said for the rest of the lads. The mickey-taking bordered on cruelty. I felt so at home among these men.

'Barden wants ter see yer!' called the site agent through the snow. 'He wants ter see both o' yer!'

'Bloody Jesus!' blasphemed Jimmy. 'It's about you! I've a feelin' yer might o' dropped me in der shite!'

'Sorry, Jimmy!'

We walked to the builder's cabin like a pair of errant school-boys heading for the headmaster's study. For me this was still a vivid memory. Barden was pacing angrily up and down when we walked in. He spun round and thrust an angry finger at me.

'You!' he yelled hysterically, 'can get your stupid arse off my site before I kick you off!'

'Yer can't do dat, Paul!' said Jimmy unsurely. 'He's me engineer, I need him!'

'What sort o' firm are you runnin' if you need a useless bastard like him!' spluttered Barden. His fist thumped the table to emphasize each word. He was a man out of control.

'He's a good engineer!' said Jimmy, which I thought was very nice of him.

'He's a brainless pillock, just look at him,' sneered Barden. 'He doesn't *look* as if he's got any sense.'

'You don't *sound* as if you've got any sense!' I retaliated.

These were the first words I had ever spoken to Paul Barden. I wasn't being very diplomatic but there's just so much you can take. Barden, like most bricklayers, lacked self-control. He took a petulant swing at me. What was it about me that made people want to hit me all the time? It was a wild, scything swing, which left me ample time to take evasive action. Taking evasive action was becoming one of my talents. The force of his misdirected punch carried him stumbling out of the door. He tripped up over my outstretched leg, which was only outstretched as a result of my evasive action and not through any malicious intent. There was an eighteen-inch drop outside the cabin door; a proposed step had never materialized, as is often the case with site huts. Barden flew out headlong and landed face down, severely winded, in the mud. I turned to Jimmy.

'This could be a good time for me to hand in my notice!'

'I tink yer might be right!' Jimmy held out a reluctant hand of farewell as Barden tried to heave himself, cursing, out of the mud.

'Tell him you've sacked me,' I suggested.

Jimmy had already thought of that. I left the hut, using Barden's slowly rising back as a step, squashing him back down into the mud. A childish but satisfying act.

'Yer fired, Foxcroft!' shouted an angry Jimmy in my wake. 'Don't come lookin' fer money, yer useless bastard!'

He was very convincing. He seemed to have convinced Barden, who ungraciously accepted Jimmy's helping hand then turned and shook a furious fist at me as I climbed into my car. I sat and watched as Jimmy followed his employer into the hut, turning round to give me a farewell wink and a mimed indication that he'd send my money on. I'd enjoyed my time with J. P. Docherty (Engineers) Ltd. But what next?

Twenty-Eight

Once again I was in it and once again I thought of Helen. I didn't know where she was staying but I knew someone who did. There was a telephone booth behind the King's Arms in Netherton.

'Hello, is that Mrs Onions?'

'Yes.'

'Could I speak to your Fanny, please.'

It would have sounded better had I omitted the possessive pronoun. I winced.

'Who?'

'Fan— er, Frances.' The chances were that her mother didn't call her Fanny.

'Right . . . Who is it?'

'Billy Foxcroft.'

'Oh, you.' She didn't sound impressed, despite my erstwhile fame. 'I'll get her,' she said, after some hesitation.

'Hiya, Billy.'

Fanny sounded more receptive. Maybe she knew what being a persona non grata was like.

'How're you doing?' I wasn't actually interested in how she was doing, but I was always a polite lad.

'Not bad. I'm working at Wetherstone's shirt factory.'

'Very nice.'

'It's crap actually but t' money's not bad, three an' six an hour. What about you? As if I need ask. Keep reading about yer. Sorry to hear about yer uncle. Helen thought he were a nice old feller. Never met him meself.'

'How is Helen?' I interrupted her.

'She's at university. I hope yer not gonna mess 'er about again. She were really upset wi' you. I thought what yer did were rotten. I saw Henry yesterday, he's working in Lands Lane post office. He's put a lot o' weight on.'

Her conversation was disconnected. Flitting from one subject to another as random thoughts escaped into her mouth and came blurting out.

'I had a baby. Did yer know?'

I'd heard about this, but thought it better not to bring the subject up. She made her little announcement with some pride, which was typical Fanny. Unmarried motherhood was very much frowned upon in 1957.

'Congratulations,' I said. 'I bet you're a great mother.'

'Thanks. He's a little lad, he's lovely. I've called him Martin. I hope your mate wouldn't have minded.'

'You mean Utters? Why should he mind?

'Well, yer know. With me baby bein' illegitimate an' all that.'

I almost made a crack about Utters being a bit of a bastard at times but I didn't. He wouldn't have minded. I tried to keep her pinned down to Helen.

'Have you got Helen's address or phone number?'

'What? I hope yer not gonna mess her about again.'

'No, I just want to get in touch with her. I haven't seen her since—'

'Since she caught yer at it wi' that tart?'

'If you like.'

'I didn't like it one bit . . . and I'll tell yer one thing for nowt. Helen dun't want yer within a mile of her. She hates yer, does Helen.'

'I don't blame her, but I'd like her address if you've got it.'

'Hang on.'

I pushed another two pennies into the slot in response to the pips and prepared to write Helen's address down on the back of the telephone directory. She came back on.

'I'm not sure I should be giving yer this.'

'Fanny, I'm running out of time and I've got no more change.'

There was a brief silence as she weighed up the pros and cons of the situation. She saw things my way.

'Flat B, 13 Ashburton Place. It's in Durham somewhere. I haven't got her phone number. Oh, and by the way she's getting—'

The pips went but I had what I wanted.

I parked my Humber outside the dark Victorian house. It had a neat but tiny front garden. The thirty-mile journey to Durham had taken me almost two hours, mainly due to the bad visibility. The snow had thinned out a bit now, just a few thin flakes accompanied by a shivering chill. I turned up my collar as I stood at the door. There was a plate on the wall with three bells for the three flats. I read the names beside flat three: A. Monkton, J. D. Gresham and H. B. Ash.

I was wondering what the B stood for, she'd never mentioned a middle name to me. A bell sounded on the first floor as I pressed the button, I could hear it from the doorstep. Above me a window scraped open and a young woman's head looked down at me.

'Looking for Amelia?' she enquired.

'Er . . . Helen Ash, actually.'

'I wish someone'd come looking for me.'

She had an intelligent face, but not one to write home about. I smiled up at her.

'Is she in?'

Her face lit up as she smiled back. 'You're Billy Foxcroft, aren't you?'

'Er, yes,' I admitted.

'Thought so. And she's invited you, has she?'

'Yes.'

I'd no idea what I was saying yes to, but it seemed like a good idea.

'She's already gone, she left about ten minutes ago, her and Amelia.'

I suspected that if I'd been invited I should know where they'd gone. Girls can be very protective of their friends.

'Are you going?' I enquired. 'I could run you there if you want.'

'That'd be lovely. You can wait in here if you like.'

She was opening the door within a minute and introduced herself. 'I'm Jane, Helen's flatmate – or one of them.' She looked at her watch, seven fifteen. 'Crikey! They're kicking off in quarter of an hour and I'm nowhere near ready.'

She was ready in ten minutes, during which time I'd had a good look around the flat, including a sneaky peek into the room Helen shared with Amelia. Maybe I was hoping to see evidence of me. There were photos of Pat Boon, Elvis and Lonnie Donnegan, but no sign of Billy Foxcroft.

'Would you sign this for me?'

Jane's voice came from behind me as I stood at the door of Helen's room. She had a photo of me in her hand, which she'd cut from a newspaper. My one and only publicity shot, done by a Leeds photographer. I had a couple of hundred ten-by-eights at home. They'd never been in great demand.

'Yes, sure.'

It wasn't the first autograph I'd signed. When we were on tour it was customary to go to the theatre bar after the show, where the punters would clamour for our signatures. The idea was to boost the bar takings. I took her pen and scribbled my name across the paper.

'You're probably the most famous person ever to come into this flat,' she cooed. If she was coming on to me she was in for a disappointment.

'Are you ready?' I enquired, politely.

She didn't look any more ready than she had when I'd first arrived. The same green cardigan over the same pleated skirt. Maybe a hint of lipstick now and she'd definitely given her hair a comb.

She smiled, demurely. 'Ready as I'll ever be.'

Jane directed me into Durham City centre, where I parked in a cobbled square near a statue of an odd-looking man on a horse that looked too small for him. Jane led me up a street, past a gigantic cathedral, and into the Central Hotel. Very posh. I'd no idea what the occasion was, Jane was prattling on about my exploits. She seemed to know more about me than I did.

'I'll let you escort me in,' she smiled. 'That'll be one in the eye for Amelia.'

An upstairs suite had been reserved for the function. A group of blazered students were leaving the downstairs bar and making their way up the carpeted stairs to the Aysgarth Suite.

'It looks like being a posh do,' I said to Jane, still trying to glean information.

'Well, it would be, wouldn't it, with Richard's parents being who they are.'

'Yes, I suppose it would,' I agreed, wondering who Richard was.

A four-piece band were tuning up on a small stage at the far side of the room. Groups of people were standing around, talking. I scanned the room for Helen, but there was no sign. Jane and I were standing at the back as the bandleader came to the microphone.

'Well,' he announced. 'If everyone's here, it's my pleasant duty to get the festivities under way. And what better way to do this than have our guests of honour start the dancing. Ladies and gentlemen, would you put your hands together and give a warm welcome to Richard Lovelace and his beautiful fiancée, *Helen Ash.*'

A cold stab of pain lanced into my stomach as Helen and a young man entered the room from a door behind the stage. I couldn't describe him, because I didn't take my eyes off her. She looked radiant and beautiful and happy as he took her into his arms and swept into the middle of the floor amid a hail of clapping hands. Above the bandstand I noticed for the first time a banner saying HAPPY ENGAGEMENT, RICHARD AND HELEN.

I excused myself to a surprised Jane and was back in my car within minutes. Heading out of the city, cursing myself for my stupidity in not contacting her earlier. Not making any effort to put things right with her. I hadn't written, phoned or anything since that night she'd caught me with Vicki. Not one word of apology. What did I expect? Tears of self-pity swamped my eyes. Everyone who was dear to me had deserted me or didn't want to know or had just died on me. What had I done to deserve this? I stopped at a pub for a pint and a phone call to Pauline in Scarborough.

At last something to lighten my spirits. Not only was she in, but she had a few days off and a visit from me would be most welcome.

Twenty-Nine

The snow came down heavier as I aimed my old Humber towards the comforts of my lovely nurse. If the heater had worked I'd have felt a lot more comfortable. The windscreen wipers weren't really up to the job either. The wedge of visibility they struggled to clear was becoming increasingly smaller. I kept on having to get out to wipe off the surplus snow with my hands, which would have been a lot warmer if I'd had the sense to buy myself a pair of gloves.

I was about five miles east of Netherton when it became obvious that I wasn't going to get to Scarborough that night. I turned off and headed towards the King's Arms, not wanting to spend a cold night in the car. The car was all over the place, eventually coming to a snow-crunching halt in a deep drift. What I hoped to achieve by getting out I'll never know. I had a shovel in the boot, with which I made a vain attempt to dig the snow out from under the wheels. In the meantime I'd stupidly left the keys in the ignition and by the time I accepted the futility of my efforts and went to get back in the car, the locks were frozen solid. It was snowing a blizzard by now, picked out in all its dramatic glory in the car headlights, which I'd left on, so, no doubt, if ever I did get back in my vehicle, the battery would be flat. But that was the least of my worries. I huddled my all-too-thin coat round my shivering shoulders and tried to find a stone or something to break back in with. But the snow was many inches thick by now and if there were any stones about, they weren't immediately obvious. Besides, my hands were paralysed with cold and I could scarcely have coped with *picking up* a stone, much less hammering one against my car window. I gave up and settled down on the sheltered side of the car, intensely cold and intensely miserable. They say that your *whole* life passes before your eyes when you're about to die. I found some comfort in this theory insofar as very little of *my* life was passing before my eyes. I found myself remembering odd things. Like my first time on stage. It wasn't the Swillingfield Labour Club. It was the Central Pier at Blackpool. I was six years old and Uncle Peter Webster was inviting anyone brave enough to come on stage and do their party piece. No one was more amazed than my dad when I stepped up and recited a poem I'd just learned at school. It was called 'Jonathan Jo had a mouth like an . . .' I was trying through chattering teeth to recite it to myself, but I couldn't remember how it went. 'And a wheelbarrow full of surprises . . .' Yes, that was the next line . . . No, I couldn't remember any more. Uncle Peter Webster had given me a stick of rock that said *Peter Webster* all the way through. 'If that doesn't make you sick, nothing will!' he'd said, and I laughed because everybody else was laughing, but I didn't know why. I understood it now after all these years. I tried to brush the snow off my head but it was a futile exercise. What was that song that Tommy Newton sang at school? 'Lavender Trousers', that was it. How did that go?

'I know what you're lookin' at me for, wotcha gotcha eyes on I can tell . . .' I was singing but I couldn't hear myself. 'It's these old pair of Lavender trousers, don't you wish you had a pair like them?'

It was round about this point that I must have shivered myself to sleep. If I'd managed to travel another hundred yards down the road I'd have spotted another car stuck in a drift, facing the other way. The driver of this car was a young woman who had far more sense than me. She also had a tent and a sleeping bag and plenty of warm clothing.

Madeleine Proctor, or Maddy, as she was better known, had abandoned her Morris Minor and pitched her tent in the lee of a high stone wall in an adjacent field. She'd intended camping anyway, as there was no way she was going to spend a night on her own in that big old house. She'd loved spending her summers there when Uncle Arthur and Auntie Maureen filled it with their laughter and their animals. It should have been filled with children but sadly they never arrived. Uncle Arthur had been a farmer but had sold out to a neighbouring estate when Maureen died of smoking too many cigarettes at the age of fifty, although at the time cigarettes weren't the chief suspect. Arthur's smoking and drinking caught up with him and he died a couple of unhappy years later of lung cancer but mainly a broken heart. Maddy had been one of the great joys of their life. Her mother had died in childbirth and her father had, albeit unconsciously, held it against her. He was neither cruel nor unkind, but they were never close. Arthur, realizing the futility of trying to persuade his brother to love his only child, invited Maddy into his home at every opportunity.

She was twenty years old and up to a month ago had been a student at the Leeds College of Music, studying piano and clarinet. Maddy was a gregarious girl and generous with her affections. It was a bout of spontaneous generosity on top of the grand piano with her clarinet tutor which led to their expulsion from the college. Their passion would have remained undiscovered had it not been for the wonky piano leg which caused the ancient instrument to noisily and tunelessly collapse at the crucial moment. The trombone tutor and various pupils rushed in from the next room to find them disrobed and still at it among the wreckage of the Steinway. Had it been the Wills and Moffitt overstrung upright, they might have got away with it, but not with the Steinway. The Leeds College of Music had its standards.

Her vivacity was matched only by her height. Maddy was six foot tall, six foot three when she wore her favourite stilettos. The fact that she was a former Yorkshire Ladies Junior Shot Put Champion and had the powerful body that went with it would normally have qualified her for a deep voice and a moustache. But Maddy had a beautiful singing voice, with which she was now trying to eke out a living in the clubs and the only hair she had was an unruly cascade of red curls framing a pleasant, freckled face.

Uncle Arthur had left her his house in his will and she'd been on her way to meet a man who'd offered her an extraordinarily good price for it. Had it not been for the snow, the contract she had stuffed in her rucksack would have been signed that afternoon, making her potentially five thousand pounds better off. A sum not to be sniffed at in 1957.

A lesser girl would have struggled to pitch a tent in those conditions, but Maddy was not a lesser girl. She was attempting to warm up a billy-can of Heinz tomato soup when she noticed the car headlights through the blizzard. At first she ignored it, being more concerned with getting some warmth inside her cold body. Half an hour and a mug of lukewarm soup later, curiosity got the better of her. Wrapping a fleece-lined ex-RAF flying jacket around her (a gift from a grateful but exhausted suitor) she battled her way through the driving snow towards the dimming light.

I wasn't apparent at first. I was round the far side of the car. Just a big lump of snow. It wasn't until she tripped over me that she realized I was in fact a person not a big lump. Although there are those who would tell you otherwise. I'm glad it was Maddy who was camping in that field and not just any Tom, Dick or Harry. She saved my life that night and she did it in some style. Grabbing my frozen body under the armpits, she dragged me through the blizzard back to her tent, where she detected some faint sign of life.

I have two vivid memories of that night. Firstly a memory of utter dejection as I slumped down beside my car, shivering uncontrollably in the intense cold and reciting childhood rhymes. I don't remember going to sleep. Passing out would be more accurate. But I do remember waking up. It was evidently several hours later, perhaps in the early hours of the morning. Someone was snoring gently. I thought, *Surely it's not Uncle Stan*, because there was nothing gentle about his snoring. Then I remembered that Uncle Stan was dead and whoever was snoring wasn't very far, barely inches away – and *barely* was right. Whoever was snoring had got no clothes on! Nor, for that matter, had I! The snorer was hugging me very close to *her* body. I didn't need to be a student of biology to identify the sex of the body. It was doing a good job of identifying itself. This body seemed to be in excellent condition. The body spoke.

'I suppose you're wondering where you are!' it yawned.

'Well, I've woken up in worse places, but you're right. I am a bit curious.'

'You'd gone to sleep outside your car, which I thought was a bit daft. Anyway, I figured you'd be more comfortable in here. Any longer out there and you'd have been a goner.'

'Well! Thank you for your, er, hospitality.' It seemed an inadequate thing to say. 'I locked myself out of my car. You've saved my life, haven't you?'

'Yes, I suppose I have. You were freezing when I got you in here, so I had to get you out of your wet clothes and get you warmed up. I zipped two sleeping bags together. I, er . . . I couldn't think of any other way of thawing you out. Every bit of you was frozen.'

'*Every* bit?' I asked.

'Every bit. One bit in particular. Mind you, if you planted him, you'd finish up with a lovely big oak tree.'

I could see her grinning, her face only inches away, vaguely illuminated in the snow-reflected light which shone through the tent. It was the oddest experience of my life. Waking up in a sleeping bag, embracing a beautiful naked woman with a sense of humour. The outcome was inevitable, I was only human. Helen and Pauline couldn't have been further from my thoughts.

'Hello!' she said. 'I think someone else is waking up.'

'Ah! That'll be my acorn. Where do you suggest I plant him?'

'Somewhere warm and shady. He'll need to thaw out first. Oops! He seems to have found somewhere on his own. Clever things, acorns.'

'Ah! So he has . . . Sorry!'

'My pleasure.'

'By the way, my name's Billy.'

'My name's Maddy.'

'Pleased to meet you, Maddy!'

I much preferred *my* Good Samaritan to the one in the Bible.

The snow had stopped at daylight. Maddy pulled back the tent flap to reveal a Christmas card landscape. No sign of any tracks where she'd dragged me through the snow. It was pure and white and virgin.

Unlike some.

She had a complete change of clothing with her that fitted me. This was just as well because mine were still saturated. There was little chance of us getting the cars out until the roads were clear and as this was only a minor road it wasn't going to take priority. A plume of wood smoke betrayed the location of a farmhouse beyond a nearby hill. It took us the best part of an hour to get there, due mainly to the time we spent laughing like big daft kids and pushing each other over in the snow. Maddy had a similar mentality to me, which is unusual in a girl. It's unusual in anyone. On our arrival, we were treated to a real farmer's breakfast, for which I insisted on paying, knowing that we might need to impose ourselves on their generosity again before the roads were clear. The farmer's wife packed us enough food to last a week, saying, 'There, that should see you through till tomorrow if needs be.' It was noon when we arrived back at the tent. The place was as still as when we'd left it. Just two snowy humps in the road told us where the cars were.

'It's a relief that they haven't been stolen,' said Maddy.

We cleared the snow off them and Maddy thawed out the lock on mine with a lighted match. After a spot of lunch we built an obscene snowman right beside the tent. It was Maddy's idea to finish him off with two snowballs and an icicle. Then we had a marathon snowball fight, which I brought to an exhausted end, as I was being badly beaten. Dusk fell and I fell.

Madly in love with Maddy.

I felt her staring at me as we sat exhausted in the tent. 'What did you say your surname was?'

'I didn't say, but it's Foxcroft.'

'Billy Foxcroft! I knew I'd seen you somewhere before!'

'Ah, you've seen the act. I don't do it any more. Not since my Uncle Stan died. It was more his act than mine. No, I've gone back into the construction business now. I'm sort of a site engineer. Well, I was until yesterday, when I got the sack.'

'I don't suppose getting the sack had anything to do with the Netherton Winter Horse Fair?' She was giggling now – not a silly girly giggle, a real dirty chortle.

'How did you know?' I was quite surprised that she knew.

'It was in yesterday morning's papers, like everything else you get up to. Actually, I've never seen your act, never got the chance . . . but I know all about your exploits. You're quite famous.'

'I know,' I grumbled, 'but for all the wrong reasons! My dad won't be too pleased when he finds out that I've been kicked off Barden's site.'

'Barden? Would that be Paul Barden the builder?'

'No! Paul Barden the bastard . . . who also happens to be a builder.'

'It's him who's buying my uncle's house!' She'd already told me about selling Uncle Arthur's house.

'What would he want with a house? He builds 'em, he doesn't buy 'em.'

'I've no idea, and I don't care. He's offered me a brilliant price for it, twice what it's worth.'

This didn't sound like Paul Barden, there was a catch in this somewhere. I told Maddy as much. It was not what she wanted to hear.

'I don't want to hear that!' she moaned. 'You've got me worried now. Surely he can't do me out of my money?'

'Well, I don't see how he can, it's just that it doesn't make sense, him paying over the odds for a house right out in the sticks. I bet there's something he's not telling you. Whereabouts is this house?'

Maddy described a house I knew well. Danny and I had even been in it, just to have a look round. It was an old brick house with a few outbuildings, adjacent to his site at Netherton. There was a bit of land attached to it but not enough to justify Barden's inflated offer. It was all a great mystery to me.

'I don't suppose you've got the plans with you?'

'Well, I've brought a contract with me for him to sign and there's a deed plan attached to it. He insisted on me bringing it.' She ferreted around in her rucksack and produced a ribbon-bound set of documents. 'Here they are.' She handed them to me. 'Take this torch, then you'll be able to see them.' She smiled at me, her face open and honest – and a bit worried.

It was something I'd overheard the site foreman say, when I'd been in his cabin one day using his telephone. Something about a ransom strip, and how Barden looked to be *buying himself out of the shit for twopence ha'penny as usual, the crafty bugger*. I remembered this as I looked at the plan. I'd asked Jimmy Docherty what a ransom strip was and he'd told me it was usually a piece of land that blocked off a building site from a road or sewer. A piece of land which, for whatever reason, the builder had failed to buy. Without that piece of land the site was useless. I thought no more about it at the time. I was thinking about it now.

The ransom strip stuck out like a sore thumb. The land attached to the house had been shaded green. There was a long track, maybe twenty feet wide, leading from the garden, right across the front of Barden's site to another field about a quarter of a mile away. It wasn't apparent on the actual site, because the hedges on either side had been cleared away during the site clearance. I knew this because we'd done it. Barden had been particularly keen for us to grub up these hedges first. I stabbed a finger at the green-shaded track.

'What's that?' I asked. 'What's that track?'

'That's how Uncle Arthur used to get to and from his fields. He used to bring his cows along that track when he brought them in for milking. The land at either side belongs to Netherton Hall Estates.'

'Not any more, it doesn't!' I was getting excited as the

implication of what she owned dawned on me. 'It belongs to Barden Homes!'

'How does that affect me?'

'It means that your house is worth a hell of a lot more than five thousand quid! Barden can't sell a house until he buys your land, and he's building over a hundred and twenty houses on that site!' I made a mental calculation. A hundred and twenty houses at roughly two and a half thousand each.

'Three hundred thousand.'

'Pardon?' Maddy wasn't reading my thoughts.

'His site's worth three hundred thousand quid when it's sold. You'll be able to squeeze a lot more than five thousand out of him!'

'How much more?'

She didn't sound as excited as she should have been. Maddy, it turned out, wasn't a greedy girl but an opportunity like this was too good to miss.

'Look, Maddy, it's not as though you're dealing with an honourable man. He'll have picked up the rest of the land cheap because without your piece it's worthless. He should have offered you a proper price for it in the first place, before he started building. No doubt he thought that as a young girl you were an easy touch.' I could see I was beginning to strike a chord here.

'Will you help me?' She placed both arms gently round my neck, knowing full well that I couldn't refuse.

'It'll be my way of paying you back for saving my life. With a bit of luck we should get a lot more than my life's worth!'

'I don't think there's a piece of land on this earth that's worth more than your life, Billy Foxcroft!'

She kissed me gently and closed the flap of the tent. It would be a long time till morning. There was more thawing out to be done.

The following morning we woke to the welcome sound of a snowplough forcing its way through the still-deep snow. The driver stopped to help us drag our cars out and even produced a set of jump leads for me to get mine started. Maddy and I drove in a skidding convoy of two back to Netherton. We booked into the King's Arms. Pauline sounded relieved when I rang her to apologize for not turning up. I explained my predicament and promised to get across there as soon as I could. Before she put the phone down she told me that she loved me. I told her the same and what I couldn't understand was that I meant it. But now there were three!

'Hello! Could I speak to Mr Barden please? It's Madeleine Proctor.'

I could just imagine the panic at Barden's end when Maddy had failed to turn up for the meeting. He was still on site. There was no way he'd leave until she'd signed her land away. He'd wait till Christmas if he had to.

'Hello, Miss Proctor.'

He was trying to sound matter of fact, but I could detect the anxiety in his voice as Maddy held out the earpiece for me to listen in. We were closeted together in the phone box behind the King's Arms.

'Did you have a problem with the snow? It's terrible, isn't it? It took us all by surprise. When will you be able to get here?'

'Well, I wasn't sure you'd still want it when I didn't turn up.'

'No, I'm a man of honour, I'm prepared to stick to my word if you still want to sell.'

He was unsuccessfully trying to unflatten his flat Yorkshire vowels. Always a mistake.

'And the price?'

This is where greed got the better of him.

'Well I did incur certain wasted expenses, Miss Proctor, when you failed to turn up, but I'm willing to split them with you. Shall we say a reduction of a hundred ? It's still way over the market value.'

This told Maddy all she wanted to know about Paul Barden.

'I won't be able to come myself, Mr Barden, so I'm sending my representative. He'll be with you at three this afternoon. His name? His name is Foxcroft, Billy Foxcroft – I believe you've met him already!'

I tried to imagine the reaction at the other end of the phone but it beggared *my* imagination. One of my worries was how all this would affect Jimmy Docherty. Barden might not take too kindly to being screwed by one of Jimmy's men, even if he'd ostensibly sacked him. I formulated a Foxcroft plan as I drove round to the site. Danny was the first one I saw. He looked uncharacteristically worried, everybody on site knew I was coming, but nobody knew why.

'Billy. If yer drop Jimmy in der shite, we're all outa work!'

'I know, mate. Tell Jimmy not to worry – I've got a plan!'

This didn't seem to fill Danny with confidence. I saw a worried Jimmy standing at his own cabin door as I went into the builder's cabin. Barden was white with rage when I entered.

'Just take this cheque and give me the contract and get off my site, yer big long streak o' piss!'

Not the most civil of openings to business negotiations.

'You know as well as I do, Mr Barden, that contracts have to be signed and exchanged in front of witnesses.' I'd spoken to Maddy's solicitor before I set off, to clue myself up on procedure.

'Are you telling me she hasn't signed back at her solicitor's?' He seemed genuinely taken aback that the deal wasn't going through as planned.

'I'm telling you that I'm here to negotiate a fair price for her house – and land!' I emphasized the last bit.

'We've already agreed a price verbally,' sneered Barden, uncertainly. 'You probably don't know this, but a verbal contract is binding.'

'Bollocks, Mr Barden!'

This was a legal term that Maddy's solicitor had told me to use in case Barden tried the 'verbal contract' ploy on me. I decided to lay my cards on the table.

'Look, Mr Barden, I know that without Miss Proctor's strip of land, your site is worth sod all. Not one purchaser's solicitor will allow his client to sign a contract until that land is in your ownership, and I gather you've reached contract stage on several houses already.'

Maddy's solicitor had instructed me well. Barden visibly blanched. This was the worst possible thing that could happen to him.

I continued with a growing confidence. 'There are two conditions of sale,' I said, 'neither of which are open to negotiation. The first is to sign a new contract with Jimmy Docherty, with a stipulation that, should his contract be cancelled by you for any reason, the amount outstanding on the contract be paid immediately and in full to J. P. Docherty (Engineers) Ltd.'

Barden's mouth opened and shut, there were beads of sweat on his face despite it being freezing cold. A vein in his neck stuck out like a piece of old clothes line. The man looked ill.

'Are you all right, Mr Barden?' I thought it only decent to show concern. He nodded dumbly. 'I suppose you'll be interested in knowing our selling price.' I was enjoying being a land negotiator, perhaps I had a calling in this field. Maddy's solicitor had told me to try him at twenty-five thousand and see what he'd settle for.

'The price is fifty thousand pounds and, of course, this is non-negotiable!'

I was having my little joke, of course, just to see what his reaction would be, before I told him our real price. There are some people who just can't take a joke. The Foxcroft evasiveness was caught off guard, he knocked me clean out. I flew backwards out through the cabin door. Some of Jimmy's lads saw what had happened and rushed to pick me up, among them was Danny. He looked down at me and said solemnly, 'Will I still tell Jimmy not to worry?' He then broke into the grin he was trying to suppress.

When I got back to the King's Arms I told Maddy what I'd done and how Barden had reacted. 'I'm sorry Maddy, I'll go back when he's calmed down and start again. I was only having a joke with him.'

She was furious – not with me, with Barden. She marched to the telephone and rang through to the site office.

'Barden? It's Madeleine Proctor here. You've half an hour to get your miserable arse down to the King's Arms and sign this contract on the terms just put to you, or the deal's off and I'm going home! And when I say *off*, I mean *off for good*! And when I say half an hour I don't mean thirty-five minutes!'

She slammed the phone down and rang her own solicitor. He was also furious – not with Barden, with me. He did arrange for a local man to come round and sort out our side of the contract should Barden turn up. Twenty-five minutes later, a subdued Paul Barden walked through the pub door, complete with pen, chequebook and defeated white face. I stayed diplomatically out of the way. I'd done enough.

Madeleine became a wealthy young lady that day. Foxy Foxcroft could have become a wealthy young man had I accepted her proposal of marriage that night, after she'd sneaked into my room to thank me in her own unique way for her good fortune. I was madly in love with Maddy, but even *I* knew that you've got to draw the line somewhere. She lay back on the bed, saddened but unsurprised at my gentle rejection of her very kind offer of marriage. Had she known my true age I doubt if the proposal would have been forthcoming.

'How about a honeymoon instead?' she offered. This seemed a highly acceptable alternative.

Three weeks later, on Christmas Eve, I walked through the door of number fifty-seven Elmtree Bank, wearing two expensive items, a sheepskin coat and a Caribbean suntan. The latter, courtesy of the Bahamas, which is much warmer than Unsworth at that time of year. My only concern was how I could explain things to my dad. He'd been at work when I'd popped home to get my birth certificate, which I needed to take over to Liverpool to get my passport. I'd left him a note to say I'd left Docherty's and was going away for a couple of weeks. He gave me a despairing look that told me he already knew everything.

'Merry Christmas, Dad!'

He shook his head. 'Merry Christmas.'

I handed him the gold watch I'd bought in Bay Street, Nassau. He unwrapped it, and drew in a short breath before saying, 'This must have cost a nice few bob. Where's all this brass come from?'

I knew what he was thinking. Unsworth lads didn't wear Christmas Eve suntans and buy gold watches for their dads. What was the world coming to?

I told him all about how Maddy had saved my life and then I told him about how we'd relieved Barden of fifty thousand pounds and he nodded his approval; then he displayed how the mercenary streak in the Foxcrofts was not restricted to Uncle Stan.

'Did she give you a cut, lad? Had it not been for you, she'd have been forty-five thousand quid worse off!'

'She did save my life, Dad!'

'Aye, there is that,' he conceded, giving me the distinct impression that I'd overpriced myself.

Maddy had offered me a very generous cut but I'd suspected there might be strings attached. In the event she'd kissed me a tearful goodbye at the end of a memorable holiday and stuffed a cheque for a thousand pounds into my pocket. I handed it to my dad, who held it like a wounded bird and placed it carefully in the second drawer down, where all the valuables were kept, such as the rent money and my birth certificate.

'How come you haven't spent any?' he asked.

He was referring to how my suntan must have cost a few bob.

'Ah! That was a bit of a bonus. Maddy paid for that.'

'I'll not ask too much about it then.'

'Best not.'

He gave me a grudging smile and patted my shoulder. The nearest I'd ever get to a hug. But it was enough for me.

Thirty

C hristmas 1957 was a good Christmas for the Foxcroft family. We decided to have a New Year's Eve party, it was the first proper party we'd ever had at fifty-seven Elmtree Bank (wakes excepted). Ethel Nesbitt and Desmond came, so did Mr and Mrs Jigger Jackson and the Rosenbergs from next door. I'd tried to invite some of Uncle Stan's old show-business pals, but New Year's Eve was a busy night for them so I was disappointed. Especially at not being able to see Mary, who was doing *Puss in Boots* in Nottingham. She sent me her love and she'd see me soon. Pauline was working, she sent me her love. Maddy was still in the Bahamas, where I could easily have been. Helen would no doubt be with her fiancé. I found this hard to deal with. If I'd become promiscuous, it was her fault. It seemed as if I was constantly searching for someone to replace her. I'd found three likely contenders, but none of them completely filled the void she'd left within me.

I'd thought about inviting Voluptuous Vicki, but I suspected my dad wouldn't approve. There were those who would.

Jacky and Henry arrived. Fanny Onions turned up with baby Martin in a second-hand pram. Prior to her arrival a discussion had been taking place as to the identity of the father. There were many suspects. Even my two pals looked a bit nonplussed when I joked about them being possible candidates.

Sprunty turned up with his girlfriend, with whom he seemed overly obsessed. She made Fanny look like Brigitte Bardot. Jacky didn't look too good and we joked that he should lay off the beer and fags. Mostyn and Marion Mallinson turned up early, parking Mostyn's Flying Fish Emporium outside our

276

house and doing a couple of hours' business before coming in to the party. Mr and Mrs Utterthwaite popped in with their daughter Maggie, who was a year or two older than me and a lot prettier than I'd remembered. We talked about Utters as though he were still alive. It occurred to me that this is where the Utterthwaites' faith in the hereafter came in handy. To them, Utters was in a better place. I just hoped he hadn't had too many impure thoughts before falling out of that tree – still, knowing Utters, he'd probably *talk* Saint Peter into letting him into heaven. Maggie wasn't quite as daft as her brother, but she had something of his spark inside her, which immediately drew me to her.

'Can I get you anything?' I asked her. 'Like excited?'

I was only seventeen and knew that girls fell for chat-up lines such as that. How could anyone resist handsome Foxy Foxcroft and his Caribbean suntan. Maggie smiled and resisted me. I tried again.

'I'm licensed to handle explosives, and you're dynamite!'

'Look, Billy, the last time I spoke to you was to tell you off for having that disgusting belching competition with our Martin!'

This knocked the wind out of the Foxcroft sails. She was having trouble seeing me as a sophisticated man of the world.

'I'm sorry,' she laughed, 'I'll have a lager and lime if you can manage one.'

I went to conjure up a lager and lime and in passing stuck Elvis's 'Blue Suede Shoes' on my brand new Dansette record player. If nothing else, I would impress Maggie with my rock-and-roll expertise. This, coupled with my suntan and comedy chat-up lines, would win her over before the night was through. As I went through to the kitchen, Elvis had them all on their feet, bopping away; even my dad was at it, dancing with Mrs Rosenberg, who hadn't learned to dance like *that* in any synagogue. As I was trying to figure out how much lime to put in the lager I felt a tap on my shoulder.

'Hello, Billy!'

I didn't have to turn round to know who it was. Even after all that time I was red with embarrassment.

'Helen?'

She spun me round as she'd often done in the past. 'You're embarrassed, Billy Foxcroft, and so you should be!'

'Well I—'

'Don't even think about telling me all the lies you've no doubt cooked up.'

'Right . . . I wasn't going to, I mean . . .' She looked dazzling. She'd taken my breath away.

'Oh, by the way, congratulations,' I said, with unimpressive sincerity.

'Congratulations? What for?'

'On your engagement. I heard you'd got engaged. When's the big day?' I tried to sound interested.

'Oh, that . . . no, that's off. Richard was nice, but, God, was he boring? It was your fault we broke up!'

I no doubt made a very bad job of hiding my delight at this piece of information.

'Blimey! I get blamed for everything! How was it my fault?'

'Well, he knew that we'd, er . . . you and I, that is, had been er, going together and you were forever in the news. Everyone up at Durham followed your exploits and I suppose to Richard you were something of a rival. I could never convince him that you and I were a thing of the past. I don't know whether you realize it but you've become something of a cult hero.'

'I've been called many things but never a cult. Something very similar at times.'

'Now then, Billy Foxcroft, don't be coarse!'

As she laughed I realized that the other great loves of my life were second-teamers compared to Helen. I saw my dad smiling at me over Helen's shoulder and knew he'd planned this one himself.

'Anyway, it was at our engagement party that I realized my mistake.' She looked at me quizzically. 'I understand you were there.'

'Er, yes. I just happened to be nearby so I called in on the off-chance. Your pal Jane took me there.'

'Why did you leave without saying hello?'

'Well . . .' My mind was racing.

'Billy Foxcroft, you're thinking up a lie. Why don't you tell me the truth for once?'

'I've never actually told you a lie in my life,' I protested. But she was right, for some reason I was embarrassed to tell her the real reason for my being there that night.

'All right,' I said. 'If you must know, I didn't know you were getting engaged. I just called to see you on the off-chance. It was all a coincidence. When I saw you and him together it . . . it was a bit too much for me to cope with . . .' My voice tailed off. I didn't want to tell her about my sadness. It wasn't her fault.

'Whatever you felt that night, multiply it by a hundred,' she said. 'That's how bad I felt seeing you with that stripper.'

I took her hand. 'Sorry about that. I'm easily led.'

She looked at me, amazed. 'That's it? That's your excuse? You're easily led?'

I shrugged. 'It's the truth, what can I say? I never stopped loving you, though. It'd never happen again.'

She nodded and squeezed my hand. 'Older and wiser, eh?'

'Something like that. What happened between you and Richard?'

She grimaced at the sound of his name. I liked that.

'Richard's a third-year law student. He was discussing conveyancing law over a glass of Harvey's Bristol Cream with some other sherry drinkers when Jane came over and told me you'd been and gone. Just the sound of your name made me realize I was making a mistake getting engaged to Richard. I went off to look for you and when I came back everyone was talking about the latest in the Foxcroft saga.'

'The Netherton Winter Horse Fair!'

'The very same. They were all laughing about it when Richard said how he thought it was an act of mindless vandalism and how he hoped they'd lock you up and throw away the key!'

'There were those who were thinking about it. So, what happened?'

'I lost my temper with him. I told him if I thought you'd have me back, I'd go like a shot!'

'Blimey! I can see how that would break an engagement off. You say daft things like that when you're drunk, don't you? *Were* you drunk?'

'Then I threw my drink all over him!'

'That would do the trick. Did you mean it?'

'God! You should have seen his face, it was a picture.' She laughed to herself at the memory.

'Did you mean it?'

'Mean what?'

'You know very well what. Would you come back to me like a shot?'

'One thing at a time, Billy Foxcroft. I'm not sure I'm ready for such a challenge.'

But she hadn't said *no*.

We went through to the lounge and danced to 'Love Me Tender', which Marion Mallinson had put on to *Slow things down a bit*. Maggie thanked me for her drink and gave me a cheerful smile which told me she could never get serious with someone who'd been in a belching contest with her brother, suntan or no suntan.

Jigger placed an avuncular arm around me and told me how sorry he was to hear about the Barden affair. 'I heard a whisper . . .' he intoned, with drunken confidentiality, looking furtively around to check that no one was listening. 'I've heard a whisper that there'll be a job opening in the new year. I'll stick a good word in for you. Mark my words, Billy, I'll make a sewage man out of you yet.'

He was a lovely man but this news did not inspire me with joy.

'Our Desmond wants a word with you,' said Ethel. Basically all *I* wanted was to be left alone with Helen. 'He's learned a bit of Stanley's act, and he wonders if you'll do it with him. It's only a bit of fun.'

'Go on then. But I don't know how much I remember. I don't have to dress up as a tramp, do I?'

'No, you'll do as you are, they'll never know the difference!'

I suppose I'd asked for that.

A space was cleared and our expectant audience gave a roisterous round of applause as Desmond made his entrance from the kitchen.

'Ladies an' gennermen,' he announced. 'It gives me great pleasure – an' it always has –' he paused here for the traditional titter – 'to hintroduce a young man what has performed in front of the Queen an' the Duke of York. Not to mention the Horse an' Trumpet an' the Pig an' Whistle!'

I strode out to further applause and held up my hands in a quieting gesture, saying, in a pained voice, 'I hope you all realize that I got out of a sickbed to come here this evenin'!'

'Ooohhh!' went everybody in traditional mock-sympathy.

'What's been the problem?' asked a concerned Desmond.

'The wife's sister's got flu!'

Our audience laughed and I knew that the bug had never left me, it was simply hibernating. Like my grandad's grizzly bear.